PARIAH

ROBERT C. SWETZ

To order additional copies of this book, contact:
Bookwhip
1-855-339-3589
https://www.bookwhip.com

DEDICATION

For the times that we've shared, the good and the bad
For holding my hand, no matter how sad
For the roads that we've walked, and the paths yet to take
For the care that you've shown, that nothing can shake
For believing in me, when doubt held me down
For holding me up, not letting me drown
For dreams that came true, and those that still wait
For knowing my heart, and also my faith
For holding me close, to keep me alive
For trusting in me, and letting love thrive
For giving yourself, with nothing held back
For love so complete, where nothing can lack
For my wife, Letitia
I love you.
It is only through my wife's help with editing,
ideas, opinions, and especially her support that this
book is even remotely possible. Thanks, Tish.

CHAPTER

1

"If I find her, will you feed me?"

I don't think I'll ever forget those haunting words. Just as I know I'll never forget…him.

The first time I met him, I was working out of the FBI office in Atlanta. Dusk was just beginning to settle as I escorted Mr. and Mrs. Holcomb out to their car. Their daughter had been missing for several days now and I was trying to reassure them that we were doing everything possible to find her. The truth is though, we had absolutely no idea where to continue looking. So many girls go missing every year – permanently. And already, this was looking like another one.

Mrs. Holcomb was understandably beside herself. All the way out to the parking lot she argued that there must be something else we could do to find her daughter. But what could I tell her? The truth is that we were already doing everything possible. What I didn't say though, is that we had absolutely no leads at all. Nothing.

How he got there, I have no idea. Why he found his way to that parking lot, I also have no idea. But suddenly, there he was, looking like some kind of a monster in some grade B movie. The sight of him was… disgusting! The smell from him was just as bad.

"If I find her, will you feed me?"

His voice was nasal and raspy, as if there was something wrong with his throat. When I looked closer, I could see that his nose was bent permanently to the side. I wondered if he could even breathe out of it. He was missing all of his front teeth and his full grey beard was stringy and a mess. His clothes…tatters! And there was something about his eyes that spoke…insanity. Another of the many homeless people in the city, only definitely one of the worst off.

Mrs. Holcomb screamed a bit at the sight of him and I automatically reached toward my gun. He should have run off, but he didn't. He just stood there and repeated his question. "If I find her, will you feed me?"

"Get lost!" I ordered as I pulled my gun into view to scare him away. "Get out of here! These people are upset enough. They don't need anyone like you around to make matters worse!" But he didn't run off. He didn't even back away.

"I can find her. I can."

"You can't even find a toothbrush!" I argued and was about to tell him to go away again, but that was when Mrs. Holcomb stepped forward.

"How?" she asked. "How can you find her?" What surprised me was that she was clearly frightened of him, yet her need to find her daughter outweighed her fear.

He held out his bare hands, and I almost puked at the sight of them. It wasn't just that they were filthy, they were so bent and gnarled that they could hardly be called hands. "Touch me," he said.

Mrs. Holcomb drew back in fear and I didn't blame her one bit. I wouldn't want to touch the creature before us either – with a ten foot pole!

He lowered his hands, and his head. "Don't blame you," he said sadly. Then he lifted his head again and turned around. He sat down right in the parking lot with his back to all of us. "Put your hands on my back," he said.

"What the heck?" I yelled. "Get lost, you bum!"

He turned his head back toward us again. "I can find her. I promise! Put your hands on my back."

"How is that supposed to help?" Mr. Holcomb asked, beating me to the question.

The creature looked back up at him. "I have no link to her. You do," was his only answer.

"What's that supposed to mean?" Mr. Holcomb asked.

"Don't know her. You're related. You have link."

"What link?"

"What are you, some kind of psychic?" I asked. "You can see the future? No wonder you're so down and out. And obviously you're no good at it if you're this hard up."

He shook his head. "Don't see the future. Not at all. I only know I can find her."

"Get lost!" I yelled again, more fiercely this time. Yet he never moved from his spot on the pavement.

He turned his head toward Mrs. Holcomb. "What can it hurt?" he asked. "Try."

Mrs. Holcomb looked to her husband.

"He's loony and just after money," her husband argued.

"Obviously!" I agreed. "You don't even want to consider this!"

But her distress over her missing daughter was more than her fear. "What can it really hurt?" she asked as she looked back and forth between us.

I rolled my eyes and shook my head. "Of all the dumb things…."

"What can it hurt?" she asked again.

"You can't really be serious?" I said.

Instead of answering, she handed her purse to her husband and approached the wretch of a figure in front of us. "Put my hands on your back?" she asked. "Nothing else?"

He looked back at her and nodded. "Touch me, and think about daughter. Think hard."

I pointed my gun at the creature. "You make one wrong move, and so help me, I'll shoot you before you know what's happened!"

Mrs. Holcomb looked back at her husband one more time. Then she reached out, tentatively, first with one hand and touched his back, then with the other. I was definitely ready to jump in and kill the guy if he made the least little wrong move. "Like this?" she asked him.

"Harder, if you can," he replied.

She stooped down so she could be lower and reach him better. I saw her pressing a bit more firmly on his back. "Like this?" But he didn't answer. "What's next?" she asked. But still he didn't answer.

I walked around in front of him and saw that his eyes were closed. He looked almost peaceful. "This is ridiculous…" I started to say. But that was when he started speaking.

"She's in a car. Passenger seat. Boy is driving. Black boy."

Mr. Holcomb looked up at me with an angry expression. I couldn't have agreed more.

"Is she alright?" Mrs. Holcomb asked.

"Yes," the wretch answered. "She is fine."

"Is she tied up in any way?" she asked.

I saw him shake his head a little. "No." After a moment, he continued. "Wearing short blue-jean cut-offs…stringy at bottom. Blue and white check shirt."

Mrs. Holcomb seemed more excited now. "Yes! She has a shirt just like that!"

I didn't want to tell her that it sounded awfully vague to me. Most girls probably have something just like it in their wardrobe.

"It's lighter where she is than here. Sun isn't going down yet."

That was something I hadn't expected. Obviously the guy had a good imagination.

"I see…corn fields. Nothing but corn fields. Lots and lots of corn."

I wanted to add that most of the corn was in his delivery, but I kept silent. The one thing I could see was that his words, as vague and as dumb as they were, were some kind of comfort to Mrs. Holcomb.

"Highway. Rural. Two lane. Don't see other cars yet. No road sign yet. Let you know."

Oh brother! The guy was a real con artist for sure!

"The car is…red. Older car. I think…a muscle car. Wide black stripe down the hood."

At that, Mrs. Holcomb turned back and looked straight at her husband. There was something about the set of his face that disturbed me.

I started to ask a question, but the creature suddenly said, "Wait! She's talking."

Con artistry at its best was foremost on my mind. Yet I wanted to follow up about the car thing. There had been some recognition about that between the husband and his wife. What came out of the creature's mouth next was something I was totally unprepared for. It took me a few moments to realize that he was repeating, supposedly, every little thing that was being said in the car, word for word. Since he just kept speaking, it was hard to pick out what was being said by which person in the car.

"Are we going to get somewhere soon? I gotta' pee again. Shit! You just went a few hours ago! Tough shit Hank! It's been more than a few hours. Besides, I'm getting hungry. I want a snack. Damn! Oh, all right. We need some more gas anyway. Reaching down into big straw bag by her feet. Gun! Big gun! We need some cash too! Yeah, we could stand to get a little more of that too. Putting gun back in bag. All we need is someplace to stop! I'm so sick of seeing nothing but farms. There'll be something…eventually."

He finally stopped talking and just sat there with is eyes closed. If nothing else, the wretch was entertaining. But that part about the girl having a gun, it just didn't wash. And I could especially see that the mother and father clearly didn't believe it. To put the icing on the cake and clearly show them that this guy was nuts, I asked the father quietly. "She doesn't know anyone named Hank, does she?"

The father and mother passed discomforting looks back and forth, and I think I silently steeled myself for the bad answer.

He nodded. "About six months ago, maybe a bit less, we had it out with her. She had been running around constantly with a black boy named Hank. But we forbid her to see him anymore. Yeah, there were a few tears and some drama, but she didn't see him anymore…as far as I know."

His words were not exactly what I wanted to hear. "And…does this Hank…have a car like that?"

He nodded. "Just like that."

Shit!

"Sign up ahead. Little sign." The creature said. We all waited. "Shaped like…shield. Number 56 in it. Could be State highway or something."

Or something, my skeptical mind repeated silently. But he had shook me a bit by pulling Hank out of the air, imagined or not.

"Another sign ahead. Gas station. And store. Bill's Highway Spot."

It was hard to tell exactly what he was talking about half the time, since he was obviously trying to give us the rundown of what he was "supposedly" seeing, as well as exactly what the two kids in the car were saying – all at the same time.

"Hey, there's a place. Yeah, I see it. You better stop! Don't worry. Like I told you, we need gas too. You go in and go to the bathroom while I pump some gas. Give the guy at the counter a twenty to keep him happy before you go take a leak. Then let me take a piss before you pull that gun out! Ha! Poor little Hanky has to go too? Damn straight! Don't worry. You know I can do this."

That was when Mrs. Holcomb took her hands off of his back and stood up again. "I can't listen to this anymore. You're wrong! You're dead wrong! My daughter would never do the things you're saying. You're nothing but a big fat..." But her anger didn't let her finish. And I could clearly see that Mr. Holcomb felt exactly the same way.

"Haven't figured out where she is yet," the creature complained.

But Mr. Holcomb pulled his wife away. "We're not listening to any more of this shit!" He turned to me. "Please let us know the minute you find anything, Agent McNair!"

I nodded. "Of course! You know I will."

He bundled his wife into the car as quickly as he could. A minute later, he practically roared out of the parking lot. The wretch had gotten to his feet and was limping away. I noticed that his legs appeared to be twisted a bit and that walking was difficult for him...or at least appeared to be. I wasn't sure just how much of it might be an act. "And stay away!" I shouted after him.

He turned slightly back to me. "Could have found her. I was there. Saw what I saw."

"You saw...nothing, you bum!"

He shook his head sadly. "Wasn't going to feed me anyway."

I watched him for a few more moments before going back inside. It was late and I was ready to head home for the day. So were the last two members of my team who had stayed behind and were waiting for me upstairs.

When I got back to the office, I could see that both Hannah and Billy were ready to leave. And just because I had nothing better to say to either of them, I turned to Hannah and said, "Do me a favor. When you come in tomorrow, see if you can find anything on a black dude named Hank. Evidently he used to be one of the girl's boyfriends a while back. And if you find him, find out what kind of car he drives. Especially if it's a red muscle car with a black stripe down the hood."

Hannah looked at me with some surprise. "Why didn't we hear about this before?"

I shook my head. "Heaven only knows."

"You get a tip?" Billy asked.

A tip? How could I call any of what had just happened a tip? I shook my head. "No, just something I…overheard. And Billy, while Hannah's checking out the boyfriend, see if there's any place called 'Bill's Highway Spot' along a highway 56, somewhere near some corn fields."

"Bill's Highway Spot? What's that got to do with this case?"

How could I honestly answer that? In fact, the whole request was a total shot in the dark. But desperate is desperate! "Probably nothing. In fact, most likely nothing at all! But check it anyway. Humor me."

"No problem. You got it," Billy replied brightly as he grabbed a notepad and wrote something down.

I almost told Billy to forget it. There was no way I was going to place any credence in anything that dirty bum had said. But he had pulled Hank's name out of thin air. Maybe asking Billy to check it out was my way of proving just how wrong the bum had been. Besides, like I said, we were desperate for any kind of lead.

While Billy and Hannah went home to their families, I went home to my cheap apartment and put a TV dinner in the oven. I had been divorced for two years now and had never bothered to move into anything nicer. I hadn't even bothered to fix my place up. I had the basic furniture, all battered and used, but comfortable. And I had a bed. What more did a guy like me need?

I also had a daughter named Shelly who recently turned six. But like her mother, I rarely ever saw her. They now lived up in Connecticut, where it snows in the winter. Heck, we get snow here in Atlanta – at least every once in a blue moon. Sometimes more often!

As I waited for my dinner to cook, I went to the bathroom to splash some water over my face, with the intention of trying to clear the disturbing cobwebs from my mind. It didn't work. When I looked up into the mirror, I was still haunted by images of, "The Creature from the Parking Lot!" Whew, I could never imagine anyone being that much of a mess! How did anyone get into the kind of shape he was in? It was a puzzling question that I couldn't get off my mind.

As I stared into the mirror, my mind tried to compare my simple features with the bum that I couldn't seem to forget. My neatly trimmed, dark brown hair was nothing at all like the long stringy gray mess covering that creature's head and face. Even after a long day, my clean-shaven face held only a faint sign of a five o'clock shadow. It was hard to not feel good about the way you looked when you compared yourself with anything that twisted and battered. Not that I considered myself all that good looking, but compared to him, I was a virtual movie star.

I tore my gaze away from the mirror to go back and check on my dinner. The truth was, I had always considered myself to be the most average guy on the planet. At five foot ten, I wasn't exactly small and scrawny, but I had towered over his bent and twisted frame. And while I wasn't exactly big and muscular, compared to him I looked like a fitness guru. The truth is, there was simply no way to compare myself to him. He was plagued with far too many problems to count, while I was…average. Simply average. But being so average was a trait that had helped me many times earlier in my career when I had gone undercover working narcotics instead of missing persons.

As I sat down with my TV dinner on my battered old couch in front of my nice new TV set, I looked around my messy, dingy apartment. "Way to go, Clifford McNair," I berated myself. "The way you live isn't much better than that bum today!" But as usual, I never got up the energy to do anything about it.

Don Wimberly, my immediate boss, liked to start his days with a morning meeting to make sure he was caught up on everyone's business. It's not that I minded so much, but there were better things I could be doing with my time than listening to cases that had nothing to do with me. Rarely did I ever have anything to say in those little meetings, but that morning I tossed out that we had gotten a lead on an old boyfriend in the Holcomb case the night before and were in the process of checking on it.

After the meeting, I walked back to our offices with John Thomas, my equal, who shared the other "inner" office in our shared room. John and I had worked with each other for six years now and I couldn't remember a single time we had ever clashed. In fact, we both often sat across from each other's desk and bounced ideas off the wall. The fact that we "shared" the six agents in the outer office never once had been an issue. Although there were two that worked more often exclusively for me, and John had a few that he leaned on mostly as well. Hannah Montrose and Billy Waincross were my two. Darla Cunningham and Brent Foster worked more often with John. Charlie Whitmore and Ben Wortham were our two youngest and newest agents. We pretty much shared their use equally, often sending them on errands the others would rather not be bothered with.

"When I left last night," John said as we walked the halls, "I wasn't aware that the Holcomb's had mentioned anything about another boyfriend."

"I didn't get that till I was out in the parking lot with them. We're going to check on it, but trust me, this one's like grasping at straws – where they don't exist!"

He grunted. He knew exactly what I meant. So many of the leads we chased down were nothing more than that.

I had barely gotten to my desk when Billy barged into my office. "Took me about five minutes to find your 'Bill's Highway Spot'," he told me. "Kansas. Definitely in the middle of some corn fields. And you know that car you mentioned? They had a robbery there last night. Black guy and a white girl. Report says they were driving a red car with a black stripe. So what's up?"

And that was when Hanna appeared at my desk too. "Boss…that Hank character you asked about last night has to be Hank Petrone. I already talked to one person who says he and the Holcomb girl used to be really big on each other. I'm still trying to find someone who's seen him recently though. And he drives an old Ford Torino. Hopped up. Red with a black stripe like you mentioned.

I stared from one to the other. "Crap!" I looked to Billy. "Tell me the girl in the robbery was wearing a blue and white checked shirt."

He looked down at the papers in his hand. "Girl…denim shorts and a blue shirt."

I cursed again as I got up from my desk to pace behind it for a moment. "See if there's any surveillance video of that robbery. If so, I want it here like yesterday! All of it!" I stopped my nervous pacing and faced them. I couldn't believe what I was about to ask. "Where do we find bums in this city?"

"You got to be kidding!" Hanna replied. "Bums? For what?"

"You don't want to know!" I told her. "In fact, I know – and I don't want to know!"

It took me three phone calls to three different police precincts before I found someone who knew him.

"Pariah!" the desk sergeant told me before I had gotten half-way through my description of the wretch.

"Yeah, he certainly is," I replied.

"No," the guy replied. "That's his name, or at least what he calls himself. I don't remember his real name. As far as I know, he harmless. Why?"

"He ever try to pull any kind of scams or cons on anyone? Or has he ever claimed to be a psychic or something?"

"Not as far as I know," the sergeant replied. "You want me to pick him up?"

"No, just tell me where I can find him."

"I have no idea, but I'll ask some of the guys and see if I can get an answer for you."

"Thanks!" I replied. "And the sooner, the better!"

We got halfway lucky with the video surveillance. We got film outside showing the car and the guy pumping gas, and we got video inside showing both the guy and the girl holding a gun on the cashier, but the video was so grainy and the angle of both was from so high up, we couldn't get any real details. Especially since they both wore big sunglasses and the girl had a wide brimmed hat on. There was no way we could see her well enough to tell if she was the girl we were looking for or not. We couldn't even see the license plate on the car. Still, the details seemed to match.

I had Billy put out an APB on the car with Hank Petrone's license tag. We also put out a warning that both the driver and his passenger could be armed. We were fairly confident that we'd hear something on the car soon. At least we hoped we would.

While we waited, we debated whether to bring in the mother to see if she could ID the girl from the video, but we finally decided against it. There was no use putting her through something so traumatic. Especially when we couldn't tell anything from what we saw ourselves.

I didn't get a call about the Pariah wretch until late in the afternoon, just before we were getting ready to leave. The call came from a police officer who worked the downtown district.

"Agent McNair?"

"That's me."

"The sergeant says you want to know about Pariah."

"Yeah. Anything you can tell me."

"What's he done? As far as I know, the only thing he's ever done before is to make a nuisance of himself trying to get food."

"Sounds about right," I replied. "Most likely, that's what this is all about. But there's an off chance he may have some information about a missing girl case we're working on."

"Him? I doubt it. But you never know. So what can I tell you?"

"Where can I find him? He showed up here last night in the parking lot."

"Way out there? What the heck was he doing up where you are? That's not his usual territory."

"So I guessed."

"Most of the time we hear about him, he's making a nuisance of himself at the back door of the restaurants in the middle of town. Check the back alleys and behind the buildings. He doesn't make an appearance much out where most people can see him."

"I wonder why?" I mocked.

"Yeah! For sure! The guy's a sight if I ever saw one. Listen, I'm going off duty right now, but you want me to have the guys pick him up tonight if they see him? Or if it can wait till tomorrow, I'll try to find him myself. I got to tell you though, finding him may not be that easy."

I thought about it again, but really, what could we gain from picking him up? "No. Don't bother. This is all probably nothing anyway."

And that was when Billy charged back into my office again. I said a quick thanks and hung up the phone.

"Boss, that robbery in Kansas last night? That wasn't the only one they pulled. I found three others in the last two days alone, stretched between here and there. Looks like it's always the same kind of shit they're pullin'."

I was surprised…but I wasn't. "Okay, check to see if we can get any better info from any of those places. Especially video! I want to know for sure that it's the Holcomb girl before we jump on any of this."

"You got it!" he replied. "You want me to work late tonight?"

"No. Just put the requests out and we'll sift through whatever we get tomorrow."

When you're working on a missing girl case, you seem to get requests filled faster than usual. Fortunately, or unfortunately, that was the case here. The following morning, Hannah, Billy, and myself all gathered around Billy's computer to watch the videos. And right from the first one, there was no doubt in my mind at all that we were watching the Holcomb girl rob another convenience store. One of the other videos only confirmed what the first one had told us.

I dreaded making the call, but there was no way I couldn't. We had to get the girl's parents in to verify that we were looking at their daughter.

We didn't pull any punches, but I did warn them on the phone about what they were going to be looking at. I warned them again as soon as they got here. I could clearly see they didn't want to believe me that their daughter would do such a thing. I couldn't blame them. If it was me, I wouldn't believe it either. I was just grateful they agreed to come in and see what we had. Five seconds into the first video, I could tell by the set of both their faces that we were looking at their daughter.

"There's got to be a mistake!" the mother said. "She had to have been coerced. Forced to do that!"

"There's no way my daughter would rob anyone…willingly!" the father added.

I went with it. "That's possible. We don't know yet. Right now, we just need to find them. After that, we can get the real story."

"This all came about, because of that…creature?" Mrs. Holcomb asked.

I shrugged. "The big lead was the boyfriend," I suggested instead, trying to throw the light on information other than what the bum had told us.

"But it fits with everything he said," she countered.

I nodded and agreed. "So far."

"Was there a video from that place he mentioned in the parking lot?"

Reluctantly, I nodded again. "Billy, bring up the first videos we got. The ones from Kansas."

They both watched the videos from Kansas all the way through without saying a word. "Why didn't you call me when you got this?" she asked.

"As you can see, there was no way to identify your daughter in them. Her face is hidden all the time."

"What are you doing to find her now?" Mr. Holcomb asked.

"We're looking for the car now. It's just a matter of time."

"It's taken way too long already!" he replied.

I had to agree. For now, the case still belonged to us, but it was starting to look more and more like a case for Robbery instead. "We'll find them," I assured them. "It's only a matter of time."

Mrs. Holcomb looked at me, and her wide open eyes warned me of what she was about to ask. And I dreaded it. "Couldn't we find her faster if we ask that…creature? The sooner we find my daughter, the sooner we can stop her from being forced to do things she would never do!"

But finding that bum was the last thing I wanted to do. "I don't think that's a good idea," I replied. "And believe me, it's just a matter of time now until we spot the car. We'll let you know the minute we find them. I promise!"

But she wasn't backing down. "Agent McNair, I want to find my daughter. You said you're doing everything possible. But isn't asking that… man, part of everything possible? He told us exactly what was happening with her the other night. And even though I don't like it, it seems he was exactly right. Maybe he can help us find her faster!"

I would have argued with her, but after questioning as many people as I have in my career, you know when it will do no good. "We don't even know where to find him," I countered. "We know nothing about him."

"Well, you're the damn FBI!" she returned vehemently. "You're supposed to be able to find people! Although to me, it looks like you're not very good at it!"

As soon as she walked out, both Billy and Hannah looked at me questioningly. "What's up?" Billy asked. "This have anything to do with you asking where to find bums yesterday?"

I hadn't told them because I was hoping the crazy wretch would be wrong. But so far, he had proven to be nothing but right. So I pulled them both into my office and closed the door – and swore them both to secrecy. This wasn't the kind of thing I wanted anyone else to know about. It was embarrassing enough that I was even considering finding the damn wretch now.

As soon as a bewildered Hannah and Billy left my office, I called the same police sergeant I had talked to before and asked him to have his guys find the homeless wretch. Pariah, he kept insisting was the guy's name. Or at least, that's what it seemed everyone called the bum. Pariah. And I couldn't think of a more fitting name for the creature.

For the rest of the day I wondered who would be found first, the girl and her boyfriend, or would the police downtown find the Pariah. I was really hoping it would be the girl and her boyfriend. I was still hoping the same thing when I pulled another TV dinner out of the microwave and sat down to eat it in front of the TV. I had just barely started eating when my cell phone interrupted me.

"Agent McNair?" the voice on the other end asked.

"That's me. What can I do for you?"

"We found Pariah for you. You want to come down and get him? Or if you like, I can bring him straight up to you. To tell the truth, we don't really want him in our jail."

"You know where our offices are?" I asked.

"No problem. I can have him there in twenty minutes. Probably less since he's being such a pain in the ass – as usual."

"As usual?"

"See you in a few minutes," he replied.

I wondered what "as usual" meant as I phoned Billy and asked him to come in for a few hours. I didn't call Hannah because she preferred spending the evenings with her family whenever possible. Billy didn't seem to care as much.

Then, against my better judgment, I phoned the Holcombs and told them that the police had found the bum and were bringing him in. The rest of my TV dinner got left in its tray, forgotten.

I was glad that the squad car pulled up in front of the building before the Holcombs arrived. The policeman got out of the car and came around to open the back door for me. I'd rather he hadn't. The wretch was far more wretched than he had been two nights ago. He was handcuffed to a ring on the floor of the car and was whining pitifully.

"I didn't do it! I didn't do it!" he kept crying. "Please! It wasn't me! I didn't do it!"

"Didn't do what?" I asked, but I didn't get an answer before the policeman leaned in and freed the bum. He got out of the car nervously and fell to his knees in front of me – a scared rabbit, never taking his eyes off of me. Still crying, still whining the same words over and over again. "I didn't do it. It wasn't me. I didn't do it."

"He's all yours!" the policeman said with a smirk. He got into his car quickly and drove off just as fast, obviously glad to be rid of the bum. I didn't blame him. But now, what was I going to do with him?

"I didn't do it!" the bum kept insisting.

"I didn't say you did," I replied as I knelt down in front of him. "Do you remember me?" I asked, trying to sound at least a little bit kind. "We met here in the parking lot two nights ago. You asked the woman to touch your back and said you could find her daughter."

He stopped whining his pitiful song and I could see a light of recognition in his eyes. "The girl. You found her. Was she where I said?"

I was saved from answering by Billy walking up. "Holy crap! This is the guy you told us about?"

I didn't feel like an answer was needed. "Let's get him upstairs before the Holcombs arrive," I suggested as I stood up again.

"I didn't do it! I didn't do it!" he insisted again. Fear seemed to be his biggest problem once again.

"Didn't do what?" Billy asked.

"It wasn't me! It wasn't me. I didn't do it!?"

"I haven't found out what he didn't do yet," I replied. "And frankly, I don't think I care." As I started to walk off, I heard a horrible scream from the creature that made me turn around quickly.

"I'm just trying to cuff him," Billy said as he fought to catch the wretch's arm. One end of his cuffs was already attached to one of his wrists.

"Don't bother," I said. "Take them off." I walked back to the wretched bum. I did my best to sound kind again – which wasn't all that easy. "We'd like your help again," I told him. "We'd just like your help. Like you did the other night. Can you do that? Please? That's all we want."

He stopped whining and stared up at me with wide eyes. Eyes that didn't exactly look sane – at all! "If I find her, will you feed me?" he asked, just as he had asked the Holcombs the other night.

What could I say? "Sure," I replied. "Sure!" Although finding him food was the last thing on my mind.

I was happy to see the creature climb to his feet. Slowly and painfully he walked next to Billy toward the building. But it seemed to take him a moment to find the courage to cross over the threshold and actually enter. His head kept turning all around as we walked through the lobby. He looked like a hunted creature watching out for the animals he knew would devour him very soon. Getting into the elevator and up to our floor seemed to be particularly difficult for him, but he came.

"If I find her, will you feed me?" he asked several times.

"I said I would!" I replied – several times. To shut him up, I sent Billy to the vending machine with a couple of dollars to buy him some candy bars while we waited on the Holcombs. The moment Billy got back and handed them to him, he went crazy trying to rip the packaging off with those gnarled fingers of his that didn't seem to work very well. Billy finally had to do it for him. And then he couldn't get the candy into his mouth fast enough. There was a look of pure relief on his face the moment he started chewing. The bum was hungry. Really hungry! I didn't have a doubt about that in the world.

By the time the Holcombs arrived, the look of total insanity was somewhat diminished from the bums eyes. He still didn't look sane, but there was a definite improvement. He looked up directly at Mrs. Holcomb before she had a chance to say anything and asked his same question. "If I find her, will you feed me?"

She looked at me and I shrugged. "We just gave him some candy bars," I told her.

She looked back at him. "Of course," she said. "That's what you asked the other night. If we find her, I'll see that you get something to eat."

The wretch closed his eyes and bowed his head. "Thank you," he muttered softly. Then he stood up and turned his back to her. "Put your hands on my back, like before," he said. "Think of your daughter. Think hard."

I said nothing. Billy and I just stood back and let the drama unfold in front of us.

"Wouldn't you rather sit down?" Mrs. Holcomb asked as she set her purse on the nearby table – well out of his reach.

He turned around and looked shocked. "Thank you," he replied as if it was the kindest thing anyone had ever said to him. Maybe it was. He pulled the chair out and turned it around so the back was to her, and he sat down again.

Mrs. Holcomb hesitated again, but only for a moment. With one final look at her husband for support, she pressed first one hand to his back, then the other. Knowing now what was going to happen, I ran to my desk and pulled a mini recorder out of it. I just barely got it turned on before he started talking.

"In bed together. Room not dark. They're…Oh! I…They're…"

He looked up at me. It was something I hadn't expected. "Are they having sex?" I asked.

He seemed relieved as he nodded. "Don't want to talk about it. Don't want to watch."

Game over! I was actually relieved. "Well," I said to Mrs. Holcomb, "we tried." I was about to tell her that it was a bad idea anyway, when the darn wretch began to speak again.

"I guess…" he said, "Could try to find where they are. Would that help?"

Oh gee! But Mrs. Holcomb beat me to it. "Yes! That's what we really need to know!"

He seemed to nod, then bowed his head again. Mrs. Holcomb's hands were still on his back.

"Hotel room. They're still…. The door! Sign on door. Framed. Tiny print. Says…oh, talks about room rates. Going outside. Look around."

"You can do that?" I asked.

"Motel. Not many cars. Sign says Motel Six. Number twelve on door."

"Where is it?" Mrs. Holcomb asked.

"Don't know yet. Need to look around more."

"Do you see any corn fields?" I asked mockingly.

"No. None that I can see from where I am. See motel lobby. Going in."

If this was a con guy, he was suddenly opening up a whole new bag of tricks.

"Not much," he said after a few moments. "Wait! Letters on the desk. Motel Six, Boise City, Oklahoma."

"Boise?" Mrs. Holcomb asked. "What are they doing out there?"

I suddenly saw Billy run off to his desk.

"Going back to room," the wretch said. A few minutes later, he added. They're still…you know." He looked up at us then. "Can't watch what they're doing!"

Mrs. Holcomb took her hands off of him. "So they're at a Motel Six in Boise City?"

The wretch nodded.

"Boss!" Billy called as he ran back. Highway fifty six goes straight into Boise City. And there is a Motel Six there!"

I silently cursed to myself. I wanted so badly for this wretched bum to be wrong. "Okay, call Boise. Ask them to be polite about it, but let's see who's in room twelve. And warn them to be careful just in case! There's a good chance they have a gun."

While we waited, mostly silently, the wretch seemed to ignore us completely as he happily worked on the candy we had given him earlier. Watching him trying to eat it was almost as disgusting as he was. With no front teeth, he either tried to stuff the whole bars into his mouth at once, or he tried to break them with his hands – which seemed to be very difficult for him.

The phone rang and I answered it. A few minutes later, I hung up again. "They got them, your daughter and her friend. The police there are taking them into custody for now. We have agents in Oklahoma who will get them for us in the morning."

Mrs. Holcomb looked relieved. "It's definitely her?"

"Without a doubt."

"Can I talk to her? I really need to talk to her!"

"We can probably arrange that later, but it's going to be a little while." I didn't want to mention that she was being arrested and booked first on a number of robbery charges.

And then the creature was there again. "I found her. Will you feed me?"

We were all somewhat taken aback. "I don't have any food on me right now," Mrs. Holcomb apologized.

"Wait a minute," Mr. Holcomb said. He pulled out his wallet and started pulling out bills.

"No!" the creature said, holding his gnarled hands up as if to ward off something bad. "No money! Can't take money! Food! I need food!"

"But you can buy food," Mr. Holcomb insisted.

"No money! Can't use money. Can't take money!"

"Why not?"

"Can't take money for finding someone. Not right!" He replied.

In a night full of surprises, this was just one more. "But you can take food?" I asked.

"I'm hungry. Very hungry!' he insisted. "Will you feed me?"

"Suppose we just give you the money, out of kindness," Mr. Holcomb suggested.

"Can't take money!" the wretch suggested. "Can't spend it. Others just steal it. Always!"

"What do you mean you can't spend it?" I asked. "It's money. Good old American money!"

He shook his head. "Can't go into stores. Don't want me. Won't let me."

I had a better understanding all of a sudden. Heck, I still didn't want to be in the same room with him.

"I don't have any food with me right now," Mrs. Holcomb said again.

He hung his head sadly. "I thought so," he muttered. He looked up at me. "Can I go now?"

I nodded. "Yeah, sure. Thanks for helping us."

He ignored us and shuffled his way painfully out the door. Billy "thoughtfully" escorted him out of the building.

As he left, I felt nothing but sorry for the man. But at the same time, I was glad he was gone. And I was glad I'd never have to see him again.

Oh how wrong I was!

CHAPTER

2

I had thought that the wretch was out of my life for good, when he showed up again two weeks later. It was late in the evening, but this time I had come out of the building alone, heading home. And there he was, out on the sidewalk, waiting for me. It's a wonder that nobody had run him off earlier. I didn't have much choice in talking to him since he came right up to me, and I almost gaged at the smell of him. "What do you want?" I asked.

"Hungry," he said. "Very hungry. If I find them for you, will you feed me?"

Not again! "Look," I said, "I don't need your help. I don't want your help! Now get out of here!"

The look on his face was so pitiful. "I'm hungry," he muttered as he turned his back. "Very hungry." He began shuffling away again.

Why did I do it? It was really the last thing I wanted to do, but I couldn't help myself. The pitiful wretch might be the worst scourge of humanity, but he was still a person. Besides, he had helped us out before. "Wait!" I called. Oh damn why did I say it? "You found the Holcomb girl and all you wanted was food. I guess I owe you something to eat for that."

He brightened immediately. "Please!" he said. "Please! I'm so hungry!"

I nodded. "All right! Will a hamburger be good enough? That's what I was going to get for myself." I was ready for something other than TV dinners.

"Hamburger great! Please. Please. I'm so hungry! Anything!"

Oh why did I say it? I pointed toward the parking lot. "My car's over this way." As we walked, I wondered if the Bureau would pay to have my car fumigated tomorrow. Somehow, I doubted it. I had more misgivings about letting him into my car as soon as I unlocked it. But the odd thing was that he was very hesitant about getting in. "Look!" I said, "Either get in, or forget it. I don't have anything to eat here." Unfortunately, he got in.

I tried to hold my breath all the way to Burger King – even with the windows open. I pulled into the line for the drive through because there was no way I was going into the place with anyone like him. In fact, after riding with him, I was seriously thinking of taking a good hot shower before I tried to eat anything. I ordered him a large hamburger meal with large fries and a large drink. Actually, I ordered two of the same meal, one of them was for me – as soon as I finished my shower. He seemed to be ecstatic over it though and kept thanking me over and over again as he stuffed French fries into his mouth as fast as he could. Hungry! So hungry!

"Where can I drop you?" I asked. "Can I take you back downtown?"

It was a moment before he could answer since his mouth was full and he didn't have a lot of teeth to chew with. "Anywhere," he replied. "It doesn't matter."

I decided the least I could do was to take him back to his usual territory – which was further away from where I lived. The further, the better! But we didn't get out of the Burger King parking lot before my phone rang. It was my boss, Don Wimberly.

"Cliff!" he said somewhat urgently. "We caught another one! Young boy about four years old. Been missing for almost three hours now." He gave me the address of the parents.

Shit! I realized where I was and where the address was – not two minutes from my location. "Okay, Don, I'm almost there now. Let me call my team and I'm on it. We'll find him." I sounded so sure of myself, but the truth was, it was usually a crap shoot.

And that was when the wretch said, "I can find him for you."

Damn! I didn't want to deal with him again. Why didn't I just kick him out of the car? I had already given him something to eat! Without answering him, I called Hannah and Billy. I told Hannah especially to get a move on. She was a mother and I really liked having her around when I talked with the parents. Unfortunately, I was too close for her to get there before I did.

The house was what I would call extremely middle class. Not fancy, not poor. "Stay in the car!" I ordered the wretch as I got out. I'm not sure he even heard me as he was busy just then trying to rip little pieces off of his hamburger that he could stick in his mouth. I realized how much trouble not having any front teeth had to be for him.

The mother was just plain hysterical, as I expected she would be. The father was just plain nervous. I asked them everything I could think of. Where they had last seen their son and when? What was he doing? Was there any way he could get out of the house by himself? Where were they when it happened? So on, and so forth. Somewhere in the middle of it, Hannah came in and stood by me. Her presence alone added moral support to both me and the parents. I turned to her as soon as I got the chance. "Call everyone in. We need to canvas the whole neighborhood."

"How about the police?" she asked.

I nodded. "Them too." Billy showed up two minutes later, and right on his heels was the wretch. The mother screamed at the sight of him. "What's he doing here?" I yelled. "I told you to stay in the car!"

He ignored me and turned to the mother instead. "If I find him, will you feed me?"

"Get him out of here!" I yelled again.

But Billy didn't move. "Um…boss…. If he can do what he did last time, he could save us a lot of time."

As much as I hated to admit it, he was right. And…the damn wretch was there. I turned to the mother. "Ma'am, you don't have to do this. In fact, in many ways, I'd rather you didn't. But this…person, has helped us out in the past with very good results."

I could see that she wasn't very convinced. "What does he do?"

Before I could answer, the father had his own question. "Why are you asking us? Don't you usually do everything possible to find someone?"

"Yes we do. But this is…not…normal."

"What the hell does that mean? Can he help find our son or not?"

"Maybe." I replied.

"I can find him," the wretch added, sounding awfully confident.

"So find him!" the father yelled.

"He doesn't work like that," I started to say.

But the wretch stepped forward. "If I find him, will you feed me?"

"Feed you?" both the mother and father asked incredulously.

I shook my head. "Don't worry about it! I turned to the bum. "I'll feed you…again!" I replied for them. Will you do it?"

With a broad smile on his face he turned around and sat on their living room floor. "Put your hands on my back," he said. "Think about your son."

"What is this," the father asked, "some kind of joke?"

"I wish it were," I replied. "But we've been lucky with him in the past."

"Somehow I don't think luck and…him, seem to go together," the father replied sarcastically.

"I can find him," the wretch repeated.

His words seemed to somehow galvanize the still mostly hysterical mother. "We just put our hands on your back?" she asked.

"Just one of you," he replied. "Just one."

The father and mother seemed to look at each other. "Oh damn!" the father replied. Kneeling down, he stuck his hands directly on the tattered clothes on the bum's back. "Now what?" he asked, clearly not happy with the situation.

"Think about son," the wretch replied. "Think hard."

"Is this really necessary?" the father asked me. I nodded. "Trust me." Why had I said that? This was something I didn't really want to be trying.

"Okay, I'm thinking hard about him!" the father replied. "Very hard."

But there was no answer from the wretch. I noticed his head bowed and his eyes closed. Billy got down on the floor close to him so he could hear better.

"Car again," the wretch said. He's in back seat looking out window. Man in front seat driving.

"Is the boy alright?" I asked quietly.

"He's fine," the wretch replied.

"Can you describe the car?"

"White. Nothing fancy. Oh! Turning onto interstate…I-20 heading… east."

While I listened, Billy backed away and pulled out his phone. "Go for it," I urged. He called the police.

"Pariah," I said, trying to use what I was told he preferred for a name, "what else can you tell us about the car. We need to find it."

"Wait," he said. "Moving back, back. License tag is TTG-3248."

He had surprised me again. "That's good!" I urged. "Now what kind of car is it? You said white."

"I see Chevrolet on it."

I could hear Billy relaying the license tag to the police in the background. "Pariah," I said again. "Can you describe the driver? Is there any way you can tell us his name?"

"Don't know his name. I only know what I see and hear." He paused a moment. "Bald on top. Totally bald. Not fat, not skinny. Little mustache."

The father suddenly turned to his wife, in the process his hands came off of Pariah's back. "It's Pete from next door! It has to be."

His wife's eyes went wide. "It could be!" she admitted.

"Can't stay with boy if no connection," Pariah told them. "Haven't found him yet!"

"Oh! You mean I have to keep touching you?"

"Yes! I have no connection. You do."

While the father once again put his hands on Pariah's back, I turned to the mother. "Who's Pete?"

"Our next door neighbor. He's always seemed to like Todd. He's always been very kind to him."

"Is he married?" I asked.

She shook her head. "Divorced. A long time now I think."

I turned to Hannah. "Go check!"

"Blue lights way behind us!" Pariah suddenly said.

The wait was long. The only thing Pariah added was after a few minutes. "Lights coming closer. Man keeps checking mirrors."

Hannah wasn't long. "Nobody home next door. No car in the garage either."

"Going faster now. Man looks nervous."

We all stopped everything and just stared at the filthy creature on the living room floor waiting breathlessly for whatever he might utter next.

"Lights are closer. Speeding up more. Speeding up more. More. Slowing down quickly! Not passing other cars. Staying in middle lane behind another car. Still watching mirrors. Lights are close. See police cars – three! One very close. Driver looks nervous. Boy watching police cars now. Pointing and laughing. Boy having fun! Siren! Police car next to us! Boy is laughing! Man looking around. Pulling into right lane…now to side of road. Police cars staying with us. Slowing down. Slowing down. Stopping. Stopped. Police running toward us. Police has his gun out. The man is letting window down. What's wrong officer? Out of the car! But. Out of the car! Now! But my son and I were just going for a ride. Out of the car! And let me see some ID!"

We all sat raptly listening to the blow by blow description of what was going on. We listened as Pariah told us word for word what was being said. We listened as the police asked the four year old boy his name and he told them. We listened as they took the man into custody and put the boy, still delighted over all the police lights, into the back seat of one of the patrol cars. And we listened as the patrol car drove off, on its way to bring the boy home.

And…we listened as Billy, still on the phone, told us they had the boy. That the boy was just fine. That the man who had him was the next door neighbor, and that they were now bringing the boy home.

And while everyone breathed a sigh of relief, and the father finally removed his hands from Pariah's back, I watched as the human wreckage slowly worked his way to his feet. And I marveled at what he had just done – seemingly so easily. Why was this creature so down and out if he had that kind of power? What had happened to him?

I had one other disturbing thought about him. What would someone else do with him if they knew what he was capable of? I didn't want to dwell too much on that one because it disturbed me almost as much as the wretch himself.

He turned to the mother and father. "I found him. Will you feed me?"

"Wait a minute!" I interrupted. "Pariah, you just ate. I'll buy you something to eat myself if you'll let me."

He seemed to think about that for a few moments before finally nodding. "I found him," he said. "Like I said I would."

"I nodded. You did indeed." My problem now was, what was I going to do with him? Did he have any idea how valuable he was? Somehow, I got the impression that he didn't consider himself to be valuable at all.

It was very late when we got back to my car. Once the doors were closed, I was again assaulted by the smell of him. I opened my window again in self-defense. "Do you want to eat now?" I asked, trying to honor my bargain, "Or will you take a rain check and let me buy you something better tomorrow night?"

For answer, he opened up his Burger King bag and pulled out what was left of his hamburger – which was most of it. "I can't eat much at one time," he replied. I got the impression he was a lot saner now than at any time since I had met him.

"Tomorrow night then?" I asked.

"I would be very grateful," he replied. "Very grateful. I get so hungry!"

"I'm sure you do. Where can I take you?"

He looked around. "Drop me here. It's good enough."

"But where do you usually spend the night?"

"Anywhere. Nowhere. Wherever I am."

There was no way I was going to invite this creature home with me. No way in hell! "You're sure?" I asked.

"Here is fine," he replied.

I pulled over and he got out. "Thank you," he said before closing the car door. I was so hungry."

"You're welcome." I replied. "And thanks for your help again tonight."

He nodded and reached to close the door again. Then he stopped. "I can find them," he said. "If I find them for you, will you feed me?"

I wanted to say hell yes! But there were too many big red flags waving in front of my eyes. "I'll think about it," I replied.

That night, I dreamed all night long about what had happened. Over and over again I played it through my mind. I didn't sleep much at all.

CHAPTER

3

In our morning meeting the next day, Don praised me for finding the kid so fast. "I think that was some kind of record," he added. "And the kid wasn't even still in the neighborhood. The guy from next door was taking him off to…who knows where!"

There was no way I was going to admit what really happened. So I just said, "We got lucky." But when the meeting broke up, Don asked me to stay behind. "Where'd you get the tip from on the neighbor?" he asked.

"You don't want to know," I replied.

"That's why I asked. I do want to know!"

I shook my head. "No you don't. And my report is just going to say a tip from someone nearby, and that's it!" There was a bit of a brief stare down between us, but he finally backed off with a nod of his head. "I'll look forward to seeing the report."

Hannah and Billy both were waiting for me in my office when I got back. I took it as a troubling sign when Billy closed the door after I got in. "Boss," he said somewhat excitedly. "Do you know what kind of opportunity we got here?"

I looked back and forth between them. "Don't say it! Don't even think it! We don't want to go down that path!"

"But why not?" Hannah asked. "Cliff, if he can find them so easily, think what he could do for our backlog of old cases. Maybe we can find some of the ones we thought were impossible!"

I didn't want to tell either of them that those very thoughts had been running through my head all night long. The possibilities were… incredible – if he could really do what we thought he could. But if someone found out…. "Look," I said, "the Bureau has worked with psychics before, probably many times. But they're never reliable. If this doesn't pan out, we'd be the laughing stock of…everyone!" The arguments weren't exactly accurate, but they were close enough to get my point across. Unfortunately, neither Billy or Hannah seemed to want to agree.

"Cliff," Hannah said as she leaned across my desk, "think of Shelly. What would you do if she were missing for…months! Would you be willing to go out on a shaky limb if there was even the slightest chance of finding her?"

I hated her. She had hit my soft spot. One of the reasons I was so passionate about this job. I knew what parents went through when their child was missing. I had been lucky with mine. That was a few years ago now, but you never forget that fear. Never! "Okay," I finally agreed. "But if we do this, we have to find a way to do it…quietly!"

"We'll think of something, boss," Billy replied with a big smile. "We'll definitely work something out."

Hannah just leaned over and kissed my cheek.

"But if we do this, we can't let up on any of our other cases!"

Billy looked shocked. "Boss! As if we would!"

I threw them both out in disgust! Unfortunately, the vacuum created by them leaving pulled John Thomas into my office. He immediately sat back in the chair in front of my desk. Actually, it was more like he lazed back in the chair. "That was good work last night," he said as he sat down.

"We got lucky."

"I'll say!" There was this strange look on his face that made me wary. "Some of the guys mentioned something about a really nasty looking bum that came out of the house when you left. Did the tip come from him?"

That had been one of my big worries. When you bring everyone in to look for someone, everyone comes – including the agents that were closest to John. And just like I would expect Hannah and Billy to keep me up to date, most likely Darla or Brent had already talked to John. But I wasn't ready yet to tell John about the Pariah, even though I realized he would have to be brought into the loop very soon. I was cautious with my wording. "Sort of," I replied.

He looked at me quizzically.

"John," I said. "Listen. We're working something that's…off the wall right now. Not normal at all."

"A case? I understand if it's something personal."

I shook my head. "It's not that. But I promise you, I'm going to let you in on it very soon. It's just that…" I shook my head as I tried to find the words. "This isn't anything I can tell you about." I could see he was going to argue with me but I continued speaking before he could say a word. "But…instead of telling you, maybe it's something you have to see for yourself. But I'll warn you, it's probably going to make the hairs stand up on the back of your head! I know it does me. Still!"

"What the heck?"

"John, trust me! Give me a day or two, then you'll see for yourself. But I'm going to ask you this one favor…no, I'm going to beg this favor…."

"What?"

"You can't tell a soul! Not a single stinking soul! Not your wife! Not your mother! And especially not Wimberly!"

I could see he was suddenly hesitant. "Something…illegal?" he asked.

"No. Nothing like that. Not even remotely like that. It's for…someone's protection." It was as close as I was willing to come.

It took him a moment, but he nodded his head. "Okay. I'll play."

Billy and Hannah were understandably anxious to get started. Together we sat down and picked out a case involving a teenage girl that was about six months old now. Her name was Terri Sterlaki. It was one of those cases where we all felt like we'd never find the girl. In my mind, it was a perfect test case. But where they wanted to start immediately, I decided to wait a few days. The last time we had used Pariah was still too fresh in everybody's mind. And just so there would be fewer people around, I decided we'd do it later at night.

That evening, I bought the Pariah another hamburger meal from Burger King and he was just as delighted as he had been the night before. I had considered getting him a decent steak, but there was no way I was going to let him go into any restaurant. And besides, I had a feeling he probably couldn't chew it. After I dropped him off again with his still full bag of food, I told him that we would try using him again, but not for two more days. "Eight o'clock at night!" I told him.

"Don't have watch," he replied. Can I come when it gets dark?"

"Yeah sure. Fine." It would have to do. As he walked off, I still wasn't sure if I was glad or not that he agreed to help again.

Getting the girl's parents to agree to it was a foregone conclusion. They were desperate, and I played it that we were equally desperate too. Well, we were. I warned them in advance of what we were going to try, but as I said, they were desperate. I think they were also reassured that we were still trying to solve the case.

The evening we were going to try it, instead of going home after work, John and I went out for dinner and a beer. I paid for a second beer for both of us. "You're going to need it," I told him.

I had put Billy on "Pariah watch" since we had no idea when he would actually get there. Hannah was detailed to wait for the parents. Pariah was already up in our room by the time John and I got there. Billy had found him another candy bar that he was munching on happily. Hannah was still downstairs waiting for the parents.

I went over and said hello to Pariah. He didn't speak, but he held up the candy bar appreciatively. I was glad to see his eyes didn't look quite so insane this time.

"You couldn't clean him up a bit?" John asked me quietly a few moments later.

"He really needs it," I agreed.

"Now I know what you were talking about with that second beer."

I shook my head. "No you don't. Not yet."

Mr. and Mrs. Sterlaki showed up and were immediately somewhat put off by Pariah's appearance – not to mention smell – despite the fact that I had tried to warn them sufficiently beforehand. At least Pariah had finished eating the candy before they arrived. The way he ate would have probably grossed them out of the building since he always chewed with his lips wide open. I'm pretty sure he really couldn't breathe out of that nose. Maybe that's why his own smell didn't seem to bother him either.

We explained what they needed to do. Billy pulled a chair in place for Pariah, but before the wretch sat down, he turned to the parents. "If I find her, will you feed me?"

I was embarrassed that he would ask. I had already planned on getting him another hamburger later from Burger King.

Both parents looked to me for advice. "Don't worry, Pariah. I'll feed you," I promised.

Pariah finally nodded and sat in the chair with his back to everyone. Mrs. Sterlaki braced herself, then put her hands on his back. She closed her eyes. I had no doubt she was thinking as absolutely hard as she could about her daughter. Billy turned on the recorder the moment Pariah closed his eyes. And…we waited. Much longer than usual.

Finally, he spoke. His words seemed hesitant…and distressed. "I…don't think I'm finding her. I can't get usual sense…like she's not really here. Connection is…so weak. Very weak. But I'm…somewhere. So dark. Can't see much. Trees…and…bushes. Can't see anyone! Don't understand! What's that? A car! Heard a car drive by. Road! Road over there! Keep getting drawn back to this spot. But I don't see anyone! Where is she?" He lifted his head after a few moments. "Never had this problem before. Never! I'm sorry. Don't know what to do. I…I think…."

I could see how distressed he was. "What do you think?" I asked quietly.

He looked back at the mother who had taken her hands off of his back now. "I'm sorry," he said. I…think she's…dead."

It was the one thing we were all worried about. The one thing not one of us was willing to say. The mother broke down in sobs that wracked everyone's heart.

"This doesn't mean she's dead!" her husband declared boldly.

"No, it doesn't!" I agreed wholeheartedly, even though I didn't really feel that way. "This is just something we wanted to try. We're at our wit's end looking for her. We all felt it was worth the effort."

He seemed somewhat placated. "Hear that honey?" he said to his sobbing wife. "She's not dead! This…guy, just couldn't find her. That's all."

She looked up and hugged him tighter, but she didn't say anything.

Pariah got up from the chair. "I failed," he said. "Never done that before. Sorry." He started shuffling out.

"Wait!" I said. Then I addressed everyone in the room. "Let's try it again. Please, for my sake." I could see how dubious everyone looked. "What can it hurt?" I asked.

Pariah nodded and made his way back to the chair. The mother nodded despite her sobbing. We gave her a few moments to somewhat collect herself. Then, still in tears, she put her hands on his back.

Pariah started speaking much sooner this time. "Same place again. Same patch of woods. This spot, right here. But I still see no one. Nothing but trees and brush. Can hardly see that."

"Pariah," I said softly. "Look around, try to find something that might help us. Anything!"

"It's dark. Hard to see anything." He said. "Big tree fallen right here. Nothing but brush and bushes around it. Can't see much. Too dark!"

"Okay, that's fine," I said. "You said earlier that there was a road, can you get to it?"

We waited a few moments. "Road not far. Just up little hill. No cars now. Hard to see, but looks very straight. No lights nearby."

"Pariah, you said no lights nearby, but can you see any lights at all?"

"Stars. Kind of a big red light way up in the sky. A tower maybe?"

"Good, Pariah. We need to figure out where that tower is."

"I guess, maybe…if I go up…."

"Up?" I asked.

"Up high. Going up. Higher. Above the trees now. I see the tower a little better. Higher now. More lights. Lots of lights in the distance. City. A car! On another road. Going a different way."

"Pariah, you said it's going a different way. Can you get to that road from where you are?"

His answer was a long time coming. "Maybe. The connection is weak. Very weak. Almost not there."

"Please try. See if you can find a sign at the intersection so we know where the road is."

"Going that way. Going…going…. See it! Long way from where I was! Trying to get there. Trying…. Made it! I'm there! Weak though, very weak."

"It's okay, Pariah. You made it. Now look for a sign. Anything to tell us where you are."

"Yes! A sign! I see it. Right at intersection…."

We waited, but he said nothing more for a while. "What does it say, Pariah? What does the sign say?"

"Having trouble reading it. Too dark. No light. Too weak."

We were at an impasse. I was just about to call it quits when he said, "Wait!"

"What is it?" I asked.

"A car. Car is coming, but still long way off."

"Can you wait for it?" I asked.

"Think so," he agreed with a nod of his head. "Can try."

We waited for what seemed like forever. You could have heard a pin drop the whole time. I think we were all afraid to even breathe hard.

"Coming…coming…closer…wait…Timberline! Think it said Timberline. Car passed fast. Couldn't see much."

"Good job, Pariah!" I praised somewhat excitedly. It was half of some information, but that was about it. "Look at the sign again, Pariah. Is there a sign for the other road?"

"Yes, but can't read it," he replied. "Too dark. Too weak. Like I'm hardly here."

"But you are still there, right?" I asked, guessing at what I thought was happening.

"Yes," he replied. "For now."

"Okay. Is there another car coming?" I asked. Can you maybe go higher to see if there's another car coming."

We waited a few moments. "No car. Nothing," he replied.

I looked at the others. "Suggestions?" I asked quietly. I was all out of them.

It was Hannah who finally spoke. "Only that we try it again tomorrow, during the day, when he can see something."

I looked at everyone. Surprisingly, it was John who added. "I agree."

I physically pulled the mother's hands off of Pariah's back. As distressed as she was, she seemed to be absolutely determined to find out more – despite the pain I knew she had to feel. She started crying again and hugged her husband.

"Are you willing to try this again tomorrow?" I asked. "During the day?"

Mr. Sterlaki shook his head. "This doesn't prove that she's dead!" he argued. "As far as I can see, it proves nothing!"

I nodded. "You're right. Completely! But I for one am curious to find out exactly what he saw. Aren't you?"

"What he saw? Get real! He didn't see anything at all! This is all bogus! All of it!"

I nodded. "Think what you may," I said. "We have no proof that anything he saw was real. I only know we've had very good luck with him in the past."

"And how many times has he been wrong?" the husband countered, as if that argument alone would dispel all of my arguments.

I hated telling him. "Not once. Not about one tiny little bit of data. He's been one hundred percent right…about absolutely everything… so far."

That seemed to shake him a bit. "I don't believe it," he finally said. "I don't believe any of this!" With that, he pulled his wife closer to him, and with nasty looks to all of us, led his wife out the door. Hannah followed close behind to escort them out.

I turned to John. "Sorry. I promised you something special, and it didn't happen. This is the first time we haven't been able to get anything," I said.

"You said it would be hair raising, and you were right!"

I shook my head, "No, not this time. This wasn't nearly as good as what he's done twice before now."

"It isn't?" He seemed to have a hard time believing that. "Look, I've worked with psychics twice before, once in Arizona, and the second time in Oklahoma. Neither of them was anything like what I heard tonight.

Not even close! If that wasn't hair raising, then I'm not sure I want to see what he can really do."

"I nodded. Thanks for taking this so well. But unfortunately, tonight, we learned nothing."

Billy broke into our conversation at that point. "No! We did learn something. He can't see well in the dark."

John laughed. "Neither can I for that matter!"

Pariah was on his feet. Without a word, he started shuffling his way toward the door. He looked very dejected. "Pariah," I called. "Thanks. You did great."

He stopped and looked at me, sadly. He shook his head. "Didn't find her. Hoping for something to eat, but I didn't find her."

"Don't worry. I promise I'll get you something tonight, as soon as we leave. Will that be all right?"

"But I didn't find her," he argued.

I shook my head. "I think you did. But even if you didn't, I'm still buying you something to eat."

He brightened a bit and went back to the chair he had been sitting in a few moments earlier.

"And when you're done with him," John said, "I'll have another beer already poured and waiting for you as soon as you can get there. By then, I'll probably be finishing up my first entire pitcher. I may get very drunk tonight. My wife is going to have a fit!"

CHAPTER

4

The following day, John was more than a little worse for the wear, but he was managing. We all felt somewhat dejected over the night before. To raise spirits, I was thinking about suggesting another test, another chance to see if we could find someone who had been missing for a while now. But I never got the chance to suggest it because before I could say anything, Mrs. Sterlaki called.

"Agent McNair?" she asked.

"Yes, Ma'am. I'm sorry about last night, I added quickly. We tried."

"That's just it," she replied. "My husband is at work right now. He's pretty adamant that we not do that again, but I think we should. If you like, I'm willing to come up there and we can try again, this time during the day so that hopefully that…man, can see something – if he can see anything. I really want to know, one way or another, what happened to Terri. We just can't tell my husband about this."

I was shocked. But at the same time, I was excited too. But there was this one little problem. Well, several actually, but the biggest one was… "Um…I think you're absolutely right in this choice, Ma'am. But…I first have to find Pariah."

"You called him that last night," she replied. "It seems like an awful thing to call someone. Especially someone who seems so…unfortunate."

"I couldn't agree more," I replied. "But from what I understand, it's what he wants to be called. I don't even know his real name," I admitted.

"Seems strange for the FBI to not know something as simple as that."

She had a point. A big one! "You're right, Ma'am. And that's something we're going to fix…soon. But in the meantime, can I call you as soon as we do find him? Will you still be willing to try again?"

"As long as my husband doesn't find out," she replied.

"I think we can manage that."

"And Agent McNair…"

"Yes?"

"What was that thing about him wanting us to feed him?"

"He's hungry," I replied. "I think he gets very hungry. It's why he agrees to do this."

"I'll see if I can bring him something," she replied. "It's the least I can do. I'll try to make a small donation to his wallet as well for his trouble."

"Don't bother," I replied. "That's the strangest thing. He won't take money. Just food."

She said nothing for a little while. "I think I understand," she finally replied. "Call me. I'll come. Just try not to call when my husband is home."

I put the word out immediately for the police downtown to find him. But no word came back that day. The next day, I asked them to keep looking, but again nothing. In the meantime, I asked Hannah to start quietly checking on him. Who was he really? What was his story?

By the following day, we were starting to worry about the wretch. What had become of him? Hannah came back with a very small folder on the guy. She and Billy and John all crowded into my shoebox office while Hannah went over it.

"His real name is Thomas Clayton. No one seems to know where he got the Pariah name, but it does seem to fit. Still, it's an odd name for someone to give him."

We said nothing at that.

"Now here's the juicy part," Hannah said. "He got out of prison about three years ago for child molestation and rape!"

We all stared aghast. "What?" I said, totally incredulous.

"That's it! Convicted of raping a sixteen year old girl and sent to prison. Looks like he got a really stiff sentence. Sixteen years. Been on the street ever since he got out."

"Oh damn!" I muttered. "We've been playing with a child molester. Asking a child molester to find…children! Damn!"

"No wonder he was so good," John added.

I shook my head. "He was good, but I don't think it had anything at all to do with him liking kids. I think he's just talented."

John nodded. "Sorry. I agree. It was just a thought."

"There's some other stuff that I think I should add about him," Hannah said.

"What's the point? He's a child molester!"

"Still, I think you should know."

I shook my head resignedly. "Go ahead, let's hear the rest."

Looks like between the court ruling against him and the fact that he no longer had a job, he and his wife lost not only their house, but all their possessions."

"He has a wife?" I asked incredulously. "Maybe he's with her!"

Hannah shook her head. "She died shortly after he went to prison while they were selling her stuff out from under her. The stress killed her. He literally lost…everything!"

I nodded. "I get the picture." A thought occurred to me. "He's a real mess – physically. How did he look before prison?"

She pulled a picture out of the file and held it up. The guy looked… nice. Very middle class, but nice. Nothing messed up about him at all. "So the question is, what happened to him?"

Hannah looked though the papers in the file, but there was nothing more about his physical problems. "Just one other thing about his case," Hannah added. "The girl he raped…was Stacy Chermont.

There was something about the Chermont name that seemed to ring a bell, but I just wasn't placing it.

"The father is William Chermont," Hannah tossed out when she saw all our blank faces. "Huge political financier."

My jaw dropped. That William Chermont! One of the richest son-of-a-bitches I knew of. And very powerful! I wasn't sure, but I thought he had moved on to the national political scene now and not just Georgia.

"You may have also heard of the lawyer they used, Nathan Brecker."

The name meant nothing to me, but I heard John give a small grunt. "Isn't he one of those big Washington lawyer's now? High profile cases only? Charges about the amount in Fort Knox for his services?"

Hannah nodded. "That's him."

We were all thinking it, but it was Billy who uttered it out loud. "Shit! He sure picked the wrong girl to screw!"

None of us could agree more.

"So what do we do now?" Hannah asked.

"Nothing," I said. "It's over. The guys a damn child molester. We can't have him anywhere around here."

I saw John nodding his head. He got to his feet. "I got to tell you though, it sure was interesting while it lasted. I just wish I could have seen those first few cases you solved with him. That had to be something!" With a shake of his head, he walked out.

"It was something!" Billy agreed, as he too left."

Hannah laid the report on my desk. "Back to the basics, I guess," she said before leaving.

I was tempted to toss Pariah's file into the trash. I hid it in a bottom drawer instead. Hopefully, I'd never find it again. I called the downtown police and told them to stop bothering to look for the bum. It was a courtesy call only. I was fairly sure they weren't bothering to look anymore anyway.

And once again I made the mistake of thinking the wretch was out of my life – for good!

CHAPTER

5

The following morning, I hadn't been out of our morning meeting and at my desk for ten minutes before my phone rang. When I picked it up, I was, and I wasn't, surprised to hear Mrs. Sterlaki on the other end.

"Agent McNair, I haven't heard from you. What's happening on me getting together with that poor psychic again?"

"Well, that's just it, Ma'am," I replied. "To be perfectly honest, we searched for him for days without finding him. But then yesterday we finally got more information about him that we didn't have before. I'm afraid we're not going to be able to use him anymore."

"And why is that? Has he left town? Or did he somehow manage to get a job somewhere? I would think he would at least be findable."

"Actually, he wasn't. The police couldn't find him at all. But that's not the main reason we won't be using him anymore. I'm afraid…" I didn't want to be honest, but I knew I had to be. "I'm afraid it's come to our attention that the man spent a long time in prison for child molestation and rape!"

The silence on the other end was mostly what I expected to hear. "Oh dear!" she finally said. "Oh…dear!"

I couldn't agree more! Those two words pretty much said it all.

"But Agent McNair, you still said he had been successful in the past. If my daughter is dead, I don't care what he's done…if…he can indeed find her. And what we went through in your offices a few nights ago seemed to be…depressing, but…promising. If you can arrange it, I'm still willing to try again — as long as my husband never finds out."

I was somewhat surprised. "I just can't, I'm afraid," I told her. "With a background like that, we simply can't use him. We can't even have him anywhere around here."

"Oh dear," she repeated. "Well, if you can't use him, there's no reason why I can't. How can I get in touch with him? There has to be some way. You found him before."

Now I was shocked. "Ma'am, I don't think that's a very good idea."

"Well I do!" she countered. "As far as I can tell, you've done nothing for months now. This is the closest we've come so far to discovering what's happened to her…and I for one intend to follow up to the fullest! Now how can I find him?"

"I really don't know," I admitted. "As I said, even the police downtown couldn't find him. And that's where he usually roams."

"Thank you very much then," she replied. "I'll concentrate my search downtown. Perhaps the police there can be more help than you've been. Goodbye Agent McNair!"

The click was loud as she hung up the phone. "Damn!" I swore to myself. I couldn't believe she would be so adamant!

Hannah walked into my office then. "Hey Cliff, here's the file you wanted on the Bryant's finances. So far, it looks clean to me."

"Thanks, Hannah," I replied somewhat sourly. I couldn't get Mrs. Sterlaki out of my head.

"What's got you so down all of a sudden?" she asked.

"Mrs. Sterlaki! She just called. She wants to find Pariah herself and try to find her daughter!"

"Can you blame her? I mean, wouldn't you if you were in her position?"

I tried to dismiss her words. I tried very hard. But they kept haunting me all day long. They haunted me as I stopped for a quick drink on the way home. They haunted me as I ate my TV dinner – not even realizing what was on TV. They haunted me so badly, that as soon as I had finished eating, I got in my car and headed downtown to look for the bum. The police couldn't find him, and it was their territory. They knew it better than I did. But that didn't mean I couldn't look.

They had said to check the backs of the restaurants. So that's what I did. I drove around lots of them with no luck at all. Finally, I parked my car and started wandering the streets. I found…bums. Homeless people really. The unfortunate down and outs who litter every big city. The ones who life has thrown such a hard curve ball that they have no way to recover. The ones who are barely surviving. And all any of them want is a good fair chance. Well, most of them. A few really only wanted a bottle of cheap liquor or some drugs.

I wandered around for hours checking the faces of all of them. Asking many if they had seen him. Some recognized his name. More knew who I was talking about by his description. But none knew where he was. I kept at it though because I knew I wouldn't be able to sleep that night. What would I do if it were my daughter? That answer was easy. I'd never rest! Never leave the slightest stone unturned. No matter what!

And very late at night, near the back of an Italian restaurant, I heard someone knocking on a door. The sound is what caught my attention and I wandered closer simply to take a look. And there I saw him, in all his glory…or lack thereof. He was about to knock again when I called him. "Pariah!"

He turned toward me and looked surprised to see me. Even in the dim spot lights behind the building I could see the craziness in his eyes. "I'm hungry," he said. "Will you give me some food?"

"What are you doing here?" I asked. "We've been looking for you."

"I'm hungry, he replied. "Very hungry. Just a scrap of bread would be wonderful. Anything! Please!"

There was something really wrong with him. "Pariah, do you remember me?"

He left the door and walked closer. I was even more struck by how wild his eyes looked. He nodded. "I couldn't find her. I tried, but I couldn't."

"That's right! We need you to try again. Please."

"I'm hungry," he replied. "Very hungry. Do you have any food? Please?"

"I don't have anything on me right now, but I can get you something."

"Hungry," he repeated as he turned away from me. "Very hungry." He seemed almost in a daze. He was about to knock on the door again, but he suddenly stopped himself and came back to me. "Stay away! Don't interfere! No matter what! No matter what you see! No matter what they say! Please don't interfere! Promise me!"

I was confused. "Sure, if that's what you want."

"I'm hungry," he repeated as he turned back again. "Very hungry."

He seemed almost in a fog again as he went back to the door. Before knocking, he turned to me. "No matter what!" he repeated. "Hide! Don't let them see you. I need food now. I'm hungry!"

I was confused, shocked…I don't know what. But I wandered back behind one of the dumpsters where I could watch, hopefully without anyone seeing me. He was knocking again before I reached my hiding place. He knocked again, louder. Then louder. I watched as he hung his head and turned away. But then he quickly turned back to the door again – and it opened.

"Please!" I heard him say. "I'm hungry. Very hungry. Can you spare some food? Please? Please?"

He sounded so damn pitiful! I would have taken him somewhere and got him something tonight! Why had he decided to go to the door instead? Did he just want Italian food or something?

"Scram bum!" I heard the man who opened the door say. "Beat it! Now!"

"But I'm hungry. Very hungry. Please."

There was a slight pause. "You want food? You want food?" The man had said it as if he didn't believe it.

"Please!" Pariah pleaded. "I'm so hungry."

"Damn! You want food? I'll give you food! You stay right there!"

The door closed then, but Pariah stayed put. He glanced in my direction and seemed satisfied that I was hidden well enough. A few minutes later, the door opened and the man stepped out into the light. He was a somewhat heavy man dressed in a white t-shirt, and had an apron covering most of his bottom half. A small white hat sat on his head. I guessed that he was the cook.

He carried a plate from the restaurant mounded with what looked like spaghetti. He strode away from the door over next to the other dumpster. "You want food, you bum? You want it that bad? Then here it is!" With that, he dumped the whole plate full of spaghetti out onto the ground in front of the dumpster. I heard another man laugh and saw someone else framed in the doorway.

"Oh, you need some sauce for it?" I was horrified to see him let out a big globule of spit right on top of the pile, then he put his foot right in it and ground it all into the ground. "There! There's your food. Now eat it!" When Pariah didn't move, the man yelled at him. "I said, eat it! You wanted it that bad, now let me see you eat it!"

The man in the doorway was laughing harder now. "Give it to him good Joe!"

I was about to pull out my gun to bully these men a bit, but Pariah glanced back at me and gave me a slight shake of his head. Against my better judgment, I stayed put. But I really wanted to ram my fist down Joe the cook's throat!

I watched totally horrified as Pariah got down onto the ground and began picking up some of the spaghetti with his gnarled hands, and shoving it quickly into his mouth.

"Not like that! You're no better than any of the stray dogs that roam around here! You want it? Then you can eat it like they do, without your hands!"

I had had enough! I started to step into the light, but again he glanced back at me and slightly shook his head. I nearly had a fit as I watched Pariah lower his head to the ground and try to eat what was there with just his mouth. Disgusting! I vowed that as of tomorrow morning I was going to do everything in my power to shut that restaurant down! And I was sure I could come up with some way to put Joe the cook into jail! Even if I had to invent something!

Why the heck did Pariah let them do this to him? I would have fed him! Didn't he know that?

Joe the cook soon gave up watching Pariah make even more of a fool of himself than he already was. A few minutes later, both he and his partner disappeared inside and the door closed again. I was surprised to see Pariah look up at me with what I was guessing was a look of triumph. I came out from behind my dumpster and was further astonished to see Pariah pulling a folded up paper bag out of his pocket. As I watched, I realized it was one of the Burger King bags from the last time I had seen him. He scooped up all the spaghetti on the ground and dumped it into the bag – dirt and filth and all. Then he carefully rolled up the top of the bag to seal it.

He held it up to me with an air of accomplishment. "See," he said happily. "Food. He gave me food."

I wanted to puke. I wanted to kill the two guys inside. "Don't eat that!" I said. "Throw it out. I'll take you right now and get you anything you want!" I meant it too! "Why did you put yourself through that?"

His answer was to simply hold the bag up again and say, "Food."

He turned and headed further back behind the building toward a little grassy strip where he wouldn't be disturbed. I followed him, wondering what he was up to now. Once he reached the grass, he sat down on it and opened his bag. His gnarled hand reached into the bag and pulled out a little of the spaghetti…and transferred it directly into his mouth. Yuck! It was all I could do to keep what was left of my TV dinner down! And I realized, he was happy about it!

I sat down next to him and watched as he put another handful of spaghetti into his mouth. "Why do you do that?" I asked. "I swear, tomorrow I'm going to ruin that guy for life! I should have stopped him! Why didn't you let me stop him?"

He looked horrified at me. "He fed me," he said simply. "He gave me food. Sometimes, when I'm really hungry…I come here. He feeds me. Feeds me when no one else will."

"It doesn't look worth it!" I commented. "How can you eat that, after what he did to it?"

He shrugged as he grabbed more out of the bag and stuck it into his mouth. "Been through worse. Much worse. Deep down, he has a good heart," he said. "Only does that because of others."

Others? I was guessing he was talking about the second man who stayed inside. Or…was he talking about more homeless people that he didn't want hanging around. Either way, I was going to ruin the guy. "I promise, tomorrow I'm going to have it out with him. I'll make him very sorry for what he did tonight."

"Don't! Please don't!" He seemed awfully distressed about it. "He has good heart. Feeds me when I'm most desperate. Where will I go when no one else will give me food?"

"You call that feeding you? I call it torture!" I realized then that some of the crazy look was starting to fade from his eyes. I was beginning to sense a pattern to it, the hungrier he was, the more his insanity took hold. I tucked that fact away for the future.

"Look," I finally said as he stuffed a bit more spaghetti into his mouth. "Remember a few nights ago when you couldn't find the girl?"

He shook his head sadly. "I tried. I really tried. But I couldn't find her. Only that place. But there was nothing there."

"Well, we think you did find her. We think you were right, she's dead, and probably either buried right there, or she was killed right there. Mrs. Sterlaki wants you to try again, only this time during the day when you can see better."

He shook his head. "I don't know if it will help. The connection was so weak. It was like I was there, but she wasn't."

I wasn't exactly sure what he meant by that, but I figured it didn't matter. "Look, please, can you meet with her tomorrow and we'll try it again?"

He turned to look straight at me. "If I find her, will you feed me?"

How many times had he asked that question? "Hell yes!" I replied. "In fact, I'll feed you tonight too."

He just shook his head and held up his bag of spaghetti as if it were some kind of prize. "Tomorrow would be good."

"Thanks," I told him. And despite my better judgment, I meant it. Now I had to fix a few other things. "Look, you're a hard person to find. Can I drive you somewhere closer to our building?"

He seemed to think about that. "No, I'll walk."

"But you'll be walking all night!"

He only shrugged again. "Don't like riding in cars. Too closed in."

"Well, we won't be doing this till tomorrow afternoon sometime. I've got some arrangements to make first. But I need someplace where I can find you when we're ready."

He shrugged. "Be there tomorrow."

But that in itself was one of the things I needed to fix. "Um… I think it would be better if you didn't hang around the entrance. One of our other agents would probably throw you off the property.

He seemed to think about that for a minute. "Your car. I know where you parked. I'll be at your car."

Something told me that somewhere deep inside, this guy was a lot smarter than anyone gave him credit for. "Good enough," I replied. "I'll see you then."

There was a smile on his face as he dug his hand one more time into the bag of spaghetti and stuffed it into his mouth. I could see a piece of spaghetti that had gotten stuck in his filthy stringy beard. Disgusting! Tomorrow, no matter what, I was going to get this guy something better to eat!

C H A P T E R

6

The minute I got out of our morning meeting and back to my desk, I called Billy and Hannah in…and shut the door.

"What's up, boss?" Billy asked.

"I found Pariah last night."

"You what? Why?" Billy asked.

"Good for you!" Hannah said at almost the same time.

It seemed they both viewed the situation differently. "I found him because I'm not going to let Mrs. Sterlaki go it alone."

"So we're on again?" Billy asked, his excitement growing.

I nodded. "Yeah, we're on. But we need to do it somewhere else. Not here."

"How about at Sterlaki's house?" Hannah suggested. "Besides, if the girl is dead, she may be buried closer to there, than here."

"Good point," I admitted. "I was thinking of going there to try it too."

"We need some better organization this time," Billy said.

I agreed, but decided to see what he had in mind. "What do you mean?" I asked.

"Last time, all he came up with was Timberline road. I checked and found several Timberline roads between here and North Carolina. And none of them are anything close to being short."

"Okay," I replied, knowing he was going somewhere with this. "What did you have in mind?"

"There's only one that's anywhere close to the girls home, so hopefully that's where she is."

"If she's there!" I pointed out.

"Yeah, if she's there," he agreed. "We can divide up into teams with cars spread out at the most likely areas along the road. Then, if he comes up with something, we can get there fast. Maybe he can even guide the cars right to the exact spot."

Everything he said had already gone through my mind a long time ago. I smiled. "Keep at it Billy. My job has your name on it in a few years!"

He beamed with pleasure. The truth was, he was a bit young and inexperienced yet, but he was going to go far. No doubt about it. As soon as I chased them out of my office, I wandered over to John's office and lounged back in the chair across from his desk.

"What's up?" he asked.

"Oh…just wanted to know if you're up for another little experiment with Pariah again this afternoon? Besides, I think I'm going to need everyone on the team to help out."

He raised his eyebrows. "You told me he's a damn child molester. We don't dare!"

I nodded. "I know. But the mother insists on going it alone with the bum, and there's no way I'm going to let her do that!"

"In other words, you're just as curious as everyone else to see what Pariah can do!"

"I didn't say that," I replied as I got up from the chair. "But you're right!"

By one o'clock in the afternoon, our office was deserted. Before any of us left, I checked the parking lot and found Pariah sound asleep – under my car. I almost missed seeing him. If it wasn't for the smell, I wouldn't have looked that close. A few minutes later, I dispatched our three two-man teams to head for the places Billy had suggested they wait. John, Pariah, and I got in my car and headed for the Sterlaki residence. We stopped at McDonalds on the way and I got Pariah another hamburger to munch on in the back seat while John and I suffered with the smell in the front.

"We gotta find a way to clean him up some!" John complained.

"I couldn't agree more!" I replied as I turned the air-conditioning up higher.

Mrs. Sterlaki greeted us at the door and led us through into her family room. I had been there many times before when the case was fresh, but it had been a while now.

"I guess we do this the same way?" she asked as we entered the room. "I just put my hands on his back?"

I looked to Pariah. "Back, or hands," he said as he held out his filthy gnarled appendages.

I wondered if his fingers hurt him much, even when he wasn't using them. "Why don't we just stick with the way we've been doing it," I suggested. Everyone seemed to agree. "That's it then," I said. Whenever you're ready."

"I've been ready for months," she replied. "I want to find my daughter! One way...or another!"

At that, Pariah stepped forward again. "If I find her, will you feed me?"

I was startled. Why did he have to ask her that? I had told him I would buy him a good meal just as soon as we finished! "I'm sorry..." I started to say to her. But she wasn't paying any attention to me.

"Yes, I promise to feed you. Even if you don't find her. It's the least I can do."

Pariah looked at her and nodded. "Thank you," he replied as if she had just granted him the greatest gift in the world. "I hope I do better this time."

"I'm sure you will," she replied. She motioned toward one of the comfortable chairs in the room that would be one she could easily stand behind. "Why don't you sit here," she suggested.

Pariah looked at the chair, but he made no move toward it. Then he shook his head. "No! Too dirty!"

"Don't worry," she reassured him. "It will clean."

But he refused to sit in the nice chair. "Sit on floor," he offered instead and started to sit down on her rug.

"Of course not!" she replied, stopping him cold. "Tell you what. How about one of my kitchen chairs. You certainly can't hurt them! Will that do?"

Pariah considered it for a moment, then he nodded.

"I'll get it," I offered. I already knew where the kitchen was. Two minutes later, I was back with the chair. I set it right in the middle of the room. Pariah sat down. Mrs. Sterlaki glanced at both John and I, then said. "Okay…" Then she put her hands on Pariah's back. I saw his eyes close and his head bow down. We didn't have to wait as long this time.

"Same spot," he said. Woods. Trees. Brush all around. Fallen tree here. Dense brush, hard to see much."

"Try, Pariah," I coaxed. "Check the ground all around if you can. See if you can find anything that might tell us if the girl was ever there."

"Down low," he said softly. "Very weak again but much easier in the light."

"Good," I replied. "Pariah, is it possible to check under that fallen tree too?"

He nodded very slightly. "Some. Gaps under it in places. Um… Um…"
"What?" I asked.
"Don't know what it is? Something…yellow!"
"Yellow? What is it?"
"Don't know. Maybe some…material or something. Hard to tell."
Mrs. Sterlaki was looking intently at me. When her daughter had disappeared, she had most likely been wearing a yellow dress. "Can you pull it out a bit to see?" I asked.

"Can't do that. Can't touch anything. Go right through it. Like ghost."
I should have known. "Okay, Pariah, you're doing great." It was time to try something different. "Pariah, can you find that intersection of the roads again? The one you were at before?"

"Think so," he replied. Going up where I can see. Going up…going…. There it is. Going…going…. Getting weaker. Going. Weaker. Still going. I'm there."

"Can you read the sign now?" I asked.
A moment later, he nodded. "Timberline Road," he replied.
"Yes. Now, does it say anything about what the other road is?"
He nodded. "Can read it now. "Thompson Highway."
Before I could say anything, John had his cell phone out. "If that's where I think it is, then Brent and Charlie shouldn't be too far away!" He suddenly spoke intently into his phone. "Timberline and Thompson! Let me know the minute you get there!" He nodded. "Five minutes!" he said to me.

I looked back to Pariah. "Pariah, they'll be there in five minutes. Can you stay there?"

"He nodded. I can stay, like last night. But it's difficult, very difficult. Connection is weak. I'm weak. Would be better if I can get closer to spot again."

I thought about that. "Okay," I replied. "But can you go up high again and let me know when you see the car?"

He nodded. A few minutes later he said. "Closer now. Much closer. Up high. Can still see intersection.

We waited.

"I see…cars! Several. And a truck!"

"Watch for one that stops at the intersection."

"Cars slowing down. One turned, the rest kept going. Truck too."

"Not ours," I replied. "Ours will stop at the intersection so you can recognize it." I lifted my head and saw John speaking softly into his phone, relaying those instructions to the car.

"Another car. And another. One from the other direction. Another truck. First car went through…second car is slowing down…slowing down…stopping…at the intersection."

I heard John relaying the information to the guys in the car.

"Car is turning now. Not them. Going the other way."

I looked up at John. We both had the same thought at the same time.

"You're going the wrong way! Turn around!" he yelled quickly into the phone. A minute later Pariah reported that the car was heading back towards him.

"Coming closer…closer…."

I wondered why it seemed to be taking so long for the car to reach him. "Pariah, is the car still coming?"

"Yes. Not going very fast. Barely moving."

"How far away from you is it?"

"A ways."

They don't want to miss the spot," John announced. "Go faster!" he ordered into the phone.

"Coming faster now. Still coming."

"Pariah," I asked. "How high are you?"

"Very high," he replied. "Very high, but going down now. Car is coming closer. Closer."

"Slow down now!" John ordered.

"Closer…going down. Almost there!"

"Slow down more!" John ordered.

"Coming closer… Almost there… Stop!" Pariah suddenly said. John had already repeated it through the phone. "Car pulled over. Two men getting out. Can't talk to them. Can't tell them where to go."

"Just tell us," I told him. "We'll tell them."

"Need to walk back up road a few feet," Pariah said. "Opening in the brush there." John relayed the information immediately. "There! Tell them to go into woods right there."

"They don't see anything yet," John said.

"Go straight," Pariah said and John relayed it. "Fallen tree is just ahead of them. They see it! Searching ground now. Both looking all around. One is pointing to something. Telling other that he sees little bit of yellow. Both looking in that spot now."

I looked up at John and he nodded. Once again we were getting a blow by blow description from Pariah's point of view – while the events were actually unfolding.

"Trying to move bushes aside to see better. One is pointing further under the tree. Both looking. Breaking more brush to see better. Pointing again."

I happened to look up at John. He nodded his head and silently mouthed. "Found something!"

For the protection of Mrs. Sterlaki, I told her that's all Pariah could do and asked her to remove her hands from his back, breaking Pariah's connection. Fortunately, she did. I had visions of her wanting to hear Pariah explaining exactly what the guys found. And one way or another, that could have been bad.

John shook his head. Very quietly he said to me, "They're pretty sure there's a body in there, but they're going to have to dig it out. They're calling in forensics now. I'm calling the other cars too to lend a hand. Vegetation is a bitch out there."

I nodded. If the remains were old, then a proper ID would be almost impossible. It would be a case for the lab guys. Most likely we were looking at several days before we knew if it was the daughter – at least several days. "Forensics is going to have to take over now," I told Mrs. Sterlaki. "As much as I hate to say this, it's probably going to be at least several days before we know one way or another. Maybe longer."

I could see the disappointment in her face, but there was something else too…hope. As bad as the news would be, if it was her daughter, there was hope that she would finally know one way or another.

Since she was so worried about her husband finding out, I suggested that we leave as soon as possible.

She shook her head. "I promised this gentleman that I would feed him, and I'm going to. I have a dinner all prepared in the kitchen. You can all have some." With that, she led the way to the kitchen, followed directly by Pariah. I picked up the kitchen chair and carried it in with me while John issued more commands over his phone. Fried chicken, mashed potatoes, and collard greens. Very southern. I had to cut Pariah's chicken up into tiny pieces for him so he could eat it while he happily shoved mounds of mashed potatoes into his mouth.

The dinner was great, but all I could think about while we were eating was my ex-wife and daughter. I used to come home to dinners like that – once in a while. All too often my job got in the way. I missed it.

Finding out that someone you've been looking for is dead, is nothing at all like finding someone alive – even though we didn't know for sure yet that it was the Sterlaki girl Pariah had found. As I walked into work the next morning, I had a pretty good idea of the biggest problem I would be facing. Namely, how do I explain how we found the girl without telling anyone about Pariah.

I had discussed it briefly with John the night before over another beer and he somewhat shared my opinion that nobody should know – especially since the guy was a damn child molester. But he hadn't offered any suggestions as to what we should tell everyone. And without a doubt, everyone would want to know how we just happened to find that body in such a remote and hidden location. Especially whoever got assigned to finding out who murdered the body we found out there. The other person I was worried about was my boss, Don Wimberly.

"Who called in the tip on the body?" Don asked us in the morning meeting.

I looked briefly to John who didn't offer up any explanations. "We're not sure," I replied.

"Anonymous," John threw out.

"And you needed so many people to check out one anonymous tip that should have gone to the police in the first place?"

"Uh… He mentioned the Sterlaki girl," I replied. "That made it our case."

He nodded. "I still don't know why you needed everyone."

John came to my rescue. "It's nothing but woods out there and the description was more than a little vague. We were lucky to find it."

I nodded. "Lucky is right!"

Fortunately, Don seemed reassured. "So was it the Sterlaki girl?" he asked.

"We think so, but we don't know for sure. The lab will have to confirm it."

He nodded and moved on. John and I both breathed a silent sigh of relief. We decided to stick with the same anonymous tip every time we needed to from now on, and we made sure everyone on our team would give the same story. They were all happy to agree. Each of us now knew how important the Pariah was to our work. Anyone finding out that a child molester was helping us would only make things more difficult.

It took the lab four days to come back with a verdict on the body – Sterkaki for sure. We were all both elated and sorry. Elated because we had found her, sorry because we didn't find her alive.

It was John who walked into my little office the day after the lab results came back. It was John who threw the case file down on my desk. It was John who said, "I want to try the Pariah on this one next." And it was John's case that changed things and made all my worst fears come true.

The case file wasn't that different than many others that clogged up our unsolved file list. It was about a fifteen year old girl named Brianna Forsyth who had gone missing five months earlier. Like many other cases, we never had much to go on. In this one, we never had the slightest clue. The girl just vanished off the face of the earth. One minute she was there, laughing and smiling…the next, someone turned around and she was gone. The fact that none of her things appeared to be missing from her room pointed us toward abduction – or murder. Most likely, both.

The parents were understandably reluctant about us bringing in a psychic, especially when we made sure they understood what a foul looking and smelling bum the Pariah was. That was something we dared not surprise them with. It was only the hope that we held out to them about how successful we had been with Pariah that won them over. Heck, we were just as anxious to find their daughter as they were! In all these cases, we hunt and we hunt and we try and try to find them when they go missing. But despite all our resources and hard work, all too often we simply can't find them. We each lose a little bit of ourselves with every failure – and believe it or not…it hurts!

It took me four days of searching this time to find the Pariah. Well, three nights and part of the next day. Each time I went out looking, I armed myself with another meal from Burger King. I'd start looking as soon as I could leave the office, and I kept looking till late at night. I was beginning to think that he had disappeared from the face of the Earth as well, just like all the missing people we were searching for.

But the third night I got lucky. There was an area in one of the parks where many of the homeless spent the nights. When I asked around about him, a few finally admitted they had seen him – recently. They would all point in the same general direction which eventually led me out of the park and into the small forested area beyond. It seemed that even the other homeless didn't want him around either. But searching at night is difficult, especially when you're in an area where there are no lights at all. I was forced to give up again.

After our morning meeting the next day, I went out looking again, starting from that same part of the park. What I saw in the daylight almost deterred me from looking any further. Nothing but woods and trees. Where was I supposed to start? Fortunately, I didn't have to. Instead of me finding him, he found me. I was just about to give up again when I heard that nasal voice of his call my name, "Agent McNair?"

I turned and saw him looking out between two bushes not far from where I was standing. "There you are. I've been looking for you," I said to him. "What are you doing here?"

He looked around a bit. "Sleep here sometimes," he replied.

"Why here?"

He seemed confused. "Why not? Nobody chases me away."

I left it at that. "We need your help again. Will you help us find another one?"

His reply was exactly what I expected. "If I find them, will you feed me?"

I took him straight to Burger King before heading back to the office. Then I dropped him off at another park with instructions that we would come looking for him later that afternoon when I could get everyone together again. I had been trying to find him for so long that everybody had almost given up hope of using him again.

Both Mr. and Mrs. Forsyth arranged to get off of work early so we could do this from their home. Since we didn't know what Pariah would find,

John and I decided to go together again, but everyone else was to stay back at the office on alert in case we needed them.

The Forsyth home was beautiful! Very upper class. Mrs. Forsyth herself was also beautiful. Very! Both of the Forsyth's were more than a bit put off by Pariah's offending nature, so much so that they almost didn't let him into their house. But since we had warned them in advance, they did relent and let him in.

"Why do we have to do this here?" the husband complained. "Does he need to be around her things or something?"

Since it was technically more John's case than mine, I let him take the lead. He shook his head. "No. We can do this anywhere, but if we find out she's close, then we can get there that much sooner."

That wasn't the reason – by a long shot! But it actually made sense to me. Fortunately, it made sense to the Forsyth's too. At my suggestion, we went into their kitchen so Pariah could sit on one of their kitchen chairs. They both looked a bit relieved over keeping him out of the rest of the house.

I pulled a kitchen chair out for Pariah to sit down on. But before he sat, he turned to the two parents. "If I find her, will you feed me?" he asked.

"No, Pariah. Don't worry, I'll feed you. Just like I always do. I promise."

Mr. And Mrs. Forsyth both looked startled and confused. I couldn't blame them. Pariah only nodded and sat down. Mrs. Forsyth put her hands on Pariah's back, Pariah closed his eyes, and I turned on my recorder and leaned in close to hear him better.

"Far away," he said. Then he lifted his head up quickly. I could see that his eyes were still closed. "Sick! She's sick!"

I looked up and saw immediate concern in the mother's face.

"What do you see Pariah, describe it."

"I don't see her sick, I feel it. But not regular sick. Different sick."

"What do you mean, Pariah? Can you explain it…or describe what you feel?"

"Woozy! Floating… Sick." He lifted his head again. "Drugs! I think it's drugs. Bad drugs. Strong drugs. I think it's the drugs that make her sick!"

I looked up at John. It was all too possible. But at least we knew she was alive. In fact, in view of the fact that nobody had heard from her, the drugs were highly probable. "Pariah, we need to find her. Where is she?"

He shook his head. "Far away. I'm far away."

"Can you look around like you did before?"

He nodded his head. "Looking. The other two girls in the room with her look sick too. They're all in their beds. Sleeping."

We were all suddenly shocked. "Other two girls?"

"Two others in the room. Two other beds. Three beds. The room looks...old...shabby. I don't see much to go on. I see...a brick building out the window."

"Window? Pariah, can you go through that window and look around?"

"Going out. Outside between the buildings. Can't see much. Going up. Going higher...higher... Oh! It's a city. Going higher. Oh my! Higher. Wow! Oh my! Big city. Very big city. Going higher...higher... Can't see the end of the city! Big! Very big city!"

"Pariah, do you think it's Atlanta?"

He shook his head. "No. Far away."

"Okay, Pariah. Go back to the girl. Let's look around more to figure out where she is."

"Going back. Wow, big city. Wow. Going back."

We waited only a moment before he said. "Back with the girls. Sick girls."

"Pariah, could they be in a hospital room?"

"No. I'm sure it's not. Looks like a bedroom."

"How about outside that bedroom. Can you explore other rooms for us?"

"Going through the door." He chuckled. "Without opening it. Man there...watching TV. Living room is shabby too. I see a kitchen beyond. Looks old too."

"Pariah, look around closely. Try to find anything that can tell us where they are. Maybe some mail or something."

"Looking around. Looking. Gun! The man has a gun on the table next to him."

I think my blood pressure went up ten points just then.

"Hand gun...pistol...whatever you call it. Black. All black."

"Pariah, how about the man, is he black too?"

"No, not black...not white either. Odd, can't tell. Dark skin but not black."

"Okay Pariah. You're doing great. Now go back to looking around. What else do you see?"

"Doors. Several doors. Going through one of them. Dark…small… closet. Back out again. Next door. Oh! I'm out in a hallway. Lots of doors with numbers on them."

"An apartment somewhere!" I stated. "Pariah, what number is on the girl's apartment?"

"Sixty-two," he replied. "Going back inside again. Two more doors. Going through first…bathroom. Going out. Last door…going through."

There was a pause. We waited, but he said nothing.

"Pariah? What do you see?"

It was a moment before he answered. "More girls. Three more. All sleeping. All look sick too."

Six girls with a guard outside the room. My blood was beginning to boil. "Pariah, this is bad! We have to find these girls. We have to help them!"

He nodded. "Sick girls. Have to help."

It was John's suggestion. "Pariah, can you maybe go through some of the other apartments? Maybe you can find out what city they're in some other way."

He nodded. "Got to help sick girls!" A moment later, he said, "Next apartment. Two men playing cards…drinking beer. Looking around, not much here. Don't see any mail. Going through to bedroom." He suddenly shook his head violently. "Two more girls. Look sick. Going out. Other bedroom. Two girls! All sick! All sick girls! Going out. Leaving!"

I looked to John again while we waited. Things really didn't sound good at all!

"Not good!" Pariah said. "Three sick girls in this room!" A moment later he added. "Three more in the other room."

We had to find out where they were! "Pariah," I said. "Go outside again. Go down this time, down to the street."

"Going out," he said. "Away from sick girls. Going down. Down to the…alley."

"Go around the building, try to find the front."

A moment later, he declared, "Got it."

"Pariah, is there a building number?"

"Four thirty two," he replied. "City street. Not clean. Typical city street."

"Okay, Pariah, find the corner. Is there a street sign?"

It took him a minute. "East Ninety Second Street."

"Great, Pariah! We're getting somewhere now. We just have to figure out what city it is."

"New York," he said matter-of-factly.

"You're sure?" I asked, totally surprised.

He nodded. "Pretty sure. That's what it said on the yellow taxi that just went by."

That fact alone pretty much clinched it for me. We were going to need help on this one. Big time help! How much more did we dare check through Pariah?

"Pariah, I said. "Go back to the girl. Is she still sleeping?"

It was only a moment before he answered. "Yes. Still sleeping."

I looked to John. "Pariah, how long do you think it would take you to search all the apartments around there. We need to know how many girls…I mean, how many sick girls are there."

"How many men with guns too!" John added quickly. I nodded my appreciation at the thought.

"This apartment, six girls. Next apartment, four girls. Third apartment, six girls," he replied quickly.

"Yes, we know that much. How about the other apartments?"

A minute later, he started talking again. "Two girls. Three girls. Two men. One man. Three girls. One girl." There was a pause.

"What is it Pariah?"

"Lots of people in this apartment. Counting."

"Are they sick?"

"No, not these. Eleven! Lots of guns! Big guns!"

I wanted so badly to say, "What the hell?" But I stopped myself.

"Pariah, we need to know what apartment number they're in."

"Seventy one."

That surprised me. "Pariah, did you go up to the next floor?"

He nodded. "Yes. Do you want me to keep going?"

"Not this time," I replied. As much as we were going to need to know, there was too much going on here that I didn't want to talk about in front of the parents. I looked up at Mrs. Forsyth. "You can take your hands off him now."

A moment later, Pariah looked up. "Lots of sick girls there. Lots."

I nodded. "Yeah. We're going to help them, Pariah. But not right now."

I turned to Mr. Forsyth. The look on his face was total shock. I think his wife was shaking slightly. "We may have to do this again, and soon, so we can know more about exactly what we're facing up there, but right now we have to make some phone calls to alert our people in New York."

He nodded, but his head hardly moved. I don't think he even blinked.

"The good news," John added, "is that it looks like she's definitely alive!

That statement alone seemed to bring them back to life. "You're sure?" Mrs. Forsyth asked. "You're absolutely sure? I mean…psychics…it's all so…unbelievable."

"I know, and I agree," John replied. "But I've seen what Pariah can do before, and this sounded awfully real to me! I for one think she's alive and in New York somewhere."

His certainty seemed to reach right into the wife because she suddenly broke down sobbing into her husband's arms.

"Thank you," he said to us. "We have more hope than we've had in a long time now."

As soon as we were back in my car, John said, "You once mentioned the hair standing up on the back of your head? I think mine not only stood up, it fell out!"

I nodded. "Yeah, but what's going to happen now? We can't go this alone anymore. We're going to have to let Wimberly in on this."

"Wimberly – and a lot of others too!"

CHAPTER

8

We dropped Pariah off at the same park where I had met him earlier, with a bag containing two large orders of chicken strips, French fries, an apple pie, and a large coke. I don't think he had been that happy in years. We also left him with instructions that we were probably going to need him for the next several days – at least. He promised to stay somewhere in the area. It was as good as we were going to get from him.

With growing nervousness, we headed back to the office. I don't think either of us said a single word as we entered the building and rode the elevator upstairs. We were just as silent as we headed up the hallway. I'm fairly sure that John felt the same sense of determination that I felt as we entered Don Wimberly's office together. His secretary / executive assistant was in his office with him. Not very politely, John grabbed her by the shoulders and pushed her out the door, which he quickly closed behind him.

Don looked up at us with two big wide eyes. "I take it the world is about to come to an end?"

"Something like that," I replied. "Maybe...something exactly like that."

As much as I had dreaded telling anyone about the Pariah, it now had to be done. Together, we filled him in on all the cases we had done with the wretch so far. Then, we filled him in on what had just occurred at the Forsyth's.

Don finally shook his head. "You expect me to go stirring up a bunch of a ruckus…over some homeless psychic?"

John leaned across his desk. "He may be a homeless bum, but I've never seen anything like him. Anything!"

"But he's still a damn…"

I cut him off quickly. "One…hundred…percent!" I said. "Everything he has seen so far is one hundred percent correct. Totally!"

He seemed a bit unnerved by that. But again he shook his head. "I still don't think…"

"Don't think!" John quickly argued. "Play him the recording, Cliff!" he suggested. "Just listen!"

I pulled out my recorder and started it at the beginning of today's session. It took about ten seconds for the look on his face to show total interest. About ten more before I could tell he was completely hooked. By the time I turned it off, he looked nothing but flabbergasted. "And that's what he does?" he asked.

"That's what he does," I confirmed.

Again he shook his head. "But still, you're asking me to…"

"I leaned over his desk. "One…*hundred*…percent!"

He shut up and stared at me. Then he stared at John. Then back at me again. "Shit!" he finally uttered. He got up from his chair and headed for his door. He stopped before he reached it and turned back to me. "Better give me that recording. I think I'm going to need it." I handed the small device over to him and he turned away again. "Don't leave the building!" he ordered without turning around. "Either of you!"

The hungry eyes of our team nearly devoured us as we walked through the door. Neither of us got to our offices before the questions started. We gathered them all together so we could go through it all at the same time. Then we told them about our visit with Wimberly. There were a few shocked looks, but not nearly what I expected. Based on what we had learned from Pariah, he had to be told.

"So what happens now, boss?" Billy asked.

"We wait," I replied. "Then, we'll see."

And that was about it. We waited. But as much as we tried to go through the motions of everyday life, we were all waiting for my phone to ring, which it did several times, but not with any information any of us were really interested in.

Eventually our team went home and John and I were left alone. He came into my office bearing two cups of coffee, one of which he set in front of me. "What do you think?" he asked.

"I think he's playing that recording for anyone he can get to listen."

He nodded. "I think so too. I have a feeling we're opening up a big can of worms here."

"Huh!" I grunted. "More like Pandora's box!"

"Maybe," he agreed. "It's certainly possible."

My phone rang – finally! It was Don's secretary with orders for both of us to get our asses to his office. I took another swig of the coffee for courage and got up from my seat.

"Close the door," Don said as we walked in. Then he motioned toward the chairs in front of his desk and we sat down. I took that as a good sign.

"They're buying it…mostly," he said. "All the way to the top…and maybe then some."

I wasn't sure exactly what that meant, other than I hoped it was good.

"But every last one of them is skeptical about this too."

That part I could easily believe. Heck, I was skeptical at first too.

"The consensus is…that they all seem to want to see him for themselves. See what he can do."

And that part sent up a few big red flags. "Uh…are you sure that's necessary?" I asked.

He looked at me like I was crazy. "Of course! I want to see him for myself too. Why would you ask?"

I heard John chuckle next to me. "Because…" I started as I searched for a way to describe him, "seeing him is not…exactly…pretty."

"Smelling him either!" John added humorously. I had to nod my agreement.

Don rolled his eyes. "Don't give me that crap! I want him in here tomorrow morning. Let's set up some kind of demonstration. Say…ten o'clock. I'll get as much of the brass as wants to see it here by then."

I shook my head. "It may not be that easy."

"Why not?"

"Because every time we try to use him, I have to find him again. And he seems to be notoriously hard to find! We may be lucky though, because he said he was going to stay in the area."

"What do you mean you have to find him?"

"He's homeless. He wanders…everywhere. I've found him in places all over this darn city!"

He shook his head. "Ten o'clock. We'll use interview three so we have enough room. Start looking for him now if you have to!"

Then John spoke up. "You know, Don, if it's a test you want to see, why don't we try to get the Forsyth's in here too. No use wasting the opportunity to learn a bit more about this case."

Don nodded. "Sounds good. Make it happen!"

And that was it. It was a good thing I didn't have anything planned for that evening. Well, I did. But it didn't involve anything more than another TV dinner and a beer.

I didn't know if I should get Pariah anything to eat or not, so I erred on the cautious side and got us each a fast-food hamburger. Then I drove to the park where I had let him off. Carrying both bags, I hunted around for about half an hour before I gave up and found one of the picnic tables that I was fairly sure rarely got used. I opened my dinner…and he magically appeared beside me.

"I saw you looking for me," he said. "I called, but you didn't hear me."

At least he took the time to let me know. I held up the bag that still contained food. "Want some?" I asked.

He moved to the other side of the table and sat down…with what was left from the bag of food we had gotten him the last time. Actually, I wished he had moved to another table, in another park before he sat down.

His smell wasn't exactly the most appetizing thing in the world. I handed over the rest of the bag of food I had just bought and he opened it.

"We need you tomorrow morning," I said. Fairly early."

"You said you would need me. That's why I'm still here." He stopped what he was doing. "If I find them, will they feed me?"

It was like a broken record with him. I wondered why he always had to ask. "Don't worry. I'll take care of you myself – before and after. Will that be okay?"

He just nodded and broke off a bit of his hamburger and stuck it in his mouth. I turned my head away. I didn't want to watch him chewing with his mouth that wide open.

Surprisingly, he finished eating long before I did, but only because he didn't eat much of his sandwich. I watched as he carefully wrapped everything back up, then he put it all back in the bag, along with what was left from his lunch earlier. He had saved everything he could. He slowly nursed his large drink while I finished my meal.

"We know that your real name is Thomas Clayton," I said. "Would you mind if I called you Tom instead? I don't like calling you Pariah."

"Pariah is me!" He said emphatically. "Clayton is dead. They took everything away from Clayton. Everything! They killed him. Nothing is left. Only Pariah now. Only Pariah!"

There was a bit of that wild look he had in his eyes again when he got really hungry. I could see that this was something he felt very strongly about, so I dropped it…for now. I would spend more time thinking about what he said later. I left him with the promise to pick him up early in the morning.

The following day, I stopped at McDonalds first because it was along the way. Then I was lucky enough to find him waiting at the park for me right where I had dropped him off the day before. Him and the same bag of leftover food from the day before. A few minutes later, I was escorting him into our offices where I handed him the bag from McDonalds to work on while I gathered up John and we went to the morning meeting.

"Before we go any further," Don said as soon as the door was closed, "I want to set the record straight on any rumors you may have heard. We're going to be working with and testing a new psychic here this morning."

He looked to me and I nodded. "He's here," I confirmed. "I got lucky."

"Good!" he replied. "Anyway, all indications are that this guy is pretty good. Different than any of the others we've worked with in the past."

"If you need a test case," one of our colleagues from homicide asked, "we've got a boatload you can choose from."

"I don't think he could help there," I replied. "He doesn't work like that."

"You mean you're just trying to hog him all for yourself!" the guy replied.

"Settle down!" Don interjected quickly. "Right now we don't know for sure what he can do."

"We told you," I replied.

He looked straight at me and repeated. "We don't know for sure what he can do!"

I got the hint and shut up.

Don turned to John. "How about the Forsyth's, are they on board today?"

"Yeah," John replied. "The husband isn't happy about being called off of work this quickly, but they both will be here by ten."

"Good! We'll use this case as a marker to see what this guy is capable of…if anything! I want the Forsyth file on my desk right away." He turned to me. "Anything you have on the psychic too."

I wasn't too happy about that request, although I should have realized he would ask. "We've dug out a little on him," I admitted.

The meeting quickly turned to more normal affairs as he went around to everyone else to see what they were up to. At the end, I stayed while everyone else was walking out. I grabbed John so he would stay too. As soon as we were alone I turned to Don. "You're not going to like what we found out about the Pariah," I told him.

"Why's that?" he asked.

"He's got a prison record." I replied.

"Figures. But then so do half the people in the state. Okay, we'll downplay it."

John of course had to be the one to add, "Child molestation."

I watched as Don closed his eyes then opened them again, obviously trying to control his temper. "And we've got him looking for missing kids?"

"We didn't know till just recently!" I argued. "Besides, what can he do? He's here with all of us around him. Not anywhere near any of the kids."

"It still looks bad!" he replied. "The brass isn't going to like this one bit."

"We didn't like it either," John replied. "We weren't going to use him again, but the Sterlaki woman was desperate and we didn't want her going alone with him."

He seemed to consider that. Then he nodded. "Get out of here before I find a reason to hit one of you two!"

We purposely didn't warn Pariah about who was going to be watching us since we didn't want to scare him. In retrospect, maybe that was a mistake. Maybe if he knew, he would have refused to do it and left. It would have saved everybody a lot of headaches if he had. But as much as possible, we wanted to keep this as much like we usually did it as possible.

It was about ten minutes early that we brought him down to the interview room. The hallway outside had a few people who were lingering around, waiting for the show. Every last one of them looked shocked by Pariah's appearance. I have no doubt that every last one of them were shocked again a few minutes later by Pariah's screams after he got into the room.

The minute we closed the door, he started looking around nervously, especially at the large mirrored window set in one wall where all the observers would be watching from the other side.

He went over to the window, glancing left and right, over and over again, faster and faster. "I didn't do it!" he suddenly yelled. "I didn't do it!" He pounded on the window with his fists. I didn't know those gnarled hands could hit that hard. I had to run over to grab him. He collapsed to the floor in my arms, crying and still saying, "I didn't do it! I didn't do it!"

The door opened and Don rushed in. "What's wrong?" he asked quickly. But I didn't pay him any attention.

"You didn't do what?" I asked Pariah.

"Please don't send me to prison again. Please!" he begged. "I didn't do it! I promise, I didn't do it."

"Didn't do what?" I asked again. "Pariah, we're not here to arrest you. We just need your help. Just like you've helped us before."

But his only reply was, "Please don't send me back again. I promise I didn't do it."

"What's he talking about?" Don asked.

"I don't know!" I replied. "He was carrying on this same way when the police found him once and dropped him off here."

"But what is it he didn't do?"

I turned back to Pariah who was still crying pitifully. "Pariah, it's all right! We're not going to arrest you. Now what is it you didn't do?"

"I didn't do it," he replied again through his tears. "I didn't rape that girl. I didn't! I promise, I didn't!"

"Pariah, that's old business," I said sternly, trying to break him out of his tearful mood. "What's done is done! We're not going back through that again!"

"But I didn't do it!" he argued.

I didn't have much of an answer for him. "Maybe you did, maybe you didn't. I don't care. Now we need your help. Please. You have to help us find those girls."

Something in his eyes seemed to change, but what I saw spoke volumes toward his mentally unbalanced side. "The sick girls?"

"Yes! The sick girls. Help us. Please!"

"The sick girls. So many sick girls," he said.

It was like he had totally forgotten about what he was crying about. I got him up and into a chair. "Are the Forsyth's here yet?" I asked Don.

"They're outside," he replied.

"Then let's get going with this." He nodded his agreement. He could clearly see I wanted to keep Pariah's mind off of whatever was bothering him before.

Mr. and Mrs. Forsyth came into the room with John a minute later. "Geez," you still didn't clean him up at all?" Mr. Forsyth complained. "He looks worse than yesterday."

"Don't worry about it," I replied. "All that matters is that he can help us."

"We hope," Mrs. Forsyth added.

"Are they ready?" I asked John.

"Close enough," he replied. "I heard someone say they were getting New York on the line."

I hadn't known they were going to conference New York in on this too, but I quickly realized it was a good idea. They would know a lot more about what was happening up there than we did.

"We're ready," an unseen voice announced over the intercom. The voice had startled me. I hadn't expected that.

"Pariah, are you ready?" I asked.

"Find the girls," he replied. Then something in him seemed to change and he stood up again and faced Mrs. Forsyth. "If I find her, will you feed me?"

I was dumbfounded that he would ask that again! "Pariah, I told you earlier I would take care of you."

He looked to me, nodded and sat down. I nodded to Mrs. Forsyth. "Let's do it."

She put her hands on Pariah's back and he closed his eyes and bowed his head.

"She's still sleeping. Other girl is sleeping too. One is awake though. A man is with her giving her some medicine. Giving her a shot."

"A shot?" I asked, startled by what he had said.

He nodded. "Man is sticking needle in her arm."

"Is he a doctor?" I asked.

"Doesn't look like it," he replied.

That was more bad news, but not much worse than we expected. "Pariah, this woman's daughter. How is Brianna?"

"Still sick. Still sleeping. Like last night," he replied. Man is pulling out the needle now. Other girl is laying back down. Going to sleep. Sick girls sleep a lot. Man is leaving now."

"Pariah, follow him. See where he goes."

It was a few moments before he answered. "Going into the other bedroom. Girls are all awake! Talking. Me first! Please. No me! I have to have it! Me! Hurry! Man is grabbing arm of one of them but the others are still begging for their medicine. Girl getting shot looks…odd. Relieved? She's laying back on her bed. Man is pulling needle out. Girl is closing her eyes. She looks happy, but I can see she's still sick. Man is going to next bed. Giving girl her shot. Next girl, next shot. Man is leaving now. All girls going to sleep. Sleep sick girls, sleep.

"Man is back out in living room, heading for the door. Man watching TV asks if the girls are good. All good. Man with needle is leaving. Do you want me to follow?"

"Yes, Pariah. Follow him!"

We listened as Pariah described going into the next apartment and giving all the girls there shots as well, putting them to sleep. I felt it was time to move on. We need to learn more about what was up there. "Pariah," I said. "Do you remember where that room was with all the men and guns?"

He nodded. "Upstairs."

"Can you go there?"

A moment later, he replied. "I'm there."

"That was fast."

"I went the quick way today, up through the floor."

I should have expected that. He said he was like a ghost. "Pariah, what do you see?"

Three men in the living room. One is counting money. One is by the window. Other one is watching TV."

"How about the guns?"

"Still there. Still stacked in the corner."

"You said there were a lot of guns."

"Yes. A lot. Big guns. Shot guns. Other kinds I don't recognize. Some smaller ones on the floor too."

Before I could ask another question, the unseen voice came softly over the intercom. "New York wants to know if they can ask some questions."

"Pariah, we have some help in New York City listening in. Can you talk to them, just like you talk to me?"

"I guess," was his only reply.

"Patch them through," I said to the air.

A moment later, someone asked. "Can you hear me?"

"We hear you," I replied.

"This is Agent David Lu. I'm with the New York office. I'm almost at the site right now. I want to see from the outside what we're dealing with. You said they have a cache of guns. How about drugs? Do you see anything like that?"

I turned to Pariah. "Pariah..."

"I heard him," Pariah replied. "I don't know what to look for though. I see...lots of things in this room. But I don't know what to look for."

"Okay, just describe what you can."

"Guns, lots of guns. I don't like guns."

"Yes, you told us about the guns. What else is there?"

Man who was counting money is putting it into a bag now. Picking up his phone, calling someone. Come get it. Yeah, right now. Putting his phone down again. Man by the window asked if he should go too. No. It's fine."

Agent Lu's voice came back. "What was that last part about?"

I answered for Pariah. "He mixes what he sees with what he hears. Sometimes it's hard to figure out what's what."

"Hold on," Lu said. "I'm there, trying to find a place to park."

"Man by the window is looking out now. Watching something."

"Okay," Lu's voice said. "I'm right across the street. Now I don't want to sound skeptical, but the truth is, I am! I'm only here because my boss told me to go. So I need to know if your man can see me."

I didn't blame him one bit. "Pariah, can you find Agent Lu? He's parked outside the building."

"Looking out the window where the man is watching something. Lots of cars parked on the road. What car?"

"I'm driving a white one."

"I see a white one. It looks like the man is watching your car too."

"Can you see what I'm doing?"

"Waving...wait! Man is talking. Hey Bo! Some guy just pulled up across the street and is waving to someone. Who? How the hell should I know? I don't see anyone around! Keep watching him."

"It sounds like you've been spotted," I said.

"Sorry, but it doesn't prove anything to me at all."

I knew exactly how he felt. I also knew he need more direct proof. Something I was sure the rest of the people watching us would like to see too. "Lu?" I called into the air. "Are you still in your car?"

"Yeah, still here," he replied.

"Stay there!" I turned to Pariah who was still sitting with his head down and his eyes closed. "Pariah, can you go down to his car?"

"Yes. Going through the window. Going down. Man in the car is looking up. Looking around. He can't see me. At his car. Going inside. Next to him. He's looking all around. Can't see me. Shouldn't bother trying."

"This certainly doesn't prove anything!" Lu said.

"Pariah," I said, "Describe the man."

"Grey suit jacket. Black pants. White shirt. Red striped tie. Black hair. He looks Chinese, maybe Japanese, I can't tell the difference."

"Chinese American – two generations now! But that still doesn't prove anything. You could have some really good cameras set up somewhere and the Chinese you could have deduced from my name! Wait! What am I doing now?"

"Man in reaching into his jacket. He grabbed a pen. Picking up a notepad from the console. Writing. Moving the pad lower down trying to hide it, but I can still see what he's writing. S…T…A…R…L…A. Starla!"

"Jesus H Christ!" Lu screamed. If you've got cameras somewhere they've got to be really good ones, because I was writing that down where nobody could possibly see it!"

"Who's Starla?" I asked.

"Can your man tell me?"

"Don't know," Pariah replied. "I have no connection to her. I am only connected to Brianna. Sick girl. Sleeping girl."

"Heard enough?" I asked Lu.

"Enough for now," he replied. "For now, let's just say I'll go along with it till I can figure out some other way you're seeing me. And for the record, Starla's my daughter."

"Can we go back to finding out what else is in that building?"

"Go for it!" he replied. "For one, I want to know exactly how many girls are in there. And what else we might be up against."

For the next thirty minutes, we had Pariah exploring that building in detail. He had found twenty five girls the day before, today he only added three new ones, twenty eight total. Not all of them were drugged to unconsciousness though. There were also a number of bedrooms that were empty but looked like they would be otherwise occupied by women who simply weren't there yet.

In the end, it looked like we needed to concentrate mostly on the fourth through the seventh floors, at least. Or the New York people would have to concentrate on it. We were a thousand miles away.

I finally called a halt to things. I could see that Pariah was getting tired. Mrs. Forsyth kept sighing and making noises like she was tired too. She had kept her hands on Pariah's back the entire time.

"Get some coffee in here!" I yelled into the air, hoping that someone would have the sense to bring us something to drink. We all needed it!

The door opened, and the Director of the whole Southeast Division walked in, followed closely by Don. His eyes met mine and I saw almost a nod, but he turned directly to the Forsyth's instead. He introduced himself to them and shook Mr. Forsyth's hand. I was glad to see him reassuring them that their daughter was our highest priority. I was also surprised when he told them that they should remain in close touch as something major would probably be happening very soon – within the next day, maybe within hours.

"Maybe we should take a few days off from work," Mr. Forsyth suggested to his wife.

"In light of what we just saw here, that might be a good idea," the Director agreed. "You might…want to check into the price of some airline tickets to New York too. But I wouldn't book anything just yet. Let us do our jobs first and we'll see what happens from there."

His words were almost as good as us telling them that we had already rescued their daughter. The two looked tired, but they now looked excited too.

The Director looked at me again, then walked up to Pariah and held out his hand. Pariah looked up at him, surprised that anyone would want to touch him. Pariah extended one of his gnarled, twisted hands, but he seemed very nervous about doing it. The Director grabbed his hand and shook it. "You're a remarkable person, sir. I just wanted to thank you personally for your help. From what I understand, all your help."

"The sick girls?" Pariah said, "You'll help them?"

"You bet we will! As soon as possible!"

Finally he looked to me and actually spoke. "We'll talk later." It was more than I deserved I guess. But then he pointed at Pariah. "See if you can clean him up a little."

It seemed like such a harmless little command. It was the same thing we had continually suggested ourselves since we met him, but never did anything about. But now that it had actually been said by someone else... what it caused!

"No!" Pariah suddenly screamed! He jumped up out of his chair, totally hysterical. He ran around the room. "No!" he shouted at the mirrored window wall. He ran to the back corner where he huddled down on the floor. "Don't touch me! Don't touch me! Please don't touch me. I didn't do it! I promise, I didn't do it!"

The Director looked horrified. "Deal with him!" he ordered. "Straighten him out!" Then he motioned to the Forsyth's. "Why don't you come with me. You don't need to go through this too."

When they left, I wondered how many people were on the other side of the mirror still watching. Pariah was still huddled in the corner, that wild look was still in his eyes. What could have possibly scared him so much about getting cleaned up a little? I would think he would welcome it!

"Don't touch me," he pleaded again as I approached.

I knelt down next to him. "I don't understand," I told him. "What's wrong with getting cleaned up a little?"

"Don't touch me! Please don't touch me," he pleaded again. "I didn't do it! I swear I didn't do it!"

It was getting a little frustrating! "I didn't say you did! Now what's wrong with cleaning up a little?"

"Don't touch me!"

I was getting nowhere. "Okay," I agreed. "We won't make you clean up. If you want to stay that filthy, then I won't make you do anything about it." Did those unalienable rights that the Declaration of Independence talked about include life, liberty, and the pursuit of being filthy? I wasn't sure, but I thought it probably fit in there somewhere – like it or not. As far as I knew, there was no way I could actually force him to clean up a little. But it was another little piece of the puzzle that I stored away to look into later.

CHAPTER

9

The phone at my desk was ringing before I got back to my office. As soon as I finished with that call, I had to answer another one…then another. I spent my entire day either on the phone or in meetings. Somewhere early on, I had figured out that someone somewhere had given the order to go in after the girls right away. And whoever once said that the Government moves slowly wasn't talking about the FBI when they had a reason to move.

There were a thousand questions, a thousand tactical decisions that all had to be made immediately. And someone early on had suggested that we ask Pariah for his help again. Which also involved asking the Forsyth's for their help too since Pariah's only connection in New York was through their daughter.

"I'm not sure that's wise," I cautioned. "They'll be listening to all the gory details of what goes on."

"Can't he do this without them?" someone asked. "I mean, he's been there now. He can just go back to the same place he was before."

"He doesn't seem to work that way," I replied. "He needs some kind of physical connection with the parent. As soon as they stop touching him, he loses it and he's back here immediately."

"So it's one of those little things we're going to have to live with then?"

"Something like that. I still don't think they should be part of this." My advice was duly talked about and kicked up and down the chain, but eventually New York decided that with all the weapons the opposition had, every little bit of intel was of the essence. Lives were at stake…more lives than just the girls they were trying to save.

John handled the Forsyth's. Pariah was already being handled by Billy and Hannah. Hannah had sprayed him with air freshener shortly after they got back to our room. Pariah had a fit over it! After that, I made sure that everyone did everything possible to keep Pariah as sane as possible. I emphasized that lives were at stake, but what I didn't tell them was that I didn't want to go through his hysterics again.

The few times I saw the Forsyths that afternoon, they both looked more and more worse for the wear, but there was no doubting their determination. John had thoroughly tried to explain how grueling the coming ordeal would be, especially emotionally, but there was no way they would miss out on anything involved with rescuing their daughter.

As for Pariah, I had given Billy a few bucks to buy him another hamburger, which I was told he immediately added to the food already in his bag. Then he laid down in a corner and promptly fell asleep. I couldn't have been happier about that.

Go-time was set for three-thirty that afternoon. It was the earliest that they dared try for with everything we were trying to coordinate in two states so far apart. I had the impression that a lot of the coordination involved officials from all over the government. As I had feared, word about Pariah seemed to be spreading quickly.

Go-time may have been set for three thirty, but I figured four o'clock would be more like it. I was wrong, they made it by three forty-five. I already had Pariah back in the conference room along with the Forsyth's. I was so glad that Pariah seemed to be much more sane this time. He even smiled at me once and asked, "Are they going to help the sick girls now?"

"They are…and so are you, Pariah. What you do is directly going to help those girls."

"I found them," he replied happily.

"Yes, and I'm going to buy you whatever you want for dinner later," I replied before he could ask about food again. I was lucky, he smiled and seemed perfectly fine with that.

We finally heard that everyone was on their way to the target. Word came down that they wanted Pariah to give them the latest on what was happening inside. All I had to say was, "It's time."

Mrs. Forsyth hugged and kissed her husband. Then, instead of just putting her hands on Pariah's back, she put her arms around him from behind and hugged him tightly, clasping her hands together in front of him. "Please find my daughter for me again. Please. I'm praying so hard for her safe return."

Pariah reached up with both gnarled hands and put them over top of hers. "I'll try, pretty lady. I'll try. I'll find her, and they'll all help make her well again. They have to!"

She did the most remarkable thing then, she kissed his back. I think she whispered, "Thank you."

Pariah bowed his head and closed his eyes. A moment later, he started speaking again.

"She's awake. Your daughter is awake, but very sick. Sicker. She wants her medicine. She needs her medicine. She's crying. The others are awake too. Also crying. Why don't they get up and ask for the medicine?"

The unseen voice was back again. "They need him in the room with the guns."

"Pariah," I said, "they need you upstairs in the room with all the guns. They need you to see what's happening there."

"Don't like guns," he replied. "Scare me."

"I know, Pariah, but they can't hurt you right now, can they?"

He shook his head. "No, not now. Not this time."

I wondered what he meant by that. "Can you go upstairs?"

"Yes," he replied. Then quickly, "Wait! Man from the other room is yelling at someone. I want to see."

"Pariah, they need you upstairs!"

"Man is coming to this room now. Opening the door. "Wake up! Get your asses dressed! Man is gone now. Girls are crying harder. One is getting up. Now the daughter is trying to get out of bed too. So sick. Going to the dresser. Clothes there. Pulling things out."

"Pariah, upstairs!" I urged.

"Going to the closet. Lots of pretty clothes."

"Pariah!" I urged again. "Please, let them get dressed without you spying on them!" It was all I could think of. "Go upstairs to the other room!"

He looked up with his eyes still closed and turned his head toward the mother. "Sorry," he said. "I won't watch while they're getting dressed."

"It's okay," she whispered. "You gave me a little bit of news about my Brianna. Now go, help the others so they can rescue her. Please!"

"I'm going pretty lady. I'm there. In the room. More men again like yesterday. Guns are still in the corner."

It was a different voice that came over the unseen connection, I was guessing someone from New York. "Do they look angry or agitated in any way?"

"No," Pariah answered. "Just playing cards, watching TV, talking. Don't know why they're all here. Wait! Someone by the window just yelled shit! Others are running over to look now too."

The unseen voice from New York uttered, "Shit!" but it was for himself.

"All men looking out the window now. One man backing away. Giving orders! Bo, Lam, Riz, get as many of the girls out of here as you can! Take them out through the basement! Hurry! Grab the guns! Men all running for pile of guns. Grabbing them, checking them. Running to the window. Bull, take some guys and cover the third floor stairwell! Hash, you cover the back stairs!"

Something in there had caught my attention though. "New York," I yelled into the air, are you still there?"

It was a moment before the voice came back. "Yeah, I'm here, but I'm busy. Looks like they know we're here."

"Listen, it sounds like they're trying to move the girls. They said through the basement. Do you have that covered?"

"Not yet," the voice replied, "I didn't even know they had some kind of escape route there!"

"I'm sending Pariah to find out where they're taking the girls, he can lead your men right to them."

"But…" The voice paused for a moment. "That's a go. Keep us informed!"

I heard a gunshot just then.

"They're shooting!" Pariah yelled. Bad men! Shooting. So loud! Bad men!"

"Pariah!" I yelled to get his attention. "Go back and check on Brianna! Now!"

"Going! Bad men! Loud guns! Brianna is scared! Very scared! Other girls too! Man running in. Get your asses out here now! Forget that! Just go! Go! Out the door! Follow them! Now! Follow! Going out to the hall. Going. Going. Down the stairs. Going down. Down. Another flight. Many girls. Going down. Down. Another flight. Still going down. Another door. Going through the door. Many girls going through. Not much light. Running. Everybody running. Following men. More men way behind making other girls run faster. All running. Running. Stopped! Men are doing something with metal cabinet. Trying to move it. Heavy cabinet. Moving. Moving. Hole in the wall! Hole! Going through now! Everybody going through. More men coming! More men running for the hole! Going through! Running! Everybody running again! Stopped again. Men pushing on something. Pushing. Opening another hole. Going through! Everybody going through. Not much light here again. Everybody stopped. Waiting for rest of men to come in. Waiting. Here they come. Closing up hole again. Everybody tired. Not going anywhere. Many girls are crying."

"Pariah! We need to find what building they're in. Can you go up and outside and see where it is so we can find it?"

"Going up. Going up. Up. Going outside now. Shooting! Lots of shooting! Loud! Scary!"

"Pariah, what building are the girls in?"

"Across the street. Not in front. Behind. Street behind. Across the street behind. Loud shooting."

"Okay, Pariah, go back to the girls again." I looked up toward the air. "New York, did you get that?"

"We're already on it Atlanta! Thanks! Great info!"

I had an idea. "Pariah, find a way out of that room. Find out how the police can get down to them."

Pariah only replied, "Going. Stairs, more stairs. Going through doors. See daylight now. This door goes down."

"Now see if you can see the police entering the building."

"Going through building. Going outside. Oh! Many men here. Police. FBI. Many guns all pointed at building. All pointed at nobody. Nobody around except in basement. All must be hiding from the guns."

"New York, did you hear that?"

"Already on it Atlanta. Keep it coming!"

"Men running at building now. Checking carefully, but nobody there. Going in through door. Need to turn left, not go straight. Door to basement is to the left. Men turning now. Going back, going right way. Need to go to end of the hall. Staircase there. Men running. Running. Opening door. Going down."

"Pariah, go back to the girls. What's happening?"

"Girls are scared. Many crying. Men all look nervous. Holding up guns. Looking toward hole in the wall and door going out. Watching both ways."

"Where are the police now?" I asked.

"Stopped on stairway just outside basement door. Yelling now. Put your guns down and come out with your hands on your head! Wait! Men inside are looking toward hole in wall again. Men trying to move cabinet blocking it again."

"It's okay Atlanta," the unseen voice from New York said, "We've got men heading that way right now. They're almost in place."

"Going back out," Pariah said. "Police can't open door."

"Pariah, how many men are inside with guns?"

It was a moment before he answered. "Seven. Seven men with guns. Men have hole in the wall open again. Running through. Two men left with the girls. Staying there. All other men running back through hole." It was a few moments before he spoke again. "Shooting! Very loud! Yelling. Shooting! More shooting! Bad shooting! Girls are scared!"

"Pariah, go see what's happening in the tunnel! They can't hurt you, remember?"

"Going into tunnel. Dark. Not much shooting now. Foggy. Can't see. Men are all coughing. Bad coughing. Lights coming. Lots of lights. Men with lights running, men yelling. Bad coughing. Men running back to room. Men with lights chasing them. More fog. Men with lights are shooting fog. Everybody coughing. Crying. Falling to the floor. Bad fog. Hard to see."

"Pariah, is it safe for the men on the stairs to come in yet?"

"Men all coughing and crying. Girls all coughing all crying. Maybe safe. Maybe. Door opening now! Men from stairs coming in. Men wearing… gas masks. Men with lights from tunnel here now. Going everywhere. Pointing guns at men. Some going to girls. Taking guns away from men. Many men with lights and gas masks. Men talking to girls. Girls just crying. Won't answer." Pariah looked up then, his eyes were still closed. "Brianna is crying too. Crying and hurting. Want's medicine badly. Needs medicine. I think she's confused. Crying badly."

I saw Mrs. Forsyth hug him tighter for a second. "We'll get her whatever she needs she whispered."

Pariah bowed his head again. "Men with lights are putting plastic things on bad men's hands. Binding them."

"Pariah, you're doing great. Really great. Now, please, can you go back to that same room where the guns were? Can you go there quickly? We need to check that whole building as fast as we can for more danger. Please!"

"Will go," he said. "I think girls will be safe now. Going through tunnel. Going upstairs through the floor. Going fast. Room is empty. Nobody here. No shooting anymore."

"I think we've got it, Atlanta. Thanks for your help."

"I'll have Pariah do a quick check around anyway. You don't need any more surprises."

"Do that please!" the voice came back. "It will be much appreciated."

Over the next fifteen minutes, I sent Pariah through the whole building as fast as we dared. He saw bodies and lots of blood, but no more threats. Once again I called into the air. "New York, can we finish here? Not much else we can do."

"We're bringing the girls up now," the guy from New York said. "Your help was much appreciated. We'll be in touch – of that you can be assured!"

I looked to Mrs. Forsyth and nodded. I saw her squeeze Pariah one more time and kiss his back. "Thank you," she whispered again. "Thank you."

I didn't know if I felt more exhilarated, or exhausted. Both I guess. Two minutes later, our room exploded with people who had been watching from the other room. Pariah got congratulated and his hand shook more times than he could probably count. If it wasn't for everyone being so happy, I have no doubt he would have been scared to death. I also shook hands and was congratulated by a lot of people, many of whom I had no idea who they were.

I thought it was over. Finally over. But I was so wrong. So very wrong. Earlier I had joked with John about this being like opening Pandora's box. But I doubt Pandora's box ever held anything like what the future was going to bring us.

It was three o'clock in the morning when my phone buzzed. I had only been asleep about two hours and I was still a little woozy from all the beer I had downed to try to get the day out of my mind – it didn't work.

"Hello?" I said groggily.

"Cliff, we've been ordered to bring Pariah into headquarters here… right now." It was Don Wimberly's voice, and he sounded awfully tired.

"What's happening?" I asked, coming awake quickly.

Don paused a moment before speaking. "I'd rather not talk about it now," he replied. "Just get him here."

"Ugh!" I grunted. "I'll have to find him first, and that's going to be almost impossible in the dark."

"Call as many people as you need to help you, but find him and bring him in."

It was such an unusual request – worded so importantly. "Does it have to be right now? Can't it wait till morning?"

"Find him! Get all the help you need, but find him! Now!"

I was suddenly holding a dead phone in my hands. Something had Don awfully upset. From the tone of his voice, there was no doubt about that. Cursing a bit, I rolled myself out of bed. Once I got to the bathroom, I debated over whether or not to shave and shower. If I found him, then hopefully I could go home again for a few more hours of sleep and I could shave later. Fortunately, I thought better of that idea and took the time to clean up, and wake up…somewhat. I still noticed the effects of too much beer in my system.

But did I need anybody else's help? I decided to wait on that for now. I'd go to the park where I dropped him off earlier. If I didn't find him in an hour, I'd call the others in to help search…maybe. I still didn't see any need to hurry that much.

The park was totally deserted. At least it looked that way to me. It was mostly dark except for the few street lights near the parking areas. But of course, Pariah wasn't near any of those places. I grabbed my flashlight and started hunting around the park. But I found nothing, no sign of him. But then, he had only agreed to stay in the area, not the park itself. Thinking about that, if my daughter went to play in the park every day, I wouldn't want someone like him hanging around anyway. But where was he?

Don had said to call the others in, but after the day we had just been through, I decided that whatever Don's big problem was, it could wait. I got back into my car, leaned the seat back as far as it would go, and hoped that no stray cop would disturb my sleep as I waited till daylight.

I didn't get quite that lucky. One minute I was blissfully sound asleep, the next, a loud banging on the window next to my head startled me awake. At least the sun was up, but not by much. I opened my car door as I was still struggling to get my wits about me.

"This isn't a hotel!" the cop said. "Let me see your driver's license."

I pulled out my FBI badge instead. "Maybe you can help me, I'm here looking for…a bum. The most filthy, disgusting, homeless bum you can imagine."

"What's he done?" the cop asked.

I doubted he'd believe me, but I told him anyway. "Saved the lives of about thirty missing girls yesterday."

He laughed. "Yeah right! Anyway, we've had a few reports lately about someone like that hanging around the row of stores about four blocks back." He pointed with his stick in the general direction. "Personally, I haven't seen any sign of him though."

"Thanks," I replied as I got back into my car. "At least it gives me a place to start."

The row of stores turned out to be an old strip mall. I drove across the front, but it was pretty much deserted. I headed around back and found nothing either. I parked my car and got out for a closer look. "Pariah!" I called, hoping he might actually hear me. But the only answer I got was the buzzing of my phone.

"Where is he?" Don's irritated voice asked.

"That's what I'd like to know." I replied. "He's homeless, and very hard to find!"

Don muttered some words I was glad I didn't hear. "Call me as soon as you find him. I've got people here waiting for him."

"Who?" I asked.

"People!" he shouted. Once again I was holding a dead phone in my hands.

"Pariah!" I called over and over again as I walked from one end of the row stores to the other. I was about to give up when I saw his head poke up from the other side of the curb where a rain culvert was located. "There you are!" I said as he struggled to climb up over the curb. I reached him and helped him get back to the street level. As I did, I looked down and saw the top of a cement pipe sticking out about four feet down. From what I could see, he had been sleeping on top of that cement. He had trouble getting up because he was carrying that bag full of food in one hand.

"If I find them, will you feed me?" he asked.

I smiled. "You found them yesterday. Lots of them."

He paused for a minute. "The sick girls. I found them."

"You certainly did. You were a great help. We appreciate it."

"Do you need me to find someone else now?" he asked.

I didn't know how to answer that. "I don't know. Someone wants to see you though, and it must be important because they've had me out looking for you all night."

"If I find them, will they feed me?"

I wish I knew why he insisted on asking that so much. "I'll make sure of it," I replied as I pulled out my phone. "We're ten minutes away," I said as soon as Don had answered the line.

The parking lot at our building is never empty, it's just a lot more full during the day. It wasn't very full when I pulled into my usual unmarked parking place. I led Pariah upstairs, then down the hall to Don's office. His secretary wasn't there, but he had three strange men with him instead.

"I take it this is Pariah?" one of them asked as he stepped forward and held his hand out toward the bum next to me. "I'm Jack Vasco. CIA."

Pariah shook his hand, but it was a very tentative shake.

I was simply shocked. "What's the CIA got to do with this? Is someone there missing? Although I wouldn't be surprised."

"We're taking charge of him now," Vasco said. "We appreciate all the help you've been so far."

Taking charge? All the help? What was going on? "I don't understand," I replied. "What do you mean you're taking charge?"

Instead of answering my question, he motioned toward the two men with him. "Take him down to the car. I'll be right behind you."

I could plainly see the fear on Pariah's face. Did he have something to do with them before? One of the men reached out to grab Pariah's shoulder and I saw the start of the insanity coming back into his eyes.

"Why?" I asked again.

My question never got answered, because one of the men made the mistake of taking the bag of food out of Pariah's hand, checking it, then throwing it into the trash. Pariah went berserk! You don't take food away from a homeless person, especially when it's the most precious thing in the world to them. And especially not when they're insane to begin with!

Pariah yelled and screamed and tried to run. The other man grabbed him before he could get out the door, which only made him struggle all the harder. "I didn't do it!" he screamed. "I didn't do it!"

I tried to step in to help, but Vasco got in my way and held me back. "He's our responsibility now, not yours!"

"Why are you arresting him?" I asked over top of Pariah's screaming.

"We're not. We're going to use him."

Before I knew it, the two men had a good tight hold on him and were dragging him down the hallway, still struggling and screaming as loud as he possibly could.

"You don't have to do this!" I argued.

"Yes we do!"

"No!"

"Back off Agent McNair!" he ordered suddenly. Pariah's screams suddenly stopped. I realized that the elevator doors had closed with him inside.

"He can't help you!" I argued.

"Think about it," he replied. "Someone like that can walk right into the middle of a nuclear reactor in the middle east and tell us what's going on, and they'd never know he was there! Or he could tell us where the enemy is hiding out and what their intentions are – and no one would ever get hurt. And think of the information he could get for us so easily. Anything at all! From anywhere! He could be the greatest asset this country has ever had!"

"But he can't do any of that!" I argued, much more calmly now. "He needs a physical connection with someone to go anywhere. As soon as that connection is broken, he's right back here again."

"How do you know? With a little training, anything might be possible!"

I shook my head. "He can't do it!"

"Like I said before, he's not your responsibility now. He's ours. Forget about him! Forget he ever existed!"

With that, he turned and walked out of the office to follow his men. I could only think about Pariah, trapped with those people. I suddenly realized that he must think he was being arrested again and going back to prison. Maybe he was.

"I've been up all night with the Director, arguing about this," Don said as he opened his bottom desk drawer. "For what it's worth, we did everything we could to keep him here. So did the Director of the whole damn FBI." He put two glasses on his desk. "It didn't take long yesterday before this whole thing turned into a shooting match between every government agency you can imagine – at the very top level!" He pulled out a bottle of brown liquid that I realized was bourbon, and started pouring it. "The CIA won by playing their trump card – National Security." He shoved one of the glasses in my direction and hoisted his. "It was great while it lasted." With that, he downed the entire glass. I had a feeling that one glass wasn't going to be nearly enough for me, but I started with that one.

Once again I made the mistake of thinking that Pariah was out of my life – for good. And once again I was wrong. I should have made the most of the time I had while he was away, enjoyed it to its fullest.

How was I to know that eventually he would come back. And things would get worse.

CHAPTER

11

For three months we tried to put Pariah out of our minds. But to tell the truth, it was simply impossible. If we weren't making jokes about him, then we were sitting around making up fanciful stories about what kind of things he might be doing. And trust me, some of the things we came up with were really wild! But the point is, he was simply unforgettable.

In the meantime, we got back to business the way we had always done it. We solved a few easy cases. We worried about the ones we couldn't solve – and wished whole heartedly that we had the Pariah back again to help us.

And then one day, Don suddenly showed up in my office – in person. "Follow me," he said before turning around and heading back out.

Curious, I followed. He never said a word as he headed for the elevators.

"What's…" I tried to ask, but he quickly shook his head and stopped me from saying anything else.

Silently, I rode down in the elevator with him – further down than I usually went. We had several detention rooms for locking up and holding criminals when we need to. That's where we went. Many of the rooms were like prison cells, but some were more like the interview rooms upstairs only more secure. He led me into one of those – but on the "good" side of the mirrored wall where all the monitoring equipment was.

Don pointed to the room on the other side of the glass and I looked, not seeing anything at first. But a closer look showed me someone huddled on the floor in the corner. His arms were wrapped around his body and his knees were drawn to his chest. It looked like he was sleeping. I had a hard time seeing his face since his head was down. It took me a minute before I realized who it was. "Geez!" I exclaimed, not believing my eyes. "He's back!"

From what little I could see of him, he looked totally different. His clothes were decent, his hair was cut, his beard appeared to be gone, but that's all I could tell. The CIA had cleaned him up! But why was he back? "What's he doing here?" I asked.

Don just shook his head. "I have no idea. I got a call from the Director in the middle of the night telling me to come in and pick up a package. They delivered him down here. Under the circumstances, I decided to leave him right there. The Director said he'd be in to see us as soon as he could make it."

I spent a few moments staring at the sleeping form in the corner. "He looks miserable," I noted. "Even cleaned up, he looks miserable." I headed for the door. "I'm going in to talk to him. Let's see what he can tell us."

He grabbed my arm. "Let's wait. I want to hear what the Director says first. They brought him back in handcuffs last night and he was raving like you wouldn't believe."

I stared from him to Pariah and back again. In handcuffs! What had he done? We'd have to wait for the director to get our answer.

Waiting on the bureaucracy usually takes forever. But I stayed for a while to watch while Don went back to his office. In that entire time I was there, Pariah never moved a muscle. If I hadn't been able to see him breathing I would have thought he was dead.

Don was back about twenty minutes later. "The Director is on his way," he said. Together we waited and watched the unmoving figure in the corner.

There were no trumpets, no fanfare. The door simply opened and the Director walked in. He stared at the miserable figure in the corner too. "I got a call last night from the CIA," he finally said, still watching Pariah. "They gave me a choice, either we take him back, or they were going to put him in the loony-bin themselves. You know the CIA, they're so paranoid that it's amazing they even admit to themselves that their organization exists. I figured that politically, they thought it would look bad if they stuck another of their people in a mental hospital somewhere. So they were trying to con him off on us again to do it for them."

He looked to me. "I don't know how bad he is, but I figure he's even worse than before. You seemed to have a pretty good relationship with him last time, I thought I'd let you decide what we should do with him. If you think you can save him so we can use him again, then I'll give you the go ahead to try. Otherwise…we have to find an institution for him. Either way, he probably needs a good doctor."

"He definitely needs a doctor!" I agreed. I stared at the miserable huddled figure a few moments more while I considered the offer. Did I want to try to save him? Of course I had no idea how bad he really was. He hadn't moved a muscle since I had been there. Was it possible that he was worse than before? Knowing what little I did about the CIA, it was entirely possible. Especially the way they had dragged him out of here a few months ago.

And then I thought of all the times over the last few months when we had wished we had him back again.

"Yeah," I said. "Let me try to work with him. At least give him a chance. We owe him that much, if not more. We can always commit him somewhere later if we have to."

The Director smiled. "I thought you'd say that. He's all yours." He walked out. That simple. And the Pariah was mine. I suddenly felt like a huge lead weight had been dropped on me. But in a way, I was glad to have that weight too. There was no reason to put it off any longer. I had to talk to him.

"Cliff!" Don said as I was leaving. "We can't just let him go free. Especially if he needs help."

I nodded. As much as I hated to agree, if he needed help, then he needed help. And if we just set him free he would never get it. We owed him that – and a lot more! He wasn't going to like it, but for now he would have to basically be – a prisoner. Or maybe that was "remain" a prisoner, because I had no doubt that he had been pretty much kept that way since I last saw him.

I entered the room quietly. He never stirred. I knelt down next to him and softly said, "Pariah," as I touched his shoulder. His whole body jerked as he came awake fast.

"Don't touch me! Don't touch me!" he cried.

I wanted to say something but I was too shocked by what I saw. His eyes of course were wild, more insane than I had ever seen them. But what shocked me the most was his face. There was thick scaring all down one side of it. I realized the wounds looked old. Very old. They had been covered by his thick beard before so we could never see them. His beard, as dirty and awful as it was, was definitely an improvement over what it hid.

"I couldn't help saying it. "What happened to you?"

But instead of answering, he just kept crying and softly pleaded, "Don't touch me, please don't touch me."

I wondered if he recognized me. "Pariah, do you recognize me? Do you know who I am? I'm Agent McNair. Remember?"

His crazy eyes just kept staring at me as if he was seeing me from a thousand miles away. His pitiful whining never stopped. "Don't touch me. Please don't touch me," he mewed.

"Pariah, it's me, Cliff McNair! Think! We worked together. You found those missing people for us." I thought of something else. "The girls! Remember all the girls you found in New York?"

I could see that something inside his mind clicked, but it wasn't much. "The girls?" he asked. "The sick girls?"

"Yes! You found them, remember? You were great! You helped rescue them all!"

"The girls? They were rescued?" He seemed to mull that over in his mind for a while. "I was there," he said, his eyes focused far away. "I was there. I saw them." He became more agitated. "All the shooting. All the bad men! I was frightened but I kept trying."

"Yes! Yes! That's right Pariah. You didn't quit. You were a hero!"

He finally looked straight into my eyes. "I was?"

I don't think it had ever been said aloud before, but the truth was all too plain. "Yes, you were! A hero! A real hero!"

His eyes glassed over again for a moment, but it was only a moment. "Me?"

"Yes you!"

He looked down at the floor as he seemed to study that fact for a minute.

"Pariah, do you remember me?" I asked again.

Finally he looked at me again. He reached out with one of his twisted hands and touched my arm. And he nodded. "Yes. You fed me. You gave me food. Lots of food." He looked down at the floor again. "It's all gone now. All gone."

"Don't worry about it," I told him. "We can get you more. Lots more!"

He shook his head and refused to look at me. "Everything I ever had was taken away. Everything I got later was taken away. Everything I will ever get will be taken away."

He was starting to drown in his own self-pity again. "No, Pariah! No! It won't! We won't let them!"

But his only reply was to turn away and start crying again. "Don't touch me. Don't touch me!"

I didn't know what to do, but I wasn't going to give up that easily. "I'll be back in a few minutes," I said softly. He never acknowledged that I had said anything. I left him still crying softly.

I went back to the observation room where I could think. One thing I knew I had to do right away. I pulled out my phone and called Hannah. "I'm downstairs in detention five. Bring Billy down. And if John is there, ask him to come too."

By the time they got there, Pariah had curled up in his little ball again and looked like he was once again sleeping.

"What's up?" John asked as they came in.

I pointed toward the room beyond the window. They all looked for a few moments before any of them reacted.

"Holy shit!" Billy exclaimed suddenly. "Is that…"

"Pariah," I finished for him.

"He's back!" Hannah said excitedly.

I shook my head. "It's him…but it isn't. I don't know what they did to him, but he's more insane now than ever. According to the Director, if we can fix him, we can use him again. But right now, it's not looking too good. I'm guessing the CIA finally gave up on him. Totally!"

"Geez!" Billy breathed softly.

"So what do we do?" Hannah asked.

"I don't know," I admitted. "But I'm going to keep trying everything I can to get through to him again."

The four of us tossed around some ideas, but there were two things that stood out as most immediate. Where was he going to stay? And Hannah asked the most immediate question – when was the last time he ate? That one I jumped all over. In the past, the hungrier he was, the more insane he seemed to be. It was late morning for the fast food restaurants. I whipped out my wallet and handed some money to Billy. "Get him a hamburger and some fries if you can. He likes them. If it's too early, get him something he can eat easily. And hurry!"

When he left, John went back upstairs while Hannah and I went exploring, looking for ideas as to where we could keep him. But we didn't go far. It became obvious immediately that if we were going to have to keep him there, then he was going to have to call one of our little cells home for a while. I didn't like that for him. I knew he would like it even less. But we had no choice. It was either that or a mental institution somewhere – where I knew he really belonged.

Was it just selfishness on my part to keep him here for ourselves? I didn't want to pursue that question at all.

Billy rushed back after managing to score a hamburger and some fries. I carried them in, but Billy and Hannah followed me into the room. They held back though, as if afraid to go near him. I felt it was probably better if they didn't get too close anyway.

He was sound asleep again. "Pariah," I said softly, remembering how he had jerked awake the last time at my touch. "Pariah," I called again. I was rewarded to see his eyes open and his head move slightly, but only enough to see me. "Food," I said. "We brought you some food. A hamburger and some fries. Just what you like."

His eyes looked down at the bag in my hand, but he made no move to touch it. Did I see a light of interest in his eyes though? Or was it just my wishful imagination? He only stared at the food bag and nothing else.

"Are you hungry?" I asked. I started pulling everything out of the bag. I unwrapped the hamburger and spread the wrapper out on the floor in front of him, laying the burger on top. The fries I set in their little container on the same wrapper.

His eyes seemed to stare more intently. But he didn't move. Not knowing what else to do, I backed away. After a moment, his hand reached out and tentatively snatched a French fry – which disappeared into his mouth immediately. His body seemed to jolt a little the moment he tasted it. We all watched him chewing – as disgusting as that was with his mouth open the whole time. When he was done, he grabbed another, then another. His eyes started glancing back and forth from me to the food. All of a sudden, he swept the whole wrapper with the food on it further into his little corner and turned his back to us, as if protecting the food so we wouldn't steal it from him. He seemed so much like a wild animal that I was momentarily frightened.

He didn't eat it all, but he ate most of it. The hamburger he pulled apart into bite sized pieces like I remembered he used to do before he stuffed them into his mouth. When he was done, he carefully wrapped everything that remained back up and stuffed it back into the bag. He cradled the bag to his chest and turned back to the corner and closed his eyes again…and fell asleep as we watched.

"Geez," Hannah exclaimed softly. "Has he had any sleep lately?"

It was a good question. I had no answer.

An hour later, we roused him and moved him into one of the regular cells. At least there was a bed there for him to sleep on. He carried his bag of food with him and cradled it in his arms again as he fell asleep. I didn't dare try to take it away from him. We left him then, locked in our little jail cell, where we knew he didn't want to be. We had other work we still had to worry about.

We each checked on him at various times throughout the day. We always found him sleeping, till Hannah phoned me late in the afternoon to tell me he was awake and eating what was left of the meal we had gotten him earlier. I hurried downstairs. I can't tell you how much I hated seeing him behind those prison bars. Something in me remembered what a free spirit he had been three months earlier. An insane free spirit. A hungry and needy free spirit. But free none the less.

I had an idea. I knew immediately that it was dumb and would probably cause more trouble than we already had, but I was desperate to help him as fast as possible. I turned to Hannah. "Call upstairs. See if Billy has time to come down for a few minutes. If not, get someone else."

A few seconds later, Hanna reported that Billy was on his way down.

I had the guard open Pariah's cell and I went in. He had been staring at us through the bars like a hunted wounded animal. His eyes never left me. I'm not even sure he blinked. I still saw the insanity in his eyes, but the other thing I saw hurt me more – distrust. He obviously didn't trust me anymore. And I couldn't blame him one bit. Somehow, I had to win back that trust again. Somehow. And maybe my insane stupid little idea could be the start.

"Pariah," I said softly. "You're looking good." Not exactly true, but I was trying. "We're really glad you're back with us again." He still stared at me, his expression never changing. I might have been speaking Chinese for all the notice he gave my words. I sat down on the edge of his bed with him.

He immediately curled up as far away from me as he could get. "Don't touch me! Don't touch me!"

"I'm not going to touch you," I said, trying to calm his fears. "Don't worry, I'm not going to touch you. I'll stay a little distance away if you like." He seemed placated, but not by much. What had they done to him?

Knowing Billy, I figured he would be there pretty soon. It was time to move on. "Pariah…" I paused, searching for the best way to ask and decided to skip the buildup. "Would you like to go for a walk outside?"

The change in his face astonished me. His eyes lit up. I almost saw hope there. Yet he never said a word.

I heard Billy outside the cell now with Hannah. I needed them. If we took him outside for a walk, I needed them to make sure he wouldn't run off.

I stood up and backed toward the cell door. "Come on, Pariah. Come take a walk with us. Outside where the sun is shining."

I think he mouthed the word more than said it. "Outside?"

"Yes, Pariah. Outside."

He got up, but slowly, distrustfully. I backed out of the cell to give him plenty of room. Hugging his bag of leftovers to his chest, he approached, but only so far. I backed up more, and he moved more. We led him all the way down to the elevators like that, giving him plenty of his own space. But when the elevator door finally opened and he saw the empty chamber, I heard him let out a little sound of distress.

"Get in and move to the back," I whispered to Billy and Hannah. They squeezed in and Pariah immediately jumped back as they got closer to him to get past. Just he and I were left in the hallway.

"Pariah, we can't get out unless we go up. We won't touch you. It will be okay. This is the only way outside."

Tentatively, he inched his way into the elevator. Careful not to touch him, I got in too and pushed the button for the main floor. Getting out of the elevator was much faster than getting in, especially when he saw the sunlight through the big plate glass windows. We had to hurry after him to keep up. Fortunately, his misshapen legs didn't let him move all that fast.

The guards at the front entrance saw him running and us running after him and moved to intercept him, but I waved them off. "Let him go!" I shouted before he even got close. They backed away and we all hurried past.

I had wanted to take him out behind the building to a little grassy area for the employees, but he saw the door and headed straight for it. I let him go…with us close on his heels of course.

He got out the door, and stopped. I saw him looking all around. Taking a deep breath. He just stood there for several minutes breathing deeply, staring at the parking area a short distance away.

"Pariah," I said, "Would you like to take a walk? I know where there's a nice grassy area not far away. Almost like a park."

"Park," I heard him mutter. "Trees." Then he turned his head to me.

"This way," I said as I turned to walk along the length of the building. He followed. I whispered to Hannah and Billy, "Stay behind us. Don't let him run off."

Together, Pariah and I walked along the length of the building, then turned down the side and headed that direction. A short while later, we were behind the building and the manicured lawn came into view. He headed straight for it as if in a trance. Once on the grass, he ran a little, first this way, then that, as if he didn't know which way to go. His head was always up as if he was searching for something…something he couldn't find. The three of us backed off a bit, always somewhat surrounding him, but giving him all the space we could. I had no doubt that if we weren't watching him so closely he would be gone in an instant.

Eventually he settled down. He walked here and there, staring at things, looking at things, but he didn't try to run off – fortunately. We eventually moved into the employee picnic area where I had wanted to take him to begin with. At that time of day, there was nobody there except us.

I sat at one of the tables. "Pariah, would you like to sit down?" He stared around a bit, then he walked over and sat, but it was at the far side of the picnic bench I was sitting on. "Is it better out here?" I asked. But he ignored me completely, as if I was no longer there. He simply sat and looked at everything…except us. As if we were something he wanted to block completely from his mind. Maybe he had good reason.

We let him stay there for quite a while before I decided we had to get back inside. It would be going home time soon. "Pariah," I said, "we have to go back in now." He ignored me. I stood up and walked closer, getting right in his line of vision so he couldn't ignore me. "We have to go in now," I repeated more firmly. He turned his head away to look somewhere where I wasn't.

I had no choice, I reached out and touched him.

"Don't touch me!" he said all too quickly.

I pulled my hand back. "Then get up and go back in with us!"

It took a moment for that to register with him, but he got to his feet and started back the way we had come. "This way," I prompted him instead. "It's closer." He stopped, and reluctantly turned slowly in my direction. It was a few more moments before he moved, but at least it was where we wanted him to go. He paused for a few seconds and looked around again before walking through the door. The elevator again gave him even more distress than last time, but he went.

By the time we got him back to his cell, he was crying. I watched as he collapsed on his bed, curled up in a ball with his bag of food hugged to his chest, and cried. I felt so bad, but what could I do? "I'll be back later," I said. "I promise." But he gave no indication that he heard me.

I breathed a sigh of relief as we rode back up to the offices again in the elevator. But that relief was mixed with grief. I couldn't help it. I felt for the poor guy.

John tackled me as soon as I walked in. "Don is looking for you. Wants to see you right away," he said. "You can tell me what happened when you get back!"

I smiled. I had no doubt he wouldn't let me get out of the building without talking to me first. No doubt he would be grilling Hannah and Billy while I was gone.

Don's secretary was at her desk and his inner office door was open. She saw me and just motioned me to go inside. Don was working on paperwork, the never ending job of all of us. Hannah and Billy do their paperwork. I add to it, plus my own paperwork. Don adds to all of it, plus his own paperwork. The cycle never ends. And this is under a system where we're trying to go "green" and use less paper. Yes, much of it has to be done on the computer now, but there are still stacks and stacks of files and papers that have to be handled.

Don motioned me to a chair and I sat down. "How goes it?" he asked.

I knew what he was talking about. "It's tough!" I admitted. "We just took him for a little walk out back. It was like it was the first time he had seen the sun in months."

"So you think you can work with him?"

I considered that. "I sure hope so. Certainly not right now. But I hope so later. The guy is a mess! A total mess! What did they do to him?"

He shook his head. "Your guess is as good as mine. How about a doctor? Have you thought about that yet? I think the guy needs one. Or do you think it would be better to commit him somewhere first…at least for a while. Then maybe we can see if we can use him again."

I thought about that. "No." Maybe it was wishful thinking on my part. Maybe I was just naive. Maybe I was just plain stubborn. "I think he's responding to me a little bit. It's too soon to tell much. Give us some time."

He nodded as he considered that. "I didn't really expect much this soon."

He searched his desk for a minute and finally found a piece of paper that he tossed my way. I picked it up and read it. On top was the name, address, and phone number of a mental institute in the city. Below it was a list of psychiatrists with their names and numbers.

"Since we're ruling out the institute for now, we need to bring in someone to help," he said.

As much as I hated to admit it, he was right. Pariah did need help. Serious help. By someone who knew what he was doing.

"You see anyone on that list that you recognize? They were all recommended by our medical chief."

There were five names on the list. None of them meant anything to me. I threw the list back across his desk. "One's as good as the next, I guess. You pick one. Just let me know."

"I'll take care of it," he replied.

I left, wondering what a qualified doctor would do with Pariah. I guessed that I would be finding out soon.

Yeah, one doctor is as good as the next. And I know that some are better than others. But I've always wondered if Don didn't have a sense of humor…or at least an ulterior motive with the one he did pick.

Of course, he could have warned me.

CHAPTER

12

I spent a few minutes that evening with Pariah again before I went home for the day. He was eating the food the guard had brought him on a tray. I wasn't sure if it was better than fast-food hamburgers or not, but I was fairly certain it was more nutritious. I tried talking to him, but he never answered. And when he was done eating, all the leftovers went into his bag with the other leftover food. I started worrying about how safe that junk was going to be to eat. But I realized he probably didn't care and had eaten a whole lot worse in his life. Probably many times.

I was back early again the next morning, bringing an egg McMuffin with me to eat while he ate his breakfast the guards had brought. His breakfast certainly looked a lot better than mine. Again I tried to talk to him. But again he refused to say anything. I left him when it was time to go to the morning meeting. I was grateful Don didn't ask any questions about Pariah, his silence had me stumped.

After lunch, I gathered up Hannah and Billy again and we took him back outside. This time we went the easy way to the grassy area – through the back door. Again he ran for the grass. He seemed very relieved the moment he got there, as if it was the very stuff of life and it had been denied him for a very long time. This time, we all sat on the picnic benches and just watched as he rolled around in the grass. He was certainly dirtier by the time we brought him back in, but the guards would help clean him up later.

It was late in the afternoon when the doctor finally showed up. I was sitting at my desk filling out forms on the computer, when the longest pair of legs I had ever seen walked in. I was momentarily stunned as my eyes worked their way up her body, up past her curvaceous hips, up past the softly rounded mounds of her breasts that teased out from behind the neckline of her dress, up to the softly rounded features of her face that almost begged me to reach out and touch them, features that framed a pair of gorgeous blue eyes, and finally up to the long black hair that fell from her head. "Can I help you?" I asked, standing to welcome her.

"Agent McNair?" she asked.

"That's me," I replied. "What can I do for you?"

"I'm Doctor Westmore. I'm here to perform the initial evaluation on Mr. Thomas Clayton," she said.

I had seen her visitor's badge and had somewhat registered that it had said Dr. C. Westmore, but it took me a moment to realize that she was the doctor that Don had picked for Pariah. It took me another moment to remember that Thomas Clayton was Pariah's real name. "He prefers to be called Pariah," I told her.

"Not with me!" she replied. "Now can I see him? Evidently, you're the only one who can grant me permission."

That surprised me. I guess when they put me in charge, they meant totally. I motioned to one of the chairs across from my desk and I sat down. She didn't take the hint and remained standing. "How much do you know about him?" I asked.

"Nothing at all," she replied, "other than his name and some kind of code word called Pariah. Your Director was most insistent that discretion was needed in this case."

I hadn't been aware that the Director himself had talked to her. I nodded. "Maybe you better sit down," I said.

"I'd rather go see my patient!" she insisted. "Now are you going to let me see him, or can I just go back to my office. I have a lot of other patients who need my help."

"I'll let you see him, but not till you know more about him."

"I'd rather find out for myself!"

I ignored her words and asked. "How much do you know about psychics?"

She rolled her eyes. "Oh give me a break! Of all the idiotic…"

"How much experience have you had with them?"

"Some!" she shot back. "But I seriously doubt I need any!"

I shook my head. "I don't think you're the person for the job!" I decided.

"What?" I could see her temper starting to boil. "I'll have you know that I was first in my class at…"

"Hold it lady!" I stopped her quickly. "Don't hand me that crap! You have no idea what you're getting yourself into here."

"I'm a doctor! A psychiatrist! And a very good one!" she replied. "I've seen it all…believe me!"

I shook my head. "No you haven't! Not anything like this."

Now it was her turn to shake her head. "Oh brother! And now you're the expert on his psyche? What kind of degrees do you have?"

"My degrees don't matter!" I replied. "I've been with him. I've worked with him. I'm still working with him. I probably know him better than anyone alive right now!"

She stared at me. "When I'm done evaluating him, then I'll want to talk to you too."

"Talk to me all you want, but you don't see him till I spend some time explaining what you're getting into."

"Ugh!" she grunted. Frustrated, she let her body flop down into one of the chairs. "Okay, Agent McNair. Explain away!"

But now that I had the opportunity, where did I start? Instead of talking, I pulled up one of the first audio recordings we had made. This one was of Pariah helping us find the Holcomb girl who had been off running around looting convenience stores with her old boyfriend. "I'm going to play you a recording," I told her. "It's from the first case we worked with him. I'll let the recording speak for itself." I clicked the play button on my computer and Pariah's voice started explaining that the Holcomb girl was in bed having sex with her boyfriend. It took almost a minute before I saw the look on Dr. Westmore's face start to change. By the time the recording finished, I could see she was completely fascinated.

"Is this for real?" she asked at the end.

I nodded. "As unbelievable as it sounds. And that…what you just heard…was nothing!"

"Before I leave tonight, I'd like a copy of that recording I just listened to, and any others you may have. They could give me valuable insights into what's going on with him."

"I'm sure you'd like them, but none of them are going to leave this building." Before she could complain, I added. "Not my decision. We're talking about security here!"

She stared angrily at me, but said nothing.

"I'll see that you get total access to all of them. There's not a lot… unfortunately. But they can't leave this building."

She seemed to think about that for a moment. Then she nodded. "Very well. Can I see him now?"

I shook my head. "Not yet. There's one more thing I want you to listen to, because it's important."

"Is it different than this?" she asked.

"Different? Different isn't exactly the word I'd use. But oh yeah, I think you could say it's different."

"Get on with it then. Play me the next one so I can finally go down there!"

I stood up. "Unfortunately, you're going to have to hear it somewhere else. This one isn't so simple."

She followed me down the hallway to one of our communications rooms. "This is Doctor Westmore," I said to the tech on duty there. "Play her the Pariah tape from the New York raid."

"Number one on the hit parade!" the tech joked. Then he motioned for her to sit in one of the chairs. He clicked about a dozen times with his mouse then asked. "Ready?"

"Can we just get this over with?" she asked.

The tech looked at me and rolled his eyes. "She doesn't know about this, does she?"

"That's why she's here," I replied.

He nodded and clicked another button. Sound filled the room, but it wasn't just the Pariah's voice we heard, it was every sound made by every microphone of everything that went on between here and New York. What she was getting was an audio bird's eye view of the whole operation. Less than thirty seconds after the session started, I saw her eyes go totally wide. "Oh my God!" she declared as she leaned her head closer to the speakers.

This was about the fifth time I had heard it all like this, and every time it still brought goose bumps to my arms. When it was over, she stared at me wide-eyed. I leaned over closer to her and whispered. "That night, the CIA took him from us. He's been gone for the last three months. Last night, they mysteriously returned him to us with the suggestion that we put him in a mental institution. I know it's where he belongs, but I'm not ready to let that happen."

"The CIA?" she asked.

I nodded. "Heaven only knows what they put him through. He was insane when he left us, but when we got him back, he was worse."

"And you don't know what they did with him?"

"Lady, my bet is that if the President of the United States called and asked, they would tell him they never heard of Pariah."

"Clayton," she said. "Thomas Clayton!"

I shook my head. "Not according to him. You want to see him now?"

She was shaken, but not that much. "More than ever!"

I took her down. Pariah was sleeping when we got there. I asked the guard to open his cell.

"How dangerous is he?" she asked a bit uncertainly.

"Not at all, as far as I can tell."

"Then why the bars?"

"We have no better place to keep him yet where he won't run away. If we let him go, he won't get the help he deserves."

"Agent McNair," she said with more than a hint of anger in her voice. "That's the whole purpose of the special hospitals we have for these people! He'll get better treatment there than here."

"No he won't!" I replied. "For one, because there's a lot of people here who want to help him…personally! And secondly…because I won't let him go!"

"I think you're the one who's deranged!" she replied angrily. "He needs our hospital!"

"Stop pushing it, because he's not going. If you want to treat him, then you're going to have to do it here, not there. If you don't like it, there are a lot of other doctors out there who would probably jump at the chance to work with someone like him."

She seemed startled. Had I hit a raw nerve? Was she that curious about working with him already? Was it a greed thing with her to work with someone so special?

"What's it going to be?" I asked.

"You're despicable!" she said nastily.

"That much I've known for years. You're not telling me anything new. Now, do you want in? Or out?"

She glared angrily at me for a few moments. "Out of my way!" she said. "You're blocking the access to my patient."

"Let me wake him for you," I offered.

"Let's get one thing straight," she replied. "You may hold his keys, but he's my patient! I'm his doctor. Not you! And if I give a medical order, then I expect it to be followed. To the letter! Understand?"

Now it was my turn to glare at her. Darn the woman was feisty! "Agreed," I replied. I really did want what was best for him. I was simply convinced that a mental hospital was the wrong solution. Once he got in, he'd be a total prisoner again – just like he was here…just like he was with the CIA. Here, at least we could keep an eye on him. And we all wanted him to get well again. Or at least better.

"Stay out of my way," she said before she went around me and entered his cell.

We had woken him up with our arguing. When she went in, he was cowering on his bed, pressed up against the back wall. She stood back and spent a long time just looking him over. "Why is he so dirty?" she asked.

"Dirty? Lady, that's the cleanest anyone has seen him in many years. You have no idea how filthy he usually is."

"Thomas," she said. "I'm Doctor Westmore. I'm here to help you. We're going to help you get better. Completely better. You'd like that wouldn't you?"

Pariah didn't move, didn't say a word. He simply continued to cower against the back wall.

She moved closer to him and appeared to be studying him closer. "What happened to your face?" she asked. But Pariah still refused to respond. She reached her hand out to touch him…and I knew instantly that it was a bad decision.

"Don't touch me! Don't touch me!" he cried as he tried to push himself further up against the wall.

She pulled her hand back, startled. "So you can speak. Can you tell me your name?" But Pariah remained silent. "I'm a doctor," she said kindly. Your doctor. I can help you if you let me. Can't you please tell me your name?" But as far as I could see, she was talking to the cement wall behind him.

After a few more minutes and a few more wasted questions. She nodded and got to her feet. "I'll be back tomorrow and we'll talk more," she replied. "I hope you'll consider letting me help you then."

Pariah never moved as she left the cell. "I'll be back in a little while," I said to Pariah. Then I motioned for the guard to lock it up again.

Once we were back in the elevator, I said, "I'm sorry you couldn't learn much. We had more success with him earlier when we took him for a walk outside."

"On the contrary," she replied, "I learned a great deal. Where did he get all those injuries? From what little I can see, they look fairly old. Not recent at all."

"We don't know," I replied. "We don't know much about him. And when the CIA took him, they took what little we had dug up about him. When we got him back, the file didn't come back with him."

"You must know something about him."

I nodded. "A little. I know he did prison time for child molestation and rape."

I heard her breath catch a little, but she recovered quickly. "I hadn't expected that," she admitted.

"Neither did we."

"I'd like to see him again tomorrow," she said. "I'll probably prescribe some medicine for him then. I want to see him one more time before I do." She looked up at me. "I don't suppose you'd let me take him to a regular hospital for a proper examination…and x-rays."

"Actually, I think it might be a good idea."

She seemed surprised by my response. The elevator door opened. "I'll be in touch tomorrow," she said.

"Anytime," I replied. I was then treated to the view of the back of her legs as she surrendered her visitor pass and walked out of the building. Why did the really beautiful ones always have to be such a pain in the ass? Oh well, she was probably married anyway. Not…that I'd have anything to do with her. Especially since she was here professionally!

But I was a man. And a man has to have his dreams.

CHAPTER

13

Once again I ate my breakfast with Pariah, trying to spend every possible moment with him. He seemed more resigned today than before, a bit calmer, but he still wouldn't speak to me. Before I left, the guard wanted to talk with me.

"We tried to get him into the shower, but he put up such a fuss we decided to hold off and ask you about it first. Do you want us to make sure he gets cleaned up?"

I had noticed that Pariah's beard was starting to grow again and that his clothes looked just as dirty as they had the day before – from rolling around on the grass. "No," I decided. "But lay out some clean clothes for him. Let's see if he changes himself. Don't make him do anything he doesn't want…for now. I'm sure the doctor will be down later. She may have some other ideas."

Doctor Westmore called me late in the morning. "I've set up an appointment for tomorrow afternoon for Mr. Clayton at the hospital. Will you make sure that he gets there?"

"No problem," I replied. "Will you be there?"

"I'll meet you there, but it will be later. I've set up with another doctor, Doctor Richter, to do a thorough examination on him."

"Okay," I replied. "Are you coming back today?"

"Yes, definitely. But not till later this afternoon again. I have other patients to take care of here."

"I have a suggestion if you're interested."

"Of course."

"We've been taking him outside for a little while every afternoon. He's been more responsive then than he is in his cell. Would you like to come along?"

"More responsive? Yes, I'll definitely be there. What time?"

"About three?" I suggested.

"Um…Can you make it more like three thirty or four?"

"No problem. We'll wait till you get here."

I tried to talk to Pariah again at lunchtime, but as usual now, he remained silent and distrustful. One of the guards stopped me again before I went back upstairs. "He still doesn't seem to want to do anything to take care of himself."

"Yeah," I agreed, I saw the clothes on the foot of his bed. "Let's give him some time."

He nodded. "Will you be taking him outside again later?"

"Yeah, the doctor wants to be there this time so it will be a bit later than we have been."

He simply nodded. "I wish you luck. He seems frightened of everything."

"That he does," I agreed.

Doctor Westmore showed up about three-thirty. Something inside of me was a bit disappointed that she hadn't worn a skirt today. But it would be very unprofessional to mention anything like that.

Billy was busy with another case involving an elderly man who had gone missing two days ago. He promised to be down later, but I told him not to bother. I seriously doubted that Pariah would be running anywhere yet. And both Hannah and the doctor would be there to back me up. Besides, Pariah couldn't move all that fast under the best of conditions.

We went down to get him. "Pariah, would you like to go outside again?" I asked.

I was rewarded to see the look of interest in his eyes. He picked up his bag of food and got to his feet, but he didn't approach the open door…not till I had everyone back off again. He was still afraid of anyone coming near him. Getting him into the elevator was still a bit of an exercise, but I thought it went a little easier today. We were able to steer him toward the back door again, and of course, the moment he saw the light from outside he hurried straight for it. Out through the door, across the patio, past the picnic tables, and straight onto the grass – where he again rolled around on it.

"Curious," Doctor Westmore muttered as I took her over to one of the picnic tables. "Is there any way you can get him out of that dark basement? Put him somewhere with windows?"

"I'm working on it," I replied. "I'd like to set him up in an apartment somewhere, but the issue is still security."

"You know of course, we have windows and plenty of security at the hospital. And he can go outside much easier and much more often!"

I said nothing. She was right…but I wasn't about to give in. I still felt that he was better off here with us.

We all noticed the man walking around the corner from the far end of the building, but we paid him no mind. In fact, none of us thought the least thing about him, until he suddenly turned off the sidewalk that ran along the building and he started heading straight for Pariah. It wasn't until he was already well on his way that I reacted. I stood up and yelled. "Hey! Back off! Stay away from him!"

The man stopped and stared at us for a moment. I was fairly certain then that he would turn around and keep away, but that's not what he did at all. Before I knew it, he whipped out a gun, aimed it directly at Pariah… and fired! To my horror, I saw Pariah's body jerk as the bullet hit. I was so surprised I couldn't react fast enough. The man turned and started running before I realized that I needed to run after him. Trying to pull my own gun while running slowed me down a bit, but once it was clear of its holster I was able to run faster. The man was shorter than me so my longer legs help me to gain on him.

"Stop!" I yelled, but I really didn't expect him to stop at all. He turned the corner out of my sight but I kept running. I paused at the corner only long enough to make sure he wasn't waiting to shoot at me. I didn't see him at all. I should have looked more carefully. The moment I turned the corner to start after him again, I saw him crouched down behind one of the bushes that bordered the building. I also saw him aiming his gun at me. I threw myself to the ground the same instant I heard the sharp report from his gun. My side exploded in pain!

He was up and running again. From the ground, I took careful aim and fired. I was rewarded to see him fall, but I had only hit his leg. Ignoring the pain in my side, I got up and went after him, keeping my gun trained on him the whole time. He twisted around on the ground and sat up, bringing his gun around toward me again. I had no choice but to fire as I ran at him. My gun went off a split second before his. I hit him – fortunately – well enough that it deflected his shot at me as his body jerked back to the ground.

His gun was still in his hand as I got to him. I kicked it away. He was alive, and that meant more to me than anything just then. I've never killed anyone in my career, and I didn't want to start now. I heard someone running up behind me and saw Hannah with her gun out…also with her phone out. She was already calling in help. I was ever so glad!

"Who is he?" she asked.

"I have no idea. How's Pariah?"

"I don't know. I ran to help you."

The man was hit bad enough that he wasn't going anywhere. I took a moment to examine my side. Blood, lots of blood was soaking through my clothes. But surprisingly, it didn't hurt all that much…yet. I couldn't tell much about the wound through my clothes though.

"Lay down!" Hannah said forcefully as she pointed toward the ground. The ambulance will be here soon."

"I'm okay," I replied. "I think."

"Don't think! Lay down before you fall down!"

"I want to check on Pariah."

"Don't bother! I'm sure the doctor is doing everything she can for him."

"I'm fine!" I insisted.

"Cliff! Be smart! Don't try to be a hero. There's nothing you can do back there anyway!"

She was right, of course. I sat on the ground and saw swarms of men running around the side of the building. I started to hear the faint sound of sirens heading our way. I cleared my gun and set it down on the ground beside me. I had shot someone. Even though I hadn't killed him, there were procedures that had to be followed.

Before help had a chance to actually reach us, I crawled over to the man I had shot. "Why?" I asked.

He looked up at me and grinned broadly through his pain. "New York, you fool. Did you think you could get away with it?"

I didn't get a chance to ask him anything else as we were both swarmed with people trying to help.

Three ambulances. I was the last one to leave since I was deemed the one in the least amount of danger. I kept asking about Pariah, but all anyone would tell me was that he was alive, but hurt. At least he was alive. And as to hurt…now that the adrenalin was wearing off, my side was beginning to burn like hell!

At the hospital, people were hurrying everywhere, but not so much for me. I took that as a good sign. Every time I asked about Pariah, nobody would tell me anything. That part I considered bad.

Don was allowed through to me shortly after I got there. I wondered how many times he had flashed his badge to manage that. "How you doin'?" he asked immediately. I could see the concern written all over his face.

"Let's just say that I don't think the morphine is doing much. How's Pariah?"

"I don't know yet, I came to see you first. I know he's alive but I don't know much else."

I wondered if he really didn't know, or he wouldn't tell me. "And the guy I shot?"

"Bad, but it looks like he'll live."

"Good," I replied. But I now knew that he probably knew more about Pariah than he was saying. "Don, after I shot him, I asked him why. He said something about New York and did we think we would get away with it."

Don was clearly surprised. "I'll check into it."

I nodded. "Good." I have no doubt that he would – probably at levels far above my pay grade.

"This is the second time you've been in a gunfight and the second time you've been shot," he said. "I hope you're not going to be making a habit of it."

Despite my pain, I chuckled at his little joke. "Don't worry, this is one habit I'd be glad to break any day!" Over his shoulder, I noticed Doctor Westmore peering at us between a break in the curtains. "Come on in," I told her.

She came in, but tentatively. "I didn't want to disturb your conversation," she said.

I laughed. "There was nothing to disturb. How's Pariah?" Somebody was going to give me an answer.

"He'll live."

I could tell immediately that it was all I was going to get out of her on the subject.

"But how about you?" she asked.

"Huh!" I looked up at Don. "This is nothing. It seems that getting shot is starting to become a habit I have to work on breaking."

Don laughed while she looked puzzled. "I'll be back later," he said before he walked out. "I've got things to check on."

I knew what he planned to be checking on. He wasn't wasting any time.

"So how are you really?" she asked.

"Hurts like hell!" I replied. "I wish the doctor would finally get here and do something for me. They seem to be running everywhere out there except in here."

"From what I could find out, the man you shot, he's pretty bad. They think he'll live though."

"But you won't tell me anything about Pariah?"

"He's got…a lot more injuries than just that bullet."

Somehow, I could believe that. A doctor finally breezed in and she left. A few minutes later I forgot all about the pain I thought I had as I learned what real pain was. The good news was that it wasn't too bad – according to the doctor. Yeah right! A gunshot wound? Minor? With that much pain? Who was he kidding? Evidently the bullet went right through me and never connected with anything important. Nothing important? Damn! Everything in my body was important!

At least they gave me a nice hospital room to spend the night in later… along with some very good pain killers. Ah, sweet bliss….

Sweet bliss, disturbed by thoughts of New York…gunshots…and Pariah.

CHAPTER

14

For a guy who is essentially single, with no family in the area, I sure seemed to have a lot of visitors. People who were distant work acquaintances suddenly became close friends and showed up briefly to see how I was doing. To tell the truth, I was kind of touched by it all. Everyone from our office showed up that night. I wish the pain killers hadn't made my head so woozy, I would have been better company. As it was, I was continually fighting sleep to talk with them all.

The next day there were no pain killers though because the doctor wanted to "see how I would do without them." Oh thanks! Throw a man a little bit of comfort, then rip it out from under him. At least I was more awake and lucid without the drugs. Sore, hurting, and irritable…but lucid. The doctor also told me that if I was doing well enough later that afternoon then I could go home. Home sounded good, but what would it really gain me? And empty apartment and TV dinners? Oh joy! Still, I took that to mean I was on the mend.

One of the nurses came by soon after the doctor left and said I needed some exercise. Like it or not, I was forced out of bed and had to walk the halls. It's amazing how much you can hurt from taking a few simple steps. Every movement seemed to pull on my stitches, making the pain flare up over and over again. I can't tell you how much I "enjoyed" that little walk. But at least I got through it, and I now knew that I could move around – somewhat – if I was real careful!

Later in the morning, I was surprised by a visit from the good doctor –
no, not my doctor, Pariah's Psychiatrist, Doctor Westmore. Of course
she asked how I was doing, and of course I lied. "Pretty good!" But I had
already had plenty of time to worry about me. "How's Pariah?" I asked.

"You mean Thomas Clayton?"

"Not according to him."

She shook her head but didn't reply to that directly. I guess she wasn't
going to go back down that path with me. "Still sleeping," she replied.
"Actually, he's been heavily sedated since shortly after he got here. It was the
only way we could do anything with him. We did a lot of x-rays last night.
We've got some CAT scans scheduled for later today. Basically, he's a mess."

"Can I see him?"

"I don't see why not…unless you mind the fact that he's probably
going to be asleep."

Instead of replying, I started cautiously easing myself back out of bed.

"Oh yeah, I can see you're really doing pretty good," she said
sarcastically. "You want a wheel chair?"

"No. I need the exercise – according to the nurses."

"At the rate you're moving, he may die of old age before we get there."

My speed wasn't quite as bad as that, but it did take me a while. I
was glad to collapse into the chair next to his bed. My side was burning
something fierce from the effort. Doctor Westmore sat in a chair across
the room.

Pariah was sleeping. His right shoulder was heavily bandaged. If my
wound hurt me as much as it did, then I was glad he was sleeping through
his injuries.

"From what we were able to see," she said, "almost every bone in his
body has been broken over and over again. Based on what we've seen so far,
we're fairly sure there's some brain damage. His hands and nose seemed to
be the worst. His nose… It looks like it's been fixed, and broken and fixed
so many times that it may not be fixable anymore. His fingers the same
way. It's amazing they work at all."

"They don't work too well. I can tell you that much," I replied.

"I believe it! The blood tests haven't shown us anything surprising so
far, except perhaps absolutely no alcohol in his system at all. I've ordered

some special tests that I should get back later today. So what the hell happened to him? What's he been through?"

"Your guess is as good as mine," I replied as I reached out and grabbed Pariah's arm. Every bone broken over and over again! What had happened to him?

"You said yesterday that this wasn't the first time you were shot," she said. "What happened the first time?"

"The first time?" Did I dare go down that path with her? Open up so many raw wounds? I looked at her. She was a psychiatrist. Probably a good one, even though I had yet to see much sign of it. Did I want her to psychoanalyze me? She was also a damn fine looking woman, not that it made any difference. But what the hell? I wasn't up to walking back to my room yet…and she had asked.

"I was working a narcotics case about three years ago. The monster I was after thought he was a major drug lord and wasn't afraid to do anything to prove it. I finally got word through a snitch of a major deal going down. I'm pretty sure the snitch told the drug lord that I knew about the deal. We found the snitch decapitated in a dumpster a day later. The day after that, he kidnapped my three year old daughter."

"Oh my God!" she exclaimed. "Your daughter? What happened?"

"He demanded that I stay away from his operation…or else! I didn't believe in 'or else' back then. I got lucky and tracked him down to a very nice looking hotel…that the guy owned. Long story short, I found him… we shot at each other…we both got hit…him worse than me.

"I got my daughter back safe and sound though. The only problem was, my wife couldn't stand it anymore that I was a cop. Even if I worked for the FBI, she still thought of my job as a cop. She was always afraid I'd go out in the morning and be dead by suppertime. To try to ease that situation, I transferred into missing persons where there was very little chance I would get shot at – till now I guess. Unfortunately, she still didn't like it and took off with my daughter for the great white north. Divorced, childless, and dumped out in the cold with nothing. Basically anyway. And that's the big story. No big deal. It just happened.

"No big deal? It sounds like more than that to me? Do you miss them?"

I nodded. "Yeah. A lot. My daughter especially. Shelly. She just turned six not too long ago. She's bright and sunny and…"

"She's happy," the body in the bed next to me suddenly said. "She's sitting at a long table with a lot of other kids. She's in school. She has a female teacher with long brown hair who looks very young."

"Pariah," I exclaimed. "You're back!"

But it was as if he didn't hear me. "The teacher is asking who has read the lesson for today. She's raising her hand."

I suddenly realized I was still holding onto his arm. As much as I wanted to hear about my daughter, I let go of him quickly. His head jerked a bit and his eyes flew open. Two seconds later, his face screwed itself into total anguish and he let out a howl of pain. Westmore was already at his side taking his pulse.

"It's alright," I told him. "You'll be fine. I know it hurts. I'll try to get you something for that pain." I looked at her and she nodded. She grabbed his head for a minute and held it still while she looked into his eyes, then she hurried out.

Pariah reached up with his other arm and grabbed his shoulder where all the bandages were. "Wh…w…what…"

"You got shot," I replied. "So did I." I pulled on my hospital gown to emphasize that fact. "Wh…why?" he managed to get out.

I saw tears starting to fall from his eyes. Was it because of the pain? Or something else? "We don't know," I replied. "We're still trying to find out."

Doctor Westmore hurried back in. "I've ordered some pain meds for him. The nurse should be in shortly. She grabbed his other arm.

"Don't touch me," he said quickly.

She was so surprised she dropped his arm. "Why not? What's wrong?"

"Don't touch me!" he repeated.

"I have to touch you," she replied. "I'm a doctor. We have to get you well."

He started crying more heavily and turned his head towards me. "I want to go home," he said. "Please let me go home."

How could I reply to that? "Pariah, you don't have a home anymore. Remember? You have nowhere to go. Besides," I added, "we've got to get you well first."

The nurse rushed in and quickly injected a drug into his IV line. Pariah kept his eyes on me the whole time. "I want to go home," he said again as he eyes started to close. "My wife."

A few minutes later, he was sound asleep. I looked up at Westmore. "I'm surprised you didn't try to ask him any questions while he was awake."

She shook her head. "I'm not his primary physical doctor, I'm his mental one. I am working with his physical doctor though. So far, Thomas seems to be responding far more to you than he does to me. I don't think he's ready for my kind of questions right now. From what I've seen, I'm going to learn more watching him and you together than if I try to hammer him myself. I just ordered him something for his pain and to keep him asleep a while longer. After what we went through with him yesterday, we think he'll be better off sleeping through the worst of the pain for a day or two. Besides, he's a lot easier to deal with for testing if he's asleep."

Her answer surprised me…a lot! She seemed more on top of things than I had thought.

"There's one more thing I think you should know," she told me. "The FBI will cover some of his expenses, but it doesn't look like they're going to cover much. He's homeless, he has no money, no insurance. He's lucky the hospital is required by law to do something to help him. But they're only going to do the minimum and that's it. I've been able to push those boundaries a bit further. If it wasn't for the FBI's interest, he'd probably be leaving way too soon. They'd rather not touch him at all."

"He can't pay," I said. "That figures. At least he's getting better help with you here than if you weren't."

She nodded. "I can't do much for him, but one thing I'm doing that I think is important, is all the tests. All those x-rays yesterday and the CAT scan later today. I have a feeling those are going to be important. Wouldn't you think so?"

Her question caught me off guard. "Possibly," I admitted as I eased myself to my feet to head back to my own room. "But right now, I can't see where they're going to help anything."

Why is it that an outsider can so often see things that we ourselves can't? Things that are right in front of our face?

John picked me up late that afternoon and took me home, along with a prescription for some heavy duty Tylenol for the pain and an appointment to have my bandages changed again in two days. I laid on my bed, but my brain was too wide awake and active to go to sleep. I turned the TV on, but there was nothing interesting to watch. I checked my supply of TV dinners and was glad to see that it was ample, for now. But what about the rest of my meals? Well, three TV dinners a day wasn't going to hurt me. Maybe I could get one of the guys to bring me something else once in a while too.

I was bored out of my skull inside of my first hour home. With nothing else to think about, I thought about Pariah. He had seen my daughter in school today. I had been surprised, but overjoyed to hear about her, as little as it had been. But one thing stood out about that, he still had the power. He still had the ability to find people, if we could get him to help again.

Hopefully, Doctor Westmore could help. Hopefully. My bored mind lingered momentarily on remembering her legs the first day we had met. Why did she have to be such a pain in the ass sometimes? And more importantly, what the heck was her first name?

John was back again two days later to take me to the doctor's office. I had spoken about a thousand times with him and everyone else over the phone about what was happening at work…particularly what was happening related to me being shot! John, Billy, and Hannah didn't seem to know much, but I could tell that Don knew more than he would say.

Once my bandages had been changed, John tried to take me home, but I wouldn't let him. "Take me to the office instead," I told him.

"You're not supposed to go back to work yet."

"I can't take being cooped up in that apartment any longer! I'm going stir crazy!" I got lucky, he drove me to work, but only after I promised to sit in my office and not make a nuisance of myself. I promised, but we both had different definitions of what constituted a nuisance.

Everyone was surprised to see me there, but they shouldn't have been. I didn't have any other outside interests other than my job. As soon as John had seen me installed back at my desk, I got to work, not on any of the paperwork that had been piling up for me, but on the phone – directly to Don. "What's happening?" I asked.

"I told you yesterday," he replied, "we're looking into some things."

"Can I come to your office and you can go over it with me directly?"

"You know you can't come back to work yet. We'll discuss it then."

"I'm back!" I replied. "I'm sitting at my desk right now. I couldn't take being home anymore." I put up with him telling me that there was no way I should be at work just then along with a lot of other garbage about not listening to orders…blah, blah, blah! To which I simply replied, "Fine!" And I put it all straight out of my mind. "I'll be there in five minutes. Just have a chair waiting that I can sit in!" I didn't bother listening to the rest of his angry ranting. I knew he was glad to have me back. It's so nice to be loved and appreciated.

Don's office door was open when I got there. Mrs. Secretary / executive assistant asked how I was doing and if she could get me anything. I told her I was fine and I continued straight into Don's office.

"I'm glad you're back," he said sincerely as I sat down. I knew all that other junk he had given me over the phone had been a lie!

"So what's happening?" I asked.

"Unofficially?"

"Yeah. You might as well give it to me straight. I'm going to find out one way or another."

"The New York office now thinks we may have stumbled into something bigger than we thought. They can't find any real proof of it yet though."

"Bigger? It seemed pretty big to me."

He nodded. "It was. Definitely! But what if what we found was only a branch office?"

"Huh? What do you mean, branch office?"

"That's just it, we have no proof. Right now it's just a theory."

"A theory about what?"

"That what we found was just a small part of a big organization. Maybe international."

I stewed over that for a moment. "Where would they be headquartered?"

"Who knows? Maybe nowhere."

I nodded. It wasn't much for me to look into – yet.

"And what about the guy who shot me? What's his story?"

"You mean Willy Wonka?"

"Wonka?"

"It's actually William Wonjakowski, or something like that. Serbian. He's suspected of at least three murders in the New York area."

"Serbian? Is there some kind of terrorist lead here?"

He shook his head. "We think he's more of a hit man."

I thought about that for a moment. "He sure seemed like he knew what he was doing when he shot me. First he waltzes in like he works here, then before we knew it, he was blasting away. And when I chased him, he turned the corner and was smart enough to hide in the bushes with his gun already aimed at me. Someone who definitely knows what he's doing."

"Yeah," he agreed. "Unfortunately, what little bit he told you is all we've managed to get out of him so far. And right now the doctors have him drugged to high heaven so talking to him isn't much of an option yet."

"Keep me informed," I told him. But I had a bigger question now. "If he was after Pariah, how did he know where and when we would be outside? And we were later that day than we had been."

"Later?" He looked surprised.

"Yeah, we waited till Doctor Westmore could get here so she could observe him when he was more responsive."

I'm fairly sure the thought hit both of us at the same time. Someone had to tell the hit man when we were going to be there. And right now, the good doctor was our prime suspect. We both stared at each other for a moment. "Shit!" he exclaimed finally. "I'll put someone on her right away."

"Don't bother," I replied. "I'll do it myself."

"You're not even officially here!"

"If she's innocent, then all the better. Besides, she's expecting to use me now to get through to Pariah since he seems to respond better to me than anyone else."

He thought about that for a moment. "Be careful," he finally said. "If she's working for someone who can send that kind of trouble, the next bullet could kill you."

I shook my head. "No, I'm breaking that habit. Remember?"

At least my brain had something to deal with now. The problem was, it was something I didn't want to deal with. Not with her at least. So how did I want to go about it? As much as I hated to do it, I decided that bringing her in and confronting her directly about it would be the fastest way. If she got angry and decided she wouldn't help Pariah anymore, then so be it. At least she hadn't really done much with him yet anyway.

I called her and had to leave a message for her to call me back. Now I just had to figure out what questions to ask.

It was over an hour before I heard from her. She berated me severely and called me crazy for being at work and not home resting. I told her I would be crazier if I stayed home. I only told her we needed to sit down together and discuss Pariah's case, nothing more. She agreed to be here but not till very late. It was either that or she would have to put off consulting on the CAT scans until another day – possibly next week. I thought that for now, the scans were more important than my questions.

I was beginning to give up on her for the day when she finally waltzed in – and again something inside of me was disappointed that she wasn't showing off her legs. I took a closer look at her visitor badge as she walked into my office and sat down. Doctor C. Westmore. Nothing more about her first name. Should I ask her?

"What did you want to talk about?" she asked. "Because I've got a few questions for you too."

That surprised me. I didn't want to talk to her here in my office though. I wanted everything she said to be recorded. I just didn't want her to know that. "Let's find someplace more private to talk," I suggested. "This time of day everyone's going to be coming in here like a parade with end of the day business for me."

"Don't you need to be here then?"

I smiled. "You forget, I'm home on sick leave." I picked up my phone. "Barry? Is the executive conference room available? Thanks." What I didn't tell her was that I had arranged for one of our technicians to stay behind if necessary to record everything. Silently.

Slowly and still painfully, I walked her down to one of our executive conference rooms where we could talk more "privately." I figured the richly appointed surroundings would put her at ease so she wouldn't feel quite so much like I was grilling her. The room was outfitted with more electronics than most people would imagine. I had no doubt that the tapes were rolling the minute we walked in the door.

"What kind of questions did you have for me?" I asked as I sat in one of the rich leather chairs.

She chose a seat across the table from me where I could see her. Perfect! "Lots of questions," she replied – which told me nothing. "But you first. You called this meeting and you're the one who's supposed to be home recovering."

I jumped right in to it. "After I talked to you on the phone the day I got shot, who did you tell you were coming here?"

The question threw her for a loop. "Why?" she asked.

"Because someone knew exactly where we were going to be and when we were going to be out there!"

She was more startled and immediately grew defensive. "And you think I told that crook? Get real! Why would I?"

"I don't know. You tell me?"

"I didn't!"

"So who did you tell?"

"How should I know? Maybe lots of people. Maybe no one!"

"Lots of people? Like who?"

"I didn't say it was lots of people. And I know I said it might not be anyone!"

"So who might you have told?"

"I don't know! I don't remember! It could have been any of a dozen people."

"That many people know about Pariah?"

She stopped to think for a moment. When she spoke, it wasn't so confrontational. "They didn't. Not then. They know now of course because of the work I'm doing with him at the hospital."

I made a mental note to make sure we put a guard on Pariah – just in case! "So who are these people?"

"My staff. Other doctors. Nurses. They all have to know where I'm going all the time."

"Why is that?"

"In case of emergencies. When you got shot, that doctor was called in for you because it was an emergency. We all get called for emergencies, even psychiatrists…like me!"

"So they all knew about Pariah – before the incident?"

She shook her head. "No. Only that I was consulting on a case for the FBI. I've done that a few times now. They don't have to know who or what my consultation is about."

"So they didn't know."

"Like I said, not back then."

"But they do know now."

She nodded. "They have to. I can't arrange things with the hospital for Mr. Clayton without their help."

I thought about that for a moment. "But bottom line, none of them knew before the shooting?"

She shook her head. "No. Like I said, I kept the details of my consultation to myself – as your Director requested."

There was too much about what she had said and the way she had said it for me to doubt her word. She was clean. I knew it down to my bones. Or was it just that I wanted her to be clean? I had to be careful with this because I was attracted to her…even though I couldn't let her have any inkling of that.

"Thanks," I said quietly. "I'm sorry I had to ask. Please believe me, it was important."

She continued to glare at me and I let her. She seemed to fume silently for a very long time before I finally saw her face soften. "So am I cleared?"

I couldn't lie. "For now. As far as I'm concerned anyway. I'm scratching you off of my suspect list, but you're only one of a lot of people I'm going to have to talk to."

"So this wasn't directed at just me?"

It had been, but it was obvious now that our search would have to expand a bit. "No. If we didn't ask you about it, then we wouldn't be doing a very good job, would we?"

It was a moment before she answered. "No, I guess you wouldn't."

"And now we've gotten this out of the way early in the investigation."

"Until you decide you want to look at me again."

No doubt about it, she was smart. "Let's hope not." I replied. I wanted to change the subject. Get her away from the accusations. "So what questions did you have for me?"

She stared at me for a moment. "I don't think I'm in the mood to ask them," she said as she stood up and gathered her things.

"Why not?"

"Because I'm still mad as hell underneath!"

I could believe it. I guess I would be too.

I got to my feet and she stayed with me as I slowly walked back to my office. Maybe she thought I might fall down or something. I was getting really tired and my wound was starting to hurt again something fierce. So even though she was angry with me, I was glad for her company. Unfortunately, when we got there, the office was deserted.

I was fairly sure that most of them had already gone home for the day, but I couldn't believe that John would abandon me. A quick check of his office showed that his computer was still up, so he was in the building somewhere, just not there.

"It looks like I'm going to have to wait around for my ride," I said as I sat down in one of the chairs across from John's desk to wait for him. "Either that, or my car is still down in the parking lot. I guess I can always drive myself home."

"You can't drive!" she declared. "You're not even supposed to be out of your apartment!"

"Well I am out, and I'm here. Driving wouldn't be all that difficult." I replied. "But in any case, John is still here. I just have to wait for him to get back. Thanks for the talk. I'm sorry I had to ask those questions."

"I know you did, but I still don't like it."

"Nobody does."

I expected her to leave, but instead she stared at me for a few moments. "I guess I could drive you home if you want."

There was no telling how long it would be before John got back. And I was getting really tired now. Besides, how could I possibly say no when a beautiful lady offered to give me a ride? Not that there would ever be anything between us. Besides, as much as I was hurting, any form of physical activity was strictly out of the question. She was simply…good for my ego.

I left a note for John to tell him I hitched a ride home and followed her down to her car – a snazzy little BMW sports model. Very nice! It seemed to suit her perfectly, as if it was another accessory she put on when she got dressed – which it probably was.

I gave her directions to my frowzy little apartment, and it seemed like no time before we were there.

"You live here?" she asked.

I held up my door key as my only reply and got out of her car.

"Can I come in?"

Now that one shocked me. "You want to come in? Really? Why?"

"I'm sorry," she said backing off quickly. "I didn't realize you would have anyone else there with you. I just thought that since you had said you were divorced...."

"There's nobody there...yet," I replied. "At least not till I go in. And if you want to see it, then you're welcome. But I warn you, it's not much." I'm not sure if I was surprised or not that she got out of her car to follow me.

"The truth is," she said, "since Mr. Clayton responds to you better than anyone else, I have to study you both."

"Oh thanks! Now I feel like a lab rat!"

"Sorry," she said. "But that's the way it is."

What a way to burst a man's bubble!

I unlocked my door and went inside. I was immediately embarrassed by how bad the place looked. But heck, this was the first woman that had been in there since I moved in – since I had split up with my wife! I watched her looking carefully around my living room. "Sorry," I said. "It's not much." The look on her face with the raised eyebrow told me she agreed.

"Remind me not to ever work full time for the FBI," she said. "It certainly doesn't look like they pay much."

"What company does?" I replied.

"That's why I became a doctor!"

Okay, I had asked for that one.

"I know you've been laid up a little," she said, "but I guess you've got food here for dinner?"

"Plenty?" I replied. "No problem."

"Good, just checking," she replied. "What are you having tonight?"

"I don't know. Whatever's on top, I guess."

"On top? On top of what?"

"On top in my freezer."

She didn't bother asking, she simply went straight to my kitchen and opened my refrigerator. "There's nothing in here but beer!" she exclaimed. Then she opened my freezer. "TV dinners? Nothing but TV dinners?" She gave me one of those looks like she was asking if I was nuts or something.

She closed my refrigerator and quickly started opening every cabinet in the kitchen. I didn't have much because I didn't need much. A few plates, a few glasses, a few coffee cups. What else could I need? So most of the cabinets were empty…except for one. She finally stopped when she got to it and stared.

"Two cans of chili?" she asked. "That's all you have is TV dinners… and chili?"

"The chili is really just for emergencies, or when it gets really cold outside. I like it in the winter."

She closed the cabinet and stared at me. "You really need help!"

I wasn't totally sure how to take that since she was a psychiatrist. "And you just happen to be a doctor," I replied.

"I think you're way beyond even my ability to help you! What about nutrition? What about something that…that tastes halfway decent?"

"Hey, there's plenty of nutrition in those dinners. They've all got vegetables and stuff in them. And as for something that tastes good, well… I eat out a lot."

She rolled her eyes – big time. "Moronic males!"

What could I say? "Sorry. I don't keep much of anything else. I'm not here that much and I wouldn't cook it anyway."

She stared at me for a second. "Idiot!" she swore softly as she walked past me back to the front door. She stopped there and turned around. "I'm eating out tonight – someplace decent! Are you feeling well enough to join me?"

First she offers to drive me home, then she berates the way I live, and now she's asking me out to dinner? As tired and hurting as she knew I was? "Just let me pop another pain pill and I'll be all set."

"Where are we going?" I asked a few minutes later as we drove out of the parking lot.

"You're a moronic male," she replied. "So I'm guessing you like Italian."

Oh yeah! Well, doesn't everybody? "As long as it's not one little place I know downtown. I have major plans to murder the chef there."

Fortunately, downtown was too far out of the way and she knew of another place that she claimed was really good. Fifteen minutes later, we were comfortably sitting across the table from each other. Well, I'm sure she was comfortable, my side was still burning horribly. The pain pills didn't seem to do a whole lot.

She ordered a glass of wine, and then told me the beer I had ordered wasn't a good idea on top of some medications. I ignored her suggestion.

She waited until our drinks arrived and we had ordered before she said anything else. "Let me ask you something," she began.

I took a small swig of beer. "Ask away."

"When you were in the room with Thomas…"

"Pariah."

"Thomas!"

"Pariah!"

"His name is Thomas Clayton!"

"His name used to be Thomas Clayton. It's Pariah now!"

She glared at me. "When you were in the room with…the subject…"

I marveled at how she had gotten around that one.

"We were talking, and then he suddenly started talking about your daughter," she said. "Was that one of his…seeings?"

"Yes. I stopped it quickly though. I kind of felt like I was spying on her. It didn't feel right to do that."

"But he was asleep. I'm trying to figure out what triggered it."

"Me. I had grabbed his arm and I made the mistake of leaving my hand there. Then when I started telling you about my daughter, it triggered him to go straight to her."

"So how does it work then? You have to just think about someone and he can go to them…instantly?"

"He says you have to touch him. Most of the time, everybody just puts their hands on his back so they don't have to touch his hands. Then they just have to think hard about someone and he finds them."

"You need to touch him? What about his clothes? Don't they get in the way?"

I shook my head. "It doesn't seem so. He always had clothes on his back for every session we've done so far. As ragged as his clothes were, they didn't seem to hinder anything." I watched as her eyes seemed to get wider and wider.

"You touch him, and you think about someone…."

I nodded. "Right."

But her head was somewhere else. "You touch him… Darn it! I was wrong! All wrong!"

She suddenly seemed very agitated with herself. "Wrong about what?"

"I thought that his fear of being touched had something to do with his injuries. But that's not it at all! Look. What must that do to his mind every time some weird piece of him goes off to somewhere else? He can see and hear and interact with everybody around him where his physical body is, even talk to them and hold conversations. While at the same time, another part of him is halfway around the world – where he can see and hear everything there too! What kind of traumatic experience is that for his brain? How does it process all that activity at the same time?"

I suddenly realized she was smarter than I had given her credit for. I hadn't thought of anything like that. But then, I'm not a psychiatrist. "Or maybe," I replied. "his fear of touching is a combination of both."

She stared at me for a moment. "There's that possibility too."

Score half a point for me!

"So how is it that he responds better to you than to anyone else?"

"I don't know? He's just always been that way. But I wouldn't call his behavior lately very responsive."

"But he'll tolerate you more than anyone else."

"It seems that way."

"How did you find him?"

"I didn't. I think he found me."

"What do you mean?"

"We had this missing girl case we were stumped with. I was escorting the parents down to the parking lot, when he just suddenly showed up and offered to find their girl – for food of course."

"For food?"

"Yeah, it's kind of a problem with him. He always asks them if they'll feed him if he finds who they're looking for."

"Always?" she asked.

"Always. Even though I feed him before – and tell him I'll feed him afterwards too."

"Why don't you just pay him?"

"He won't except it. Only food. Nothing else."

"Some wages!"

"I have noticed one thing though, he's a lot more sane when he eats than when he doesn't. And there can be a big difference. At times, he can almost seem…normal. Well, not really normal, but closer anyway. At other times, I think he's just so desperate for food that something more goes haywire with his brain."

"So keeping him well fed keeps him sane…or better anyway?"

"Exactly."

She was looking at me, but it was more like she was staring off into space for a few minutes. Finally she cocked her head. "Is it possible?" she asked…herself?

"What do you mean?"

She suddenly snapped back to reality. "Nothing. I was just considering something."

Our meals arrived then, but I don't think she was paying much attention. When the waiter offered to grate some fresh cheese for her she waved him off like she hadn't heard.

She said nothing for a few minutes as her far-away look seemed to be back again. I let her sit there and think while we ate in silence.

"And you said he found you?" she suddenly asked.

"Yeah, he just showed up in the parking lot. I tried to get rid of him."

"But he managed to stay."

"He can be more stubborn than you!" I quipped.

But she didn't take the bait. She continued thinking silently while she ate. Suddenly she said, "Excuse me," and dug her cell phone out of her purse. "Is Doctor Richter there?" she asked after she had dialed. "This is Doctor Westmore. Please ask him to call me back as soon as possible! Yes… Thank you."

"What's going on?" I asked.

"Doctor Richter is the primary medical doctor assigned to Clayton. I got the special blood tests back this afternoon that I had asked for. There were minute traces of a mix of powerful anti-psychotics there. I'm guessing left over from his trip to the CIA. As wild as this sounds, his brain simply may not function the same as everyone else's. So I'm wondering if all the drugs are actually having the opposite effect on him than what we want. In other words, the drugs are more of a problem than his brain damage."

"So he definitely has brain damage?"

"Definitely. But not so severe that he can't function."

Her phone suddenly rang and she answered it. "Thanks for getting back to me so fast. I want to stop all the anti-psychotic drugs on Thomas Clayton right away. I have some vague evidence that they may be causing the opposite reaction than what we want. ... Yes, the normal pain stuff should be just fine, but please make sure he's wide awake tomorrow morning. ... Yeah, cutting back might be a good idea for now, even if it means he has to hurt a bit more. I'm going to need him wide awake tomorrow morning when I get there. Oh! And one more thing. Please make sure he eats well in the morning. Tonight too if it can be arranged. The more food, the better! ... Yes... Thanks."

She hung up her phone and looked at me very seriously. "I really need to talk to him tomorrow morning. Which means I'm going to need your help."

I shrugged my shoulders. "Sure." What else was I going to say to a beautiful woman?

Since she had been so busy thinking, I was finished with my dinner long before she finished hers. I ordered another beer and watched her eating. "Now that you've got some things straightened out, can I ask you a few more questions?"

"Are they anything like the ones you asked earlier?"

"A little," I admitted.

She gave me an irritated dirty look, but replied. "Ask them now!"

"Now that your staff knows about Pariah, do they have any idea of what he can do?"

She shook her head. "None. Not even Doctor Richter knows that."

That was good news to me.

"What else?" she asked, but she didn't sound quite so irritated.

"What does the 'C' stand for?"

She looked up at me and blinked. "What 'C'?"

"The 'C' in your name. Doctor 'C' Westmore."

I was relieved to see her smile. "Cynthia. Now it's my turn. What does the blank stand for?"

Now it was my turn to blink in surprise. "Blank? What blank?"

"Agent Blank McNair."

It's the little questions that can make life so interesting!

CHAPTER

15

It was after ten o'clock the next morning when she finally picked me up – snazzy little sports car and all. This time she was wearing a white lab coat over her clothes – which again I lamented did not include a skirt. What had she done, worn one that first day just to tease me? Darn! It worked!

"No Stethoscope?" I asked as I got into her car.

She looked at me strangely. "What would I need one of those for?"

"We have a problem," she said as she pulled out of my parking lot. "The hospital wants Clayton gone as soon as possible."

"Because he can't pay?" I asked.

"They won't come out and say it, but that's exactly it. I took the initiative to call your Director about it this morning. Sorry I didn't talk to you about it first. I just thought since he's paying the bills so far, then he ought to know right away."

"Yeah," I agreed. "I'm glad you called him. I'm not sure he'd listen to me about it."

"Anyway, he said he'd look into it. Whatever that means."

"No telling," I replied. "But I'm sure he'll do something."

At the hospital, she stopped at the nurse's station to ask some questions while I hung back out of the way. It didn't take her long. "They gave him a snack late last night," she said when she came back. "And he ate this morning too, although he didn't eat much. They said he put up quite a fuss when they tried to take what was left of his breakfast away, so they left it with him."

"I'm surprised he didn't ask for a bag to put the left-overs in."

She gave me a strange look for that one. I don't think she believed that I was serious.

Pariah was sitting up and staring out his window when we walked in. He never turned to look at us, even though I said "Hi Pariah," the moment we entered the room.

I sat down in the chair next to his bed again, which was at least somewhat in the direction he was looking. Doctor Westmore dragged the other chair over next to me. "Pariah," I said, "please talk to me." But he did his best to totally ignore me while he just looked out the window at… nothing but the blank wall of another wing of the hospital. "Pariah!" I said again, trying to get his attention. "Pariah!"

He finally turned his head toward me. His eyes still looked glassy, not focused well. "Pariah, we need to ask you some questions," I said urgently.

"I want to go home," he said softly.

His plea pulled at my heart, but it was something I could never help him with. "Pariah, Doctor Westmore needs to know some things."

He looked over at her. "Doctor?" he asked.

"Yes," she replied. "Thomas…"

"Needles and pills. Needles and pills. Needles and pills." Then he closed his eyes for a moment before he looked at me. "Please take me home."

"I wish I could, Pariah. I wish I could. But right now we still have to know some things."

He looked back at the Doctor for a moment then back at the window. "Doctors ask questions. Many questions. No answers. Just needles and pills, more needles and pills. He looked at me for a moment. No more needles and pills. Don't let them give me any more. Take me home. Take me home." His head turned back to the window again.

I looked questioningly at the doctor.

"Mr. Clayton, will you please talk to me?" she asked. "It's very important. And I'm not going to give you any more needles or pills. I promise. In fact, I asked that they stop some of them."

She may as well have been talking to the wall for all the reaction I saw in his face. But she pressed on anyway.

"Mr. Clayton…"

"Pariah," he said without turning his head.

She jumped. "I don't want to call you that! It's not your name and it's not nice!"

"Pariah," he said again without looking at her.

"That's not your name!" she insisted.

"Pariah," he said just as he had repeated before.

The look she gave was leveled at me, not him. And beside the anger, what I read was another one of her moronic male comments from last night. I'm just glad she didn't say it.

"Why do you insist on being called Pariah?" she asked.

"It's who I am," he replied, still looking out the window. "Clayton died. Completely. Only Pariah is left. Only Pariah."

I could see she was practically gritting her teeth. I was so glad she didn't argue about it anymore with him. Whatever happened to the nice understanding therapist who would go along with whatever you told them? That certainly didn't seem to be her!

"Very well, Mr. Pariah." Her voice didn't sound exactly tolerant at all. But she softened it now as she tried to get down to business. "When someone touches you, do you always go somewhere else?"

But he didn't answer. He didn't even act like he heard her.

"Pariah? Pariah?" she repeated.

Again, she might as well have been talking to a brick wall.

"Pariah," I urged, "please answer her question. Do you always go somewhere else whenever someone touches you?"

He turned briefly to look at me. "No," he replied before turning his head toward the window again.

The doctor looked a bit relieved. "What if they're thinking about someone when they touch you?"

I don't even think he blinked as he continued to stare out the window as if she didn't exist.

"Pariah," she said. "Did you hear me? What if they're thinking about someone when they touch you? Do you always go somewhere else then?"

The awful sound of silence was the only reply she got.

So I tried again. "Pariah, please answer?" But he didn't reply. "Pariah, do you always go somewhere when someone is thinking about someone and they touch you?"

Slowly he turned his head toward me again. "I'm not sure. I think… most of the time."

"Can you control it at all?" she asked.

And again all she got was ignored silence.

I jumped in quicker this time. "Pariah, can you control it?"

"Sometimes," he replied, this time without turning to look at me.

I looked at the doctor and she was looking at me. It seemed that Pariah had his own version of games – as frustrating as they were for us to have to play.

"Pariah, what do you have against Doctor Westmore?" I asked.

"Needles and pills. Needles and pills."

"I'm not going to give you any more pills and certainly no needles!" she argued. But again, she got ignored. She finally rolled her eyes. "I guess we'll have to do this the hard way. Ask him…for me…why he came directly to you that first time you met."

"Pariah, why did you come directly to me that first time? Would you have gone to anyone, or was it me particularly you were looking for?" This time, I was the one met with stony silence. "Pariah, did you understand the question? Were you looking for me particularly?" The man could be so incredibly infuriating at times. "Let's move on," I suggested.

The doctor leaned forward again. "Pariah, did you know you were going to get shot?"

When he didn't answer, I tried again. "Pariah, did you know you were going to be shot that day?"

"I don't know," he replied.

"What do you mean?" "Felt…worried…something was going to happen. Didn't know what or when."

"How about where?" I asked.

"No. Didn't know."

I looked to the doctor, I could almost see the wheels turning in her head. Finally she nodded and asked her next question. "Have you always been able to go places like you do now? Find people like you do now?"

I waited to see if he would answer, but as before he ignored her completely. My turn. "Pariah, have you been able to find people like you do your whole life?"

Still staring out the window, he shook his head. "No. Not till…"

"Till what?" the doctor asked, leaning forward. "Till what?" I repeated.

But he wouldn't answer. Even though we both prodded him again and again. There was a secret there that he was holding onto. Something that he wasn't going to reveal, no matter what!

I looked to the doctor for her next question, but she seemed deep in thought. She finally looked at me. "This isn't going quite as well as I hoped," she said. "But at least were getting some things."

"If you don't mind, I have a few questions I'd like to ask."

"Be my guest," she replied.

I looked at Pariah again who was still staring at the same spot out the window somewhere. "Pariah, you said you were worried about something happening before. Do you sense anything is going to happen again?" I noticed the doctor leaning forward on that one.

He was a long time answering. I was about to ask it again, when he said, "Yes."

"What?"

"Don't know."

"When? Soon?"

"Don't know."

"And of course, you don't know where either."

"Only that trouble will come again."

Something about his words worried me. I was reminded of my idea last night to put a guard on his room. I hadn't done anything about that yet.

It was time for my next question. "Pariah, what do you want?"

This time he turned his head to look at me. "To go home," he replied.

I shook my head. "You don't have a home anymore. Remember? You lost it when you went to prison."

"Go home," he replied again. "Not that home."

This time, I was shaken. Another home? "Pariah, what other home? Where is it?"

Once again he lapsed into stony silence. The man was so infuriating.

"Pariah, is that what you really want? You want me to take you to this other home?"

He turned to look at me again. "No, not all I want. Something else too."

"What Pariah? What?"

But he didn't answer.

"Pariah, just tell me. What can I do for you?"

"Not time yet," he replied. "Not time. Take me home instead."

I was getting really frustrated. "What home? Where is home?"

But all he did was to continue to stare out the window.

I looked at the doctor. "What else do you want to ask?"

"I think that's enough for now. He doesn't seem willing yet to delve deeper than this on some subjects. We'll leave him be for now."

I nodded, and was about to say goodbye when I thought of just one last thing. "Pariah... Will you still find the missing people for us?"

This time, when he turned his head to look at me, I thought I saw a bit of triumph in his face. "Yes," he replied. "If I find them, will they feed me?"

"You know we will, Pariah. You know we will."

We left him then with promises that we would be back to see him later. Neither of us said a word until we got all the way back to her car.

"That was so frustrating!" I said as I got into her passenger seat.

"Yes and no," she replied. "But he was far more responsive than I thought he would be. Far more. And yet, I know his behavior before he was shot wasn't an act! And despite his unwillingness to talk about some things, we learned an awful lot."

"Like what?"

"Like the fact that his abilities are far more than we ever thought!"

Her cell phone rang just then and she pressed a button on her steering wheel to answer it. It was the Director's secretary calling to tell her about a meeting the Director needed her at this afternoon. While she was discussing it, my cell phone rang. It was Don...inviting me to the same meeting.

I had her drive me directly to work despite her insisting that I go home and rest instead. "You've seen my apartment," I told her, "would you want to spend the next week or two cooped up in there?" She didn't give me any more grief over the subject at all.

My first order of business once I was back at my desk was to get the recording from my meeting with Doctor Legs the night before and listen to it carefully – over and over again. There were other questions I could have asked, but in the end I decided they would have gained me nothing. I was still thoroughly convinced she had nothing at all to do with the shooting.

With that done, I got back to my feet and made my way out to Don's office, where I had to sit watching his secretary / executive assistant typing away at her computer while Don was talking with someone else. It was a long wait, but it was my next order of business so I stayed right there. Finally his door opened, I exchanged a few pleasantries with one of my colleagues, and I was allowed into his inner sanctum.

"I didn't know you were here today," he said as I walked in.

"I wasn't till a little while ago. I've been over at the hospital with the doctor talking to Pariah."

"He's actually communicating finally?"

"Sort of," I replied. "But it seems he has his own rules about what he's willing to talk about right now…and who with."

"Does it look like he's ever going to be useful again? Because I got to tell you, I've had serious doubts. I'm ready to wash my hands of the whole business."

"That's just it. When I asked him if he would be willing to help us find people again, it was the one thing that he seemed to be the most interested in. All the other questions, he either wouldn't answer, or we were lucky to pry anything out of him."

"He wants to help? Really? Okay, that part surprises me. And…it will probably change everything. If he's willing to be cooperative, then I think the FBI will be willing to spend more resources on him."

"How much resources?" I asked.

"We'll have to find out from the Director this afternoon. Did you talk with the doctor yet about any possible involvement in the shooting?"

I nodded. "Yeah. Naturally, she didn't like it much."

"Does anyone?"

"She came around in the end. My take is that she's completely clean. I think we can rule her staff out for now too."

"You're pointing in dangerous territory then." "I know. But if she didn't have anything to do with it, then we have to look closer to home. In the meantime, someone tried to kill him once, they could try it again. I think we should put a guard on him while he's in the hospital."

He thought about that for a moment. "I'll think about it," he replied. "It may depend on manpower."

"It wouldn't take much. Just make sure someone is always there to keep an eye on things. One man should be enough." I changed the subject slightly. "Anything new from the guy who shot us?"

"He's clammed up tight and has a rather expensive lawyer hovering over him to make sure we don't get anything else out of him."

I didn't have to say anything to that at all. Our primary lead was probably going to be a dead end. At least we had him for sure on the shooting, but we probably wouldn't get another word out of him as to why.

I didn't see Doctor Won't-Show-Me-Her-Legs again until the afternoon meeting. And then she breezed in late. Don was in the process of telling everyone what I had told him earlier about Pariah now wanting to help us locate missing people when she sat down with us.

The Director looked at me. "Is this true, Agent McNair?" he asked.

"Yes, sir," I replied. "That was the one thing that surprised me the most when we talked with him this morning."

"So he's out of his unbalanced mental state?" he asked. "He no longer needs psychiatric care?"

I looked to the pretty doctor to field that one. "Not at all," she replied quickly. "He's very unbalanced and will probably remain so for the rest of his life."

"So what made him so bad the CIA couldn't deal with him?"

"The drugs I think. Well, mostly the drugs. I think they wanted to use him so badly that they didn't take anything into account except their own needs...certainly not his needs at all or his real problems. He has a very unique mind – more so than I originally thought. And unbelievably, in his case, the drugs did far more damage than they did good. He's just now starting to come back to getting his head somewhat straight…at least as far as I think what we can expect, for now."

"And do you also think he now wants to work with us and help us?"

"I do. I'm not totally sure of his reasons, other than that he has some. His service to you would of course give him a sense of real purpose that he is missing in his life right now. As long as you don't abuse him as I'm thinking the CIA might have done, he could prove to be a very valuable asset for you."

"You're sure of this?" the Director asked.

"I am. Absolutely. Don't get me wrong, he's still psychologically damaged. I strongly recommend you keep a doctor around to deal with him frequently – either myself or someone else. But I also think that the expense and benefits would be more than compensated for by what he is capable of doing – of which, we may only be scratching the surface."

That last part surprised me. Fortunately, the Director pounced on it too and asked her to explain.

"I'm convinced that he has other very potent abilities. Please keep in mind that I've only worked with a few other psychics in my life, and none of them were anything like Mr. Clayton. But take into consideration, not only that he seems to be able to travel to places far away while his body remains here, but he also knew where, when, and who to contact with his ability when he first found Agent McNair. Couple that with the fact that he says he didn't know he was going to be shot, but he did know something was going to happen. I think we're only scratching the surface with him."

"So your bottom line recommendation is that we should keep him?"

"Absolutely! Keep him, but also keep a good doctor close by just in case. With the kind of traumas going on in his head, especially when he finds someone, you're going to need one." She paused for a moment and glanced at me for a moment. "Personally, I would relish the opportunity to work more with him. I can't imagine how his mind manages to coordinate interacting in two separate places at the same time. Such a thing would scramble any normal person's brain."

"Your thoughts, Agent McNair?" the Director asked.

What could I say? "I concur," I replied. If the good doctor wanted to hang around, it was fine by me.

"Very well," the Director said, "Now we just need to figure out what to do with him. The hospital wants him out as soon as possible and the government is not going to foot the bill to fix all his problems! He's homeless so he has no place to go, but he was shot on our turf so we have some responsibility as to taking care of him. And I'm not sure a cell downstairs is the best answer."

"May I make a suggestion?" Don spoke up.

"I hope someone has one," the Director replied. "I was all prepared to sign the commitment papers when I walked in here."

"Use one of our safe houses. Not only would it get him out of the basement, but the security would be easier to arrange. I took the liberty of putting a guard on Pariah's room at the hospital this morning now that he's communicating again. If they tried to kill him once, then they may try to do it again."

It was news to me that Don had actually taken my advice. But I was certainly glad he did.

"And you think a guard is necessary?'

I answered this time. "Yes, not only for his safety, but to make sure we know where he is at all times. In the past, he's been notoriously difficult to find when we need him."

"And what's the latest on the shooting?"

"We're still beating the bushes," another of the agents at the table replied. "We still think it has something to do with the New York business, but we don't have any real leads yet. New York is helping us, but the shooting didn't happen on their turf."

"In other words, you want me to light a match under their feet."

"Something like that," the agent replied.

The Director made a note on his pad. "Okay," he said when he was done. "I like the safe house idea. Make it happen. But only till he's well again. Then I see no other choice than to let him go his own way and hope for the best. And I'll set up a small budget to pay him too. Any ideas on how much we should budget for?"

"Don't budget in dollars," I replied. "He won't take money...so far. All he wants is food. Mostly fast-food hamburgers."

He stared at me for a moment. I was sure he thought I was joking. "We'll get together somewhere else and discuss adequate compensation for his services," he said. He looked at the pretty doctor. "And for now, you stay."

It was that easy. I thought that once Pariah was able to be up and around a bit, we'd be back in business again. I thought that we would quickly be the envy of every missing person's bureau in the world. I thought life would be beautiful and great and that we'd all be heroes. And I thought that Doctor Legs would finally wear a skirt when she met with me.

Boy was I wrong – about everything!

CHAPTER

16

The safe house wasn't anything like the typical safe houses you see in the movies, where a bunch of hulky looking agents sit around playing cards in a cheap looking room while babysitting some obnoxious looking bad guy. This was an actual house – where someone lived – all the time. Actually, it was Phil Albright's house. Phil was a retired agent who supplemented his income by offering the use of his house from time to time. And it was a nice place. Really!

Phil was there most of the time and we usually kept at least one other "active" agent there whenever one of our "guests" used the place. The house also had some other redeeming qualities. It was fairly close to work. He owned the vacant properties on each side of it, and it backed up to a dense wildlife protected area so there were no neighbors looking straight into the backyard. It had a good six-foot fence all the way around it with an electric gate to help security. And it had one hell of a guard dog. Okay, so the dog was a miniature white French poodle, but he was feisty as hell and barked non-stop at the least little thing. Talk about an alarm system!

I had insisted on driving myself home the night before, and I drove to work again the next morning. For a few minutes I felt like a teenager just getting his first set of wheels. That wore off quickly though when I realized that hitting the brake with any kind of pressure also put pressure on my wounds. But at least it was tolerable, so driving was no problem. But to pick up Pariah and get him to the safe house, I decided to use one of the company cars instead of my car – one where I could fix it so the back doors couldn't be opened from inside the car. I just had visions of Pariah jumping out at a red light and us not being able to find him again.

Doctor Can't 'C' My Legs Westmore rode with me to the hospital because I was going straight to the safe house once we collected Pariah. Outside of his room, I recognized one of the guards who had been down in the cell block with us a few days before. The guard was flirting with one of the nurses in the hallway. At least he recognized me when I got there.

"What's going on?" he asked.

"We're moving him," I replied. "The hospital wants him out."

I was surprised to see him roll his eyes. "I just got here!" he complained. "So much for my overtime tonight."

"Don't worry," I said, "maybe they'll let you help babysit with him sometime."

"Is he going back to the cells again?"

"No," I replied. "Somewhere else." I purposely didn't tell him any more than that.

Another nurse arrived then with a wheelchair for Pariah and we followed her into his room. His shoulder was still heavily bandaged and his arm was in a sling. But he was dressed and ready. It didn't look like they had made any effort to shave him though. Actually, I guessed he probably wouldn't let them.

"Okay, Pariah," I said as we walked in. "Time to get out of here. Are you ready?"

"Take me home?" he asked hopefully.

"I wish I could, Pariah," I replied sincerely. "But for now we're taking you to another home till your shoulder is well enough. Then I can let you go anywhere you want." Was I offering him too much hope? It was the best I could do at the time. "This is a really nice place we're going to. Believe me. I like it myself."

"It wouldn't take much for you to like anything better than you've got," the Doctor quipped behind me. She did have a point.

"Where's he going?" the guard asked again as we were pushing him out. "Someplace else," I replied. "That's all I can tell you."

He nodded. "I understand…perfectly."

Surprisingly, Pariah gave us no trouble at all as we got him downstairs, out of the wheelchair, and into the back of the car. The few times we tried to talk to him though, he remained as silent as a stone. I drove us out of the parking lot and headed back the way we had come.

Since Pariah wasn't talking, I figured I'd talk with the doctor instead. "So doctor, no other patients today?" I asked.

I sensed her looking at me. "Cynthia," she said.

"What?" I asked totally surprised.

"If we're going to be working closely together, we might as well use first names. So it's Cynthia…or 'Cyn' as most people call me."

Okay! "Cliff," I replied, referring to what I expected her to call me. "So is that 'Sin' with an 'S' or 'Cyn' with a 'C'?" I was shocked that the question had just come out of my mouth and I regretted asking it the moment I realized I had said it! Dumb McNair! Dumb! Definitely not professional!

But her reply surprised me. In the sexiest voice I was sure she could manage, she said. "Take your pick, big boy!" I finally realized she was attempting to sound something like Mae West in one of those ancient movies. It worked enough to leave me speechless! Then she laughed. "Sorry! I used to get that one so often in High School and College that I long ago came up with little things like that to reply. It's an old habit."

"So which 'Cyn' is it?" I asked with a big grin on my face.

"Take your pick," she replied again, only this time in a more normal but laughing voice.

Okay, I knew it now for sure. The lady could certainly tease. But was it going to be another thing like her legs, where she let me see them only once and then went out of the way to make sure I never saw them again? I certainly hopped not. Professional, McNair. Keep it professional!

The gate was closed when we got to the house. I stopped the car next to the keypad and rolled down my window, then decided to honk my horn instead. I immediately heard the yapping of a dog somewhere and a minute later the gate started to roll aside. I drove in and saw through my rear view mirror that the gate was closing again. I parked up close to the garage out of the way of any other cars that might be coming later. I saw Phil walking down the sidewalk to meet us – along with his still yapping little white poodle, Brutus. Phil had started to put on a little weight in the last few years, and his hair was starting to show small patches of gray, but his muscular body still betrayed the time he had spent in the Marine Corp before he had joined the FBI.

"Hey, McNair," he called as I got out of my car.

"Hi Phil," I replied. "How's it going?"

"Same as ever," he replied. He stopped right where he was as Doctor "Sinful" Cynthia got out of the car. "I do hope you're the one who will be keeping me company," he said as he shook her hand."

I answered before she could. "Sorry, Phil. You get someone with a whole different kind of charm. That's Doctor Westmore."

I opened the back door for Pariah to get out. But he just sat there staring at Brutus who was still barking his head off. I realized that Pariah was afraid of the little dog.

"Quiet Brutus!" Phil finally yelled. The dog actually shut up and sat down.

"It's okay, Pariah," I said. "I promise the dog won't hurt you. He's really very friendly."

It took some coaxing and making sure the dog wouldn't get close to him before he would get out of the car. When he did, he started looking all around. And what he saw first was the big tree in the front yard. He ignored all of us and headed straight for it, where he sat down in the shade near its trunk. For once, he actually looked…happy. That is till Brutus decided to investigate him further.

The dog barked and ran right for him. I could tell that Brutus was trying to be playful, but Pariah took it the wrong way and curled up into a frightened ball and started letting of the most hideous sounds of distress.

"Brutus!" Phil yelled as we all ran after the dog.

Brutus jumped and barked at Pariah trying to get some attention until Phil got there and yelled again. The dog finally backed away.

"It's alright, Pariah," I said. "The dog isn't going to hurt you. He's not even close to you now."

Slowly, he unrolled himself from his little ball and looked up. "Why don't you come into the house with us," I suggested. "Would you like to see your room?"

But he just sat there and stared distrustfully at Brutus.

"Pariah," the doctor asked as she knelt down closer to him. "Are you afraid of dogs?"

I don't know who was more surprised that he answered, her or me. "Dog's bite," Pariah said softly.

"He won't bite you," she replied. "We'll make sure of it." With that, she looked up at Phil.

"I guarantee it," Phil added.

Pariah sat a little straighter, but he made no move to get up from where he was.

Having him outside in the front yard was not my first option. Not where anyone could see him if they drove by. We wanted to keep his presence here at least somewhat of a secret. "Are you sure you don't want to come into the house and see it?" I asked. "It's a very nice house."

"Trees," Pariah said instead. But he didn't say anything more.

"Pariah," I said. "We need to get you inside where it's safer."

But once again all he said was, "Trees."

"Trees?" Cynthia asked. She looked up to Phil. "Are there any more trees around?"

"Plenty in the back," he replied.

"Hear that, Pariah," she said to him. "There are lots of trees in the backyard. Would you like to see them?"

"More trees?" he asked hopefully.

"Lots," Phil replied.

We were rewarded to see him get to his feet and follow Phil around to the back of the house. Brutus followed too, although I was glad to see that while he never seemed to stop watching Pariah, at least he stayed away. The backyard was large and very nicely landscaped – including plenty of trees. The moment Pariah saw it, he headed for the middle of a group of three and sat down. Once again, he looked happier than I had ever seen him.

"It may be a while before we can get him inside," the doctor said. But at least he shouldn't be so visible back here.

"Thanks," I replied. "This should do nicely.

"You mean, you're just going to leave him out here?" Phil asked incredulously.

"Hopefully, he'll agree to go in later," Doctor 'C' replied. But for now he seems perfectly happy and content.

"I'll be back later," I added. "I'll make sure he gets in the house when it gets dark."

Phil shook his head. "You brought me a real strange one this time."

He had no idea how true his words were.

"Hannah showed up a little while later and I took Doctor "Sinful" back to the office where she could get her car and go back to her hospital. When I got off of work, I headed straight to the safe house to relieve Hannah and check on Pariah.

When I got there, a barking Brutus met me at my car then took off again. Hannah let me in through the front door, but told me everyone else was out back. I followed her through the house. Phil was sitting there on the patio watching Pariah…and Brutus. Hannah took the seat next to him.

"What's going on?" I asked.

"Brutus is still trying to get your man to play with him" Phil replied.

"I thought we were going to keep Brutus away from him."

"I think Brutus is handling it just fine," Phil said.

I pulled up another chair to watch too.

Brutus was laying on the grass about twenty feet away from Pariah, watching him intently. But Pariah wasn't looking in his direction at all. The little dog finally got to his feet and started carefully creeping closer, as if he was stalking the wretch of a man in front of him. A moment later, the dog dropped to his stomach to wait again. He had moved perhaps five feet closer. Pariah didn't even seem to know the dog was there. Anyone else for that matter.

The dog moved again, creeping carefully forward, then he dropped down again, his eyes still intent on his target. But as before, Pariah still seemed totally unaware of his presence. The dog moved slowly forward again. Closer, closer, closer…

Pariah turned his head so fast to look at the dog it startled me. The dog turned tail and ran for the other side of the yard. Pariah went right back to looking at the trees and plants in the back part of the yard – where he didn't have to see the house or anyone else. As if he was all alone back there…except for the dog, who was once again slowly making his way back toward the man in the trees.

"They've been doing that all afternoon," Phil said. "Brutus gets closer and closer, then he suddenly turns around and Brutus runs off. They've made a game of it. And I'm pretty sure your man is enjoying himself. Don't know how he knows when Brutus always gets to that same point, but that's always when he turns and Brutus runs off."

I watched the odd game with them and Phil was right. As far as I could tell, Pariah turned as soon as Brutus hit that same place again. Was that another tiny manifestation of his abilities? That was another question for Doctor Legs.

Eventually, Phil got to his feet to make dinner, and Hannah said goodbye to go back to her family. "Can I help?" I asked Phil.

"No, I got it. What does your friend out there like to eat? Hamburgers… and spaghetti." I replied. "Actually, probably anything that's easy for him to chew."

"If that's the case, then you and I may be sharing all the steaks I bought earlier," he said.

"I won't turn them down," I replied.

"Spaghetti good enough for tonight?" he asked.

"Sounds great to me." I knew Pariah would appreciate it. And, dinner would probably be an easy way to get him into the house. A little while later, all I had to do was to yell, "Pariah, dinner's ready. Spaghetti!" from the back door, and he got up immediately and came inside…with Brutus right at his heels.

I had warned Phil about the way he ate, but there are some things you just have to experience to truly understand. It wasn't long before Phil understood all too perfectly.

After dinner, I showed Pariah where his room was. He stood in the doorway and just stared at the bed. But he didn't seem to want to go all the way into the room.

"What's wrong?" I asked.

He pointed at the bed. "Bed," he said.

"Yes. That's where you can sleep."

"It's a real bed. Not a hospital bed, not a prison bed."

"Of course not."

"And I can sleep in it?"

"Of course."

He looked at me as if he didn't believe me. Then he walked over to the bed and sat on it. Very carefully, he managed to lay down on top of all the covers. I could tell that his injured shoulder and his arm being in the sling made things more difficult for him. But once on it, he closed his eyes as if to go to sleep.

"Pariah," I said. "Do you want to watch some TV with us before you go to sleep?"

But I got no answer. He was already sleeping.

A few hours later, a security guard arrived to keep watch all night and I went home. I felt good because for once Pariah was in a place where he seemed to be happy. He was protected there. And best of all, I would have no problem finding him when we needed him. And speaking of needing him, I made the mental decision to start looking for another case to use him on as soon as I got to the office in the morning. No use wasting more time. It might even help his recovery.

I went to sleep that night, haunted by a pair of "Cynful" legs. It was a restless night.

CHAPTER

17

I needn't have bothered worrying about a case to try out Pariah on again because the office was in something of an uproar long before I arrived. I wasn't called about it because "technically" I still wasn't there.

"What's up?" I asked John as I walked past his office.

"Another case. Kidnapped boy, about four years old. Been missing since yesterday afternoon."

"What can I do?" I asked.

"Tell Don I won't be at his meeting this morning," he replied.

I had a pretty fair idea that Don wasn't expecting him today. This kind of thing happened frequently to all of us. "You got it!" I replied.

"Hey Cliff!" he yelled before I could get out of earshot.

"Do you think there's a chance that we can use Pariah if we need him?"

"To tell the truth, I was thinking of looking for a case to use him on right away," I replied.

"Thanks, buddy," he said as he picked up his phone to make a call.

On the way to my office, I noticed that Hannah was in the big room, but not Billy. That was good. Billy was supposed to be at the safe house by six in the morning to relieve the guard who had been there all night. Hannah would relieve him in the afternoon, then I would be there after work until the next guard showed up. It was really a no-problem schedule for any of us.

In Don's morning meeting, I was surprised when he didn't ask about Pariah. But he did tell me I needed to stick around afterwards for another meeting…this time with the lawyers. I hated any time I ever had to meet with lawyers – about anything! Somehow it always seemed like I wound up on the losing side of the stick. Instead of holding it in Don's office, we went down to the executive boardroom instead.

The subject of the meeting was adequate compensation for Mr. Clayton's, aka Pariah's, services. Mostly, Don and I sat while the lawyer talked…or rather read from a brief he had prepared. I only caught about half of what he was talking about. The rest was so dull and technical it completely lost me. The only problem was, they actually wanted to issue Pariah a check for each "service rendered."

"This isn't going to work," I finally said, interrupting the lawyer who I'm more than sure thought his solution was brilliant.

He actually looked surprised! "Why not?" he asked.

"Because Pariah is homeless. He doesn't have a dime to his name, and he certainly has no bank account."

"Well he can have one now," the lawyer responded.

"Except that, so far, he has refused to take money for anything. All he wants is food."

"He can buy all the food he wants."

The guy just didn't get it. "He's homeless! He's a bum! He's been in prison for child molestation! No restaurant wants him anywhere near. None of the stores want him either."

The lawyer just looked at me strangely. "Did you say he was in prison for child molestation?"

"Yes!"

"Then this can't work. We can't use someone like that to find missing children. Do you know how that would look?"

"We know! We've been through all that!" Don replied.

The lawyer shook his head. "We can't allow it. There are too many ways this could reflect very badly on the good name of the FBI."

I could tell Don was perturbed by the tone of his voice. "What would it take for you to reverse that decision?" he asked.

"I won't," he replied. "The Director himself would have to issue the order."

Without another word, Don picked up the phone from the big table and dialed. He spoke to the Director's secretary, then waited for the

Director. "Hold on a second sir," he said as soon as the Director was on the line. He passed the phone to the lawyer. The lawyer spoke his concern, then listened. Finally he said, "Yes sir," and hung up the phone. "It seems we will be using Mr. Clayton's services despite his background."

I was very glad to hear that, although I already knew we would be. But what the lawyer said next, was not so good to hear.

"However, in light of his background, we are going to require that all clients are made thoroughly aware of Mr. Clayton's past. We will prepare a statement for them to sign to cover us legally."

I was outraged. "That's not necessary!"

"Yes it is!" the lawyer responded. "It's either that, or you can't use him."

Stymied! By a damn legal head with no idea of what was really going on! It was take it or leave it, but at least we would still be able to use him.

"Better prepare that statement quick," I replied, "because we may be needing his services…today!"

I had hoped to shake him a bit, but all he did was to nod and reply, "No problem. I'll see that it gets prepared immediately."

You win some – you lose some. I guess we came out fifty – fifty with the lawyer. I suppose that's really pretty good. Most of the time I usually lost. Completely.

The call came from John late in the morning. "What's going on?" I asked.

"The kidnapped boy," I told you about. "We're helping out with about a dozen other branches. The father's a big time executive downtown, and from all appearances, they're major loaded! Ransom demand was for two million."

"And you want to use Pariah," I finished for him.

"Yeah. Don gave me permission to ask you if you think he'll do it. Even if he can just verify that the boy is still alive would be a big help."

"How about the parents? Did you tell them about what you want to do?"

"Yeah. The father thinks I'm loony, but as usual, the mother is jumping at anything."

"Well, there's one more new wrinkle…courtesy of the legal boys upstairs. They want the parents to sign a document saying that they know he's a child molester."

I couldn't agree more with every swear word I heard over the phone. "I'll get back to you," John finally said.

I walked out of my office and called to Hannah. "Stand by," I told her. "We may be using Pariah on this kidnap thing."

From there, I went directly to Don's office. His secretary / executive assistant waved me right though by saying, "He's expecting you."

I barely got through his doorway when he said, "John just called me. He was…upset…about the legal thing."

"So am I!"

"Me too, but we'll go with it for now. I'll talk to the Director more about it later. If the parents agree, then we'll do it here in the interview room again, just like last time. Full recordings of everything."

I had no problem with that. "I'd like to bring Doctor Westmore in too. She hasn't really seen him in action yet."

"Better do it."

"Now all we need is the parent's permission," I replied.

He nodded. "How about Pariah? Is he up for it yet? He's still badly injured."

Okay, he did have a good point. My gut told me Pariah would be fine with it, but… "I'll go back to the safe house right now and talk with him."

Phil was inside vacuuming his living room carpet when I got there. No surprise, everyone else was out back. I went out to the patio and took the chair next to where Billy was sitting. Pariah and Brutus were playing the same game again, but with a difference. This time, Brutus was able to get to within a few feet of Pariah before he suddenly turned and the dog took off running.

"What's happening?" Billy asked.

"The kidnapping case everyone is busting their rumps on."

"And you want to use Pariah?"

"If the parents will let us. And right now, that's a big if."

The back door opened again and Phil came out to sit with us. "I fixed your man some scrambled eggs, bacon, and toast for breakfast today. He actually said thank you to me, and he sounded awfully sincere."

"Your cooking must have scored a few points with him," I replied. "He hardly says a word to anyone."

"Yeah, well he could score a few points with me by taking a shower and changing his clothes. He totally ignores any suggestions about cleaning up in any way. Frankly, the guy is starting to smell a little, Cliff. Maybe that broken nose of his doesn't let him notice it. But it's going to become obvious to everyone else pretty soon."

"This is nothing," Billy replied. "You should have seen how he used to be!"

"Well, it doesn't make it right. And it doesn't help matters."

I had to agree, but Pariah seemed to play by his own rules sometimes. This was another one of those things we were going to have to work on with him. I decided I'd pass the information on to Doctor Tease-Me-And-Forget-Me. Maybe she could straighten him out.

I got up from my chair and headed back to the trees where Pariah was sitting. Brutus barked and ran to me. I petted the small dog for a moment then continued on toward Pariah. I had to walk around in front of him and sit on the ground for him to pay any attention to me. Brutus stayed close, but out of the way.

"Pariah," I said. "I need to know if you're well enough yet to help us again." He barely acknowledged that I was there. "We have a kidnapping case. A small four-year-old boy. He's been missing since yesterday."

His eyes suddenly focused clearly on me. "If I find him, will they feed me?"

Why did he always ask that? Someday I would take the time to get to the bottom of it, but not right now. "We'll feed you," I replied. "Anything you like. I promise. Will you help us?"

Instead of replying, he got to his feet and headed for the house. "Pariah," I called as I got to my feet too, "the parents haven't agreed to use you yet. We just had to know if you were willing to help us first." It's absolutely amazing how he can ignore people and the things they try to say to him. As if they don't exist!

My phone rang as we reached the patio. Pariah went straight into the house while I stopped to answer the call. I saw Billy getting up to check on Pariah. "Hello?" I asked without bothering to check who had called.

"Cliff? I finally got the parents to agree, well, the mother anyway. The father wasn't around to check with. What's the situation with Pariah?"

"Um… I'm checking that now."

The back door opened and Billy stuck his head out. "Pariah's sitting in the back seat of your car. Are you going somewhere with him?"

"John?" I said into the phone. "It looks like he's going to help. Bring the parents to the office though. Don wants everything recorded…and we also have to get some legal documents signed."

Billy disappeared again and I dialed Doctor "Sinthia." I had to leave a message for her to call me back right away.

When I got to the car, Billy and Brutus were standing outside of it. I saw Pariah in the back seat. "You may as well ride shotgun," I said to Billy. "Looks like we're all going back to the office."

My phone rang about ten minutes later. It was the pretty doctor. "We're going to be using Pariah on another case today," I told her.

"When?" she asked.

"I don't know. I'm bringing him back to the office now so he'll be there. No telling when the parents will show up."

"Cliff!" She called me Cliff! "Let me know! Don't let them start till I get there!" she said rather emphatically.

"I'll try," I replied. She hung up the phone, but I was hung up over the fact that she had actually called me Cliff! Sometimes, it's the little things that can mean so much.

The session was set up for mid-afternoon. I had taken the precaution of buying Pariah a hamburger and a large order of fries for lunch so hopefully he would be at his sanest. I also warned him that we would be doing this in the same room we had used last time so he would be prepared and hopefully wouldn't freak out about it.

Doctor "Sinthia" showed up shortly before we were ready to start – white lab coat and all. She was also carrying a small black medical bag.

I was rather amazed when I saw her remove a stethoscope and a blood pressure cuff from the bag. As she went over to talk to Pariah, more people arrived. Not only people I recognized as working for the FBI, but this time someone from the local police too. Too many people were going to be learning about Pariah and what he could do.

Unfortunately, the lawyer also showed up amid the crowd. I saw him sitting down and showing a document to the parents. I decided I didn't want to get in the middle of that so I went over to help the doctor with Pariah.

"Pariah," she said to him. "I just want to take your blood pressure. See…no needles, no pills. You had this done at the hospital many times. I just want to check on you to make sure you're well enough to do this."

He looked up at me uncertainly. "It's okay, Pariah," I said. "I'm right here. No needles or pills. I promise! I'll watch her closely."

It was tentative, but he finally nodded slightly. And of course, that's when all hell broke loose. Not because the doctor wanted to take his blood pressure, but because that was when the boy's father decided to become more vocal about the whole thing. And in particular, he pointed his finger angrily at Pariah and called him a damned child molester.

Pariah broke out in wails of anguish and once again started screaming at the top of his lungs. "I didn't do it! I didn't do it! It wasn't me! I promise I didn't do it!"

"He's a damn nut case!" the father yelled back. "Look at him! Why should we listen to a damn pervert? I don't like this one bit!" He turned to his wife. "We need to forget about this nonsense! This whole thing is ridiculous!"

Pariah was huddled in a ball on the floor again, crying. "I didn't do it. I didn't do it."

"Henry!" she replied mostly in tears. "What can it hurt? We're already here. I want my son back! They said this man can help!"

"How? A…a crazy loony psychic? Don't make me laugh! And now we find out he's a damn child molester on top of it? It's not right! It's just not right! And this is where our tax money goes? Crazy junk like this?"

"Sir!" John protested. "This man can help! Please give him the chance!"

"I don't believe in psychics!" the father replied. "And I sure don't believe in child molesters…letting them live that is!" That last part was aimed directly at Pariah who was still huddling on the floor whining he didn't do it.

I jumped into the argument, trying to use facts. "One hundred percent!" I yelled at the father to get his attention."

"What?" he asked, caught off guard since he didn't know what I was referring to.

"One hundred percent," I said again. "That's his success percentage. Every single time we've used him, he's been one hundred percent correct! In every single way! He has never…I repeat *never*…been wrong…about anything!"

The father seemed a bit shaken by what I had said and he backed down a little. "He should have been more right about what would happen when he molested whatever little kid he attacked!" He turned to his wife. "Let's forget this whole thing and get out of here!"

"No!"

"What?" It looked like he couldn't believe his wife had stood up to him that way.

"I said no! I want to try this. If they say he can help…and he's never wrong, then we'd be fools to turn them down!"

"Oh for the love of…" He shut up and stomped out of the room.

"Give me that paper," the woman said to the lawyer. "I'll sign it. They told me earlier that he had molested someone." She turned briefly to look at Pariah who was still crying that he didn't do it. "Are you sure he did it?" she asked.

"He was tried and convicted in a fair and proper procedure," the lawyer replied.

The woman shook her head, then quickly signed his paper. "Now what?" she asked John.

I answered instead. "Now we see if we can get him calmed down enough to agree to do this for you." Although at that point I didn't have a lot of hope about that. Pariah was still huddled in his ball crying he didn't do it and the doctor was trying her best to comfort him without touching him.

I looked around at the people there and spotted Hannah. "Get him a candy bar. Quick!" I was hoping that maybe some type of food would bring him back to some sense of normality.

I joined the doctor on the floor with him. "It's okay, Pariah," I said. "The man is gone. He's not here anymore. But the boy's mother still wants you to help." Once again I was talking to a brick wall. I tried several times to persuade him, but I got nowhere. Hannah showed up suddenly and held out a candy bar for me. I ripped the wrapper off it and held it out to him. "Here Pariah. Candy! You like this stuff. Maybe it will help."

He heard that part! His eyes locked onto the candy bar in my hand and he slowly reached out and took it. Painfully, he broke a bit of it off and stuck it in his mouth.

He was about half-way done with the candy when I felt someone else leaning over me. I looked up and was surprised to see the mother. She looked almost as distressed as Pariah. "Please," she said to him. "Please help me. I'm sorry my husband was so rude."

Pariah actually looked up at her.

"Please help me?" she said again. "I want my son back. His name is Tommy."

"If I find him, will you feed me?" he asked. I suddenly knew everything was going to be just fine.

"Feed you? You want me to feed you? Wouldn't you rather have money? I can pay…lots. I just want my son back."

Pariah shook his head. "No money. Can't take money. It's not right! I need food. Only food."

"Whatever you like," she replied. "If you can help us, I'll see you get whatever you want."

Pariah nodded. "I will find him." He stuffed the last of the candy bar into his mouth and held out his dirty hands. "Just touch me, and think hard about him."

"Pariah," I said quickly. "Wouldn't it be better to go over to a chair and sit down? Wouldn't you be more comfortable?" Brick wall time. Slowly, the mother reached out with both hands and took Pariah's misshapen hands into her own. And just as slowly she settled herself down on the floor where she could be more comfortable. Pariah's eyes were already closed.

"He's fine," Pariah said first. "In a bathroom. He's going…um… doing…." He opened his eyes to look at me.

"It's okay," I told him. "We get the picture. He's on the toilet."

He nodded and closed his eyes again. "Chain. Shiny chain. Long chain. Wrapped around his ankle several times. Padlock. Chain goes out of the bathroom."

"Follow it Pariah. We need to know where he is."

"Bedroom. It's…nice…interesting…log cabin walls Sloped ceilings."

"A log cabin?" I asked.

"I think so, don't know much yet. Bed. Massive bed. Fills most of the room. Very tall bed. Stepstool next to it to get up and down. Massive bed. Made from tree trunks. Looks heavy, very heavy. The chain is wrapped around one of the legs of the bed. Padlock. Bed is all rumpled. TV on the wall in the corner. Cartoons playing."

"Great Pariah! Now can you explore the rest of the house?"

He nodded. "Easy. Good bond. Bedroom door is closed, going through it. Stairs. Going down. Fishing poles on the wall."

"On the wall?" I asked.

"Fish too. And bears. Cute bears all around."

"Bears?" I asked.

"On the end tables, in the corner. Over the fireplace. Nice place. Looks fairly new. Log walls again. Wow!"

He said nothing for a few moments. "What, Pariah? What is it?"

It was another moment before he answered. Trees. Lots of trees. And mountains. Huge window overlooking trees. Way up high. Beautiful! Beautiful trees."

"Sounds like a tourist cabin up north," the doctor said quietly. "I've rented a few of them before."

"Trees!" Pariah said again. "Going through window. Beautiful view. Beauti…. Uh oh! Man down on the deck. Sitting in chair. Drinking something. Looking at trees. Beautiful trees."

The doctor suddenly started wrapping the blood pressure cuff around his arm. He opened his eyes.

"Don't worry," she said to him. "Try to ignore what I'm doing. I'm just making sure you're okay."

I was relieved to see him close his eyes again. "Pariah," I asked, "do you see anyone else there?"

"No, not from where I am. Beautiful view. Mountains. Trees."

"Okay, Pariah. Good. Go back into the house. See if there's anyone else around."

"Like the trees. Like the mountains. Want to stay."

"Pariah, we need you inside. We need you to help us find where the boy is."

"Want to stay," he replied softly. "Beautiful trees."

"I know that, Pariah" I said with some frustration starting to build. "Pariah, we need your help. Help us find the boy."

The doctor had pumped up the pressure cuff and was now slowly letting off the pressure. I marveled that it didn't seem to disturb Pariah's concentration.

Pariah gave a big sigh, then said, "Steep slope going down behind the house. Lots of steps going down to the water. Mountain stream. Pretty."

"Good, Pariah, can you please help us find the boy now? Go back inside."

"Going inside," he finally said and I breathed a sigh of relief. What was it with him and trees?

"Nice place," he said. "Don't see anyone. Wait! Hear something! Looking! Don't see anyone. Another bedroom. Empty. Big bed again. Covers rumpled. Kitchen. Looks nice. Another bathroom. Another bedroom. Nobody on this floor. Still hear sounds of someone else. Another stairway, going down. Oh! Pool table. Man playing pool. Gun! Handgun! On bar near pool table. Big open space. Big TV with chairs."

"Good, Pariah," I said. So there's only two men there and the boy?"

"That's all I see," he replied. "Want to see trees again."

"Wait, Pariah. "We need to find out where this cabin is."

"If it's a rental cabin, it should have a sign with a name out front," the doctor said. "It could be easier to find that way."

"Pariah, did you hear that? Can you go out front and see if the cabin has a name sign?"

"Going outside. Like it outside here. More fishing things on the front porch. Decorations. Don't see a sign with a name."

"Look out by the road," the doctor suggested.

"Gravel road. Bad ruts. Very steep. See sign with number. Twelve forty three. Here... Fishing Fiesta! Sign says Fishing Fiesta."

"Great, Pariah! Really good."

I turned to John but he spoke first. "They're already on it," he replied.

"Pariah, is there a car out front?"

"Yes. SUV I think. Big. White."

"Good. How about a license number?"

"Avis," he said.

"Avis? A rental car?"

"Sticker on the car same as license. Avis car rental."

I had no idea what to do next. I turned around to look at John. "Suggestions?" I asked. He shook his head. I looked at the big mirrored window. "Suggestions?" I asked again.

"Hold on," a voice came over the speaker.

"Pariah," I said. "Please check on the boy again. How's he doing?"

"Going," he replied. It was a moment more before he added, "Boy is in bed watching TV. Cartoons."

"Good, Pariah," I said. I turned to the mother. "Is there anything you want to know?"

"Is he hurt in any way?" she asked.

"Pariah…" But he was already ahead of me.

"He seems fine. Chain around his ankle. Some red skin there, but not bad."

"Any bruising?" the doctor asked.

It was a moment before he answered. "Don't see any."

Don's voice came over the speaker this time. "We located the cabin. State police are on the way. But it's going to take them a while to get there. Can he assist when they get close?"

"Pariah," I started to ask.

"I can stay," he replied. "Good bond. Like it here. Trees. Beautiful trees. Beautiful mountains. Going up. Going high. Going higher. Beautiful view."

I looked to the mother. "How are you holding up? Need a break?"

She shook her head. "Not as long as he can keep checking on my son once in a while."

Pariah said nothing for a few minutes. Then he suddenly said, "I see a bear. Two bears. Mother and cub I think. Very black."

The country up there was famous for having lots of black bears. "Where?" I asked. "How close to the cabin."

"Not close at all. Deep in the woods. Beautiful here. Very beautiful. Lots of trees. Like the trees."

The doctor started pumping up the blood pressure cuff again. I watched as she took his blood pressure. When she was done, I saw a look of surprise on her face. "Bad?" I asked.

She shook her head. "No, good! Very good. Wherever he is, he likes it because his pressure has gone way down."

There was a soft knock on the door and John opened it. "The father want's to come back in," he said. "Is it okay?"

I thought about it for only a moment. "No!" I said. "Keep him out. I don't want to disturb Pariah any more than I have to. He can watch from the other room."

After the way he had behaved earlier, I saw no reason to have him anywhere near.

"Man on the deck is going into the house," Pariah suddenly said. I was both surprised and glad that Pariah was somewhere where he could see it. "Going to the stairs. When was the last time you checked on the kid? He's not going anywhere! Idiot! Man walking away. Going to other steps. Going up. Going up. Opening bedroom door. Boy is still on the bed watching TV. Closing door again. Going back downstairs."

"We have one unit getting very close," the unseen voice suddenly announced.

"Pariah…"

"Going outside," he replied. "Can't see much through the trees. Going higher. There. I see a car with lights on top. Police car. Getting closer. Closer. Almost there. Driveway is just around the bend. Police car is at entrance to driveway. Stopped there. No lights. No siren. Just stopped. Doing nothing. I hear sirens in the distance. Going higher…higher… Still can't see police cars. Hear them better though."

"Should we get them to kill the sirens?" I asked the unseen voice. I got no answer. Someone else would make that decision.

"See police cars now. Two cars. Lights. Sirens. Climbing hill. Lots of twists and turns. Coming closer."

"Pariah," I said with some concern. "Go back and check on the men. What are they doing?"

Going," he said. A minute later, he added. "Man downstairs is still playing pool. Other man is…wait…I think he hears the sirens. Getting up. Going to window to look out. Sees the police car at the driveway. Reggie! We got trouble! What's up? Police! Right here! Man from downstairs running up steps. Has gun in his hand. What do we do? Other man going up other stairs to boy's room. Man with gun following. Bedroom door open now, but they didn't go in. What do we do? Shut up! I'm thinking! How the hell did they find us? How should I know? I've been here the whole time. Sirens stopped. Maybe they're not after us. Good point. Man running downstairs again. Looking out window. Shit! They're getting out of their cars. We got to get out of here! How about the boy? Leave him! We don't have time. Man running for back door. Other man with gun running down steps.

"The boy, Pariah," I urged, how about the boy?"

"He's climbing down off of the bed. Going to bedroom door. Looking out. Can't go any further because of the chain."

"Okay, good. Now find the men again."

"Outside. Running down back steps. Police yelling at them to stop. Still going. Gunshot! Man with gun shot at police! Running down steps again. First man at the water. Jumped in! Trying to get to the other side. Man with gun almost there. Shot at police again. Police shooting back. More shots from police. Yelling at man with gun to lay his weapon down. Man with gun shot again. More shots from police. More yelling! Man with gun holding up his hands. Laying gun down. Police running at him aiming their guns. Man laying down at bottom of steps. Police are there. Have him."

"How about the other man?" I asked.

"Can't see him. Trees too thick."

"Okay Pariah. Go back and check on the boy."

"Going…. Policeman in house. Has gun out. Moving slowly. Looking around carefully. Sees boy above now in bedroom doorway. Is anyone else here? Boy not saying anything. Were there only two men? Boy nodding his head. Policeman hurrying upstairs. Tommy? Boy nodding. Are you alright? Boy nodding. Policeman checking chain. Going into bedroom. Can't lift bed. Pulling out radio. We're going to need something to cut some chain."

"Great Pariah. The boy will be fine. Can you find the man in the woods?"

"Going down. Going out. Trees. Beautiful trees. Crossing water. Looking. Looking. Hear something. Looking. Thick trees. Hear something. See him! Police are all on the other side of the river. Man still hurrying through trees."

"Pariah, if those police cross the water, do you think you can guide them to the man?"

"I can do it."

"Good. Does the man have a gun?"

"I don't see one."

"Good Pariah." I turned to John. "What are they doing?"

"They're crossing the water now," he replied.

"They haven't started yet," Pariah said. "Still on the other side. One man in water. Two more. Crossing the water. Hurrying. Going the right way. Keep going straight. Up the hill. Tell them to go left."

I listened as Pariah gave instructions for a while more, telling them when the man ahead started running more. It took a while, but eventually they had him cornered and under arrest. Before I let the mother break the connection, I had Pariah check one more time on the boy. But he was in the back seat of the police car by then.

"You can let go of his hands now," I told her. But she didn't. Instead, she leaned forward and kissed him lightly on the cheek. Then she let go. The room was filling up fast now. The father came over and hugged his wife.

Don came over and held up a cell phone to them. "Someone wants to say hello." He pushed the speaker button. "Tommy? Are you there?"

"Hello?" the little voice answered.

The mother broke down in tears.

The doctor was taking Pariah's blood pressure again. I knelt back down to the floor. "You know you're a hero again," I told him.

"Trees. Beautiful trees," he said.

"I know. Maybe we can take a trip there sometime." He actually smiled.

"Yes, all my hopes and dreams were coming true…well some of them. Doctor Won't-Wear-A-Skirt was still hiding her legs, but Pariah was as good as ever…maybe even better. We were the heroes of the day.

How was I to know it was only the calm before the storm!

CHAPTER

18

That night, as I was driving Pariah back to the safe house, I asked him what he wanted for dinner. "Anything at all!" I told him. And he more than deserved it. Surprisingly, or not surprisingly, he wanted more of the eggs and bacon Phil had cooked him that morning. I stopped at a grocery store and bought two dozen more eggs and a package of bacon. Phil and I had already decided we had to eat the steaks he had bought before they went bad. Sinful Cynthia said she would join us too.

When we got there, we were suitably greeted by Brutus's best impersonation of a big killer dog – for which, I briefly petted him behind the ears. I was glad to see that Pariah didn't seem to be the least bit afraid of him this time.

Phil was out back tending to his barbecue grill. Real charcoal. In my opinion, the best way to cook! Pariah went back to his place out under the trees, but Brutus didn't join him. Brutus had decided he wasn't going very far from those steaks.

When Cynthia arrived, minus her lab coat but still wearing pants, I took over at the grill while Phil went inside to cook some eggs for Pariah.

Very shortly, we were all sitting down to dinner together. I was surprised that the doctor didn't ask any questions during dinner. I saw her stare at Pariah a few times as if she was going to say something, but I think the disgusting way he ate quickly stopped all thought of conversation with him. Instead, the meal was relatively silent, and therefore, ended quickly.

Pariah, of course, headed straight back to his place under the trees as soon as he could. Cynthia offered to help clean up, but I got there first. "I'll get it," I told her. "You and Phil go sit!"

"But you're the one who's injured," she countered.

"I think I can manage," I replied. Cleaning up didn't take all that long, but when I got outside, I was very surprised to see the doctor out under the trees – talking to Pariah. I figured the eggs must have put him in a particularly good mood. I sat with Phil for a few minutes instead.

As soon as the doctor left Pariah, Brutus jumped off of Phil's lap and went straight toward the back of the yard. We were all treated to another round of the same old game the dog played with Pariah every night. Only now Pariah was letting the dog get even closer. "He's going to get there eventually," Phil noted. We had to agree.

I was happy to see a security guard that I recognized show up later. The same one I had talked to both at the hospital and down in the cell block. I guess he managed to finagle his overtime pay after all. Good for him.

I used to like weekends, but for the last few years I've dreaded them – ever since my life got lonelier than it used to be. It wasn't so bad when I had a case to keep me occupied, but right now, I "technically" wasn't even supposed to be back to work yet. I was healing well though. I figured that was a good thing.

I woke up Saturday to a miserable gray rainy day. Phil called me fairly early. "Want to know where your friend is right now?"

I took a wild guess. "Outside in the rain."

"Bingo!" he replied.

"I guess…leave him be. As long as he's happy."

"I'm happy about it too," he replied. "It's the closest thing to a shower he's had since he got here!"

I supposed that was one way to look at it.

In the afternoon, I left my boring abode and headed for the safe house giving the weekend guard on duty the option to either stay or leave. I figured he might need the overtime pay too. He had to think about it for a few minutes before he finally decided to go home to his family.

The rain had stopped shortly after lunch but everything was thoroughly soaked – including Pariah. He didn't seem to notice though. I could tell we would be in for more bad weather. Georgia weather usually went that way. The worst storms usually came late in the day.

Since Pariah wouldn't come in the house, we spent what time we could outside as well – where we could keep a better eye on him. And keeping an eye on him was the main reason I was there after all. Phil was nice enough to keep me company. Brutus was still doing his best to keep Pariah company – as much as Pariah would let him.

We were watching the skies late in the afternoon, trying to figure how long we had before the clouds let loose, when Brutus suddenly stopped what he was doing and turned to face the side of the yard. A moment later he was barking and running for the fence.

"What's that damn dog barking at now?" Phil complained as he got to his feet to check it out. He was about halfway across the yard when the shot rang out.

I immediately looked over at Pariah and saw where the bullet had carved out a chunk of bark from a tree not far from his head. I jumped up and pulled my gun as Pariah rolled himself into a ball and tried to hide in the bushes. Phil had hit the ground in self-defense. "Get back to the house!" I commanded as I carefully eased my way toward him. He went, but he crawled, trying to make himself a smaller target that way.

I searched carefully for sign of anyone along the fence, but the clouds were blocking the sun so much that I couldn't see anything that well between the thick vegetation. Brutus though was still barking wildly and looking toward one particular area of the fence. A second shot rang, but I couldn't tell where it had gone. I hoped Pariah was okay. All too quickly, a third shot came, and so did the bullet, right past my head. I hit the ground fast! Brutus was now barking at the back of the fence, then over at the side again, then toward the back again. Multiple shooters! Not good! Not good at all!

I looked back and saw that Phil had disappeared into the house. I fired toward the side yard, not having a target to really shoot at, then I quickly fired at the back fence too. I just wanted to keep them from shooting again. It didn't work. The one in the back immediately shot at me again and the grass caught the bullet not two feet from my head. I scrambled backwards towards the patio where I dumped Phil's picnic table over on its side and hid behind it. I hoped the wood it was made of was strong enough. I was still recovering from one gunshot wound. I didn't need another one.

I tried to look out between the wooden slats of the table, but I couldn't see much. When I peered around the side, I couldn't see much either. I could see Brutus though, still barking, but now he was running as fast as he could, back and forth between the back fence and the side fence. Talk about a brave little dog. Foolish too. "Brutus!" I yelled. "Get out of there!"

He didn't move until Phil stuck his head out the door and yelled. "Brutus…. Get!" Then the little dog ran for the trees where Pariah was and promptly disappeared.

"I called for backup!" Phil said as he came out the back door to join me behind the table. That was good news. The better news was the shotgun I saw in his hand.

I heard someone shouting from the back fence in a language I didn't recognize.

"What the hell was that?" Phil asked.

"Trouble," I replied.

"Tell me something I don't know."

I could hear sirens in the distance now, but they certainly weren't close yet. At the same time, I saw movement at the side yard. "Can you fire that cannon about halfway down that side fence," I suggested.

"I see it," he replied. "He's climbed the fence!" I watched as he quickly popped his head over top of the table, aimed and fired, then got back down again.

I peered around the side again. "I don't think you hit anything," I said. I immediately fired my gun in the same direction, then just for good measure, I fired at the back of the fence too. We were quickly greeted by another shot that hit the table. The resulting thud sent my ears ringing. The good news was that the table held.

"There!" Phil said and quickly popped up again. He took bead and fired. It was extra loud though because the guy at the back of the yard fired at the same time. The top of the table was going to need replacing! We were rewarded though by a scream of pain. I looked and saw someone rolling on the ground in agony. He had gotten close enough to Pariah that his next shot would have hit for sure!

A shot hit our table again and I fired around the side again. A second later, Phil popped up with his shotgun and fired at the back fence. The sirens were getting very close now. We waited, but we didn't see or hear anything – except sirens. Phil ran back into the house to open the gate. I stayed put until the backup arrived. Minutes later, the yard was crawling with police.

I never saw anyone at the back of the yard, the vegetation was too thick – done that way purposely to help shield whoever was staying at the safe house. But this time it had worked to our disadvantage. They saw us, but we couldn't see them.

I hurried out to check on Pariah. I was greatly relieved to find him still alive and untouched. He was still curled up in his tight little ball, but this time he was holding Brutus protectively in his arms. I knew that dog would get to him eventually!

Like it or not, I grabbed his arm. "Come on," Pariah, "let's get you into the house." I had been prepared for the worst, but he scrambled to his feet, dropped the dog, and hurried as fast as his bent legs would let him. Whew! Nobody hurt! Nobody from our side anyway. Lightning blazed the windows along with an ear splitting crack of thunder. Pariah hit the floor and curled back into his ball. Only then did I realize that it had been pouring rain for the last few minutes.

It was a long night filled with police and FBI agents. No trace was found of the second gunman. Of course the rain made things that much more difficult. The man Phil had shot though was another story. He was on his way to the hospital with part of his right leg so damaged it might have to be amputated later. He wasn't going anywhere.

I think I told the same story at least two dozen times. Pariah, as usual, wasn't speaking. We had to give the "brain damaged" line over and over again in his defense. It was about two in the morning by the time everyone left. Well, almost everyone. The Director had ordered six guards to patrol the perimeter of the house all night. Brutus had a field day, which didn't help my sleep much since I had decided to take the second spare bedroom. Darn dog. I didn't know whether to love him or hate him!

For a Sunday, our office was awfully busy. We brought Pariah in just for the added security. I left him in my office under Billy's supervision while I attended a meeting called by the Director. I wasn't surprised to see so many department heads there. I kind of felt out of place.

The Director asked his first question before he even sat down. "What do we know about the gunman?"

"His name is Galleti," one of the department heads at the table replied. "Portuguese, but he's a local boy. Several trips to the pen for armed robbery. This is the biggest thing we've heard him doing yet though."

"And his partner?" the Director asked. "The one who got away?"

"We're not sure yet, but we have our suspicions. We think he's another local boy though. A friend of Galletti's."

The Director seemed to think about that for a moment. "This one was local. The last one was a hire sent down from New York. If they were related, you'd think that someone would go with the local talent first. So are they related?"

He got nothing but blank looks from everyone as his answer. "Find out people! Now, what do we do with Mr. Pariah?"

I probably shouldn't have spoken up, but I did. "I'd like to know how they knew where we were first. Wouldn't that make a difference as to what we do with him?"

"Good point," the Director replied. "What did you have in mind?"

I shook my head. "I have no idea. Sorry. But I have a feeling that we may have someone internal handing the information out."

"That's a dangerous accusation," he replied.

"I know."

He nodded his head. "In the meantime, what do we do with him? Obviously somebody wants him dead!"

"Let's keep him at Phil's…for now. Maybe we can smoke someone out. Only this time, let's increase the security…like by a lot!"

The Director shook his head. "No. If people want him dead, then we need to move him somewhere with more security. He's already been shot once, and they almost got him this time. Plus, every government agency along with the local police either know we're back in business with him again, or they soon will. It wouldn't look very good if the FBI can't adequately protect someone so valuable."

Unfortunately, I could only agree with his logic. "Part of our problem," I said, "is that he's a lot more comfortable outdoors than in. He seems to be particularly drawn to a lot of trees."

"I noticed that while he was finding the boy," the Director said. But it doesn't change the fact that we need to keep him safe, even if it's someplace he's not as comfortable with."

One of the department heads at the table spoke up. "How long are we talking about?"

"Good question," the Director replied. "Until yesterday, the plan was to let him go homeless again. Roam the streets again once his shoulder healed. But now…we would be very negligent if we did that."

The man who had asked the question only nodded but didn't offer anything more.

"Why?" the Director asked him.

"Well, it was just an idea I had. I know a place where the owners are gone most of the time. It's like one of about six houses they own. Big place. Kind of fancy inside. But it has this huge solid wall around the entire property. And since it's not one of our usual safe houses, then…."

He didn't have to say anything more. We all knew he was referring to the fact that someone in the company wouldn't know where the address was to tell anyone else.

The Director thought about that for a minute. "So, you're suggesting we keep a tight lid on where this place is — among ourselves?"

"Need to know only."

"But isn't that the way all of our safe houses are?"

"But all too many people still know about them. Most have been used for years now."

The Director didn't look too happy about what had been said, but he looked straight at me. "McNair, check it out right away. Let me hear your recommendations in the morning." He looked back at the man who had suggested it. "And nobody but you two know anything about this! Understood?"

Frank Morris worked one of the homicide teams. I didn't know much about him but he seemed to be a good man. He drove the company car as we headed north up I-75. Twenty minutes later, he turned east and within minutes the countryside became hillier. We didn't talk much as we he drove…well, I didn't talk much, he spent most of his time on the phone. Since it wasn't his house, he didn't have the keys, and it seemed that locating someone who could let us in wasn't going to prove to be easy.

By the time we got there, we were faced with a big iron gate, an even bigger wall, and no way inside. I walked up to the gate and peered in, but I saw no sign of the house. Frank was still on the phone trying to find someone to let us in. He seemed frustrated. Finally, he got out of the car.

"I finally hooked up with the caretaker," he said. "But the damn guy won't even come out here to show us anything without the owner's permission.

"And where are they?" I asked.

"Austria…he thinks."

"So it's a no go," I said as I stared at the massive wall. "Pity. The place looks like it might have some definite possibilities."

He laughed. "You think? You should see the house!"

We got back in the car and headed home. For now, Pariah would have to remain at Phil's place, along with a ton of extra guards. At least until we could find someplace better to keep him. For some reason, I was happy about that. More people to watch him.

How was I to know it would prove to be a big mistake!

CHAPTER

19

It was Tuesday afternoon when I got called to another meeting – again with the Director. There were not a lot of department heads there. In fact, it was only Don and myself in the Director's office.

"I want you to hear this personally," he said. He dialed a number and set his phone on speaker. "New York," he said quietly as we waited. Two rings later the phone was answered by a female voice. "It's me again Donna. Patch me through," the Director said.

The woman on the other end simply said, "One moment." Eventually, the line was picked up again.

"Harris here!"

"Harris? It's me again. I've got McNair here as well as Don Wimberly. You want to tell it again, just like you told me?"

"Hey guys," the voice said in what I was guessing was some kind of New York accent. Bronx maybe? "We're not real sure what kind of can of worms you've opened up here yet, but it's lookin' like you need to keep your heads down. Way down! Ya' know what I mean?"

"What's the problem?" I asked.

"Is that you McNair?"

"It's me," I replied.

"Yeah, good. Listen, the credit for that bust a few months ago may have gone to us, but the recording of your Pariah guy has bounced all over the place."

"Unfortunately!" I said.

"Yeah, right. Very unfortunately. Look, that raid turned out to be a piece of a white slavery ring. We're having lots of trouble finding the rest of it though. So far, all we've been able to dig out of the guys we captured is that they're in touch with places in Europe, Hong Kong, and get this… Texas! And that's about all we've gotten!"

"So we're talking a really big operation?"

"Yeah. We suspect there's still more to it than what we know."

"Okay, what do you want us to do?"

"Two things. First of all, find them! Use that Pariah guy if you can. I know for a fact that Washington will back you up one hundred percent on whatever you come up with."

"Okay, we'll bounce that one around and try to come up with a plan. What's the other thing?"

"Like I said before, keep your head down. We've been able to dig up that there's a one hundred G bounty on Pariah's head."

"Holy cow!" I exclaimed.

"Yeah. Let's face it, someone somewhere who's heard that tape talked to someone else!"

"I figured that out when both he and I got shot and I had some time to think about it in the hospital!"

"You're kidding!"

"No! And they tried again a few nights ago. We got luckier this time. At least neither of us have any more bullet holes in us."

"Well you might want to watch your back too McNair, because there's a five G marker on you!"

I stared at the phone in shock. "On me?"

"You got it! So watch out!"

"Will do," I said. I couldn't believe it. Somebody had put out a contract to have me killed? Five thousand dollars? And the funny thing was, I didn't know if I should feel honored…or slighted. Pariah's contract was for a hundred thousand. I only rated a paltry five!

"Thanks Harris," the Director said. "We'll be in touch." He looked at me as he pushed a button to close the phone line. "I want you to know that there's already an internal investigation underway. Most likely they'll be talking to everyone you know – including you. I want you out of that side of the investigation. We've got other people who can do it better than you."

I didn't appreciate the way he had put that, but I knew he was right. "Okay," I replied simply.

"In the meantime, see if you can come up with a plan to expose a bit more of this slavery ring. Let me know what you need. And I'm personally going to be looking into the security on you two!"

His words were comforting, but there wasn't a whole lot else he could do. I went back to my office and gathered John, Billy, and Hannah. I gave them all the good news as plainly and as simply as I could. "Come up with some ideas," I said. "We'll get together later and hash through them."

I was glad to see the serious looks on all their faces as they left. John lagged behind though. "Maybe you should move into the safe house too."

I considered it for a moment. There were pros and cons to the idea. Mostly pros! "I'll think about it," I replied.

We gathered together again late in the day to discuss what to do. There weren't a lot of ideas thrown out except to go through case logs from all over and try to pick out cases where the girls matched what we thought they'd be after.

"How about a profiler?" Billy asked.

I had no doubt that all of us could have profiled what we needed perfectly, but I replied. "I'll add that to the list."

"I have a question," Hannah said at that point.

"What's that?"

"Shouldn't we check with Pariah and see if he's still willing to do this — in light of the bounty on his head?"

It was a very good question, and not one I wanted to hear. I was very inclined to say no, we would keep Pariah sheltered and in the dark. But we did have two guys shooting at us a few days ago. It would only be right to make sure he knew what was happening. As much as I hated doing it, I replied, "I'll check with him."

As was my usual practice now, after work I headed straight for Phil's place. The guard at the gate was one of the security guys I recognized, the same one from the hospital that last day. Since he knew me, he didn't ask for my ID. He just opened the gate and I drove in. Most things looked the same now, but not everything. The one glaring change was all the security. There were always at least four men on duty all the time. I had a feeling that if the Director didn't move Pariah to another location, that number would probably be increasing pretty fast.

One of the little changes that I missed now, was that whenever I arrived, Brutus wasn't there anymore to greet me. There were so many people wandering around all the time and so many cars coming in and out, that the poor little dog was forced to ignore everything but what his eyes could see. He wasn't however above going to any of the extra people looking for a little attention. But the biggest difference for Brutus now, was the one thing I noticed as soon as I walked through the house and out to the back patio. Brutus was in Pariah's lap out under the trees.

I took the chair next to Phil. "How goes it?" I asked.

"Mostly the same," he replied. "I got a call earlier though that kind of surprised me. They're sending over a team tomorrow morning to see if there's any way to boost the security here…as if all these guys wandering around all the time aren't enough. How was your day?"

"Disturbing," I replied. "Somebody's put out a contract on Pariah… and me too."

"Phil turned to look at me with a shocked look on his face. "You're kidding, right?"

I shook my head. "I wish I were."

"At least we know now what all the fireworks were about the other night. How much?"

"A hundred grand on Pariah." He again turned to look at me and whistled. "Damn! How much on you?"

"Five thousand." He actually laughed. "I know!" I said. "I don't know if I should feel honored or slighted!"

"Listen Cliff," he said still chuckling, "we both know that there's all too many out there who will do the job for nothing more than a bottle of booze. You watch your ass!"

"Yeah, that's the advice I've been getting all afternoon."

"Well take it! And I'll change the sheets in the other bedroom. You might as well stay here too."

"I haven't decided to stay here yet."

He shook his head. "I'll change the sheets."

We were interrupted then by Doctor 'C' coming through the back door. "Hi guys," she said as she walked across the patio.

"Hi Cyn," I replied. Yes, I had finally moved onto calling her that. As usual, the first thing I noticed about her was that she wasn't wearing a skirt again. I had now pretty much figured out that she only owned one outfit that had a skirt – the one I had seen. Or…maybe she didn't own it, maybe she had rented it. She set her bag on the picnic table and headed across the big yard out toward Pariah. I saw Brutus turn to look toward her before she got very far. The little dog's tail was wagging so fast I was afraid it would break.

The doctor settled herself right down on the ground in front of him, and Brutus jumped into her lap. I saw her petting the dog while she talked to Pariah. I still marveled that Pariah was talking to her at all. She spoke to him for a little while. Then I saw her shake her head and get to her feet. Brutus went right back to Pariah's lap. Despite the fact that she wasn't wearing a skirt, I still enjoyed watching her walking back toward us.

"I see you're making progress," I noted as she got back to us.

"Not much," she said as she took another of the chairs. "Some, but not much. There are some things he's willing to talk about, and other things he's not. But despite that, I'm still learning quite a bit."

"Like what?" I asked.

"Like that shooting the other night. When I ask him about it, he won't say anything about himself except that now he's there to protect Brutus in case it happens again."

"Does he think it will happen again?" I asked with some concern.

"What I asked wasn't exactly that, but it was another or those subjects he wouldn't answer."

"There's a bounty on his head now," Phil said. "A big one! Cliff too."

I was kind of surprised that she didn't act like that surprised her in the least. Phil might as well have told her he was going to the store for a gallon of milk for all the excitement it seemed to stir in her.

"Mine's not big though," I replied.

"How do you feel about it?" she asked after a moment.

"We were just discussing that before you arrived. I don't know if I should feel honored, or slighted."

"Why is that?" she asked.

"Well, they're offering a hundred grand for Pariah's head. They think mine is only worth five thousand."

"That's not what I meant," she said. "I mean, how do you feel…personally…about having a price on your head? Are you worried? Scared? What?"

"I don't know," I replied. "I hadn't really thought about it. Like I said, I'm still trying to figure out if I should feel honored or cheated."

"In other words, it hasn't really sunk in yet," she said.

"I don't know. Maybe."

"Or maybe not?"

I nodded. "Maybe not."

"I told him I'm changing the sheets in the other bedroom for him," Phil offered. "But he won't commit to staying here."

I really expected her to jump all over me for not going along with the suggestions. But instead she said. "Well, I guess that depends on how worried he is."

And I guess that pretty much said it right there. I was still trying to figure out if I should be worried or not. Logically yes, but…five thousand… next to a hundred? Come on! Still, I also knew that Phil was right, all too many people out there were willing to kill for nothing at all. What really surprised me though…no, disappointed me…was that she didn't jump up and swoon all over me saying, "Cliff you've got to play it safe. Cliff, I'll just die if anything happens to you." Yeah right! She was so cool and calm about it that I was sure I hardly mattered at all to her. Which I was fairly sure I didn't. Why should I? Besides, what other reaction could I expect from a woman who rented her skirts when she needed one?

"I need to talk to Pariah about it," I said. "That New York deal was a bigger thing than we knew. We just happened to stumble onto a fairly large white slavery thing and that was only a piece of it. They want us to look for more of it now with Pariah's help. As much as I hate to, I'm thinking of leveling with Pariah about the dangers and make sure he's still willing to do it. Either way, we're going to keep protecting him now. With a bounty like that on his head, there's no way the government is going to let him wander around homeless again."

"I think you should level with him…completely!" she replied.

"Yeah, but I'm worried he may not fully understand all the implications."

"In other words, you want to slant his decision in your favor."

Okay, that thought hadn't really occurred to me – consciously. But she was right. "I was just planning on laying it all out for him. Let him decide."

"So you were going to slant it," she said.

"Not consciously!"

"You won't be able to help it," she replied.

She was being frustrating again! "And you're playing mind games with me!"

"Sorry," she replied. "Occupational hazard."

Oh yeah! At times she could be such a pain! But...she was so damn beautiful too! Even if she wouldn't expose her legs again. How much did it cost to rent a skirt? Something really short had to be cheaper than something long. What if I offered to rent her one for a day...or a week... or longer?

"Just make sure I'm there when you talk to him," she said.

At least she cared enough to try to help. But who would she help, him...or me?

I didn't broach the subject with Pariah until he had finished eating – pancakes this time. Phil had discovered that he liked them too. I guess it was another soft breakfast food. "Pariah," I started, "I need to talk to you about something." I was glad that he stayed in his seat and didn't try to ignore me. Maybe it was all the food Phil was feeding him. "Pariah, I'd like your help again."

"If I find them, will you feed me?"

One of these days, I had to get to the bottom of that! But I had other problems on my mind just then. "You know we will, Pariah. Anything you want."

He started to get up from his seat.

"Where are you going?"

"To find the missing child."

"No, Pariah. At least not yet. Not today." I was lucky, he sat back down. The next part was the tricky part. "Remember when we found the girls in New York?"

"The girls? The sick girls?"

"Right. The sick girls. Well, we think there's more girls like them out there that need our help. We'd like you to help us find them."

"If I find them, will they feed me?"

I ignored him this time. "There's another problem though. Remember how those men shot at us a few days ago? They tried to kill us?"

"Protect little dog," he replied. "Have to protect dog."

"Yes, Pariah," I replied. "You protected Brutus really well." At least I thought I had said the right thing. I saw the doctor's head turn quickly at me though. I ignored her. "I don't know if you can understand this or not, but some of the bad men from New York are trying to kill us. Well, you more than me. But both of us to be sure. They're offering a lot of money to anyone who can kill us." I was somewhat surprised at myself. I thought I had put that straight out – just like it was.

"Why?" he asked.

"Because they're bad men and they know we can stop them from stealing more girls and hurting them."

"They make the girls sick?"

"Yes. They hurt them in other ways too. Badly."

He seemed to think about that for a moment. "And they want to kill us so we can't find the girls."

"That's it exactly! But Pariah, even if you don't find the girls, they still want to kill us because we helped the girls in New York. So either way, they still want us dead."

I saw the fear in his eyes as he thought about that last part.

"Can't die yet. Not time. Not yet."

That was a reply I certainly hadn't expected. But it was true enough for any of us.

"I agree," I said. "I don't want to die either. I think our best bet is to find the girls along with the men who want to hurt us, and stop them forever. I don't want to have to worry about them trying to kill me either."

"And the men make the girls sick?"

"They steal them too. Take them away from their families."

"Not right!" he said. "Very bad men!"

"Yes they are. Will you help us then?"

It was the way he said it that surprised me. And for that one brief moment, his eyes looked totally and completely sane. "Of course!"

And then he got up from his seat and walked back outside. Brutus looked to follow him, but there were still food scraps on the table so he stuck with us instead.

"That went well," I said, more to myself than to anyone else.

"I wonder which of us is reading him right?" the good doctor said.

"Huh? What are you talking about?"

"A couple of things. When I talked to him earlier, I got the impression that he wanted to protect Brutus…in the future, not the past. Not what he had already done."

"The future?"

She nodded. "As if he's expecting more trouble."

The problem was, more trouble was likely. And it would become more likely with every passing day. But those kinds of psychic things weren't something my poor brain could deal with just then. "What else?" I asked.

"When he said it's not time for him to die yet. He said he can't die yet. It's not time."

"What of it. It isn't time for me to die either."

"Of course not, but that's not the point. I got the distinct impression that he has some other agenda. Something else he has to accomplish first!"

"Like what?" I asked.

"I have no idea. None. Most of what I'm getting out of him is from reading between the lines."

I hadn't known that. But another little thought hit my tiny brain. "I remember once, I asked him what I could do for him. He said he wanted me to take him home. But there was something else he wanted too. Something he wouldn't tell me about. I think he said it wasn't time yet."

She nodded. "I remember that! Maybe they're related. It adds to my list of things to find out about him."

She got up from her seat then to leave and go home. But she paused by me first and put her hand on my shoulder. "And Cliff…take the extra room here."

Heavens! She did care about me! At least somewhat…I think.

And then she leaned down and kissed me lightly on the cheek! My brain went into melt-down. Totally!

C H A P T E R

20

After our morning meeting, John and I stuck around to talk further with Don. "We've put together some things we'd like to do towards the slavery thing." I said. "Can we just tell you and you can tell the Director, or do we have to go up there personally?"

"Let me have it," he replied. "It's going to come back to me anyway."

I looked to John to start. "We want to gather the most likely missing girl cases from all over the country." He said. "All sources, not just FBI cases."

"And we want a profiler to help us sort through them," I added. "Then we start going through them one at a time with Pariah and hope we stumble on another one like New York."

"Hopefully, within the United States," John added.

I nodded my agreement, anything out of the country would be impossible to work.

"Sounds logical," Don said without giving it much thought. "Anything else?"

"Yeah," I replied. "The way we do this. I still want to use the interview room where we've been working. We're going to need the recording and communications gear in there. That's turned out to be a huge help. But no more dog and pony show. We keep the people involved down to only needed personal and that's it. And we try to stay at least a little bit quieter over what happens. Not blab all over about it."

He nodded. "Security. Maybe we should put together a core team that works all your cases. Same people all the time and only those people…as much as possible."

I nodded. "I like it. Thanks."

"Anything else?" he asked.

"Not yet," I replied. "We'll start pulling files here and going through them. Let me know who's going to help profile them."

It was late in the morning when a tall skinny black man walked into my office. I had passed him in the building a few times so I somewhat recognized him, although I didn't know him. "Agent McNair?" he asked as he held out his hand. I stood up and shook it. "Brent Jackson," he said to introduce himself. "I've been assigned to help you look over some files for something specific. They wouldn't say what though."

Ah, our profiler. "We're looking for a white slavery ring," I told him. "We stumbled over a piece of it a few months back and now they want us to try and find the rest of it."

"Was that the raid in New York where you used the Pariah man?" he asked.

Did everyone in the world know about that? "Yeah, that was it. I'd appreciate it if you wouldn't spread it around though. Too many people know too much already."

"As far as I know, everyone in the building knows all about it."

"I'm not surprised. But for the future, we're not talking to anyone about this, outside of a select few…of which you are now a part. Got it?"

He smiled. "No problem. Now, how can I help?"

I pointed to a stack of folders on my desk. "These are the missing girl files we have in our system that have occurred over the last eighteen months. The girl we rescued in the New York raid wasn't the only one from our Atlanta office. There was one other too that had been missing longer. Six others were in the FBI files from around the country. Two from Canada, one from Mexico, a Puerto Rican, one Japanese, one Chinese, and a bunch we had no idea were missing at all. We want to try to pick the most likely subjects that are still missing and have Pariah try to find them. We're hoping we'll get a hit with one of them."

"So you want my help to narrow down the field?"

"Exactly. And these files are just the tip of the iceberg. There will be more coming in from all over the country pretty soon."

"Sounds like a lot of work," he said.

"I have no doubt it will be."

"I'm going to need the particulars on the girl you found. In fact, on as many of the girls found in that raid as possible so I can look for things to match."

"I'll see that you get whatever you need. The first one is easy. I'll have Hannah get you that file right away. You can take that stack to work on for now. If you like, there's plenty of table space out in the main room behind you. We'll all meet to go over things in about an hour. Okay?"

"Sounds fine," he replied as he picked up the stack of folders.

The space where the folders had been was suddenly empty...clean. For a moment it felt like I had just finished a tremendous pile of paperwork, but I quickly realized, the work hadn't even started yet.

For our first case, we chose one from our own files. A teenage girl who had been missing for about eight months now. The parents were contacted and eventually persuaded to come into our offices to make the attempt.

We scheduled it for Monday afternoon so everyone would have a few days to prepare...or rest. I had laid in a large supply of candy and snacks – just for Pariah to help keep him under control. At the rate he was eating, he wasn't going to look so skinny for long. Unfortunately, he was also starting to look more and more like his old self with every passing day. His beard was starting to grow out and while his hair was short, it was growing too. But worst of all was the fact that he absolutely refused to bathe or change his clothes. He was starting to become intolerable, but no amount of pleading or bribery seemed to budge him from his chosen path. And unfortunately, he didn't officially work for the government so there was little we could actually do about it.

All was going well until the lawyer again walked into the room with his paper for the parents to sign, certifying that they knew Pariah was a child molester. Unfortunately, Pariah must have figured out from the last time what the lawyer was there for. The words "child molester" were spoken quietly, but plenty loud enough for Pariah to hear them. And like last time, he went into fits, screaming that he didn't do it. It wasn't him. The papers were signed though and Pariah was eventually calmed down – with two candy bars instead of one.

The father took one of Pariah's misshapen hands, and Pariah went off to find their daughter. Unfortunately, he reported rather quickly that the girl was dead. But with several repeated efforts and a lot of coordination, the body was located before the end of the day. Success in finding the girl. No success in finding her alive. And no success in finding the slavery ring.

Round one was a washout. But another of our cases went into the found pile. It would be up to someone else now to figure out what had happened to the girl.

We made the next attempt a week later with a girl missing from the Phoenix office files. Unfortunately, she too was found dead, although it took us two more days of effort and coordination for Pariah to lead the authorities to her body, which had been dumped out in the desert. From the lack of landmarks, it was amazing we were able to piece together where the body had been dumped at all. But as usual, Pariah found it and another case was crossed off.

We worked four more files, finding all four alive but under different circumstances. Three of them were hooking in different cities. The last girl, from Chicago, was actually located here in Atlanta. Talk about luck!

I was beginning to think that we'd never find the ring. Maybe it didn't really exist. Maybe they had quit! I knew better than to take that thought seriously though.

No attempt had been made against either Pariah or myself in so long now that I had mostly forgotten about it. I had never taken Phil up on his offer to use the extra room at the safe house, and now I was glad I hadn't.

I also noticed that very quietly, the number of guards at the safe house had dwindled down to two. I was only surprised that they were still there.

Our next attempt was for a file on a girl missing from Seattle – Connie Sullivan. It was starting to become old hat to us all now. The doctor showed up as usual and took Pariah's blood pressure. I had no idea why she insisted on doing that through every session, but she said it was necessary so we went with it. The lawyer also showed up as usual to get the parents to sign the paper about his child molestation. But this time, Pariah's little tantrum wasn't so little. In fact, it was so outrageous that it scared most of us...especially the parents! Eventually, we managed to get him calmed down though and the attempt was made.

Mrs. Sullivan put her hands on Pariah's back as many of them preferred to do, and Pariah went off again. But this time...this time he found something different. Something we hadn't expected.

"Far away," he said when he finally spoke. "Far, far, far away. Very far. Very good connection, but very far away."

"Pariah, did you find the girl? Is she alive?"

"She's alive. Sick. Very sick."

"What's wrong with her?" the mother asked, almost removing her hands from his back.

"Sick," Pariah said again. "The drugs."

"Like the girls in New York?" I asked.

"Worse," he replied. "Where she is staying is worse too. She's on a bed. Small bed. Tiny bed. Only big enough for her. Very low, barely off the ground. She is moaning. Sick. Very sick. Hand is chained to the wall. Curtains all around her. Heavy curtains. Very bad lighting. Very low lights. Don't see any other light but dim light. Hard to see clearly."

My hopes were starting to rise. "Good, Pariah. Really good. Can you see well enough to help us figure out where she is?"

"I think so," he replied. "Going through curtain. Um..." he paused.

"What is it, Pariah?" I asked.

"Another bed. Another curtained room like girl's room. Another sick girl. Also chained to the wall."

"Another one?"

"Moving on," he said. And then he found another one. And another. And another. By the time I was able to get him to move on, he had found twenty eight women on two floors of the building they were in. All chained to the walls. All in their own tiny curtain rooms. All in bad condition. But where were they?

"Pariah, we need you to figure out where they are. Can you go further? Try to find out?"

"Stairs, going down another set of stairs. Still pretty dark. Strange markings on the wall. Men! Four men. Um…not American. Chinese or Japanese. Can't tell which."

"Oriental," Doctor Westmore suggested.

"Oriental," Pariah agreed. "Men are…playing a game. Mahjong I think."

I was somewhat surprised that he would know the game. "Keep going Pariah. You're doing great! Try to figure out where they are. What city at least." But in my heart, I was beginning to suspect I knew exactly what city they were in. Hong Kong. That was where they suspected another piece of the slavery ring was…if this was part of that ring. There could be dozens of other rings like it…or worse.

"Going up. Going up through the floor. Going up. More floors. Outside now. Above the building. City. Big city. Dark. Very dark. See water. Big bay. Big bay. Going up. Going higher. Higher. Very high. Big, big city across the water. Very bright lights. Lots of lights. More lights across the water than on this side. Um…ocean I think. Very dark. Hard to see that way. Only a few scattered lights here and there. Boats I think."

I knew already that without a doubt we were going to have to have another session – at a time when it would be daylight in China. I looked up at John who was standing nearby. "We're going to have to come back later," I said.

He nodded his agreement.

"What does that mean?" the father asked anxiously. "What does all this mean?"

"It means she's still alive," I told him. That was the good news, the only good news. "But it also means we're going to have to try this again later today."

"Why?" the father asked. "Your people told us that this man could find our daughter. What's going on?"

"That's just it," I told him. "He did find her. She's just no longer in this country."

The mother broke down crying and removed her hands from Pariah's back. He looked up at me. "Bad place," he said, very bad place."

"Yeah, I have no doubt," I replied sincerely.

"So that's it?" the father asked. "We can't get her?"

"I didn't say that," I replied. "Now we have to try again under better conditions to figure out exactly where she is. We start narrowing things down from there. We don't even know for sure what country she's in… what city. All we know is that she's alive and somewhere far away."

"And sick!" the mother added. "Very sick!" She broke down crying again.

I looked at my watch. It was almost one thirty in the afternoon. I wondered what time it was in China.

Since I was guessing she was in Hong Kong – even though I didn't say that anywhere near the parents, we decided to try again at nine o'clock at night – our time. Hong Kong was ten hours ahead so that would make it about seven in the morning there. The Sullivan's went back to their hotel and I got Hannah and Billy busy with collecting maps and areal images of the Hong Kong area – just in case.

Late in the day, I loaded Pariah back into my car and headed back to the safe house for dinner. Along the way, the traffic in front of me started slowing down and stopping near a small construction zone. We were barely moving when the car in front of me suddenly slammed on his brakes. I was forced to slam on mine…and the side window next to my head exploded. It seemed like slow motion as the air in front of me was suddenly filled with bright shiny pieces of glass. I felt the sting as some of them slammed into the side of my face – bringing the moment back into the world of reality.

It took me a moment to realize what had happened. And when I did, I rammed the car into reverse as I automatically looked over toward Pariah. He seemed to be okay, but I noticed that the window next to him was nothing but broken glass like mine. But Pariah wasn't my first concern. I need to get the hell out of there and quick! I stepped on the gas as I was turning my body to look out the rear window. I clipped the bumper of the car coming behind me as I tried to steer around him in a desperate panic.

The windshield suddenly banged loudly. I turned my head momentarily and saw that another bullet had buried itself in the dashboard. Driving in reverse, I floored the gas pedal as I entered the lane of cars going back the way I had come from. At least I was going with the flow of traffic. A third loud bang rocked the car. I checked Pariah again, he looked terrified, but otherwise okay. I kept going, driving as fast as I could in reverse. I finally pulled into the parking lot of a convenience store, turned the car around so it was facing forward, and drove off – the right way – as fast as I dared for the office. I called Don the moment I got the car facing the right way. Now that I was facing forward, I noticed a big hole in the hood of the car.

Don's secretary answered the line and I didn't waste time asking her to get him. I shouted that we were under attack and I was on my way back to the office. And that was when I started to see the steam coming out of the new hole in the hood of my car. I cursed at the steam and I cursed at all the slow drivers in my way. I glanced over at Pariah. He was silent, but his eyes were wide with fright. He seemed otherwise okay.

Don himself grabbed the line. "Cliff! Where are you?" he yelled into phone line.

"I'm about half-way between you and the safe-house," I replied. "The shooting seems to have stopped – as far as I know. But my car may not make it all the way back. I don't want to stop anywhere close in case they're following!"

"Keep coming," he said. "I'm sending backup to your position."

"Call the police too!" I replied. "I'm not exactly driving nice and I'd like the extra support if they're available!"

"You got it!" he replied. "Just stay on the line with me."

I had no doubt that his secretary was already putting everything in motion as we spoke. I glanced down at the dashboard and noticed that the engine temperature was moving quickly closer to the red. "Shit!" I exclaimed.

"What?" Don asked.

"I think I'm going to need a new engine!" I replied. "I'm running hot and it's getting hotter."

"Understood," Don replied simply. "Do what you can."

As if I wasn't already. "You okay?" I asked Pariah.

He turned his head to look at me. He still looked terrified, but he made no reply at all.

"Don, you still there?"

"I'm not leaving you," he replied.

"Call Doctor Westmore. Tell her what happened. I want her to look at Pariah as soon as possible."

"Is he hurt?"

"Doesn't look like it, but he's scared stiff!"

"I would be too," Don replied.

I was sure he knew how scared I had to feel. The temperature gauge was all the way into the red now. I knew the engine wasn't going to last much longer. I started looking for a place to pull off the road. I could hear sirens coming from somewhere, but I couldn't tell where. The car lurched, it wasn't going to go much more. I took the next driveway and pulled into a bank parking lot. I tried to pull it into a place where I could see the road I had just gotten off of. The car didn't make it all the way into the parking space before it gave out, but it was close enough that I could see the cars coming from both directions.

"Relax, Pariah," I said. "I think we're clear now." I hoped anyway.

But relaxing was the last thing I was capable of doing just then. My heart was hammering way too fast. The police sirens never came near us. I was guessing they went to the scene of the shooting instead. I was wondering who would find me first, the police or the FBI. It wasn't even close, the police never showed up at all, but I was awfully glad to see John in the lead car as he nearly caused an accident pulling into the bank's parking lot. Three more FBI cars followed right behind him.

Once again I was back in the emergency room. This time, to have embedded glass removed from my face. At least Pariah was completely unhurt…physically anyway. I was told that Doctor Legs was with him. Somehow, I wished she was with me instead.

And then, my wish suddenly came true. She was there, at the hospital, to see me!

"Hi Cliff," she said as the doctor pulled another tiny fragment of glass from my face.

"I'm going to look like Pariah by the time they're done," I joked.

"Hmm. Think of it as an improvement."

Oh thanks! "How's Pariah?"

"Back at the safe house 'protecting' the dog. He's shaken, but fine – for him at least."

That was good news. The bad news was that I was the one who had gotten injured – again! At least it was a minor injury this time. But it still stung like hell!

"Are you cancelling trying to use Pariah again tonight?" she asked.

"Not unless he doesn't want to do it. Ouch!" I said as the doctor pulled yet another tiny piece of glass.

"He'll be fine," she replied confidently.

"Yeah, but will I?" I said jokingly.

"You want my professional opinion on that?" she asked.

"Uh…maybe not. I may not like it."

"Oh gee!" she quipped. "And I had this long detailed description of you and all your psychosis all ready to sink you and your ego down into the depths of total despair."

What could I say? "You're the soul of kindness. You shouldn't have gone to all that trouble."

"Trust me, it was no trouble at all. In fact, it was all too easy!"

"Well then, since you made the effort, I guess it's only right that I let you lay it all on me. How about over dinner tonight?"

"Fine! Then you'll find out how sick you really are!"

"Fine!" I returned. "But…I think you're going to have to drive. I'm having a little problem with my car. Something's wrong with the windows."

After all the excitement of the afternoon, I treated myself to a huge rare steak, smothered in steak sauce, and topped off with a loaded baked potato and a beer. My system needed the fortification. She treated herself to a chicken salad. Women just don't know how to eat properly. But if the way she ate kept her looking like she did, then I wasn't going to complain in the least. Even if she still never wore skirts!

We talked about this. We talked about that. But never once did either of us mention Pariah or work. She seemed to be into a lot of things I wasn't, like art and dancing. And as for me? What could I tell her? I was into work and nothing else. I didn't have any other interests. But that didn't stop me from enjoying listening to her.

Dinner was great. Life was wonderful. And I was feeling more than perfect by the time we got out of there.

How was I supposed to know that in just a few hours, the world as we knew it was going to be turned upside down!

C H A P T E R

21

I hadn't seen the Director at our first attempt earlier in the afternoon, but this time he was making his presence known to everyone. I was one of his first targets of the evening.

"You okay, McNair?" he asked.

"Yeah. It just stings a little."

"Your face looks like someone tried to make hamburger out of it."

Gee thanks! "No," I replied, "it's just a bad case of acne." At least he smiled.

"If you can, just find out where she is. The more exact the better. You can't do anything else if she's overseas. We'll leave that to the diplomatic boys."

It wasn't a lot of hope. But I already knew it was the best I could hope for. "I know," I replied. "The closer we can track down her location, the more I'll feel like this was at least somewhat of a success. And we haven't had a single failure yet."

"You haven't failed here," he said. "You know where she is."

"Close anyway. She's just untouchable."

He nodded. "Good luck."

The father walked up to me then. "What happened to you?"

"I had a little altercation with a window," I said. Well, it wasn't exactly a lie!

"You need to be more careful," he told me.

Now he tells me! Someday I'm going to take that advice.

"I spoke to several of the other agents here," he continued. "Every one of them seemed to be convinced that what your man saw was real. That it was really our daughter that was being held prisoner somewhere…in China maybe?"

"I nodded. Trust me, it's real. And I have a bad suspicion about what city she's in. We'll know for sure in a little while. I hope!"

"And what do we do if she is there?"

I pointed to the Director. "Ask him. I know for a fact he's already working on it."

My words seemed to reassure him. But he moved off to talk to the Director.

At least this time the lawyer didn't show up with paperwork to be signed, so that was a relief. Pariah seemed like his old contrary self as he munched on another candy bar while the pretty doctor took his blood pressure again. I meant to ask her why she kept doing that! Once again, I let it pass.

I asked if everyone was ready. Then I motioned to Mrs. Sullivan. "Let's find out exactly where your daughter is," I told her. Once again, she put her hands on Pariah's back. And once again, he closed his eyes.

"Lighter now, but not much," he said.

That surprised me.

"How is the girl?" I asked.

"Still sick. Awake. Just lying there. Can't go anywhere because of chain."

"Okay, Pariah. Let's find out where she is. How high can you go?"

"Don't know. Strong connection. Far, but still very strong connection. Going up. Up. Out. Bright now, very bright. Sun is up. No windows inside, too dim there. Big city. Very big. Very big. Not New York. Still going up. Very high. Getting harder. Very high. Harder." And then he laughed.

"What is it, Pariah?" I asked.

"Cloud. Little cloud. I'm in the cloud. White. Wispy. Little cloud. Very hard. Don't think I can go much higher."

"That's good Pariah, I'm sure that it's more than enough." Actually, I was completely amazed that he had gone so high. "Take a good look at the city and the land. I especially want you to look at the shapes of the land and the water. Okay?"

It was a moment before he answered. "Looking. I see wide water with more land far, far away. Water on my right. Water on my left. No water behind me."

"Good Pariah. Now, is it possible for you to look at some pictures we have on the computer here and see if any of them match?"

"Don't know, he said. "Can try."

"Good, Pariah." I motioned for Billy to bring over a tablet we had loaded with aerial pictures. "Look at some of these picture we have here, Pariah, see if they're the same."

He opened his eyes and Billy held the tablet out for him. "Hard to see," he said. "Hard to tell."

"What's the problem Pariah? Is there anything we can do to help?"

"Stop connection," He said. "Hard to look at two things at the same time."

I saw Cynthia give me a big wide-eyed look. I couldn't have agreed with her more. "Take your hands off his back for a minute," I said to Mrs. Sullivan. "Let's see what he can tell us."

Pariah had his eyes open now and was looking at a picture of Hong Kong on the tablet. He took the tablet from Billy and turned it sideways. Unfortunately, when he did that, the picture shifted around too. I saw him grunt with frustration. "Don't move!" he said to the tablet. "Don't move!"

"Here, Pariah," Billy said, "let me hold it for you and see if we can get it the way you want." He took it and held it the way he thought Pariah wanted to see it.

Pariah pointed at the picture. "That's the water!" he said. "Many boats. "I wasn't as high as the picture, but it looks the same. There, there is the other land past the water. Water on the left, water on the right. Girl is about…" He moved his finger across the picture and pointed toward a spot near the bottom. "Here!" he said.

"Billy, see if we've got anything with a closer view," I said.

"Got something better," he said. And then I watched as he pulled up Google Earth on the tablet and started slowly working his way closer and closer in on the city."

All of a sudden Pariah got more excited. "There!" he said suddenly. That's how it looked to me. That's how I saw it from the cloud."

We all crowded around the screen to look. While the picture didn't extend as far as I would have liked, it was indeed an airplane view of the city of Hong Kong.

Pariah pointed at the picture on the screen. "Girl is here."

"Wait a minute," Billy said as he made an adjustment. The picture shrank, then moved a little, putting the target area into the center of the screen.

"Yes! Yes!" Pariah said excitedly, "There. Down there!" He was pointing to the screen again."

Billy moved the view in closer and closer as Pariah kept showing him where to go. Eventually, we could clearly see the top of individual buildings quite easily.

"That one!" Pariah said, putting his finger on the screen. "Girl is in that building!"

"You're sure, Pariah?" I asked.

He nodded. "Very sure!"

With what we had now, I had no doubt we could easily find that building a dozen different ways. "Okay," I said, "let's go back and see if we can see anything else about what's in there." I looked at Pariah. "Ready to go back?" I asked.

"Yes," he said. "Can I go high again?"

"Not this time," I said to him. "We need to know more about what's inside the building."

He looked a bit disappointed, but he closed his eyes. "Ready," he said.

Mrs. Sullivan looked to me, then put her hands on his back again.

"Good connection again," Pariah said. "Very good. Girl is still lying there. Same as before. Going out now... Wait! Man coming in to see girl. Girl moving on bed. Looks very frightened of man. Man grabbing chain, unlocking it from wall. Pulling girl up out of bed. Girl struggling. Man is too strong, still holding chain. Pulling girl. Pulling girl out through curtain. Girl doesn't want to go. Still trying to pull away. Man still too strong. Stairs. Going down stairs. Girl yelling now. Keeps saying no, no, no! Man not listening. Still dragging her. Going down more stairs. Girl still yelling. Still struggling.

"Man dragging her through another hallway. Into a room. Strange room. Not nice. Wooden bed. Wooden walls. Wooden floor. Not much else. Girl struggling harder. Yelling louder. Man doesn't care. No! No!"

"What is it, Pariah?" I asked desperately.

"Man threw girl on the bed. Girl is kicking and screaming. Man chaining hands to top of bed. Both hands. Girl still kicking. Yelling. Man chaining foot to bottom of bed now. Still struggling. Girl kicking at him with other foot. Man grabbed other foot, chaining it to other side of bed. Girl trying to move but can't move much. Man doing something with clothes. Girl still screaming. Man untying her clothes. Pulling on them. Pulling. Girl is… girl is…no clothes! No clothes! Still screaming, crying now. Man walking away. Doesn't seem to hear her. Girl just lying there now. Crying. Crying. Poor girl. No clothes on girl."

"Pariah!" I said, look around that floor what else do you see there?"

"Going. Going quickly. Don't want to look at girl with no clothes. Not right. Man going into another room. Following him. Following. More men. Three more men. All oriental men. Man talking to another man. Funny words. Can't understand words at all. Different language. Understand girl, but not men. One of the men leaving now, going out of room. Following. Heading back toward girl. Going into girl's room. Girl has no clothes on. Man talking to girl. Girl struggling again. Screaming. Crying. No. No. No. Man taking off his clothes! Girl crying! Man taking off his pants. Man has no clothes! Man going toward girl. Girl crying. Struggling. No! Nooo! Nooooo!" he screamed.

"Man is angry with girl. Getting off her. Yelling funny words at her. Grabbing something from corner. Stick! Man has big stick! Long stick. Bad stick! Yelling at her. No! No! Don't! Don't! Man hit girl! Girl screaming. Girl in pain. Red bruise on girl's stomach. Man yelling at girl. Girl crying. Struggling. Man hit her again. Girl screaming louder. Noo! Noo! Nooo! Nooooo!"

Pariah was yelling now, totally transfixed by what he was seeing, just as we were transfixed by what we were hearing. I could see his face turning redder and redder the more agitated he got.

The Doctor pumped up his blood pressure cuff again. "Calm down, Pariah," she soothed.

But Pariah wasn't listening to her. He was too intent on what was happening that only he could see. "Nooo! Nooo! Don't hit! Don't hurt! Noooo!" Pariah's eyes were wide open now, but whatever he was seeing was certainly not in the room with us. He was yelling "No!" at the top of his lungs. His face was beet red! Very slowly he brought his arms up as if to reach out toward what only he could see. "Nooo!"

And suddenly the room exploded…with the horrible sound of silence. Mrs. Sullivan lurched forward a bit over the back of the chair. The Doctor was suddenly left holding a blood pressure cuff that was dangling by its tubes. And most strangely of all…Pariah was gone. Disappeared. Completely. As if he never existed.

We all stood stark still with our mouths open, staring at each other as if one of us might know what had happened. But nobody knew. A moment later, the door flew open and people rushed in. Lots of people. All wanting to know what happened. But nobody knew.

The recordings would all verify that the exact time was thirty two seconds. Thirty two of the longest, most strange seconds of my life. But just as the room had suddenly erupted into silence a moment earlier, it was suddenly filled with screaming again. But not just Pariah's screams, a high-pitched feminine hysterical scream too. The screaming came from behind us, forcing us to turn quickly to see its source. There, up against the wall, rolling on the floor, was Pariah, holding on for dear life to a naked young woman.

They were both screaming hysterically, the girl more than Pariah. We all rushed to them. The doctor helped me pull them apart. "Pariah!" I called repeatedly. "Pariah!" It was a moment before he looked at me. The wild frightened look in his eyes was worse than I had ever seen it. Worse than I ever imagined it could be. He stopped screaming and reached out to me. I held him to me and hugged him as if he were my own child. He sobbed into my chest.

Behind me, I saw the doctor holding the naked girl. Her mother and father were leaning down now to try to hug her too. "Connie! Connie!" the mother said over and over again. "Connie!"

Slowly the girl stopped screaming and started staring unbelievably around her. "Momma?" I heard her say. "Daddy?" The father ripped the naked girl out of the doctor's arms and he crushed her to him.

I eased up my grip on Pariah. My mind was still trying to figure out what had just happened. I looked around. The room was packed with people. Everyone who had been on the other side of the wall was here now. I saw Don talking on his cell phone, calling for medical help. I was glad. The Director was staring with the same open-mouthed expression on his face that still crippled my own mind.

What had happened? Miraculously, Pariah had disappeared from the room here, only to come back again – with the girl! Impossible! Absolutely impossible! I had to be imagining it. It couldn't be real!

I looked at Pariah again and noticed that his face was screwed up as if in pain. "Doctor!" I yelled. "He's hurt!"

It took only half a second for Cynthia to get to my side. "Where?" she cried.

"I don't know! But look at him."

"Pariah, where does it hurt?" she asked quickly.

Pariah did his best to point toward his back as he started crying miserably. I turned him around. His shirt was sliced in three long straight rips. Blood was spilling around the ripped places. I could tell that he had been hit by the cane more times than what was showing by the slices in his shirt. "It's okay, buddy," I said. "We'll fix it. You'll be okay."

I saw the Director giving orders now – quickly and forcefully. Posting a guard on the inside of the door. I caught on right away. Nobody inside the room was leaving. Not yet at least. Not yet.

And then the Director did something that surprised me. He pulled a chair over to the corner and climbed up on it. "Everyone!" he yelled. "Listen to me now! As of this moment, everyone in this room is sworn to secrecy about what just happened here. You don't tell your wife, you don't tell your mother, you don't even tell your priest! Got that! You tell…nobody!" He looked to the Sullivan's. "An ambulance is on the way to take her to the hospital. You go with her, but you don't tell anybody what happened. Some of our people will be with you all the time. After the hospital, we're putting you up for a while, someplace different, not the hotel you're staying in now. It's for your protection…and your daughter's!"

Then he looked straight at me. "And you! Don't even think about going back to your apartment…for a very long time!"

Ten minutes later, two ambulances arrived. I noticed that someone had given the girl a man's sport jacket to cover her body. Pariah was soon loaded in the back of one of the ambulances. Cynthia explained that she was his doctor and climbed in too. I simply didn't give them any choice in the matter. I was inside before any of them and helped to load the stretcher.

Cynthia called Doctor Richter from the ambulance to get him moving since he was Pariah's primary medical doctor. I stayed as close to Pariah as the technicians would allow. They had him lying flat on his stomach as they started cutting the back of his shirt. Beside the long cuts, I could see bad bruising starting to form all over his entire back and shoulders.

I got down where he could see me better. "How are you doing buddy?" I asked.

"Hurts," he moaned. "Hurts bad."

"I know," I replied. "If I could take all that hurt away from you and give it to myself, I would. Gladly."

I was very surprised when he reached out with one of his gnarled hands – and grabbed mine. He gripped my hand tightly and kept holding on. I held his hand all the way to the hospital.

I don't know what the Director had done, but the hospital was in something of an uproar by the time we got there. People were running all over the place to try to help us. When one of the nurses tried to get me to stay outside when they took him back to one of the examining rooms, I held up my badge. "I'm not moving from his side!" I told her in no uncertain terms. Thankfully, she got the message. I would have pulled my gun if I had to!

"What happened to him?" the nurse asked as she started cutting away more of his shirt.

"I can't tell you that, so don't ask again. Don't ask anyone!" I told her. "Just deal with what you see!" She looked at me somewhat angrily. "Just deal with it!" I told her. I wasn't in the mood for arguments.

"Cliff!" Cynthia said. "Ease up. She didn't need you snapping at her like that."

I realized she was right. "Sorry," I apologized. "Rough day."

It was another twenty minutes before Doctor Richter got there. He took one look at Pariah's back and grunted in astonishment. Then he saw my face. "What happened?" he asked. "It looks like you've both been through a war."

"I'm afraid we're still fighting that war," I told him. "And I'm sorry, but we've all been sworn to silence about what's going on."

He took a much closer look at Pariah's back. "You two need a different line of work," he said. "Something a bit safer!"

I was starting to think he was right!

I was surprised when the Director suddenly made an appearance. "How is he?" he asked.

"It looks like you ran over him with a tank!" Doctor Richter replied. "I'm going to send him upstairs for x-rays again."

"He'll be okay?" the Director asked.

The doctor nodded. "As much as possible – for him. It's just going to take time."

The Director nodded. "I'll be back."

I didn't see the Director again until much later. Pariah was back from x-rays, his back was stitched together in a few places and was covered in some kind of smelly ointment that did nothing to make him smell any better than he did. The doctor had said he had a fractured rib, but he wasn't going to touch it. But when the Director came back, he wasn't alone. He had Mr. and Mrs. Sullivan with him.

"How is he?" Mrs. Sullivan asked. I could tell she was somewhat appalled by the look of Pariah's bare back.

"He'll make it," I replied. "He just needs a bit of time."

She walked closer. Her husband followed. "Can I talk to him?" she asked.

I backed away. She came around to where she could see his face. "I never got the chance to thank you for what you did earlier," she said.

Pariah blinked, but said nothing more.

"Ever since my daughter went missing, I've prayed every single day and every single night for her to return safely. Eventually, I started praying for a miracle. You…were the miracle. A much bigger miracle than I ever expected. Thank you."

I don't know if I was surprised or not that Pariah bothered to answer. "Hurting her. Kept hurting her. Couldn't let them hurt her."

Mrs. Sullivan put her hand on his arm. "We'll make sure she gets all the help she needs," she said. "Thank you for bringing her back to us. I don't know how you did it, but thank you."

"How is she?" I asked.

It was her husband that answered. "Battered, bruised, in some kind of withdrawal from the drugs, and very, very confused."

"Just like all of us," I replied. "I'm glad she's going to be okay."

Mrs. Sullivan started to leave, then stopped. She put her hand back on Pariah's arm. "For what it's worth," she said, "I don't believe at all that you've ever molested anyone. I simply can't bring myself to believe it."

"I didn't do it," Pariah replied. "It wasn't me."

"Then why did they make us sign that paper?" she asked.

It was the Director who replied. "He was tried and convicted in court. We have to cover ourselves legally. We don't want anyone to come back at us later and say they didn't know in advance who they were dealing with."

"But did he really do it?" she asked.

"He was convicted," the Director replied.

"But," she asked, "are you sure he did it?"

"We have no reason to believe otherwise."

She looked down at Pariah. "I think you should rethink that," she told him. "I've heard about all too many cases where they convict someone and they were totally innocent. Don't you think he deserves a second look? Don't you think it's time you knew for sure?"

The Director stared at her for a moment. What he said next, surprised me. "You may be right."

I'm not sure anyone else noticed it, but Pariah gave a sigh of relief. He had told us over and over again that he didn't do it. For a long time we had no idea what he was talking about. And even when we did, we had no reason to reopen a case that had already been closed – a long time ago. Even now, it was going to take someone high up to give the go ahead. Someone like…the Director.

The Director ushered the Sullivans out of the tiny room, then turned back to me. "My office in the morning." And then he was gone.

I was surprised that Doctor Richter didn't see any need for Pariah to spend the night in the hospital. With no shirt to cover his body, Cynthia and I slowly walked him out of the examining room and out toward the door. I immediately saw several agents posted and watching everything that went on. Three of them headed straight for us the moment we came out of the room. One of them was Don. "I'll drive you back to the safe house," he said.

I figured that was good since none of us had a car there. And my car was going to be totally out of commission for a while. With the other two agents flanking us the whole way, we went outside and eased Pariah painfully into Don's car. I had started to think that maybe I should try to borrow a shirt for him from somewhere, but I got the distinct impression that anything covering those bruises on his back would only add to his pain. Sitting up in the car and riding anywhere was not going to be fun for him. I think I felt every little bump in the road just as much as he did, only because I was worried about how badly he hurt.

The first thing I noticed when we got to the safe house, was all the extra guards. More than ever before. And they weren't exactly lazing around. I had pictures in my mind of someone adding coils of razor wire around the place next. And after the day I had just had, I also thought that maybe it would be a good idea.

Brutus jumped all over Pariah the minute he walked in the door. As badly as Pariah hurt, he still held the little dog to his chest. We soon got Pariah settled in bed, minus the dog. I hoped he could sleep through all his pain.

"Geez, Cliff," Phil said as soon as Pariah was finally taken care of, "what happened to you guys? He's all beat up and your face looks like it's been through the blender. And what's with all the beefed up security?"

"Sorry Phil," I replied. "We're not allowed to talk about it."

He nodded. "Understood," he replied. I knew he did, but only because he had been an agent.

"Are you staying the night?" he asked Cynthia.

But it was Don who replied. "I think she should. We don't know yet what the threat level is to her."

That surprised me. "Maybe you should stay," I suggested.

I expected some big argument out of her, but instead, she shrugged her shoulders and said, "Why not. Got an extra bed?"

Phil smiled. "It just so happens that I do." He turned to me, "You get the other spare room. You're going to be here a while." He turned to Cynthia. "You get my room." He dropped his voice to a whisper. "It has a better bed."

"Where will you sleep?" Cynthia asked.

"Don't worry about me. Brutus and I have spent many happy nights on the sofa. It pulls out into a bed."

"Well, just for tonight," she replied.

A little while later, I was laying in my bed in the spare bedroom, staring at the dark ceiling. My mind wouldn't shut down after everything that had happened throughout the day. And then I saw my door quietly crack open as Cynthia snuck in and quietly closed the door behind her. All thoughts of the day behind me went out of my head the moment she slipped into my bed.

Let's just say that Cynthia showed me exactly how sinful she was capable of being.

And the result? Heaven!

CHAPTER

22

Don was there late the next morning to collect Cynthia and me. He looked a bit travel worn and I got the impression he hadn't gone home to bed yet. I'm sure I didn't look much better. Not only did I not sleep much last night, but because of the cuts on one side of my face, I decided not to shave for a few days.

"Can I go home now?" Cynthia asked as we rode toward the office.

"If you're careful," Don replied. "We don't think there's any threat aimed specifically at you, but you are part of the project, so be careful. It's Cliff and Pariah who have the contracts on their heads, and we found out yesterday that those contracts are still all too active. Just remember, mum's the word on last night."

Cynthia of course had no problem with that. She wasn't really talking much about this stuff with anyone – as far as I knew. As soon as we arrived, she jumped into her sporty little car and Don and I took the elevator up to the top floor. As far as I could see, everything around the building was business as usual, no special excitement at all. As far as I could see.

We entered the outer office of the Director's domain. His assistant was busy putting paperwork into a case. His inner door was open. "That you Wimberly?" his voice called from the inside office. The assistant just looked at us and motioned with her head for us to go on in.

When we got through his door, we saw him buttoning up his shirt. It looked like he hadn't been home last night either, so he had probably shaved and was just now changing in his office. "McNair," he said, "how's the face?"

"It's fine," I replied. "It just stings a bit when I touch it. As you can see, I'm growing a beard for a few days."

He grunted as he buttoned the top button on his shirt and grabbed his tie. "I'm heading to Washington in a little while," he said. "I'm going to see what can be done about shutting down that Hong Kong slave business. I've had the tech guys working all night putting together a few…special… versions of the tapes from last night.

"Anyway, I think that what Mrs. Sullivan said last night was right. Not only do we owe Pariah a big debt, but we also need to know exactly who it is we're working with here. Since you are Pariah's handler, and I don't want to bring in more outside people than necessary, I'm going to put you in charge of finding out."

I thought about that for a moment. "You know there are some very politically powerful people involved that he…upset in his past."

"If it gets that far, let me know first," he said. "I'm on my way to talk with some of the most politically powerful people in the world. If need be, I think I can handle what you need."

"In that case, sir, I think this is long overdue."

He stopped tying his tie for a moment and nodded. "Damn right! Just keep your head down, McNair. If you get shot, I don't know how much use Pariah would be to anyone. And if he gets shot…"

"I get the picture, sir."

"You're in charge of Pariah, and Don is in charge of you! Listen to him! We've been working on some new options all night. Don't get stupid! Now please excuse me, I have a plane to catch."

With that, we were quickly gone from his office. "What options was he talking about?" I asked.

Don smiled, "I'll let you know when they happen."

I love it when everyone keeps you in the dark.

"In the meantime, if you leave this building, you let me know in advance."

And now he was crippling my style. But heck, I didn't have a car anymore anyway.

"They dug a couple of bullets out of your car this morning," he said as we entered his office. "Big stuff. High powered. We don't know much more yet, but they're working on it."

He sat down behind his desk and I took one of the chairs in front. "You were lucky yesterday, very lucky," he said.

"I know," I replied. "It I hadn't had to slam on my brakes because of the car in front of me, the first bullet would have gone right through my head. Maybe Pariah's too for that matter. Two for the price of one."

He nodded. "Damn lucky! The shooter picked that construction spot perfectly. We figure he was shooting from the top of a building across the street. The angle is right and you can see that whole construction zone perfectly from it. You slow down to practically nothing. Easy pot shot."

"All foiled by the car in front of me."

He nodded. "We've got somebody out there with a good sized gun, who knows what he's doing."

"Not only that," I replied, "but he knew my car and when I would be passing that spot. Which means, he most likely knows where the safe house is."

"Exactly! And somehow, I seriously doubt he had been lurking up on that roof all day. Someone tipped him off when you left the building with Pariah."

"So how do we find him?" I asked.

"*We* find him, not you! You've got another job. And since you're marked as a target too, it's going to complicate things. A lot!"

"I'll keep my head down," I assured him.

"You better! Now see what you can dig up."

"Question," I said.

"What?"

"Can I see the Sullivan girl? I want to talk to her about what happened last night."

He thought about that for a minute."Have you talked about it with Pariah yet?" "No, he was still sleeping when I left."

"Most likely the Sullivan girl is sleeping too right now. But it sounds like a good idea – when she's able to talk. I'll let you know. I'd rather have you asking those questions instead of someone who's not in the know about this."

"I'd like to have Doctor Westmore with me too when I talk to her. Her insights have been helpful so far in dealing with Pariah."

"That's fine. She's a psychiatrist. It probably wouldn't hurt."

John wasn't there when I got back to my office, but Hannah and Billy were. I called them in for a little chat and shut the door. "We've been tasked with digging up Pariah's past. Particularly, did he actually rape that girl?"

"That's not our usual business," Hannah noted.

"I know, but they don't want to use anyone outside of the people assigned to work with Pariah now. And to tell the truth, I really want this one."

"So his file is officially reopened?" Billy asked.

"Very officially reopened. But quietly." I looked to Hannah, "First step, you re-put together all that information you found on him before…plus, anything else you can dig up. Billy, see if you can get the transcript from his trial. That's where I really want to start with this."

Two seconds later, my office was vacant except for me. I rubbed the itchy growth on the good side of my face where it wouldn't hurt. Pariah claimed over and over again that he didn't do it. But he had been convicted in a fair trial. How was I going to find out one way or another what really happened? I wanted badly to start pouring through the paperwork right away to figure it out. The only problem was, I didn't have a single piece of paper yet to pour through.

It didn't take Hannah long to dig up the information she had found once before. The trial transcript however was another matter. It wasn't until late in the day that I got that. Billy had been kind enough to print the entire thing out for me from the digital copy he had finally located and been granted access to. When I got it, I cleared my desk of everything else and started in on it. What surprised me the most about the file, was how thin it was. I had somehow expected it to be much larger.

Chermont versus Clayton. Not very exciting. Neither was the rest of the transcript. I made a few notes, mostly of names. The one big thing I realized in it, was that the whole thing boiled down to the Chermont girl's word against Clayton's – Pariah's. Stacy Chermont claimed up and down that it was Clayton who raped her, and of course Clayton claimed that he didn't. But where I saw tons and tons of paragraphs of things that the Chermont's lawyer talked about, there was very little rebuttal from Clayton's lawyer. And the Chermont's lawyer's arguments sounded all too convincing.

There were one or two little things that surprised me. Of all things, Clayton had been Stacy's Sunday school teacher. That was something I never expected. According to Clayton, the two had argued rather vehemently after Sunday School on the day in question over Stacy's behavior with certain members of the opposite sex. Stacy however, claimed that the argument was about Clayton trying to get her into bed when she wanted nothing to do with him. So yes, the two of them knew each other, and obviously well enough to argue about something. But that something that each of them claimed the argument was over, was at total opposite ends of the spectrum.

Stacy had come home late that day and promptly headed to the bathroom where she threw up. Her mother and father were naturally concerned. It was then that Stacy had sobbingly told them that Clayton had raped her. A few days later, the doctor confirmed that she was indeed pregnant. Two weeks after that, Stacy miscarried, and was rather passionately glad that she had.

It was brought out that Clayton was away from home for most of the day in question. According to Clayton's lawyer, he spent the day in the church repainting one of the Sunday School classrooms. According to Stacy's lawyer, the painting didn't take very long at all so he had more than enough time to force himself on the poor helpless girl. Stacy had only stopped back in at the church later that afternoon to collect the Bible that she had carelessly left behind before going out with her friends.

The other thing that surprised me was something that came out in Clayton's defense. His wife was pregnant. Why would he rape Stacy when his wife was expecting a baby? Unfortunately, Stacy's lawyer found all too many convincing arguments that made a pregnant wife sound like a convincing argument in favor of the rape.

There was one other little tidbit that I almost missed, and I debated whether to put it on my list of things to check on or not. It was a minor reference to material not admissible. But no other mention was made of it anywhere else in the transcript.

Overall, as far as I could see, Pariah was screwed. The whole thing boiled down to his word against hers, and her case looked awfully convincing to me. I had to remind myself that looks can be deceiving sometimes. But still, I wasn't overly confident anymore.

I got a call from Cynthia shortly after I finished with the file. "Have you had a chance yet to talk to Pariah about last night?" she asked.

"Not yet," I replied. "I've been here all day."

"Good," she said. "Because I want to talk to him about it too."

"You want to approach him together about it?" I asked.

"Together, then maybe separately some other time."

"Works for me," I replied. "How about tonight? I'll be leaving here in a little while. I need to call Don first and arrange a car to drive."

"I'll see you at Phil's place then," she said. I was already wishing she would spend the night again, but somehow I doubted that it was part of her plans. I picked up the phone and called Don. "I need a car," I said. "Time to go home."

"You're not going home!" he replied all too sternly. "Give me a list of what you need and I'll send someone to your apartment for it later. And if you're ready to leave, then meet me in my office here. I'll take you myself."

I was very surprised at how stern he was being about the whole thing. But I wasn't being given much of a choice in the matter. A little while later, we rode down the elevator together and he led me to a side door instead of the usual entrance I used. He made me wait inside until he pulled his car up near the door. I felt a bit overly protected and thought most of his precautions were silly. Then I remembered all that glass floating in the air in front of my eyes yesterday. Maybe a little precaution wouldn't be a bad thing. What surprised me more, was that he didn't pull up in his car, he pulled up in a big SUV with heavily tinted windows instead. And when I went to get in, he had me get in the back seat.

He drove me straight to the safe house, then shocked me. "Stay!" he said. "Don't get out of the car."

I glanced around. The extra security guards were all too evident. Why couldn't I get out? We were here! But I had no one to ask since he had quickly disappeared into the house.

It was about ten minutes later when he came out…with Phil, Brutus, and Pariah at his side. Pariah was wearing a new looking shirt that I was sure Phil had found for him. But somehow, despite the clean shirt, he still looked terribly grungy. Don opened the back door of the car and Pariah climbed in next to me. A minute later, we were back on the road again, going somewhere else. "Where are we going?" I asked.

"Someplace different," he replied. "A new safe house. Very new…as of today."

"You know, Doctor Westmore was supposed to meet me at Phil's tonight," I said.

"We'll take care of her too," he replied.

I got the distinct impression he was trying to reveal as little as possible – even to me!

It was a while before I realized exactly where we were going, and I wasn't surprised when we pulled up in front of the gate that led into the grounds of the house I had tried to see with Frank Morris that day. "I take it they finally located the owners," I said.

"We're the owners now," he replied. "As of earlier this afternoon. Seems the old owners were anxious to sell it more than they thought."

I immediately wondered what the government had done to arrange that – and how much they had paid for the place. It had to be millions!

A guard posted at the gate let us in and we drove past the massive walls into the winding driveway. The house finally came into view, and what a house. A mansion! "We bought it with the purpose of housing our more… important…guests," Don said. "So I guess you two are the first."

I tried to feel honored, but it wasn't sinking in. He parked in a parking area near the front entrance and we got out. All except Pariah. He just sat in the car and stared at the big house. I opened his door for him. "Come on Pariah, we're home again."

"Big house," Pariah said.

"Yeah," I replied. "And I'm sure it has plenty of room." But he didn't move yet. "Plenty of trees in the yard too," I added. "Way more trees than Phil has."

I saw him looking around more. And slowly he got out of the car. I tried to steer him toward the house, but instead he started walking toward the trees he could see. He stopped, and looked around more, then changed direction and kept going, continuing to look around. I finally realized he was taking a tour of the immense yard.

"The wall goes all the way around?" I asked.

"All the way," Don replied. "The place was built to keep prying eyes and people out so the owners could have a bit of privacy. It makes the perfect safe house for us now."

I decided to let Pariah enjoy his little walk and I followed Don toward the house. But we didn't quite get to the front door before Pariah was back again. "Ready to go in?" I asked him.

But that wasn't the reason he returned. "Little dog," he said. "Have to protect little dog."

"You miss Brutus?" I asked. "I understand but he doesn't live here."

Pariah suddenly became more insistent. "Have to protect little dog!"

I stared at him for a moment, wondering if there was more to his request than just his fondness for Brutus. I decided to err on the cautious side. Still staring at Pariah, I said, "Don, is there any way we can get Brutus and Phil here? Like maybe tonight? And I think we should make sure there are a few more security guys out at Phil's place too. Just in case."

It was a moment before Don answered. "I'll see that it happens." He turned to Pariah. "Do you think there's going to be trouble at the other safe house?" he asked Pariah directly.

"Little dog," Pariah said one more time. "Have to protect little dog." It was the way he said it that sent chills up my spine. I have no doubt that Don experienced the same thing.

"Come on in," Don said, "and make yourself at home."

I went in. Pariah turned and continued his tour of the yard.

I took the fifty-nine cent tour of the downstairs. Opulent, modern, wide-open, rich, rich, rich! I had no doubt that the government budget would ruin the whole thing completely. No doubt they'd auction some of the furnishings off for extra cash once they got the chance. But I was glad to see it the way it was supposed to be…in its original state.

I found Don again when I got to the oversized kitchen. He was still talking on the phone, giving orders to the guys at the safe house. He suddenly turned to me while he was still talking to someone else. "McNair, got any ideas on how we can smoke out our shooter?"

What a terrible question to ask someone who hadn't been thinking about it. "Not yet," I replied, "but I'll let you know."

He nodded and went back to giving orders again. When he was done, he said to me, "Phil and his dog will be here in a little while. Maybe he can help run this place while you and Pariah are using it. We haven't had time yet to look into that angle."

"Sounds like a great idea to me," I replied. "Thanks for arranging for Brutus to help keep Pariah company. He's become awfully attached to that little dog."

He smiled, "We do what we can. That was an easy one to arrange."

While we waited, I decided to go out and tour the yard. In other words, search for Pariah. The wall surrounding the property was a good ten feet high. The way it was made, nobody could see anything from the outside of what was inside the wall. Someone could climb it, but they would have to go to an awful lot of trouble to do so. The grounds were fantastically landscaped with little areas of trees and plantings everywhere. I found Pariah in the middle of one of those areas, again sitting on the lush grass under the trees.

"Don has arranged for Phil and Brutus to come here too," I told him. "They should be here in a little while."

He looked up at me gratefully. "Little dog. Have to protect little dog."

I knelt down by him. "Pariah, do you sense a threat to the little dog, or anyone else?"

He looked right at me. "Have to protect little dog."

I took that as a yes. I left him there to go back to the house. But I turned around before I got too far and stared back at Pariah. If I was a shooter, and I wanted to kill Pariah, how would I go about it? In my mind I saw Pariah sitting as he was sitting now, but I saw him sitting in Phil's yard, not this walled compound. I raised my hand as if it was a gun and aimed it right at Pariah's head. "Bang," I said softly. With renewed purpose, I strode directly toward the house to find Don.

He was still in the kitchen, sitting on one of the stools at the long counter. And, he was still on his phone. "I have an idea," I said while he was still concentrating on his conversation.

He stopped talking for a moment. "I'll call you back," he said into his phone, then he ended the call. "Shoot!" he said.

I paused for a moment at his choice of words. "Shoot could be it exactly," I replied. "If the shooter is mainly after Pariah, and Pariah is mainly in the same exact spot, and the shooter knows where the safe house is, wouldn't he know where Pariah usually spends all his time?"

Don looked startled, "Out in Phil's yard under the trees. So?"

I raised my hand like it was a gun again and aimed it at the refrigerator. "So we already know this guy is a pretty fair shot. Maybe not the best, but pretty darn good. We also know that he likes rifles and isn't afraid to shoot from a fair distance. Where would he set up shop to take out Pariah?"

Don thought about that for a moment. "The trees behind the property would probably be out. We're watching them closely and they're too thick for a decent long shot. The property on either side of his house is vacant too but the land is all cleared. So there's nowhere left."

"What about the properties next to those vacant lots. Particularly, the next house past Phil's house on the left. If the shooter positioned himself, say, on the roof of that house, or maybe in one of those big trees in the backyard there, he could see right into Phil's yard. Maybe he'd even have a chance at a shot with his rifle. It's not that far. Deer hunters shoot from a lot farther off than that."

He thought about that for a minute, then nodded. "Good thinking, we'll watch that place too. It's a good thing we got you out of there then."

"I think you're missing the point."

"And that is?"

"What if we baited a trap?"

"Go on."

It took me two minutes to lay out the basics of the idea I had…as dumb as it sounded. And the more I talked, the dumber I realized it was. So I wasn't surprised by Don's response.

"That sounds absurd!"

"Yeah, now that I think about it, I couldn't agree more. Sorry," I replied.

But instead of saying anything to me, he dialed another number on his phone and started giving orders, setting up the exact scenario I had just described. He finished by telling whoever it was on the other end of the line that he knew it was absurd, but to do it anyway.

"Satisfied?" he finally asked when he was done.

"I'm not sure," I replied. "It still sounds like a dumb idea."

He smiled. "Dumb enough to just work!"

Another SUV arrived a little while later and I was pleased to see Cynthia get out of the back seat. I could see she was rather stunned by the fancy place. "Nice digs, McNair," she said as she looked around at the front of the house. "Big improvement over your last place."

"A beautiful house, for a beautiful lady," I replied. "Would you like to see the inside?"

"I can't wait!" she replied, already heading toward the front door. "What's with all the cloak and dagger stuff?" she asked. "As soon as I got to Phil's they shoved me straight into another car and drove me out here… wherever here is. And the driver wouldn't tell me anything!"

"Security," I replied. "I think we're going to try to use Phil's place as a decoy now. Try to draw out the shooter."

"Where's Phil?" she asked.

"Still at his house. But they're going to bring him out here later. Pariah is particularly worried about Brutus. I think he's expecting another attack."

She looked around her, especially at the massive wall surrounding the property. "No worries about that here."

"That's the idea," I replied.

I led her inside and she stopped and stared around. "Okay," she said after a moment. "I'll take it. How much?"

I laughed and let her wander around, discovering the place for herself. What surprised me the most, was that she didn't just take in a whole room at a glance, it was the little things that seemed to draw her attention the most. All the pictures, the carvings, the little pieces put out on the tables.

She picked up many of them and examined them closely, then carefully put each one back in its place. Touring the house with her took a lot longer than my little run around it. And then we got to the second floor, where I hadn't been yet.

She ood and ahed over each of the guest bedrooms. Then we got to the humongous master bedroom. "Oh God!" she exclaimed. "I could live right here and never come out!" And when she saw the master bathroom, she was totally sold. "Heaven!" she declared.

I was very tempted to try to get her to try out the bed with me for a different kind of heaven, when I heard Don yelling from downstairs for us to get down there quickly. Drat! Foiled again!

We rushed down the steps. "We've got a possible bogy in that neighbor's house," he said quietly while he was listening to his phone. He set it on the kitchen counter and pushed the speaker button. "McNair and the doctor are here with me now," he said to alert whoever was on the line that it wasn't just Don anymore.

"Cliff? You there?" I was surprised to hear John's voice coming through the phone.

"What are you doing there?" I asked.

"Pretending to be you!" he replied.

"No way. I'm much better looking."

"Wanna' bet?" Cynthia said playfully.

"See!" John said. "Even the lady agrees!"

"Shut up!" I replied teasingly.

"Okay, just so you know," John continued, getting back to business, "we cleared the family out earlier. Made it look like they were just going out for dinner and a movie or something. Half an hour later, we saw a car drive by and drop someone off, then the car left."

"Was he carrying a gun?" I asked.

"He was carrying a case of some sort. It could definitely have held a gun though."

"What about the car that dropped him off?"

"Texas plates, we're still running them. We're trying to find the car now."

"I have a feeling he won't go too far."

"We agree," John replied.

"Why don't you just go in and arrest him?" Cynthia asked.

"He hasn't done much that's illegal yet. We don't want to get too close yet so we don't know if he's broken into the house or what?" The sun will be going down in a little while. If he's going to make his move, most likely it will be soon."

"The dog, John. Where's the dog. Keep him out of the way. Way out of the way. Pariah is very concerned about him!"

"Got it!" I heard him giving orders to someone to make sure the dog stayed in the house.

"Okay," John said. "We have the dog, he's not going anywhere."

"Good," I replied. "When are you going to send Phil out?"

"I'm thinking about now should be good enough," he replied. A minute later, he said. "Phil's going out now. He's yelling to Pariah to try to get him back in the house."

"Where's Pariah?" Cynthia asked, full of concern."

"Don't worry, he's here, not there," I replied.

"Phil's going out further. God, what a ham! He's waving his arms at the dummy and yelling. Now he's stomping back into the house. Community theatre 101."

"You're just jealous!" I said. "He's a better actor than you."

"Want to bet?" he said.

"You just watch your head. You're going to be all too exposed out there!"

"Don't remind me," he replied. "I'm putting the phone down for a bit. I hope I come back to pick it up again."

We waited, and we waited, and we waited. All we could hear were minor little sounds in the background. Then finally, John's voice came back on the phone. "Okay," he said, "I'm back."

"Did you go all the way out to the trees?"

"No," he replied. "I chickened out. And I'm not afraid to admit it!"

"You weren't supposed to. You were just supposed to yell from the middle of the yard then get the hell out of Dodge!"

"That's all I did. But I stayed for a bit to yell at the dummy more and also to yell to Phil that we should just let him stay there. Shit!" He suddenly yelled. "McNair! We've got a shot!"

All we heard for a while was sounds of turmoil as he ran all over, giving orders, asking questions, whatever he needed to do. None of us tried to talk to him, we knew he was too busy. Finally he came back on the line again. "I'll have to call you back McNair. I can't talk and take care of this too."

"Understood," I replied.

But he added one more thing before he hung up the phone. "McNair… the dummy took a direct hit to the head!"

"An absurd idea," Don said into the sudden silence.

"Yeah. Just absurd enough to work."

"What dummy?" Cynthia asked.

"I think they wound up grabbing a mannequin out of a store somewhere," Don replied. "We didn't have much time to set this up."

"But it sounds like it worked," she replied.

"Not yet," I said. "We still have to catch the guy."

"And whoever he's working with," Don added. "Because now we know that he's not alone!"

The problems just never seemed to end.

It was almost forty minutes before Don's phone rang again, and thankfully, it was John. "Okay, we got the guy who did the shooting. A little Mexican twerp this time. But his gun was certainly big enough. For a little guy, he somehow managed to climb way up in one of the trees in the back yard fairly quickly. We had a devil of a time getting him down. He's not talking yet, but he seems pretty happy with himself. I'm pretty sure he thinks he really killed Pariah."

"Great work John," Don said. "How about the car and his friend?"

"Nothing yet. We got the owner's name from the tags, but I don't know anything else yet."

"We'll get there," Don replied. "Go ahead and ship Phil and the dog."

"That's going to make things easier," I said as soon as Don had hung up his phone. "Can I go back to my apartment yet?"

"No!"

That was an answer I hadn't expected.

"It won't hurt you to stay here till we reevaluate the threat on you. As far as we know, that contract is still out there."

A car arrived an hour later with Phil, Brutus, and a bounty of fast food for everyone since there was no food in the house yet. I had to use Brutus as a lure to get Pariah out of the yard and into the house. But once the two were reunited, he hugged that little dog so close I thought he would kill him.

After dinner, Cynthia and I attacked Pariah with our questions.

"Pariah," I started, "We need to know what happened last night when you disappeared and came back with the girl."

He looked at me, but said nothing. I was guessing it was about to become one of those subjects he wouldn't talk about. But just as I was about to ask something else, he opened his mouth and spoke. "I don't know."

"Tell us about it," Cynthia said. "What do you remember?"

I saw his eyes sort of glaze over as he spoke. "Bad man. Hurting girl. Hitting girl with stick. Hurting girl badly. Girl crying. Hated it! Hated it! Had to stop man! Had to help girl! Wanted to help girl! Wanted to stop man! Wanted…"

He stopped talking and stared off into space.

"What, Pariah," the doctor asked softly.

"And then…I was there." He turned to look at Cynthia directly. "Don't know how…but I was there. And the bad man with the stick yelled funny words, and started hitting me with the stick. Hurt! Hurt so bad! Hurt so bad! Had to protect girl. Laid over top of her so stick couldn't hit her. Hurt so bad! Hurt so bad! Had to get away from hurt. Had to get away. No connection anymore. No way back. Told her to think of her mother. Told her over and over to think of her mother. Held her tight. Think about mother. New connection. Pain from stick was bad. So bad. Had to get away from pain. Had to…" His eyes had glazed over again and he was once again lost in space.

"Pariah?" I prompted.

He turned back to look at me. His eyes were still glazed over though. "And then, I was back. Back with girl. No more pain from man, but I hurt bad. Hurt bad." His eyes seemed to focus better on me. "And you were there." He reached his hand out and grabbed mine. I held it for a few moments until he finally pulled away and started to get out of his chair.

"Pariah," Cynthia said. "Has anything like this ever happened to you before?"

I didn't think he was going to answer. I thought he was just going to walk away. But a moment later, he turned. "No. Never happened. Don't want it to happen. Scared me. Scared me bad. No connection. No way back." He left us then with Brutus at his heels. I heard a door open and knew he was going back out to the yard.

"He's still pretty shaken up about it," I said to Cynthia. "Until now, I hadn't realized that."

"He hides things pretty well sometimes," she replied. "What I found interesting though, was that it happened because he needed it to happen. He needed it badly. But then, once he was there, he still managed to function brilliantly."

"He lost his connection," I replied. "But he still had an overwhelming desire to help the girl. He had to protect her more than he wanted to protect himself. And the pain had to be horrendous."

"Horrendous enough that he quickly figured out how to get back again. Use the girl to bring them back to us here...where her mother was."

"As dumb as he seems sometimes, once in a while I get a little glimpse of a lot of intelligence in him."

She nodded. "I've always thought that. The intelligence is there, but there's brain damage too. Brain damage that I think he's fighting. What we get, is the result."

I took that in. Intelligent, but brain damaged. That was Pariah in a nutshell.

"There's one other thing that strikes me," she said.

"What?"

"In everything we've seen him do so far...everything! His actions and the things he says are not what I would expect from someone who was capable of committing rape...especially to a child."

Inwardly, I agreed whole heartedly. Especially since I knew him better than anyone else. But.... "You haven't read the transcript of his trial," I replied. "It's awfully convincing!"

"I don't care," she said. "I don't think he did it."

"Neither do I," I replied. "But I'm going to find out, one way or another."

"Let me help you with that," she said.

"How? Most of the investigative work is nothing but digging up paperwork and making phone calls."

"I don't care. I especially want to help when you go and talk to people."

"Really? What about your other patients?"

"I've been making Pariah more and more my main responsibility. I'll cut back on my other duties as much as necessary. Especially after last night!"

The truth was, I really wanted her around, but it was completely for personal reasons, not for Pariah.

"Okay," I said. "I'll try to work something out."

Since I was technically marked for death from some unseen source, I had grave misgivings about putting her in danger too. It was simply my personal attraction to her that had made me make the decision. All I could think about afterwards was that I had made a big mistake. I was putting her in danger. I shouldn't have done it.

But heck, I liked the woman. A lot! And I had an inkling that she liked me too. Why wouldn't I want to spend more time with her?

And how was I to know the danger was only just beginning?

I was at work Monday morning, going through the court transcript again, when Don phoned me. "If you still want to talk to the Sullivan girl, her doctor says you can go over now. Do you want me to get you a car?"

"Hell yeah!" I replied. "Can I drive this time?"

"If you manage not to wreck the thing or get shot at again!"

"I'll try," I said. I felt like a prisoner who had just been released. I immediately called Cynthia and arranged for her to meet me at the hospital. She too had been wanting to talk to Connie Sullivan.

The car I got was the same SUV that Don had driven me to the safe house in the day before. It was big and a lot heavier than I expected, but it drove well and was very comfortable inside. I found Cynthia at the nurse's station going over the girls medical charts. I also found two agents from the company posted at different areas along one of the corridors.

"It's about time you got here Cliff," Cynthia said. "I've been waiting forever!"

"Sorry," I replied. "I had to wait to get a vehicle."

"I've already talked with the psychologist assigned to her and also her primary medical doctor here," she said. "She's lucid, but we're going to be fighting drug withdrawal so they're not sure what we're going to get out of her. The psychologist said her parents both described her as being a fighter, and from what we know about how she behaved in Hong Kong, I believe it. I think that's going to be in our favor."

"A fighter! Yeah, if she was still fighting back at the breaking house in Hong Kong, then I have no doubt that she'll be just fine...eventually."

I actually knew the agent that was posted at the girl's door, but he insisted on seeing my ID anyway. But to tell the truth, I was glad he did. The guy was going to stay on his feet and stay sharp. Just what we needed here.

Inside, Connie Sullivan was obviously in a bad way. I could see the sweat on her face, neck, and arms. The room stank of vomit. She was wearing a hospital gown and her body was covered by a light sheet so I couldn't see any of the scars and bruising that I knew had to be there. A man who knew what he was doing with a cane could punish them so that they hurt horribly, but not leave any permanent scars.

"Hi Connie," Cynthia said as she walked up to the side of the girl's bed. "I'm Doctor Westmore. We'd like to ask you a few questions about what happened the other night when you came back from Hong Kong."

The girl looked startled. "They said I'm not supposed to talk about it."

"We know, but you can talk to us about it. The man who brought you back...I'm his doctor. I'm a psychiatrist."

"Is he okay?" she asked. "They were beating him hard...and then..."

"He'll be fine," she told her. "He's very badly bruised though, much worse than you, but he'll be just fine."

I saw her struggling with something internal. Then she quickly leaned over the other side of the bed and started to wretch. Nothing came up though – thankfully.

It was a few minutes before she was able to continue. "Sorry," she finally said. "I can't stop doing that."

"It will get better with time," Cynthia told her. "You just have to keep wanting to get better."

"That's what my doctors keep telling me, that I have to want to get better. But I'm not sure I do! They gave me drugs for a long time, and I want them so bad now!"

"Connie," I said, "from everything we know about you so far, we know that you're a real fighter. You don't give up. Don't give up on this. Don't let them win!"

She seemed to look at me for the longest time. "I'm trying," she said. "It's just so hard. I don't think I'm going to make it."

"You will," I replied. "Trust me, you will. Just keep trying."

"Connie," Cynthia said, "we need you to tell us what happened that night."

"It was a miracle," she said. "Momma keeps saying it was a miracle. And she's right. How did that man do that? How?"

"We don't know yet," Cynthia replied. "We don't. But somehow, he did it."

"She nodded. A miracle. I want to thank him…if I ever get better."

"I'm sure he'd like that," Cynthia replied. "A lot! Now what happened when he came?"

"Jojo was beating me again because I refused to give into him. And suddenly, that man was in the room with us. I never saw him come in, he was just there. Jojo was so surprised, but he got real angry real fast and started beating the man with his cane. And I could tell he was hitting to really hurt. The man jumped on me and started telling me to think about my mother. Over and over again he kept saying it. I couldn't figure out why, but the next thing I knew, I was somewhere else…and Momma and Daddy were there." She was crying all of a sudden. "And Jojo wasn't!"

Her story exactly matched what Pariah had told us, but then I never had a moment's doubt that it would. We stayed with the girl for a few minutes to comfort her, then left. Other agents would talk to her further about her experiences. I only knew two things. Pariah had indeed gone to the other side of the planet and brought her back, and that Connie Sullivan was a fighter. She would make it! She would make it just fine!

"Lunch?" I asked Cynthia.

I love it when she smiles at me!

We found a dark little bistro to grab a bite and a nice quiet back corner to talk while we ate. "So what are you doing now to figure out if he's innocent or not?" Cynthia asked me.

"I was just about to phone the arresting officer this morning when Don called and said we could talk to Connie."

"So that's your next move? The arresting officer?" "Yeah. It's not much and it's simple, but that's it."

"Can I come?"

"I don't know that I actually need to go see him."

"So call and find out," she said.

That surprised me. I got the impression she was more anxious to clear Pariah's name than I was. I had to call and find someone in the office to go to my desk and get the phone number for me. Then I called the precinct where the officer worked. It took a while to track officer Perelli down, but I got lucky. After so many years on the force, he had a detective's badge now and his own desk…and he was there. I explained who I was and what I wanted. But the guy didn't remember the case at all.

"Tell you what, he said, "give me the particulars and I'll look it up. If you want to stop by in a little while, I'll be glad to talk to you and see what I remember – if anything."

I looked up at Cynthia. "I guess we're going downtown to talk to the police."

Detective Perelli turned out to be a bit older than I imagined, but he was nice enough. He shook my hand and Cynthia's hand, then got down to business. "Sorry I don't remember much, but there's not much to remember. My notes only say that all I did was go to Clayton's house and arrest the guy, not much else. I seem to remember that his wife was there and that she was pregnant. Funny how it's dumb things like that that stick out in your mind, but nothing else does."

"Yeah," I agreed, "sometimes it's the little things that can mean the most."

"Yeah," he agreed. "I find that out all the time."

"Did you ever get the sense that he was innocent, that he didn't do it?" I asked.

He shook his head. "Not that I remember. But I barely remember this one at all. Um…I do think he might have said over and over again that he didn't do it, but that could be a hundred other cases talking, so I'm not sure."

"Sounds like him," Cynthia said.

"Anything else you can tell me?" I asked.

"Nope! Like I said, all I did was go to the guys house and arrest him. I didn't work the case."

"We didn't get much that was useful there," Cynthia complained as we got back into my car.

"No. But he did confirm that his wife was pregnant at the time he was arrested."

"That's right!" she said. "Why would he rape the girl if his wife was pregnant? Wouldn't that help to clear him?"

"Unfortunately no. That came out in the trial and the opposing attorney found more reasons for it to cause him to rape the girl than reasons for him not to."

"Damn lawyers!"

I agreed with her sentiments exactly…for many more reasons than just this case.

"So what now?" she asked.

"Now we try to locate Pariah's attorney."

"Where is he?"

"That's the problem. We don't know yet."

I drove her back to the hospital where her car was and headed back to the office. My phone rang about halfway back. "McNair!" Don's voice came over the line. "Where are you?"

"On my way back. Why?"

"Come straight here and straight to my office when you get here!"

"What's going on?" I asked.

"Ballistics!"

It took me a moment to realize he had hung up on me. What could be the problem with ballistics? When I got to his office though, he wasn't there.

"He had to leave," his secretary told me. "But he wants you to go down and talk directly with Frank Morris instead. Second floor."

"I'll find it," I replied as I turned around and left. It seemed like so much of my job was just bouncing from one person to the next. Morris was the agent who had originally tried to show me the safe house we were in now. He must have located the owners somewhere in Austria since then.

Morris's office was much like Don's only down a level. He welcomed me inside and I took a chair that exactly matched the ones in Don's office upstairs.

"I see you found the owners of that mansion," I said.

He sat back and smiled. "Funny thing about that, I didn't even know they wanted to sell it. But once the Director had a little talk with them, turns out they did want to sell it – badly!"

"What did we have to pay for it?"

"I have no idea. Once I did the initial leg work, I was out of the loop completely. I only heard the deal went through real fast, and that was it."

"So what's new?" I asked, wanting to get down to the reason I needed to see him.

The grin left his face quickly. "You've got some kind of lucky guardian angel looking over your shoulder, McNair. For sure!"

My thoughts of a heavenly angel turned immediately to Cynthia, but not for any of the reasons he thought. "Just lucky," I replied.

"Lucky is right! And I'm told that little set up at Phil's safe house was your idea. Good work."

I hadn't known that Don had told anyone. "We kind of thought it was absurd at the time."

"I would have too," he replied. "But…we managed to snare one of them…uninjured this time. The only problem is, the bullets from his gun don't match the bullets we pulled out of your car. They were big, but not the same."

Okay, I was totally surprised. "How can that be?"

"You tell me?" He sat back in his chair. I realized he was waiting for me to put it all together.

"His friend," I finally said. "The one driving the car."

"You got it. Although he wouldn't tell us that. But it's the only thing that makes sense."

"So what were they doing, taking turns or something?"

"That's what we think. They were working together for sure."

"So there's still another shooter out there with a rifle, and he's still got it aimed right at me."

"Pariah first," he said. "But you're still definitely a target."

"What do we know about him? Did you trace the plates?"

"The plates were stolen. The owner didn't even know they were missing."

"So we have no leads at all?"

"Not a lot."

But I had picked up on the fact that he did know more. "What else is there?"

"The contract. We've been trying to trace the source. Find the money man, remove the source, and no more contract."

"So where is he? New York?"

"That's what we thought, but we were wrong. Mexico."

That one floored me. "Mexico? And they sent a hit man down from New York?"

"Don't ask me," he replied. "I'm just telling you what I know."

"So who wants me dead so much?"

"A real bad ass! A drug lord. Carlos Pacheco. Ships drugs up from Mexico a hundred different ways. The border patrol is very much at war with this guy. Plenty of trouble, no way to get at him."

"Pacheco!" I exclaimed, recognizing the name. "I used to work narcotics until I moved over to missing persons. I recognize that name very well. But I've been out of narcotics for a long time now, so there's no way he could be after me for that."

"He's not really after you, he wants Pariah dead, remember? You're only secondary."

How nice to make me feel so important. "So he's into slavery too?"

He nodded. "That and anything else he can make money off of."

And then it sunk in. "Texas! There's another part of the slave ring in Texas. They said New York, somewhere in Europe, Hong Kong, and Texas!"

He looked shaken. "You're sure? I haven't heard about that."

I nodded. "Pariah found the New York operation first. He found Hong Kong a few nights ago. We haven't stumbled across Texas yet."

"They're not telling me squat about what goes on with Pariah anymore. Somehow they're managing to keep it very well contained."

"Sorry," I said. "We need to. Security."

He nodded. "You just continue keeping it quiet. But if you want my opinion, I'd start looking for their Texas operation as soon as possible. And my bet would be that it will be located right on the border somewhere."

He was right. After spending years in narcotics, I knew he had to be right!

So now I was back to having someone who was good with a gun still aiming at my head. Well, Pariah's head first, but my head was in the equation too. And now my thoughts about the next time we used Pariah were more centered around finding the Texas operation. Because if we found it, we might also find a way to stop Carlos Pacheco, and I might finally be allowed to go back to my crummy little apartment with my TV dinners and stale beer. Oh goody. Maybe having a price on my head was a good thing. I was currently living in a mansion!

As soon as I got back to my office, I tried to put all thoughts of drug lords out of my head. I called Billy and Hannah into my office. I opened the trial transcript and found the name of Pariah's attorney – Clint Green. I turned the paper around to show it to both of them. "Find him for me." I said. "And find me Brent Jackson, our profiler. We need to make a little change to what we're looking for."

"What's up, boss?" Billy asked.

"I want to target the Texas operation specifically. The contract on my head is coming out of Mexico, and I think it's going to be related to Texas!"

Brent was in my office inside of thirty minutes. I explained the changes I wanted to make in what we should be searching for and set him to work.

It wasn't until late in the afternoon that Hannah was able to dig up Clint Green. "You're not going to believe this," she said, "but he's not an attorney anymore. He's working up at Perimeter Mall…selling shoes in Macys!"

Okay, that surprised me. How do you go from having a law degree to selling shoes in a department store? "You're sure?" I asked.

She nodded. "Want me to check him out? I love shoe shopping!"

I could believe it. "Not this time, but I'll keep that in mind."

"Going to invite the doctor instead?" she asked with a smile.

Did everyone know that I was hung up on the pretty doctor who refused to show me her legs? I'm not sure if Hannah left because of the grin on my face or the fact that I was probably blushing. Oh wait! I had two days growth of beard covering my face. She couldn't tell if I was blushing or not! Whew!

I picked up my phone and dialed Cynthia. "Want to do some shoe shopping?" I asked.

"Now that is without a doubt the first time any man has used that line to get me out on a date!" she replied. "But sure, I love shoes!"

"I have another motive," I said.

"I hope so," she replied suggestively.

"Pariah's attorney is now selling shoes in Macy's."

"How the hell does an attorney wind up selling shoes?"

I love it when she sweet talks me!

Cynthia drove up to our office and I took over the driving responsibilities in my overly large SUV. On the way, I filled her in on the latest with the shooter and with focusing more on Texas.

"How soon are you looking to try again with Pariah?" she asked.

"I was thinking about next week," I replied.

"You might want to give him a bit longer to recover," she said. "His bruises have to be awfully painful still. And after the experience he just went through, he may not be ready to try it again so quick. I'd give him some time to get mentally ready again."

"How much time?" I asked.

"A month wouldn't be out of the question at all."

"Too long. I don't think we can wait that long with such a big price on his head. I was thinking more like a few days."

We settled on an extra week, although she warned me that he might not be willing even then. I hoped she was wrong, but I could also understand why Pariah would be so afraid to try again. What he must have just gone through had to be mind-shattering! But I had faith in Pariah being tougher than he looked.

We entered Macy's together like an old married couple. It took us longer to get to the shoe department than I would have liked because she kept stopping to look at things to buy. I was there for business, but business and shopping to her seemed to be much the same thing.

I flashed my badge to a worker in the shoe department and she promised to find the ex-attorney, now shoe department manager, for us right away. We still had to wait…which gave Cynthia too much time to look over the shoes.

When he finally came out, I flashed my badge and introduced myself. "We need to talk to you about a case you tried a number of years ago when you were an attorney." I told him.

"That would have to be the Thomas Clayton trial," he said without blinking an eye. "That was a long time ago."

"Was there anything out of the ordinary about it that makes it stick in your mind so much?" I asked suspiciously.

"I'll say!" he replied. "I remember it because it was the one and only case I ever handled in court."

That surprised me. "So it was your very first case?" I asked.

"And my last."

"You quit afterwards?"

"I got fired! Laid off technically, for budget reasons. One day I felt like a hot-shot attorney, the next I was out on my ass. Well, something like that. Not really so hot-shot I guess."

"You got fired because you lost the case?"

"I don't think so. Not that they told me anyway. In fact, they were kind of conciliatory toward the fact that I had lost my first case. The other attorneys all said that losing the first one was usually expected."

"So why do you think you lost? Inexperience?"

He nodded. Nothing went the way I expected it to.

"It was your first case. What did you expect?"

"To win!"

"Why is that?"

"Because the guy didn't do it. I know that for a fact."

"You know it for a fact? How can that be?"

"Because of the video tape."

"What video tape?"

"The one from the convenience store that shows him clearly on the other side of town at the time the rape was supposed to have taken place. There was no way at all that he could have done it."

I was suddenly floored. "You had a tape…that showed Thomas Clayton somewhere else…at the time of the rape?"

"Time stamped and all."

"What happened to it? I didn't see it in the transcript at all!"

"It got killed before I could even get it into evidence."

"How did that happen?" "The judge ruled that he wasn't going to look at a tape that was grainy and inconclusive. So he threw it out."

"And was it grainy and inconclusive?"

He shrugged. "It might have been a bit grainy, but not that bad. I mean, you could clearly see who it was with no trouble. You even got a flash of his license tag so we knew it was his car too."

"And you didn't argue with the judge about it?"

"I didn't get much of a chance. It was like he knew what he was going to rule before I got there, and he had already decided he wasn't going to see it."

I was stunned. "Where did you get the tape? I talked to the arresting officer already, but he didn't mention anything about a tape to me."

He smiled. "That was the one big thing I thought I had done so well back then. I found the tape myself. I was actually proud of myself for finding it and was convinced it would prove he didn't do it. I figured that the tape would be the end of everything. Instead…well, it didn't work out very well."

"How about the appeal? What happened?"

"I don't know. They let me go shortly after the trial."

"And where is the tape now?" I asked.

"I have no idea. I don't know what happened to it after that."

I pulled out one of my cards and handed it to him. "If you think of anything else that might be useful to me, please give me a call."

He looked at the card. "I guess. But I don't know what's going to be useful or not."

"I have a question," Cynthia spoke up. "How does a lawyer who's passed the bar go from that to selling shoes?"

Clint Green didn't look so comfortable with that question. "After that case, and after I got fired, I realized I was so out of my element, that I quit. Totally. I mean, the guy I had gone up against was so much better than I was that it became obvious what a total fool I had made of myself. If they hadn't let me go, the best thing I could have done anyway was to quit. I've never even thought about going back."

I knew why the attorney he was up against made him feel like such a fool. The guy was one of the biggest lawyers in the country now. A rookie fresh out of law school never stood a chance. Why would the company he worked for send out someone like him against the likes of Nathan Brecker? Of course, I guess if I was an attorney, I wouldn't want my reputation to be soiled by the likes of someone like that. So I guess I understood the company's strategy. Send out someone they don't care about. Let him take the hit instead. The only problem was, I didn't believe that was the reason at all.

"Any other questions?" I asked Cynthia. "Only one," she said. She pointed to a pair of shoes. "Do you have those in a size six and a half?"

While Cynthia tried on shoes, I puzzled over the tape he had talked about. Obviously that had been the little note in the transcript I had almost missed. Why was it always the little things like that that could be the most important?

So now my big question was…where the heck was that tape? I didn't even have any idea where to start with that question.

In the meantime, I had sinful Cynthia all to myself and a decent set of wheels. I wasn't going to waste the opportunity.

We had dinner, we talked, and then, instead of me driving her back to pick up her car, she had me drive to her apartment – so she could "show it to me." One look at just the outside and I knew she had to be out of my league. The place was modern and sleek and looked very expensive. But once we got inside, I quickly realized that when she had said she would "show it to me," she wasn't talking about her apartment at all.

She showed it to me all right! And all I could think about was what Frank Morris had called my guardian angel. She had to be it, because once again I was treated to a little piece of heaven!

CHAPTER

24

Yes, Don was angry at me for not going back to the safe house. Major angry! Blisteringly angry! Angry enough that he gave me a major dressing down right after our morning meeting. But what was he really going to do to me? I was Pariah's handler. And right now I was very valuable to the company. But it sure is nice to know you're loved.

Besides, I had phoned from Cyn's apartment to tell him I wouldn't be at the safe house that night. You'd think that would earn me at least a little consideration. Of course, I had to turn my phone off shortly after that call because it wouldn't stop ringing. I mean, I had to get some sleep, right?

A little later that morning, Don phoned me as I was trying to figure out what to do next as far as tracking down the video tape that Clint Green had told us about last night. "I just heard from the Director," he said. "He wants you to stick right here for a little while in case he needs you."

"What for?"

"He didn't say.

So I stuck around the building – even through lunch. I knew the Director was in D.C. but I couldn't imagine what he would need me for. He followed everything about Pariah so closely he probably knew more than I did about him.

It wasn't until midafternoon when the Director finally called me. "McNair? What's the chance of having Pariah available to do a bit of sightseeing in Hong Kong early tomorrow morning?"

"I'm not sure sir," I replied. "He's still pretty messed up over what happened. I get the impression he's scared. That may take some time for him to deal with and get over. But the big problem is that he doesn't have a connection to there anymore. Not since he brought the girl back with him."

"What if he went looking for a relative of someone who has family in Hong Kong?"

I thought about that for a minute. "Use that connection for him to get to Hong Kong, and then have him try to find the original building and spy on what's going on."

"You got it!" he said. "Do you think he can do it?"

"I think it's possible," I replied. "The problem is still going to be if he's willing to try."

He didn't say anything for a moment. "I understand," he replied. "Look, I need you to keep this totally quiet. I've managed to talk the CIA and State Department into forcing the Hong Kong authorities to raid that building tomorrow. I don't think we can make it happen till about five or six in the morning, your time. We're not letting anyone else know about Pariah now or what he can do, but we'd still like another pair of eyes, especially like his, telling us what's happening when they go in. Do you understand?"

"Yes sir. I'll be happy to talk to him. But I can't guarantee anything."

"Good enough. Even if he doesn't feel up to it yet, we won't really have lost anything. I'll give Wimberly the name of someone I know that I think we'll be able to use for this. Just see if you can get Pariah to help us again. If he's scared, maybe something like this will be the best thing for him. Get back on the horse so to speak. The girl has already been rescued. All he has to do is watch and let us know what's happening. No pressure."

"I'll try," I said. "But I still can't make any guarantees. This is Pariah we're dealing with. And it's hard to say what he'll agree to and what he won't."

"Just try McNair! Now, what's the latest on his case?"

"Reading through the trial transcript didn't exactly inspire any confidence at all in the idea that he didn't do it. But I did track down his defense attorney last night and two things came out that have raised some questions in my mind. First of all, the lawyer assigned by his law firm was a kid fresh out of school. That case was the lawyer's one and only trial. Right after that they fired him. And get this, he's now selling shoes in Macy's! Why send a rookie like that up against a lawyer like Nathan Brecker?"

"Sounds odd," the Director noted. "What else?"

"Just that the guy claimed that he had come up with a video tape that proved that Pariah was nowhere near the girl at the time she was supposedly raped."

"Where's the tape now?"

"He didn't know. The judge never allowed it into evidence. He said he got the impression the judge had decided on that before he even had a chance to talk to him about it."

"Hmm… Anything else?"

"Not yet. I'm trying to figure out where that tape might be – if it exists."

"Keep on it McNair. I have a few minutes this afternoon. I think I'll drop in on a few friends over at the Justice Department. See what they think."

"Thanks sir."

"You just see if you can get Pariah to help us tomorrow."

"Yes sir," I replied.

I had some misgivings about asking Pariah to try to help again so soon…especially with something where he would be going back to Hong Kong. But what choice did I have? The Director wanted me to try.

I was starting to like driving that big SUV. It was very comfortable and offered a great view of the road. And it was so heavy that when I had to drive through a big thunderstorm on the way back to the safe house, I never had the least bit of worry about it being blown all over the road… like my car usually did. I decided then and there that even if they could fix my car, I was going to get a new one…something bigger!

When I got to the safe house, it was still raining, but lightly. Pariah of course was getting the closest thing we could call to a bath since he was out in the rain. Brutus had more sense!

"Is your lady friend coming for dinner tonight?" Phil asked as I walked through the kitchen.

"I don't know," I replied. "I haven't talked to her."

He laughed. "Not since last night!"

I just grinned and pulled out my cell phone. It was a minute before she answered. "Are you coming to the safe house for dinner tonight?" I asked hopefully.

"Not tonight, Cliff. I've got to check on some other things. Besides, I doubt I could find that place on my own."

"I can pick you up," I offered.

"Don't bother. Not tonight," she replied.

What was it, she didn't like me anymore? I wasn't good enough for her last night? But there was something more she needed to know about. "I had a little chat with the Director today. He's asked me to try to get Pariah to help out with something early tomorrow morning."

"Help with what?"

"Sorry," I said. "I can't say over the phone. But it should be something similar to his usual."

"Similar?"

I made no reply.

"Cliff! You know he's not ready for anything like that! What he went through was unimaginably traumatic! Don't even try to put him through this!"

"I'm afraid I have no choice. The Director said try to convince him, so that's what I'm going to do. Maybe it will be good for him. Boost his confidence."

"And maybe it will destroy him completely! He's not ready!"

"For the record, I agree with you. But I still have to try."

"Don't!"

"Sorry,"

"Damn you! What time are you doing it?"

"I plan to get him to work sometime around four AM."

"Cliff, that's…" She stopped talking for a moment. Then she said, "Oh my God! That's…"

"Don't say it!" I warned. "Not over the phone!"

"This still isn't right!"

"I know. See you then." I hung up. Suddenly I wasn't too sure about my relationship with her. But really, what choice did I have?

I didn't approach Pariah with the idea until after dinner. I wanted him to have a full stomach and to be at his most sane…in other words – agreeable. We had toweled him somewhat dry before we ate, but his clothes were still all wet. I knew better than to try to get him to change them. "Pariah," I said, "I need to ask you something."

He said nothing, but he looked at me. At least I knew I had his full attention.

"The Director would like you to help us with something early tomorrow morning. He's arranged for the police to go into that building you found in Hong Kong and try to rescue all those girls there. He wants to know if you can go to Hong Kong like you did before and just report what's going on during the raid. No pressure. No worries. Just tell us what goes on." I looked at him hopefully. His face changed very slowly, but it did indeed change. And not for the better.

Very slowly, I saw the fear and distress creep back into him. He started shaking. He started quietly whining. His eyes seemed to glass over – they certainly weren't focused anymore on the world I was looking at. I was pretty sure he was once again reliving the traumatic experience he had just been through and had not yet recovered from.

He finally shook his head, ever so slightly. "No, no…" he managed to get out, his eyes still looking somewhere that I couldn't see.

"Pariah," I said. "There'll be no pressure on you. Nothing at all you have to worry about. We know someone with relatives who live there. You can use that person to go to Hong Kong and then just find that building again."

But I don't think he heard me. His voice was almost crying. "No… Please no…"

"Okay buddy," I said. "If you don't feel you're up to it, then we won't make you do it. Okay? Forget about it."

I still don't think he heard me. He certainly didn't move from his seat at the table. I got up and walked away, just so he would know I wasn't going to push him anymore on the issue. And to tell the truth, I'm glad he didn't agree. I knew from the start that he wasn't ready for it yet. And maybe him not doing it would help to get me back into Cynthia's good graces.

While Pariah sat at the table staring into space, I quietly helped Phil with the dishes. Then I pulled out my cell phone and called Cynthia again. "You'll be happy to know he doesn't want to do it," I told her.

"That's a relief," she replied. "You should have never asked him in the first place!"

"If it's any consolation," I said, "I didn't want to. I only did it at the Director's orders."

"That doesn't make it any better!" she replied.

I wanted to argue something back, but Pariah was suddenly by my side. Surprised because it was so out of character for him, I told Cynthia, "Hold on. Pariah's here." I turned my full attention to the still wet wretch in front of me. "What is it, Pariah?"

"If I do this," he said, "will you do something for me?"

"Pariah, you don't have to do this. You know I'll do anything for you. Anything! Just ask." He certainly had my full attention now. He had never asked me to do anything for him before.

"Before I die…" he started, then he seemed to back up and try to start again. "All I want…" But he still couldn't seem to find the right words."

"Pariah, what are you talking about? You're not dying."

He shook his head. "All I want before I die…"

Again he paused, as if it was the most difficult thing in the world to ask.

"Is…for everyone to know…I didn't do it." His sigh of relief was such that I could almost feel it physically.

I stared at him for a long time before I answered. "Buddy…I'm already working on it. If there's any way at all…any chance…I'll make sure it happens. And that's a promise! Believe me!"

He stared at me for a moment then blinked and nodded. "I'll do it," he replied. "I'll go find the sick girls again."

Very sadly, he turned and walked away. And at the same time, I heard Cynthia's voice yelling over the phone, "Noooo!"

I felt like a total heel. I had promised the Director I would ask…and now Pariah would help again. But it was the promise I had just made to Pariah that I vowed would be my one main calling in life – until I could fulfill it – just the way he wanted.

The alarm on my watch went off at three in the morning. I forced myself to get out of bed and wash my face. The good thing about my decision not to shave for a while was that it saved me a lot of time.

As I headed for Pariah's room to wake him up, I came across one of the security guards making a tour of the house.

"Oh! Agent McNair!" the guard said, somewhat surprised to see me. He was the one that I recognized from the company's little prison where Pariah had stayed a few days. "I heard some noise and was just investigating. Is everything all right?"

"Just fine," I replied. "I'm glad you checked. I see you managed to arrange for some more overtime here."

He smiled. "I need it. I still have two years left before I graduate school. Then I can apply to become a regular full time agent."

"So that's what it's all about," I said happily. "Well, good luck. And for the record, I think you'll make a great agent. Let me know if you need my help with anything."

"Thanks sir," he replied. "Um…are you leaving now?"

I nodded. "Got to go to work."

"Well, good luck," he said as he turned and walked back the way he came. I saw him pause to look back just as I was going into Pariah's room to wake him up. He nodded and disappeared around the corner.

At least Pariah was sleeping on top of the bed. He didn't always. But he was still wearing his wet clothes and of course, not a single cover over top of him. I shook him awake. "Pariah," I said softly. "It's time to get ready to go."

He didn't startle awake like I expected. He simply opened his eyes and sat up on the side of the bed. But there was still some distress in his eyes. He wasn't looking forward to this, and I couldn't blame him. Since he didn't need to do anything to get ready, I could have left him sleeping a few more minutes. I still had to finish getting dressed. A little while later, I got him and his still damp clothes into the back seat of the SUV and the guard let me out through the gate.

There were no street lights along that stretch of road. It was too far out in the country for lights of any kind. I turned my high-beams on in an effort to watch for any deer that might be lurking – just to terrify all the unwary drivers, but even still, I drove a bit slower and more cautiously because of it.

We were almost out to the highway when I went around a bend in the road and saw a pickup truck parked on the side of the road. I automatically slowed down because I would have to go over into the other lane a bit to go around him. And then the loudest bang I had ever heard in my life came from the windshield in front of my face. It scared me enough that I automatically slammed on the brakes. My mind was still dazed by the sound when another one came, again right in front of my face. My reactions were definitely slow! I was being shot at! Again!

Just like I had done the last time, I rammed the vehicle I was driving into reverse and pounded my foot down on the gas. It was only as I was driving backwards that I realized why I wasn't dead. Bulletproof glass! This was a specially made bullet proof vehicle. No wonder it felt so heavy! And just then I was thanking my lucky stars for every bit of the bullet proof shielding!

Two more bangs hit my windshield before I got back around the bend enough to be out of sight of the pickup. I didn't want to turn around and see what the windshield looked like. I was just glad it was still there.

I realized Pariah was making some kind of distress noise as he tried to roll himself up into a ball despite his seatbelt. He didn't get far and started rocking back and forth instead. "Easy buddy," I said reassuringly, even though I myself felt anything but reassured. Okay, I was just plain scared!

I kept driving – backwards. As soon as I thought I had gone far enough, I turned the vehicle around – which took more time than I liked – and stomped on the gas once again. I could see a few dings in the windshield, but in the dark night, that's all I could see. I dug out my cell phone and in a total panic, called for help.

It's a good thing that no deer were in my way, because they would have been flattened in an instant as I pushed the big SUV back toward the safe house. My heart was still racing a mile a minute. I had been shot at…again! I desperately watched every little piece of the road I could see, checking for more snipers. I was starting to see them behind every little tree.

The driveway to the safe house finally came into view ahead and I started pounding on the horn to get the guard's attention. It must have worked because the gate was slowly opening in front of me by the time I got there.

I rolled down the window to warn the guard, but I heard him asking, " Forget something?" as I started yelling.

"Close the gate! We're under attack!" Once again I stomped on the gas and got the car rolling again. I pulled up right in front of the door. Five seconds later I was trying to get Pariah out of the car and into the house. All my commotion had alerted the other guards and they came running, fortunately, they opened the front door in the process. "Watch for a shooter!" I yelled as I pulled Pariah out of the car and ran him up the steps into the house where I finally let go of him. He didn't stop running though. I was afraid he would go straight outside, but he didn't. He ran to his room instead. When I got there, his door was closed. I found him huddling on the floor behind his bed.

Brutus ran in and straight to him. Pariah picked the little dog up in his arms and hugged it to his chest as he rocked back and forth, scared out of his wits. I did my best to try to comfort him, to reassure him, but he ignored me completely.

My phone rang and I answered it. It was Don. "What's happening?" he yelled.

"We got shot at again as we were coming in!"

"Are you okay?"

"We're fine, but Pariah is major stressed out. I can't calm him down!"

"Where are you?"

"Back at the safe house again."

"Good! Stay there!" he replied. "I'll head that way as soon as I can!"

While I waited, I left Pariah where he was and went out to check the perimeter myself. All the guards seemed to be actively watching everything and there were now two guards at the front gate. "See anything?" I asked them.

"All quiet," one of them replied.

That was good. I didn't think my nerves could take much more tonight.

The first car to come screaming up was Frank Morris, and I was awfully glad to see him. Two other cars came through the gate shortly after. I offered to go with Frank to show him where the shooting happened, but he told me to stay put. They would find it themselves. He didn't need me getting shot when there was no need for me to be out there in the first place. To tell the truth, I was kind of glad not to go. I was getting more and more gun shy with each passing day!

Don finally arrived right after Frank and his boys left. I was surprised to see Cynthia driving his car. Don was on the phone when they pulled in. Cynthia got out quickly, but he stayed in the car and talked.

"Are you all right?" she asked as she ran up to me.

"I'm fine," I replied as if I wasn't the least bit scared anymore. Hey! You've got to play it tough for the women!

"You imbecile!" she suddenly yelled full of anger. I told you not to take him tonight! I told you it's too soon! All this could have been avoided if you had just listened to me! But no! You've got to go playing the big hero. You've got to drag him out when he's clearly not ready for anything! Drag him off where there's a good chance he could get more seriously mentally hurt than he already is!"

I love it when women are so understanding.

"Now where is he?"

"In his room," I replied.

She left me and hurried straight into the house. I wasn't sure if I wanted to follow her or not. The decision was taken away from me.

"Cliff!" I noticed that Don was finally getting out of the car. "What happened tonight?"

Once again I went through exactly what had happened. He took it all in, but didn't say much. Instead he got back on his phone and started making more calls. I decided to take my chances inside now and check on Cynthia and Pariah.

I found them on the floor together, still behind Pariah's bed. Brutus of course was in Pariah's lap. Cynthia was talking softly to Pariah, but I got the impression he wasn't saying much…as usual. But he suddenly looked up straight at me. "Promise?" he asked.

"Promise!" I replied solemnly. And I meant it too!

CHAPTER

25

I didn't go into work that day, Don wouldn't let me – something about reviewing security on Pariah and me. I wasn't buying it much. I think he just wanted to make sure I stayed out of the way of the investigation into the shooting…and stayed in a place where he didn't have to worry about me. To make sure I didn't go anywhere, he took the big SUV that had saved my life – in order to have it analyzed and checked over. Okay, that part I believed and was glad of. I was hoping they would replace that windshield too with a fresh one that would continue to hold up as well as the current one had.

But having nothing to do gave me time to think…and since the last shooting was foremost on my mind, I started going through all the little details I could think of. First of all, how did the shooter know I would be driving down that stretch of road in the middle of the night last night? And for that matter, how did he know what kind of car I was driving? And now that I thought about it, since the road led to the safe house, he most likely knew where the new safe house was. How?

The answers to those questions were not something I wanted to think about, even though it was something we had suspected for a long time now. And all the answers were really only one answer – someone had to tell him! Someone who knew where the safe house was! Someone who knew what kind of car they had given me to drive! And someone who knew I was leaving in the middle of the night! Or more likely, someone who knew exactly when I had left the safe house. The shooter had been tipped off!

Because of that, I was convinced that the informer had to be someone who had been in the house last night...or at least on the grounds. I immediately eliminated Pariah, myself, and Phil. And I seriously doubted that Brutus was going to be making any phone calls. That left only the guards. I remembered speaking to the one in the house while I was getting ready, and also the one at the gate when I went out. The third one I had never seen, but I couldn't leave him out either. All of them were possibilities.

But then I realized one other horrible possibility. Doctor Won't-Show-Me-Her-Legs Westmore also knew I would be driving from the safe house to the office, and she had a pretty good idea of what time I would be on the road...and, she had been to the safe house before. As much as I didn't want to believe she had done it, I simply couldn't cross her off my list.

I would have questioned her about it, but she had already departed with Don when he left. I would have questioned the guards too, but all of them had left with the shift change. Stuck...with no one to talk to except Pariah and Phil. And Pariah didn't talk much. And Phil was busy trying to figure out how he was going to manage such a big house while we were there. So I cracked open a beer and sat out on the elegant patio to brood over not being able to do anything at all. In other words, I was bored!

Frank Morris called once to tell me that his guys had actually located four shells from the area of the shooting and he was pretty sure they were going to match the type of bullets they had pulled out of my car. I didn't know if that was good news or bad. I wasn't even sure if it was progress. But I thanked him just the same.

Don called me a little while later and I took the opportunity to pass on my suspicions about the guards. I also reluctantly admitted that I also couldn't write Doctor Westmore off my list either – although I was quick to point out that I seriously wasn't considering her a suspect. At least he thanked me and said he would look into all of them...including the good doctor. I hated that part, but it had to be done. And now, preferably by someone who wasn't so close to her.

And then the Director called. He asked how Pariah and I were doing. I told him better than expected, but I highly recommended we wait a few weeks before even asking for Pariah's help again. He told me he thought it might be a good idea – under the circumstances. And under the circumstances, I felt relieved about it.

I asked about the raid. He told me it went down, and there was a lot of shooting and a number of police were killed in the process. But "some" of the girls were rescued…alive. Others had been killed by their captors during the raid. That was bad news. But at least the place had been shut down and eliminated.

And then he asked me one more question. "Anything new on Pariah's case?"

"I wish," I said. "Right now I'm stuck here at the safe house with no way to do much of anything." I almost left it at that, but there was one thing I could add now. "Um…" I said before he could reply to my last comment. "There is one thing that I probably should add."

"What's that?"

"Last night, Pariah asked me for something. He's never done that before."

"What does he want?"

"All he wants is for everyone to know he didn't do it…before he dies. And Director, I promised him I would do everything in my power to accomplish just that. And it's a promise I intend to keep."

He didn't say anything for a moment, and then he asked. "And do you believe he's innocent?"

I don't know if I made the leap of faith then, or if I had already made up my mind earlier. But saying it fully committed me to the belief. "Yes…I do!"

"Good! Because I made a little trip over to Justice yesterday and had a chat with a few acquaintances there. They're sending one of their people down to help you on this case specifically. So you'll have good advice to work from."

That surprised me. "Thanks! That will be a big help."

"Actually, it didn't take all that much," he said. "All I had to do was to mention Chermont and Brecker in the same sentence and I think it raised a few red flags."

After the Director's call, I spent more time sitting there trying to put the pieces together. But it's hard to put together a puzzle when you're missing most of the surrounding pieces.

As I sat there, I saw Pariah and Brutus touring the yard. I guess since there was so much more yard than at Phil's house and so much more vegetation too, he didn't feel so obligated to stay in just the one spot all the time. I was glad to see him moving around. It made me feel like he was dealing with his problems pretty well. Was he really as fragile as Doctor Westmore had thought? I had no way of knowing.

As I watched his odd struggling walk, my mind started to wonder what could have damaged his legs so badly that it made him walk that way. And for that matter, what had damaged the rest of his body so badly too. It was another little puzzle I decided I had better get a handle on pretty soon. If we were trying to find out everything we could about the man, that should certainly be a big part.

Since I had nothing better to work on at the time, I got up and went out to walk with him and Brutus. I said nothing for a little while. I just wandered around from place to place with him, looking at the trees and shrubs. Okay, the place was a veritable park! A beautiful one! But staring at the bushes didn't hold the same appeal for me as it did for him. So I finally broached the question. "Pariah, how are you holding up after last night?"

He didn't look at me, but at least he replied. "Scared," he said.

"I believe it," I replied. "I think I'm still a bit scared too. And how are you feeling about your little trip to Hong Kong?"

His reply was exactly the same, and again he didn't look at me. "Scared."

Well that was to be expected too. I wandered with him for a few more minutes while he investigated the leaves on the bushes and trees. "Pariah," I started. "How did you get injured so badly? The Doctor says almost all your bones have been broken many times. How did it happen?"

It's amazing how completely invisible he could make me feel, as if my spoken words never left my mouth. I tried again. "Pariah, can you tell me how you got hurt? Please? I have to know."

I think that if he had turned in my direction he might have tried to walk right through me…because he acted completely as if I wasn't there. I knew from experience that I wasn't going to get an answer to my question. It was another of those little things he wasn't going to talk about. I'd just have to figure it out the hard way…just like everything else.

I walked back to the house and pulled another beer out of the refrigerator. At that point, I started to worry about how many I might wind up drinking all day. But what the heck, I couldn't go into the office to get anything done anyway. I grabbed my phone again and called Cynthia. It was almost an hour before she called me back. "What's up Cliff? How's Pariah."

"Better than expected," I replied. "He says he's scared, but he and Brutus have been doing more walking around the yard than I've ever seen him do. I think he's getting over everything just fine."

"Good," she replied. "But let's not push him!"

"Don't worry, I won't. Listen, in your little talks with him, did he ever tell you how he got injured so badly? How his bones got so messed up?"

"No. I've asked him a few times, but all I ever get to that one is the silent treatment."

"Yeah, that's what I just got too. I'm thinking it's long past time we tried to find out what happened to him."

"Good!" she replied. "Let me know if I can help!"

"Are you coming here again tonight?" I asked.

"No, not tonight. After last night you had me scared out of my wits! I think I'll take a long hot bath tonight and just sleep. See you tomorrow though. My schedule should ease up a bit…hopefully."

I said goodbye. She wasn't coming…again. Was my little piece of heaven gone? I hoped not.

So the new question was, how did I go about finding out what happened to Pariah? We had a picture of him from before prison that showed him as perfectly all right. So that left either prison or after prison. Hopefully, there would be one quick way to narrow those two options down to one. I grabbed my phone again and called Hannah. "How busy are you?" I asked.

"Ugh! John has us trying to match up pictures of the dead girls from the Hong Kong raid to see if we can figure out who they are."

"How many of them weren't Chinese?"

"Most of them. We think we've already identified two. We have twelve more to go."

"Geez! That's a lot!"

"Tell me about it!"

"Listen, do you think you can take a break to find me some information?"

"Sure, anything to get away from this for a little while."

"See if you can get me the number of anyone who might have seen Pariah either just before he left prison, or right after."

"Got it. I'll call you back."

Hannah was the best researcher I had. Some people just had a talent for it. And she had it!

She called me back about twenty minutes later. "Cliff, listen, if you don't want to go through the prison switchboard system, I found the name of someone who was "technically" his parole officer."

"What does technically mean?"

"It means that he was released on parole, but only just barely. The guy served almost all of the sixteen year sentence he was given. So he wasn't in the program long at all."

It was rare that someone wasn't given some chance at parole. Why wait until his sentence was almost complete? "Thanks, Hannah. I appreciate it."

I phoned the number Hannah had given me and was rewarded to hear the parole officer pick up the line almost immediately. I introduced myself, then said, "I'm trying to find some information on a former parolee of yours, named Thomas Clayton."

"Sorry," he said. "The name doesn't ring a bell at all."

"It would have been a few years ago. He wasn't on parole very long."

He seemed to sigh a bit. "Give me a minute to look him up in the computer. You said Thomas Clayton?"

"Yes," I replied. Then I spelled his last name out so there would be no mistakes. I had to wait while he apologized for his computer being so slow. I knew how he felt. There were days I wanted to throw mine through the window!

Finally he found the record. "Oh yeah, I remember him now," he said. "The monster!"

"The what?"

"Sorry," he replied. "Look, the guy was all messed up…physically and mentally. At least he was that way the two whole times I actually saw him. After that, well, I wasn't too worried about seeing him again and his parole term was so close that I didn't really care."

"So his injuries occurred before he saw you?" I asked.

"Injuries? I guess you could call them that. Were you referring to anything specific, cause I've got a picture here. Let me tell you though, I remember this one now because the guy gave me the creeps."

"Let's see," I said. "Was his nose all twisted so he couldn't breathe out of it? And how about his hands, did they look normal? And did it look like his legs would hardly hold him up?"

"Yeah, that's the guy. All of that. And, I remember he wasn't right in the head either. If I remember correctly, he could hardly talk at all.

"Couldn't talk? Or wouldn't talk?"

"Couldn't! I think it was because he was so messed up in the head. He did try though. He kept trying and trying to say things, but he couldn't seem to manage to put two words together coherently. I don't understand why they gave him a regular parole instead of a medical one."

It sounded strange to me too. I asked him to fax the picture to my office. I knew where I needed to start looking for my answers. Prison! All I needed now was a way to get there. I needed…transportation!

It was getting too late in the day to do much more anyway. Hopefully, tomorrow Don would let me have the SUV back again. In the meantime, I made another phone call to Hannah again. "It looks like we're going to have to look a lot harder into what happened to him in prison," I told her. "See if you can find out who he bunked with during his stay. Also, maybe I should start with the warden's office too. See if you can get me an appointment with him first."

"I'm on it," she said. "By the way, we've identified another girl."

"Good!" I replied. "Keep at it. That's more important than my stuff right now."

"But your stuff isn't so depressing," she replied.

"Don't be so sure," I said. "Prison is awfully depressing no matter how you look at it."

"Point taken, but it's still better than looking at mutilated bodies."

"You win," I replied. "Just do what you can for me."

It was close to the end of the day when she called me back. "Cliff, I set up an appointment for you with the warden at ten o'clock tomorrow morning? Can you make that?"

"I don't see why not, unless Don won't let me leave this place again. It's possible I may need a lift though."

"He can't keep you there forever! And if you need a ride, just let me know. I'll be happy to get out of working this stuff – even if it involves hanging around someplace like prison."

"Thanks," I replied. "Hopefully I'll be able to finagle a car."

Now that I had a reason to really need a car, I phoned Don. "I'm going to need a car again tomorrow," I told him. "I'd prefer to have that SUV again if it's available. By the way, I'm thinking of buying one – just like that! Armor plating and all!"

"Not funny!" he replied. "You have no idea what that beast costs."

"I don't care. It saved my life."

"Yeah, it did definitely do that! Four shots, all of them hit the windshield. Three of them fairly close together."

"I'm just amazed it didn't break!" I told him.

"So am I," he replied. "The shooter knew how to use that gun."

"So can I have it?"

"No. It's going to be laid up in the shop till we can get the windshield replaced."

"I'm going to need something else then," I told him. "I'm looking into Pariah's case and I have an appointment with the warden tomorrow morning."

"Does it have to be tomorrow? It won't hurt you to cool your heels for another day."

"I'm bored!" I said. "I need something to work on! And I'm better protected at work there than I am here."

"But the problem is getting you between there and here! And I'm not too keen on you driving around town either! I'll think about it and let you know tomorrow!"

That wasn't exactly the answer I wanted to hear. He didn't say yes, and he didn't say no. And I wasn't looking forward to spending another day doing nothing – even if it was in such a luxurious place. Now if Sinful Cynthia were here to keep me company…that would be a different story!

26

Heavenly Cynthia had told me she was just going to take a bath and go to bed, so I was surprised when she walked in shortly before dinner time with a couple of large pizzas. One meat-lovers, and one that was only ham and pineapple – her favorite. At least she was thinking of me with the meat-lovers…or was she thinking more about Phil? Oh well, I was just glad to see her.

"Any luck with Pariah's case?" she asked as I was extracting a slice of the meet-lover's from the box.

"I talked with his parole officer," I told her. He called Pariah 'the monster'. Says he was that way when he got out of prison. And…he also said he could hardly talk. Not because he didn't want to, but because he couldn't. He tried, but evidently it was difficult for him. He wasn't able to string words together or something. He attributed it to him being mentally messed up."

She looked at me with something of a shocked look on her face. "Couldn't talk? But he tried? Oh Cliff! That puts a slightly different spin on things. That means that for the last few years since he got out of prison, he's been trying to overcome a disability. Kind of like when someone has a stroke and they lose the ability to speak clearly. If they go through therapy, they can usually regain most of the ability they had, if not all of it. Something similar must have happened to him, only he hasn't had the benefit of the therapy. I don't understand how something like that could happen in prison – and they didn't do anything about it!"

"Neither do I. And get this. He was sentenced to sixteen years – a pretty stiff sentence since the absolute max for a first time offender is twenty. But they didn't let him out on parole till just a few months before his entire sentence was over. And if he's so messed up, he should have been out much earlier on a medical parole!"

"So why wasn't he?"

"I'm supposed to see the warden tomorrow morning about that." I looked up then and noticed Don walking in. I raised my voice a bit so he could hear me. "If...I can get that SUV back again tomorrow."

"No dice!" Don said flatly as he walked in. "All right! Pizza!" he exclaimed happily. He bypassed the one with pineapple and pulled one of the meet-lover slices out of the box and started eating it.

"I need a car!" I argued. "I have things to do!"

"Yeah, I heard you," he replied. "But that SUV is going to be laid up for a little while."

"How about another car?"

"I'm working on it," he replied.

"I can take you," Cynthia said. "I'll be glad to."

"Prison is no place for a lady!" I told her.

"Hey," she said, "I'll have you know that I worked on a special study for two years with prisoners as part of my doctorate. I think I can handle it just fine!"

Don and I both looked at her totally surprised. "What kind of study?" Don asked.

"I was looking for a correlation between the type of crimes they committed, and sleep habits."

Okay, that one floored me. Talk about dumb! "And what did you discover?" I asked.

"It was inconclusive," she replied.

I had no doubt about that at all!

"So how about it?" she asked. "Do you need a ride or not?"

I looked at Don. He looked back and forth between Cynthia and me. "Shit!" he finally said. "I guess we got to get you out of here sooner or later. I'd just rather it was later. Okay," he said. "But...you got to promise me to find a different way out of here, one that no one will expect you to take! And keep your head down McNair! We're still working on finding that shooter!"

Freedom! "What's happening with that?" I asked.

"We're working on it!" he replied.

"I'd think you'd do like those shows on TV," Cynthia said. "Where they just trace the cell phone and see where the guy is."

"What cell phone?" I asked. "As far as I know, we don't know who he is or what his cell number is. Besides, it isn't as easy as they show on TV."

"Actually," Don spoke up, "we think we do have his number."

"What?"

"Late this afternoon we got all the phone records from the guards who were here last night. One of them made a couple of calls shortly before you left here and then another one right after you left. All of them to an unregistered phone."

"Can't you trace him from that?" Cynthia asked.

"Like Cliff said, it's not that easy!" Don replied. "You can't just push a button and instantly know everything you want. It takes time and coordination. We're working on it."

"I'm sure it does," Cynthia replied. "It's just that all the shows make it look so easy."

"Well this isn't TV. Just getting through all the red-tape is half the battle."

"So what's your next move?" I asked.

"Morris is looking into it," he replied.

I knew I wasn't going to get any more out of him on the subject. It wasn't my investigation – even though I was intimately involved in the problem.

So that left me with only one more thing that I had to figure out…how did I get Cynthia to agree to spend the night? In the end, she didn't. She went home instead to take that good long hot bath she had wanted. Drat!

Cyn was back again early the next morning though and I gladly climbed into her sporty little car. Going out through the gate however sent chills down my spine. She went the opposite direction from the only way I knew, but I was still constantly searching the road for any possible threat. I never thought it would be so difficult to go for a simple little drive! Once we finally reached the highway, by a very round-about route, I started to feel much better and we made better time.

When we got there, I discovered that Cynthia hadn't been kidding about her work with prisoners. Not only did she know where the prison was, she seemed to be old acquaintances with several of the guards as they checked us in.

"I didn't realize you had worked in this prison," I said.

"Actually, I worked in several," she replied. "This was just one of them."

"Big study!"

"Very big," she replied.

"But inconclusive"

"Don't remind me!"

The warden was expecting us when we got there and we went right in. He was very surprised to see the doctor with me, and I was surprised to see that they knew each other. I was fast figuring out that Doctor 'Sinthia' got around more than I realized.

"I understand you're looking for information on Thomas Clayton?" he asked.

"Yes," I replied. "Specifically, what happened to him while he was in here."

He nodded. "That I can't really say, but I can tell you this. Booting him out of here was one of my first acts when I took over as warden three years ago. And I remember him specifically because of it."

"Why is that?" I asked.

"Several reasons. First of all, the guy was physically a mess. His medical record was one of the fattest I've ever seen! And when I met him, something had recently happened to his head, leaving him with some impaired abilities that our doctors here couldn't handle."

"Why wasn't he released on medical parole?" I asked.

He grunted. "Money and politics! Plus I was new on the block and problems like his were not the kind of thing we wanted listed on more… public…records. If I had it to do now though, it would have gone that way, only faster."

Money and politics. I didn't want to believe it, but I did. "So what happened to him?" I asked. "How did he get such a big medical file?"

He shook his head. "I have no idea. It's not in the records at all! It wasn't in the records when I took over here. You'll have to ask Hugh Ogilvie, the warden before me."

"Is there any chance I can get a copy of his medical record?" Cynthia asked.

"I can send a copy to the FBI," he replied. "Will that work for you?"

"Perfectly," Cyn replied with a smile.

"How about why he wasn't offered parole until his term was all but up?" I asked.

"Again, ask Hugh. Other than his immense medical record, everything else about him seems to be mysteriously missing."

"How about who he bunked with?" I asked.

He smiled. "Now that much I can tell you." He looked down toward his notes. "The whole time he was here, he was in with Angelo Chavez. Chavez is doing a rather lengthy term for repeated armed robbery. I wouldn't imagine he was the best of company for Mr. Clayton to live with."

"Can we talk with him?" I asked.

He nodded. "I'll set it up right away. Anything else I can do for you?"

"Just one other thing. How do I get in touch with the former warden?"

He dug into his desk drawer and rooted around for a minute. Finally, he pulled his hand out with a business card and tossed it over to me. "That should help you out," he said.

Before going in to see Chavez, I took a good look at Cynthia. "Maybe you should stay here and let me talk to him alone. Having a woman in there with him might make things awfully uncomfortable – for you!"

"Don't give me that crap Cliff! I spent two years working with the prisoners here. Remember?"

Well, I tried.

Chavez wasn't considered any kind of risk, so he wasn't handcuffed or chained in any way at all. They had simply put him into a very depressing little room with nothing but a table and a few chairs. The guards weren't in the room, but they were staying close by – just in case. When we walked in, he couldn't seem to take his eyes off of Cynthia. Actually, I couldn't blame him. I took the time to study him for a moment. Latino. Tough. Heavily muscled. He had the look of someone who had spent the last twenty years in jail and knew his way around – which I'm sure he did.

"Who the hell are you?" he asked after finally taking his eyes off of the doctor.

I showed him my badge. "FBI," I replied.

He seemed very surprised. "Why is the FBI asking me questions now? I've been here for almost twenty damn years! Nothing I did before should matter to you now!"

"I'm not interested in you," I replied. "I want to know about Thomas Clayton."

I saw him blink with surprise. "Who?"

"You heard me, Thomas Clayton. You bunked with him for sixteen years!"

"Bunked with… I shared a cell with…" And then his face seemed to change. "Geez! Was that his real name? You got to be talking about Toyboy!"

Now it was my turn to be surprised. "Toyboy?"

"Yeah, that's what we called him. For as long as I can remember."

"Why is that?"

He smiled. "You figure it out!"

"Tell me something," I said, "how did he get hurt so much?"

Instead of answering, he leaned back in his chair and crossed his arms. "I know how these things work," he said as a sly smile crossed his face. "You want answers? Then you do something for me!"

"Like what?"

He leaned forward. "Like get me out of here. I still got ten years to go. I'd like to see my old lady again before I croak!"

"How about I leave you here for an extra ten years for not cooperating?" I asked instead.

He leaned back in his chair again and re-crossed his arms. "Go ahead. I probably won't know the difference, and you won't get any info you need. And I got plenty I can tell you. Plenty!"

"Like what?"

He just smiled. "Not till I get a signed deal on the table."

The guy was going to play difficult. "If I *try* to arrange this for you, what kind of information can you give us?"

He leaned forward again. "Just about everything you want!"

"Like what?" I asked again.

"Oh…like why we called him Toyboy. Like why the guy kept getting beat to a pulp. Like who the warden made a certain deal with."

The mention of the warden and a deal had my full attention.

"And why should I get all that out of you and not simply go ask a few others around here?"

He smiled broadly at me. "Because of the reason you decided to talk to me in the first place. I shared a cell with him the whole time he was here. I know everything there is to know about him. Things that nobody else here knows."

Okay, he had a point. Nobody else would know the things that he would. "I'll be back," I told him. "And I'll look into your request. But you know I can't promise you anything."

"You want what I know, and I want that signed piece of paper on the table."

I nodded. "I'll check on it."

He looked back at Cynthia again. "And make sure you bring her back with you. Damn woman, you is the finest piece of ass I've seen in a long time."

"She's the only piece of ass you've seen!" I said angrily as I got to my feet.

The guards opened the door and I got Cynthia out of there and back to her car as quickly as possible.

"What are you going to do?" she asked as she drove out through the prison gate.

"Just what he wants," I replied. "I'll talk to someone about cutting him a deal. He mentioned too many things that I want to know about."

"I want to know too!" she said. "And what did he mean about a deal with the warden?"

"I have a feeling that I should talk to Chavez again before I go looking for the former warden. I want to arm myself with information first."

"Sounds like a good idea," she replied.

"Chavez was right about one thing though," I added.

"What's that?"

"You are definitely the best looking piece of ass I've seen in a long time!"

The comment earned me a big sly smile. Was heavenly Cynthia back again? Hope! Hope! Hope!

CHAPTER

27

Cynthia dropped me off at the office and went back to her normal "abnormal" patients. John filled me in on the latest, which was that they had tentatively identified about half of the dead girls from the Hong Kong raid now, but it was getting more and more difficult. Many of them we had no idea what country they had come from in the first place.

I phoned Don and passed on my request to look into Chavez's demand. He promised to get back to me.

While I waited, I started adding my latest notes to Pariah's file. The file was slowly growing. Not only did it now contain all my notes, but also the picture the parole officer had sent. I took a minute to closely compare the two pictures. No doubt about it, he had been through hell in prison. Something major wrong had to have happened for that kind of difference. On a whim, I phoned the tech lab and asked if they could come up with a few pictures of Pariah from the tapes we made when he went off finding someone. They said it would be no problem. I figured all of it would make good evidence – hopefully.

Pariah's file grew by a big amount when his prison medical file arrived. I had Hannah print out every single little page and bind it all into one big folder for me. I wanted to keep it separate from the rest of the stuff we had.

I had just opened the file and started trying to make heads or tails out of the medical terms when Don called, "Cliff! My office. Now!"

He could be so chatty sometimes!

When I walked in, I was surprised to see Frank Morris there. "What's up?" I asked as I took a seat.

"Remember that cell phone number I told you about?"

"You caught the guy?" I asked hopefully.

"No, but we have a general idea of where he is."

"So we know who tipped him off then."

"Definitely!"

"And of course you arrested him."

"Nope!"

Okay, I was surprised. "Why not?"

Instead of answering, he threw a stack of papers at me. "That's the translated transcript of a tap we managed to get on the shooter's phone," Don said.

"Translated?" I asked.

"My Spanish isn't all that great," Don replied. "You want the original?"

"Not really." I spoke some Spanish, but I wasn't all that great with it either.

Morris took over. "The guy's name is Raul. It was his brother Juan that we pulled out of the tree near Phil's house. Both are known to work with Pacheco. From the tap, we've managed to confirm that Raul is talking to Pacheco himself. Directly!"

"Directly?"

"You got it. Raul isn't happy about his brother Juan now being in our custody, and it seems that Pacheco isn't too happy about some other things. If you read that, you'll notice the mention of Hong Kong in there."

I smiled. "We found the right breaking house!"

"That you did," Don said. "Unbelievably, out of probably dozens, you picked the right one."

"We must be doing something right," I said happily.

"Or wrong!" Morris replied.

Huh? "Why wrong?"

He smiled at me, but it wasn't a happy smile. "You'll be happy to learn that Pacheco has cancelled the contract on both you and Pariah."

Now I was really happy. "Now that's good news!"

He shook his head. "Not really. It doesn't say *how* in those conversations there, but it looks like he's somehow managed to put two and two together and now he's blaming Pariah for the raid in Hong Kong too."

That troubled me! My happy mood started sinking fast! "And?" I asked, knowing that whatever he was about to say wouldn't be good.

"And…he's made it personal! He's declared war directly on you two!"

Okay, that much I realized was bad. My happy mood was totally gone now, completely replaced by images of bullets hitting my windshield in the middle of the night. It was a feeling I didn't like at all. Basically, it was rooted directly in fear.

"Any openings available in Alaska?" I asked. "Or how about someplace like the Antarctic?" I was dead serious, but naturally they both ignored me.

"We're not arresting anybody yet," Morris said. "We're not arresting them because the taps we have on Raul's phone and the guard he's been talking to are the only way we have to track anything that Pacheco is sending against you and Pariah."

As troubling and wrong as it sounded, I realized that was actually a good thing. They were doing their best to keep me alive. Pariah too of course…okay, mostly Pariah.

"So what has Pacheco deemed fit to hit me with now?" I asked.

"He's sending a team this time to work with Raul. No details. We only know it will be a few days before they get here since they'll be driving."

"And what do you want me to do?"

"Just what you're doing now," Don replied. "No changes in your routine. Keep working Pariah's case and anything else your office needs to handle."

No changes? I didn't have a routine lately. "Isn't there anything I can do?" I asked. The whole business sounded awfully risky to me.

I saw Don look over at Morris before he looked back at me. "One thing maybe that you could do to help us. Before you leave to go anywhere, you call either me or Frank. And if you should happen to see the same car following you more than usual, ignore it – totally. Like you never saw it there. Don't tip off anyone that someone will be following you at all times!"

They were indeed going to be watching me closely. And calling them ahead of time would give whoever was going to follow me a few minutes to get ready so there would be no surprises. The only problem was, they were staking me out as bait! And that didn't feel very safe at all. Once again I saw myself being shot at on a dark road in the middle of the night. And it didn't feel good!

"Well," I said bravely. "I guess I do have to continue with my investigations anyway."

Don smiled. "I thought you'd feel that way."

I didn't really, but like with Doctor Cynthia, I couldn't let him know that. "How about that SUV?" I asked. "How long before it will be ready again?"

"I put a rush on that new windshield. Should be here sometime Monday. You can have it as soon as it's ready."

"And in the meantime?"

"We don't think the threat is going to be much for the next few days. After that we'll begin to worry."

They weren't going to worry for a few days, but I would! "So I should just keep bumming rides?" My own car was out. Besides, it was locked up for evidence now.

"Whatever you have to do," Don replied. "Just don't go near your apartment yet!"

Yeah. Like it was so easy. Anyone I asked for a lift was immediately put in danger! 'Sinful' Cynthia and her sporty little car immediately came to mind.

When I got back to my office, I found pretty Cynthia talking with Hannah. "There you are," she said as I walked in. I came to see if the prison sent over Pariah's medical record yet."

I pointed at the file on my desk. "Feel free to browse all you want," I replied. "I don't understand any of it."

She picked up the file. "This is all there is?" she asked. "From the extent of his injuries, I was expecting more."

She had confused me. I had thought the file was huge. "More?" I asked. "It looks like a lot to me."

She just gave me one of those hopeless looks of hers. "I'll let you know," she said before she walked out to the other room with it.

I wished her luck.

Cynthia was back about thirty minutes later. She dropped the medical file on my desk with a distinct plop! "Well, that was a big waste of time," she complained.

"Why?"

"Because it doesn't say anything. "Yes, it notes a lot of broken bones and stuff, but not one thing about why or how it happened."

"Nothing?"

She shook her head. "Nothing! The most interesting section was the last. He was sent in unconscious. X-rays revealed several skull fractures. It was two days before he woke up. And when he did, the file says he refused to talk to anyone. He was released back to his cell four days later. No mention of him finally speaking or anything. Zip! Nada! It's ridiculous!"

"It's prison medicine," I offered.

"Prison medicine isn't that bad! Why was everything left out? That's not normal, Cliff. It's not normal at all!"

"I guess it's something else to ask the former warden about," I suggested.

"And I want to be there to ask it!" she replied angrily. "There's something odd going on here, something that's not right!"

"We're working on it," I replied. "The wheels of justice usually turn slowly. But we do the best we can."

"Somebody should have caught this years ago," she said a bit more calmly.

"I think somebody did."

"The warden?"

"Maybe. There are a few other possibilities too," I replied.

"Like who?"

I shrugged my shoulders. "Other possibilities."

She rolled her eyes. "When do we go back and tackle Chavez again?"

"Just as soon as I hear what they want to do about his request."

"You just make sure I'm there with you again. I want to hear it all. Something happened in that prison that was so out of line it makes me sick! And I want to get to the bottom of it!"

"You and me both!" I told her. I just wasn't too sure about taking her back to the prison though. She wasn't an agent, and with someone wanting to kill me, every place we went together put her further at risk. Not that I was going to let that stop me from seeing her.

And speaking of seeing her… "What's the chance of you driving me back to the safe house tonight?" I asked.

"No problem," she replied. "I really should check in on Pariah anyway."

I picked up my phone and called Don to let him know I was leaving for the weekend. He reminded me to keep letting him know if I went anywhere.

Since the weekend was coming up, I tried to feel good about having a few days off. Especially when they weren't expecting any danger to either Pariah or myself – yet. But the truth was, my mind was too occupied with problems concerning what had happened to Pariah, both at his trial and in prison. Too many things were simply…odd! And I wasn't going to get far finding the answers without my own car, especially on a weekend.

I had decided not to tell Cynthia about the change in the threat to me and Pariah. Actually, the threat had only changed technically, we were still in just as much danger as before – if not more. I didn't want to alarm her any more than was necessary. In the meantime, I had a few days to chill and relax – even though I didn't really want to. Was there any way I could use that to my advantage?

"What are your plans for the weekend?" I asked Cynthia as she turned off the highway onto the two-lane road.

"Nothing special," she replied. "What did you have in mind?"

I had lots of things in mind, but I think she was looking for some kind of reply that didn't strictly concern getting her into bed. "I'm not sure," I said. But the scenery was fast changing from busy metropolis to tree lined country road. Which did give me an idea. "I was thinking…" I said as I considered exactly what it was that I wanted to do. "Pariah has asked a few times now for us to take him home. I was thinking of driving him by his old house so he could see it again."

She nearly swerved off the road as she looked over at me. "Hasn't he had enough shocks to his system lately? How damaging do you think presenting him with what he used to have will be to him?"

I thought about it for a minute. "Oh, I don't know. I don't think it's going to be anything he won't already be expecting."

"I think it's a bad idea!" she said.

"But it's something he wants. And this weekend may be our best time to make it happen," I argued.

She seemed to think about that for a while as she drove. "I still think it's a bad idea," she finally replied.

We decided to tell Pariah about what I had in mind right after dinner. I already had a pretty good idea that he would want to go, but I wasn't quite prepared for how desperately he seemed to want it.

"Home," he said as soon as I told him I was thinking about taking him. And then he got up and started heading toward the front door.

"Where are you going?" I asked.

"Home," he said without turning around. "Not tonight!" I called quickly after him.

I saw him stop and reluctantly turn around. He looked sad and defeated. "Tomorrow," I told him. "In the morning."

The following morning, Pariah wasn't in his room when I got up to check on him. But that didn't surprise me. What did surprise me was that he wasn't in any of his usual places. Instead, I found him and Brutus sitting on the ground out by the cars.

"Home," he said again hopefully as I approached him.

"Not yet," Pariah," I had to tell him. "It's too early. Doctor Westmore isn't here yet to take us."

"Home," he said again rather desperately.

"In a little while, buddy," I replied. "In a little while."

Since there would be three of us riding, I managed to get Phil to let me borrow his car for the day – with the provision that if we got shot, we wouldn't blame him. I know he was only joking, but I had been shot at all too often lately, and the comment conjured up images of just how fragile his car was compared to the bullet proof tank I had driven recently.

Once Cynthia arrived, we got Pariah into the back of Phil's car and I made a quick phone call to Don to alert him we were leaving in Phil's car and the general direction we would be going. Then I went out through the gate and started heading away from Atlanta toward Lake Lanier.

"Home," Pariah said several times, rather emphatically as I drove.

"That's where we're going," I replied happily each time.

It wasn't until we were nearly there that he suddenly changed what he was saying. His voice was full of distress as he raised his voice, "Not this home! Home! Not this home!"

I nearly slammed on the brakes. "This is the only home I know of for you," I replied. "Where are we supposed to go?"

"Home! Not this home!"

I looked to Cynthia. "I don't know of any other place."

She turned back to Pariah, "Where is your home? Where is it you want to go? Can you tell us? Give us directions?"

I was now turning onto the street that my notes told me his house had been located on. Not many houses were visible between the thick forest of trees.

"Not this hoooome." His voice trailed off as he pressed his face up against the window next to his head. I realized I was approaching a driveway. The number on the mailbox was the address we had been looking for.

"Not this home," He said softly. He was crying with his face still pressed against the glass. He didn't want to be there, but he couldn't look away either.

I pulled into the driveway and stopped. There was no sign of a house, just a narrow dirt road that ran back through the trees. "I'm just turning around here," I said. "Don't worry, Pariah, we're leaving right away."

I put the car in reverse…and Cynthia put her hand on my arm. "Wait!" she said.

She turned around to watch Pariah. His face was still pressed against the glass, trying to look at the gap between the trees. Instead of saying anything, she suddenly turned back and got out of the car. She opened Pariah's door. "Pariah, come with me. Let's go see your old house."

Slowly, he got out of the car. Cynthia took his arm and led him up the little dirt road. I got out to join them, but I hung back a bit. The road continued straight for a little ways, then it turned left and suddenly opened up into a large cleared lot completely surrounded by trees. There was a nice looking house located toward the back corner. Cynthia stopped him right at that point and I watched as he looked all around.

"Trees," he said. "Trees."

I saw Cynthia look back at me briefly, but neither of us said anything.

"This was your house," she said softly to Pariah.

Slowly, he extended his arm and pointed at the house. "Laura," he said softly before dropping his hand. He was crying again.

I seemed to remember from somewhere in my notes that his wife had been named Laura. It was one of those tiny little pieces of information that I had bypassed though as having no value to us now. "His wife," I said softly to let Cynthia know. I saw her eyes widen for a moment before she turned back to Pariah.

"She's not here anymore," she said to him. "She's not with us. She's gone."

"Gone," Pariah cried softly. "Laura gone. Laura gone." He sank straight down to the ground in misery and Cynthia sank right down with him. She held him to her and let him cry.

Cynthia had said this wasn't a good idea and I had ignored her advice. Now I was regretting that decision. So why had she gotten him out of the car and taken him here?

Cynthia held him while he cried for a few minutes, then she took his head in her hands and turned it so that he was looking at his old house. She held his head there for a few moments so he would continue to look at it. "That's your old house, Pariah," she said softly. "You and Laura lived here together, didn't you?"

I wasn't sure, but I got the impression he tried to nod his head a little.

"Laura's not with us anymore. She doesn't live there. It's just a house now. Not her house. Not your house. There's nothing of her left for you here now."

He looked up at her then. "Trees," he said. "Trees."

"What about the trees?" she asked.

"Laura's trees. Wanted trees. Lots of trees."

"Is that why you moved here?" she asked. "So you could be in the middle of all these trees?"

His head seemed to fall to his chest as he nodded. "Laura's trees."

She looked back at me for a moment. I knew now why Pariah was so drawn to the trees. They were his reminder of his wife.

"Home," he suddenly said. "Take me home."

"But not this home," Cynthia replied, trying to be certain of what he wanted.

"Not this home," he replied.

"Can you show us where it is?" she asked.

He nodded his head.

We both helped him to his feet and got him back to the car. I turned it around and we headed back toward Atlanta. On the way, I passed a car that was parked on the side of the road just back from where we had been. Our followers. Our watchers. Our guardian angels – I hoped.

Pariah eventually led us right downtown, although the route was more than a bit round about since he didn't seem to be too sure of the way until we got nearer. I had this sneaking suspicion of where we were going once we reached Midtown. I was more sure when he took us to a park there – the same park I had searched for him in once before.

"Home," he said as I found a parking space nearby. The look on his face seemed awfully determined.

The moment the car was stopped, he was out and hurrying along the edge of the park. Cynthia and I followed. He never wavered in his direction as he ran toward the back of the park…and the small stand of woods beyond. We followed him right into the trees, and he kept going, turning here and there down the faintest of paths. Finally, he dropped to his knees and crawled under some brush. I crawled after him.

The little cubbyhole he had built for himself certainly wasn't waterproof, but I figured it might deter at least some of the rain. It certainly wasn't insulated either, but it would block the wind from making matters worse in the winter.

I found him on his knees digging frantically through the contents of an old black trash bag. It took him only a moment to pull something out. He looked at it. He kissed it. He held it to his chest.

"Can I see?" I asked as Cynthia managed to get just into the opening.

He looked at the picture in his hands again, then hesitantly held it out toward me. I could barely make out the faded rumpled image. It was obviously a woman, but the picture was so old and damaged from the years of use that very little details remained.

"Is this Laura?" Cynthia asked.

He nodded. "Wife."

"She's very pretty," Cynthia added.

I guess she was trying to be nice. The picture was almost un-viewable.

He took the picture back from me and kissed it again. Then he looked at me. "Ready," he said.

"Ready?" I wasn't sure for what, but Cynthia started crawling back out of the opening and he started to follow. Instead of joining them, I looked around at his little burrow. I saw a winter coat, or what was left of it. It looked like he had mostly used it as a pillow. And then there was his plastic bag full of…who knew what. I grabbed the bag and held it up. "Pariah, do you want this?"

He stopped and looked at his bag. Then he nodded and crawled out again. I was tempted for a moment to grab his coat too, but I decided I'd rather not touch the thing. I wasn't too sure about the plastic bag I had in my hand either, but I dragged it out with me.

While everyone else got to their feet, I took just a moment to quickly open his bag. I couldn't see much besides some old clothing, but I could feel a few hard items through the outside of the bag. "Can I see what you've got here?" I asked.

Not only was I curious about what he had in there, but if he happened to have any weapons of any sort it was vital that I know about it now.

Once again he nodded his consent and I dumped the bag out. A sweater. Another pair of pants. Another wadded up shirt. An old t-shirt. A used plastic plate. An old plastic cup. A plastic fork, knife, and spoon. A bottle of dirty looking water. And four empty soda cans he must have picked up along the road. Not much. I was tempted to just leave the bag here, but I figured that now it would only be littering. I stuffed everything back into the bag and started wondering if I could get away with "accidently" leaving it behind in a trash can somewhere. I kept looking, but we got to the car before I saw any sign of a trash can to dump it in.

Cynthia and I looked at each other a few times on the way back to the safe house, but we never spoke a word. Pariah was still hugging that picture to his chest as he got out of the car and Brutus jumped all over him. We watched as he knelt down and hugged the little dog, then showed Brutus the picture of his wife. Brutus of course licked it appropriately.

As soon as I got inside, I asked Phil if he could find me a twist tie or something to seal the bag up with. He didn't have one so we stuck Pariah's bag inside of another garbage bag and then I tied the thing off. No telling what kind of bugs were in there! I left the bag in Pariah's room…hoping he would never open it. I also hoped I could throw it all away eventually. But did I dare? It was all his worldly possessions…well, all except that coat I had purposely left behind. When winter came, I would make sure he had a better one – something brand new!

With Cynthia watching, I pulled out my cell phone and called Hannah. "What's up Cliff?" she asked.

"Top priority!" I said. "First thing Monday morning, see if you can locate a picture of Pariah's wife!"

Heavenly Cynthia kissed me.

"Your beard hurts," she said.

Ugh! So much for not shaving.

____

CHAPTER

28

On Monday morning I was rubbing my now freshly shaven face when my little office was "gifted" by the presence of a very large man in a very expensive suit. "Agent McNair?" he asked.

I stood up to shake his hand. "What can I do for you?"

"I'm Simon Cantrell. Justice Department." Then, just to show off, he pulled his ID out and showed me. Yes, I was impressed…somewhat. To tell the truth, I was more impressed by the guy's size. He was not only tall, but underneath the cut of his million dollar suit, it looked like he had the frame of a body builder.

"The Director told me that Justice was going to send someone down," I said as I motioned toward one of the chairs in front of my desk.

"I just came from his office," Simon replied. "I understand you and Mr. Clayton both have a price on your heads."

I smiled. "Not anymore. Not technically anyway. The contracts were cancelled. Now Pacheco has declared war on us personally. I think he's mad because we smashed two legs of his white slave business."

He actually laughed! "I can see where he might take a bit of offence at that. But that brings up another thing. Your Director wants you to fill me in on everything about Mr. Clayton. I got the impression that there's something…wrong…or perhaps different about him?"

"Wrong? Different? Those words don't even come close!" I picked up my phone. "Excuse me for making this call, but I have to make sure you're cleared to be a full part of the team."

"Team? If this is something top secret my clearance should be good. But if you're trying to protect your information, then I'm glad to see you checking to make sure. I can't begin to tell you how many problems I've had to deal with because of innocent carelessness."

I phoned up to the Director's office. Two minutes later I had not only the permission to tell Simon everything, but I was ordered to make sure he knew...*everything*! I hung up the phone. "Welcome to the team, Mr. Cantrell."

"Call me Simon," he said with a grin.

"So how did you get elected to peek into our little problem here? I would think a little thing like this would be a bit off your beaten track."

He shrugged. "When the Attorney General of the United States calls me personally into his office and says go, then I go."

Yes, I was flabbergasted. "The Attorney General?" I asked with disbelief.

He nodded. "Usually I'd have someone under me do this kind of thing, but I got the impression that Mr. Clayton has somehow become a big interest to certain parties. Unfortunately, no one was very forthcoming with what that interest is."

I nodded and got up. "If you want to know everything, then let's take a little walk. I'm afraid you're going to be busy for a while listening to recordings and watching tapes. It's the only way you'll fully understand what you're dealing with. But I'm going to warn you now, what you're about to witness is going to warp your perception of the whole damn universe!"

He laughed again! He actually laughed! But I knew for a fact that he wouldn't be laughing for very long.

I walked him into the tech lab and asked one of the guys to set him up with several of the most interesting recordings...saving the Hong Kong video for last. They set him up at a desk with a pair of headphones in front of a monitor. I patted him on the shoulder. "Don't leave today without talking to me first," I said. Then I leaned down and whispered one final thing. "You're probably not going to believe what you're about to see and hear. But I can assure you, every little bit of it is real. Very real!"

I walked off while he stared at my back. It was the only real way I knew to warn him about what was in the recordings.

When I got back to my little office, Hannah stopped by. She had three pictures in her hand that she gave me. "Pariah's wife seems to be almost as difficult to locate pictures of as him. I found the first one in a newspaper obituary, the other one is from the same paper, but way back to her wedding. The last one is from her high school yearbook. I looked at the pictures. They're great," I told her. Much better than the old one he has now."

"Old one?" she asked.

I nodded. "He has a really old one that's so mangled and worn out you can't see the picture anymore. I want to give him a better one."

"Listen, Cliff, if you're wanting to do something like that, I have the phone number for her parents. I can call them and see what I can get. Maybe we can put together a little album for him."

"That would be great," I replied as I handed the pictures back to her. "See if you can get a little album to put it all together in."

She smiled and walked out. I had no doubt that she would return with something I would be proud to hand to Pariah.

It was several hours later when Simon phoned me. "Jesus Christ!" he exclaimed rather vehemently. "You're telling me all this is real?"

"How far have you gotten?" I asked.

"I just finished everything up through the two New York tapes."

"Oh," I replied, "all that was just the warm up for the more interesting stuff."

"More interesting?"

"Trust me, Simon, you haven't seen anything yet! Ask them to cue up the recordings for Hong Kong next. I guarantee you won't sleep tonight!"

"Geez!" He grunted. "I don't think I'll sleep with what I've seen so far!"

"I tried to warn you."

"Not very well!"

It was nearly lunchtime when Simon called me back. "Where do you go for lunch around here?" he asked. "And is it anywhere where we can talk?"

I had no doubt that he would want to talk to me now. "Our best choices are not in this building. I'd drive but my car is kind of laid up for a while in the evidence department."

"Evidence!"

"Yeah, something happened to my windows."

He grunted. "I'll drive."

"In that case, I'll point the way."

I took him and his fancy suit to a bar where I knew they had the best deli sandwiches you could get. I was a little concerned about how he might feel about going into a bar to eat, but he seemed very happy with my choice of establishments. We chose a booth in a fairly dark corner and settled back, each of us with a bottle of beer. I took his choice of drink as a good sign!

"I understand completely now why the Attorney General is so interested in Clayton," he said after he took his first swig of beer. "And I'm betting that the heads of every other government agency are watching even closer. But that doesn't explain what I'm doing here."

"Did you notice his little temper tantrums in those tapes?"

He nodded. "What were they all about?"

"Twenty years ago, he was convicted of child molestation and rape."

I saw his eyes nearly bulge out of his head. "You've got to be kidding!"

"Trust me, it's true! In the process, he literally lost everything. His home, cars, stuff…and his pregnant wife died from the stress while they were selling their house out from under her."

"So he's mad."

"I don't know, but mad is definitely a term you could use for him. He's brain damaged now. Happened in prison – along with the multiple breaking of almost every bone in his body."

"What the heck did he do to deserve that?"

"I don't know yet. I'm working on it. But the bottom line is that he claims he didn't do it. All he wants before he dies is for everyone to know he was innocent of the crime."

I saw him consider that for a moment as he sipped at his beer. "Okay," he said, "It's a bit out of my usual territory but I guess I'm going to be looking into an old child molestation case. What was the girl's name?" he asked as he took another swig from his bottle.

"William Chermont's daughter, Stacy."

He spit the beer he had just sipped back into the bottle.

"I see you've heard of him."

"Oh yeah!" he replied.

"Good, because here's another little tidbit for you. The lawyer they used was someone named Nathan Brecker."

The shock that registered on his face was almost comic. "And that," he said, "explains everything!"

"I take it you know Brecker too?"

He nodded, but only after taking a very long drink of his beer. "My record against him is a losing one right now. He has two wins, I have one. I'd like to even that score!"

Now it was my turn to be surprised. "You've gone against him in court?"

"Oh yeah! And each time it was anything but fun! I take it you've got the original trial transcripts?"

"On my desk. You can have them when we get back. But I'll warn you, they don't make it look good for Pariah."

"Why is it that everyone always calls him Pariah?"

"That's what he wants to be called. He objects rather stubbornly to being called Clayton now. As far as he's concerned, Clayton is dead."

"But he still wants his Clayton name cleared."

I nodded. "We owe him a lot."

"I can see that," he replied. "I have a feeling we're going to have an uphill battle on our hands, especially after twenty years."

"I've just started investigating this," I said, "and I don't know if it will help, but I've already uncovered a few things that I think are odd."

"Odd? We're talking about what's legal and what isn't. Brecker has long been suspected of doing a lot of Chermont's dirty work for him. So throw Brecker and Chermont into the mix together, and there's no such thing as odd. But throw it at me anyway."

"First of all, Clayton was assigned a lawyer named Clint Green. At that time he was fresh out of school and that case was the one and only case he ever tried. The firm fired him right after that. He's literally selling shoes now in Macy's."

He grunted. "I'll talk with him. Do you know where I can find him?"

"Macy's! Perimeter Mall."

He looked at me strangely. "You're not kidding?"

I ignored his disbelief. "Green claimed he had found a surveillance video that clearly showed Clayton was nowhere near the girl when the rape was supposed to take place. Unfortunately, the tape never made it into evidence."

I could see that got his interest. "Where's the tape now?"

"He has no idea. He said the judge seemed to have made up his mind about not allowing the tape before he could introduce it."

I saw the wheels turning in his head for a moment. "Okay," he said. "It would depend on what's on the tape. What else have you dug up?"

"I'm in the process now of trying to talk with Pariah's former cellmate, but he's refusing to talk without some kind of deal."

"What's he want?"

"To go home. He's doing thirty for armed robbery. He has ten still to go."

"And what's your feeling on it?"

"He mentioned a few things that rubbed a bit raw. One in particular was some kind of deal the warden made."

He nodded. "I'll check on it when we get back."

I noticed that he was taking everything in, but wasn't taking any notes. That was something that scared me a bit. But the fact that he insisted on buying us another round of drinks took a bit of the edge off of that. And despite my total dislike of every lawyer who had ever lived, I was actually starting to like the guy. That is…until he asked one more question.

"What was the deal with the doctor I saw in the tapes?"

My heavenly Cynthia! He was interested in my Cynthia! "She's Pariah's psychiatrist," I replied coolly. "I don't know why she insists on taking his blood pressure all during those sessions."

"It's not a bad idea," he replied. "If anything should happen to him, you've got evidence that you did everything possible to keep him from further mental damage. Keep her!"

Oh, I definitely wanted to keep her. The problem was, as soon as he met her, he was going to want to keep her too. And once she met him…. Well, what could I say, the guy wore expensive suits and he had the physique of a body builder. What would she see in me after she met him? At least my total dislike of all lawyers was once again intact!

As soon as I got back to the office, I handed over everything we had gathered so far to Sinister Simon. We set him up with his own little work table out in the big room, complete with a phone and everything. Now I only had to figure out how to keep him from ever meeting Cynthia!

I was distracted from my thoughts by Hannah walking in. The look on her face wasn't good.

She dropped a photo on my desk. "That's all I was able to get back from Laura's parents."

I looked at the photo. What I saw was a complete photo, but it was a copy of another photo that wasn't complete. The photo showed a woman, and the picture was obviously cut all along the edge of one side of her body – where her husband used to be.

"It's the best picture we have of her so far," Hannah said, "but we can't give that to him."

"I take it her parents aren't exactly happy about their son-in-law?"

"That's an understatement. I was lucky to get this out of them."

I handed the picture back to her. "Shred it!" I said. "I don't want any chance that he'll ever see it. And see if you can find something to put those few other pictures in so I can give them to him." I wanted badly to find some way to tell the parents off…to show them how wrong they were about Pariah. But as much as I wanted to believe he was innocent, that proof didn't exist – yet. But finding it was still my main mission in life – if you don't count keeping Simon away from Cynthia that is.

They say good things happen to good people. I don't know how good I was, but I must have done something right since Don called me to tell me the armored SUV was mine again. Yes! Yes! Yes! The only problem was, I now had wheels but nowhere to go – yet.

My first thought was to go back to the prison to see Chavez, but I still needed that agreement. I went out to find Simon, but he wasn't at the table we had set up for him and nobody knew where he was. I phoned Don about it, but he hadn't heard anything yet on it either. So much for that idea. I was forced to go back to working on paperwork that never seemed to end.

Hannah came back a little while later. She had taken the few pictures of Laura Clayton she had been able to come up with and put each one into a protective plastic sleeve. The sleeves were locked together in a file folder to keep them together. On the cover of the folder, she had beautifully lettered, "Laura Clayton." As little as it was, I was impressed.

"Thanks, Hannah," I said. "I love it. I'm sure he will too."

"I just wish I could have come up with more for him," she replied.

I nodded. "Maybe someday."

It wasn't until very late in the day when Simon came into my office holding up a thin file folder. "Got it!" he declared.

"Got what?"

"An agreement to present to Chavez."

"They're letting him out?" I asked.

"Not quite. We'll offer him three more years plus move him to a less secure facility where he and his wife can enjoy some *quality* time together once in a while."

I was dubious. "Do you think he'll go for it?"

"He'll have to, it's the only shot he has."

"I've got a car again…well, sort of a car. Actually, it's an armored SUV that I've become rather attached to. Want to go out to the prison tonight?"

He shook his head. "Let's wait till morning. What I'd like to do instead is to meet Clayton. Any chance? If I'm going to be representing him, I'm going to need to talk to him."

"I can take you to him," I said, "but he's not going to be someone you can talk with easily. Most of the things we ask him about he refuses to talk about. And very often the things he does say don't always make much sense."

He stared at me for a few moments. "Understood," he finally said.

I made my quick phone call to tell Don I was leaving while Simon was gathering up his things. Then, with him in tow, I reclaimed the big SUV again and headed off toward the safe house. Halfway there, my cell phone rang, and unfortunately, it was Frank Morris.

"Where are you?" he asked.

"Halfway back to the safe house," I replied.

"Good!" he replied. "When you get there, stay there!"

"What's up?" I asked, my concern growing quickly.

"Pacheco's friends have arrived."

"Are you going to arrest them?" I asked.

"For what?" he asked. "As far as we know, all they've done is to drive up here from Mexico. And there ain't no law against that!"

"So what are you doing?" I asked.

"Listening! But since they arrived, we haven't heard much phone chatter. Just keep your head down McNair. And be careful!"

"I promise!" I replied. I was instantly nervous again.

"Problem?" Simon asked.

"Just that nice man from Mexico who wants my head on a platter. Now instead of just a couple of assassins, he's sent a team of men after us."

"Does that have anything to do with why your car is locked up in evidence and you're now driving this thing? You did say it was armored."

"Yeah. And it saved my life big time a few days ago!"

He actually grinned! "And I thought my trip to Atlanta was going to be boring," he replied happily.

He was very silent when we pulled up to the gate in front of the safe house so the guard could let us in. But the silence didn't last long once the house came into view. "This has to be, without a doubt, the best looking safe house I've ever seen!"

"The government just bought it," I replied. "Actually, I understand the previous owners were quite anxious to sell once our Director had a chance to speak with them."

And then I spotted the one thing I absolutely didn't want to see. In fact I would much rather have noticed the entire gang of Mexican bandits outside the house with all their guns aimed at me...instead of seeing... Cynthia's car.

I saw his eyes glancing over the lines of the sporty little car as he got out of the SUV. I wasn't looking forward to introducing him to the doctor, but I led him in through the front door.

"Fantastic!" he exclaimed as he looked around carefully.

I said nothing. I was dreading seeing Cynthia too much.

We found them in the kitchen, right where I expected to see everyone – except Pariah of course. Oh, and Brutus too. And the one thing that tore into me more than I expected it to, was the way that Cynthia's eyes seemed to light up at the sight of Simon. I was finished, and I knew it. "Guys, this is Simon Cantrell. He's a lawyer from the Justice Department in DC. Simon, that's Doctor Westmore," I said pointing at Cynthia."

"Cynthia," she said quickly. She certainly hadn't been that quick with me.

"And that's Phil Albright," I said, pointing toward Phil. "He kind of runs this place and keeps us all in line."

"Fantastic place you've got here," Simon replied as he shook Phil's hand.

And then he shook Cynthia's hand. There was no doubting the fascination I saw in her eyes. "It's a pleasure to meet you," she said to him.

"Pleasure's all mine," he replied.

Did he have to put it that way? To break things up, I pulled out the little folder that Hannah had put together for me with the pictures of Pariah's wife. "Look at what we put together."

Cynthia took the folder and opened it. I watched as she flipped through the few pictures. "That's all you could come up with?" she asked critically.

"That's it, I'm afraid. Her parents didn't seem to think very highly of Mr. Clayton back then. The one picture they sent wasn't one I dared let him see since he was obviously cut out of it."

"Stupid people!" Cynthia muttered.

I took the folder back and headed for the back door. I realized that everyone was following me. I found Pariah and Brutus out wandering among one of the little gardens again. Brutus showed off his best imitation of a big guard dog by barking ferociously at Simon. Good dog! For which Simon reached down and scratched him behind his ears. Bad Simon!

"Pariah, we found you something," I said as I held the folder out for him.

He took the folder hesitantly and read the cover. His fingers traced the letters of his wife's name that Hannah had so carefully drawn. He looked up at me, then he opened the folder. He stared at the picture from the newspaper of his wife's engagement announcement for a moment, then he brought it to his lips and kissed it. I was glad for the protective covering that encased the picture. His fingers traced lovingly over the face in the picture. Then he turned the page and traced the picture there. The next page he simply stared at for a few moments.

Then he turned the page again. I hadn't realized that Hannah had put a blank protector in the folder. But I watched as he opened one of the buttons on the front of his shirt and extracted the picture he had kept with him for so many years. It took him a while to manage to open the protective sleeve. I was tempted to offer my help, but I let him be. Eventually, the picture was safely secured with the new ones.

Ignoring us completely he sat down on the grass and Brutus naturally jumped into his lap. One by one, he went through the pictures again, this time for Brutus's benefit.

I felt Cynthia lightly grab my arm. "Let's go," she whispered. "Leave them be."

Silently we all walked back to the house together, but before going in, Cyn briefly hugged me and planted a kiss on my cheek. "That was nice Cliff. Thanks." Why couldn't she have kissed my lips instead?

As usual, extra company didn't seem to give Phil any problems at all. He stuck another baked potato in the oven and pulled another chicken breast out of the freezer for his "famous" fried chicken. I don't know if it was famous or not, but it certainly wasn't bad at all. For Pariah, he whipped up another batch of pancakes. For dinner, Pariah showed up with his picture folder still clutched to his chest. He sat on it while he ate.

I didn't formally introduce Simon to Pariah until after dinner was over. Simon tried to tell Pariah what he was there for, but Pariah not only didn't answer his questions, he acted like he wasn't there at all and got up to leave in the middle of something Simon was trying to say.

Simon looked questioningly at me. "That's just him," I told him. "I warned you that he could be frustrating to talk to sometimes."

"Give him time," Cynthia suggested. "He doesn't know you yet. There are too many things he won't discuss with either of us yet too."

"I can't wait forever!" Simon complained.

"You may have to do this without talking to him," I suggested.

"That's crazy."

It was Cynthia that replied for me. "You may need to plan on it though…just in case."

I could see that he didn't appear to be too happy about that.

"Can you drive me back to get my car?" he asked me.

Technically, Frank Morris had requested I not go anywhere. But… "Sure," I replied.

"I can take you," Cynthia spoke up all too quickly.

"Sounds like a good idea," he replied, "that way he doesn't have to go and come all the way back again."

Personally, I thought it was anything but a good idea, but what could I say?

I didn't say anything about it at all because that's when Pariah came and found me. He still had the picture folder in his hands, cradled against his chest. I thought he was there to thank me for putting it together for him. I guess he was, but as usual it was his own version of a thank you. One that surprised all of us – greatly.

"I will find them for you," he said.

"What?" Yes, I was surprised. Very! "Pariah, you don't have to do this yet. Give yourself some time to recover after that last one."

He looked down at the folder in his hands then back up at me. "I will find them for you," he said again.

"I don't think…" Cynthia started to say.

"I will find them!" he insisted.

"Okay, buddy," I said. "We'll go back to work again. You and me. And we'll find those missing people. As many as we possibly can."

He nodded, looked at the folder in his hands again, then back at me… and walked off.

"I can't believe it," Cyn said. "I'm not sure he's ready yet."

"We'll try to pick something easy for him to start with again. Hopefully!" I added, because we never knew exactly what he would find.

I couldn't help but watch as Simon walked out the door with Cynthia. I couldn't help but watch as he climbed into her sporty little car with her. I couldn't help but watch as she drove out the gate with him. Was she driving out of my life too? I hoped not.

I had no claim at all on her. We had made love a few times and that was really it. I liked her…a lot. Okay, more than a lot. But there was nothing "official" between us. So I had no reason to be jealous. No reason to worry about it. No reason to….

But reasons have no place when it comes to relations between a man and a woman. I would just have to see what happened and deal with it the best I could.

Now…if I could just breathe again!

Did he sleep with her? Did Simon Sinister take my heavenly Cynthia to bed last night? Or did Sinful Cynthia take him straight to her apartment? These were the demented thoughts that ran through my mind all night and all the way to work. They were still raging through our morning meeting, and especially when Simon finally arrived at the office and stopped in to say hello. I just couldn't let him know what had been on my mind. "Morning," I greeted pleasantly.

"How long before you can be ready to tackle Chavez?" he asked.

I looked at everything on my desk. Just a ton of paperwork. "Right now I guess," I replied. I knew that Cynthia wanted to be in on this too, but there was no way I was going to invite her – especially not with Simon there. Besides, it was no place for her at all!

"Are you going to alert Cynthia that we're on our way?"

Cynthia! He actually called her Cynthia! Oh how I despised that! "I wasn't going to," I replied. "This isn't the kind of thing she should be present for."

"Normally I'd agree," he replied, "but since she is a doctor and we're going to be probing into what happened to Clayton physically, she may have some insight that we might overlook."

I stared at him for probably a full minute before I gave in and picked up my phone. Two minutes and one more phone call later, we were heading down to my big heavy SUV.

Cynthia wasn't there yet when we arrived, but we went in anyway and arranged to have Chavez set up in a room so we could talk to him. Cyn didn't arrive until just before we were about to go into the room. "Did I miss anything yet?" she asked breathlessly as she hurried up.

"Not yet," I replied. "We were just about to go in."

The guard opened the door for us and I led the way in. Chavez was sitting back in his chair. The moment I walked in, I could see the look on his face change. He looked incredibly confident and satisfied. His gaze on me didn't last long as Simon followed me into the room. The look on his face seemed to cloud a bit. But his face changed to a very broad smile at the sight of Cynthia. I guess I couldn't blame him for that. He totally ignored Simon and me and kept looking at Cyn.

"Mm! You is one fine lookin' woman!" he said. "I am very glad you came back to see me." He glanced quickly at Simon and me. "You could have left them home though."

"For now," Cynthia replied, "you can just ignore me as if I'm not here."

"Ha! Why the heck would I want to do that? I'd never ignore anyone as fine as you, baby!"

It was time to bring him back to reality. "Chavez!" I said sternly to get his attention. "It's time to talk."

At least he looked at me. "I guess you got some paper for me to look at?" he asked. "And it better be exactly what I want!"

Simon took the seat directly in front of him. "Not quite!" he said, looking Chavez straight in the eyes.

"Who the hell is this bozo?" Chavez asked. "I'd rather talk to the woman...by myself!"

"Not going to happen!" Simon replied.

"And I ain't talkin' unless I get out of this place...like now!"

"That's not going to happen either," Simon said as he set the file folder he had brought in down on the table in front of Chavez. "But…we did come up with something that we think you'll find very agreeable."

"Like hell! All or nothin'!"

"Your remaining time gets reduced to another three years," Simon pushed forward.

"Three years!"

"Plus…you get moved out of here to a nicer facility…one where you and your wife can see each other…privately for a while. And what you do with her privately will be your business."

I saw Chavez staring at him, considering the offer. "No," he finally said. "Like I said before, all or nothin'! You want what I know? Then you get me what I want!"

Simon stood up and grabbed the folder with the offer he had put on the table. He ignored Chavez totally. "This is what I want to do," he said to us. "We start pulling in everyone who was around while Clayton was here – one at a time. Set them up in as many separate rooms as possible to keep them from talking to each other. Then we'll…"

"Hey wait!" Chavez complained. "What about me?"

Simon looked at Chavez. "You don't want to talk? We go around you."

"But I'm the one who roomed with him. I'm the one who knows everything you want to know."

Simon leaned over the table. His huge muscular form looked somewhat intimidating to me. I was sure it was having the same effect on Chavez. "You don't want to talk? Fine! You've had your chance. And you don't think that by interviewing all those people we can't come up with at least one or two who will tell us everything we want to know? Everything! You've got to be crazy if you believe otherwise. So forget it! You had your chance and you blew it…passed it up. Now shut up and stay out of my way!"

He stood up again and turned back to Cynthia and me. "We'll see if the Warden can help us narrow down…"

"Wait!" Chavez said again.

"Narrow down our prospects," Simon continued without looking at Chavez. "Hopefully, that should save us a lot of…"

"Wait!" Chavez said again.

"I told you to shut up!" Simon roared at him.

"I'll take the deal!" Chavez said.

"You lost the deal!"

"That was then. I've changed my mind."

"And why should we bother?" Simon asked. "We know there's a lot of others around who can help us…willingly!"

Chavez just looked at him. "Just give me the deal," he said. "What I know can save you a lot of time."

Simon slowly set the folder with the deal on the edge of the table, but he didn't push it toward Chavez. He sat in the seat across from Chavez. "Talk."

Chavez reached across the table for the folder, but Simon pulled it away. "This…will depend on how cooperative and informative you are."

Chavez sat back and looked at me, then he looked longer at Cynthia. "What do you want to know?"

I almost breathed an audible sigh of relief.

"You mentioned to Agent McNair something about a deal that involved the warden. Let's start there."

Chavez didn't say anything for a moment. Then he started speaking. "All right. Look, I don't know why or what for, but for some reason, the old warden made this deal with Bullfrog. And get this, the warden asked Bullfrog to make Clayton's life as miserable as possible while he was here. Told him he could do anything to him…just a long as he didn't kill him. The warden wanted him to suffer as much as possible and keep him suffering – for a long time."

I was stunned…as I'm sure everyone was.

"And who is this Bullfrog?" Simon asked.

Chavez looked at him like he was crazy. "Bullfrog runs this place. All of it. The warden may be in charge, but on this side of the bars, Bullfrog runs it."

I got the picture. Prisons always had an unofficial hierarchy among the prisoners. Often there was more than one as there probably was here. But it sounded like Bullfrog was the biggest honcho in the jail.

"So exactly what did Bullfrog do to Clayton?"

"Well, first off, he dubbed him Toyboy right away. And if you bother to talk to anyone else, I doubt they're going to remember him as anything other than Toyboy. I didn't! And with a name like that, you can pretty much guess what he did with him…every chance he got! And not just him. Most of the guys in here had their go with him as often as they could, and mostly because Bullfrog wanted everyone to mess with him."

It was absurd! Totally absurd! And yet, I somehow believed him. I looked at Cynthia, her face was total rage. "How long did this go on?" she asked angrily. I could tell she was doing her best to keep her emotions in check. Sort of.

Chavez only blinked at her question. "Since he got here," he replied.

"You mean, the whole time he was here? Sixteen years?"

"Shit yeah! Of course! What did you think?"

"How about you?" Simon asked. "Did you have a go at him too?"

Chavez suddenly looked very uncomfortable. He glanced briefly at the agreement on the table. "I ain't gonna answer that."

"In other words, yes!" Simon supplied for him.

Chavez said nothing.

"And what did Clayton…Toyboy…do about it?"

"Huh!" Chavez grunted. "How do you think he kept getting hurt? I got to say though, for a little guy, he didn't ever give up. He kept fighting back as best he could for as long as I knew him."

"So he got all his injuries in fights?" Cynthia asked.

Chavez considered her answer. "Sort of. Every time someone wanted to have a go at him, he always tried to stop them. So they stared breaking his bones to teach him a lesson. Usually it was just something simple, like his fingers, but one time or another I think they got around to just about everything on him. Once he was hurt, he couldn't fight back. Easy pickin."

I felt sick! I couldn't imagine how Pariah had survived like he did all those years. Talk about a fighter! Yet he never stood a chance.

Simon looked to us for a moment. Cyn took that as her cue to move in. "Tell me," she said. "Something happened to…Mr. Clayton…shortly before he left here. Something big. Something bad. He couldn't talk when he got back from the hospital."

Chavez laughed briefly. "Shit yeah! Dumb idiot made a big mistake… *big* mistake! Bullfrog wanted him to suck him off, and Toyboy, as usual, refused. Except this time, he bit Bullfrog right on his…. Well, from what I heard, he hurt Bullfrog bad. Bullfrog came real close to killing him for that. I didn't see Toyboy for quite a while. And when he came back, he was really all messed up…worse than before…in the head I mean. He couldn't talk right. Heck, he couldn't talk at all for a while. And when he could again, it was like he would say one word, and then nothing else with it. Messed up! Totally! Worse than he was.

"What do you mean, worse than he was?" Cyn asked him. "Was he mentally messed up before that?"

"Shit! He was messed up for a long time."

"In what way?"

"Heck, nothing big. He just got…weird." He looked straight at Simon. "And this is something that no one else can tell you!" He looked back to Cynthia. "For the last few years he was here, it was like he was…in another world or something. And then he would start telling me the weirdest things about the people who were porkin' him…well not about them directly, but like…he would tell me that some of the guys were thinking about someone else, not him, and then he would start making up these off the wall stories about what the person they were thinkin' about was doing. Like he was there with them or something. Weird! Really weird!"

"Did he ever do that for you?" Cynthia asked.

Chavez looked at her for a moment before answering. "There was this one time…and no, I wasn't doin' nothin' with him. We was just sittin' in the cell. I was tellin' him about the latest visit from my old lady. When he just suddenly moves over onto my bed and says, give me your hands. I wanted to knock his block off, but he just kept tellin' me to give him my hands. So I figured…what the hell? I let him hold one of my hands. The dude closed his eyes and started makin' up this crazy story about seeing my wife in the kitchen…get this, paintin' it yellow! Of all things, yellow? I knew then for sure he was makin' stuff up from way out in left field."

"What did you do?" Cynthia asked.

"I pulled my hand back quick. I mean…yellow?" His whole demeanor seemed to change. "Now here's the really weird shit. I saw my wife again a month later. And she starts tellin' me how she's been fixin' up the house and repaintin' everything. And she said she did the kitchen in…yellow! Can you believe that shit? Weird! Really weird!"

"So Mr. Clayton only started acting…weird…as you called it, over the last few years he was here. How many years would you say?"

"Shit! How should I know. Maybe three or so."

She nodded. "Thank you Mr. Chavez. Do you know if he did this with anyone else?"

"Shit! Not like he did with me. Only when they were…you know. But the few times I know of when he tried to tell the guys what he says he saw, they just beat him up for it again. I think he learned to keep his weird stories to himself after that happened a few times."

"Thank you," Cynthia said again.

Simon looked to me.

"May I?" I asked Simon, motioning toward the chair he was sitting in. He got up, and I sat down.

"Chavez," I said quietly. "How long was Clayton here before he started sharing your cell?"

"Shit!" he said. "Right from the start. They moved him in with me and that was it."

"Tell me about him back then. What was he like?"

"What was he like? What kind of question is that? What was he like! He was fresh. Stupid! Didn't know shit! And over and over again he kept saying he was innocent – I didn't do it! I didn't do it," he mocked. "He was always sayin' that! The whole time I knew him."

"And did you believe him?"

He looked at me strangely. "Man, you got to be stupid or somethin'. I'll tell you what I told him…over and over again. Don't matter whether you did it or not. You in here…you guilty! Period! End of story!"

I nodded that I understood. "How about any contact with his lawyer? Do you remember anything about that?"

"Man, you talkin' a long time ago. I don't know that he saw his lawyer but maybe once or twice. Not much at all. But I do remember that he kept writin' the guy letters, but he never got anything back. Except for one that said he wasn't gettin' no appeal. He didn't take that too good. Cried like a baby for the rest of the day. And then when they told him his wife died, man that was worse, much worse, especially when the warden wouldn't let him leave to attend the funeral."

"They didn't let him go to his own wife's funeral?"

"Ain't that what I just said?"

"Chavez, do you remember if the warden ever saw him? Did the warden know everything that was done to him?"

"How would I know?" he said. "Warden never came around here that I know of. If he knew from somewhere else, then I wouldn't know about it."

"But you do know that the warden had a deal with Bullfrog."

"Shit! Everyone knew that. Bullfrog bragged about it!"

"And no one tried to put a stop to what they did to him?"

"In here? You got to be kiddin! These guys all loved it. The guards too! He was everyone's favorite pastime."

"The guards too?"

"Of course! You don't think they were going to let something like that happen unless they got in on the fun too."

"All of the guards?"

"Well no. Not all. Just a few."

"But the others did nothing?"

"Not that I ever heard of."

I had no more questions to ask just then. I looked to Cynthia, then to Simon. "He's all yours I said as I got up from the chair.

"Do I get that deal now?" Chavez asked as Simon moved back in front of him.

"Not quite yet," Simon replied.

"Shit! Screwed! I knew it!" Chavez grunted angrily.

Simon opened the file folder, pulled a pen out of his pocket, and signed the paper in the folder. Then he pushed the folder over to Chavez. "Now you can have it."

We found a Denny's restaurant on the way back to work where we all stopped for an early lunch. "It's unbelievable!" I said as we all sat down. "How the hell could all that have gone on...for years...and nobody put a stop to it?"

"It doesn't sound likely to me either," Simon agreed. "Something is wrong here."

"But at the same time, all too much of what he said went right along with the facts. Things we know for sure. He was even able to tell us how long Pariah has been able to travel. So something had to be true about all that."

"I really want to talk to that warden now!" I declared. "And soon!"

"I think we should wait," Simon replied.

"Wait? What for?"

"I'd kind of like to have a little chat with Mr. Bullfrog."

"Now that might be interesting," Cynthia agreed.

"Yeah," I agreed as well. "It would be interesting. And we might learn something more to ask the old warden about too."

Simon just nodded and pulled out his cell phone. A few minutes later he was talking to the new prison warden, asking him to set up an interview with Bullfrog as soon as we could get back there. "It's on," Simon said after he had hung up his phone. "But the warden warned that we weren't likely to get much out of him…except trouble. He's doubling the guards around us."

The guards were indeed doubled, and a few of them looked nervous. I wanted badly to interview some of them, but right now, they weren't on my direct agenda. Bullfrog was. They had set him up in a room that was more like a cell…open bars where the guards could see and hear everything that went on. Bullfrog was seated in a chair, his hands chained to a ring in the floor. And just looking at him, I could easily see why. The guy was huge. Monstrous! Three hundred pounds wouldn't even come close! I was thinking more like four hundred! His face and hands were black as night – as dark a skin as I had ever seen. And he sat there totally calm. Totally at peace with himself. That alone seemed frightening.

"What the hell do you want?" he asked as we walked in.

He didn't ask loudly, in fact, he had said it almost softly. But his voice still seemed to send a chill down my spine. I looked to Cynthia, she looked nervous. Heck, so was I!

"We want to talk to you about Thomas Clayton," Simon said.

"Who?" Clearly he didn't recognize the name.

"Toyboy!" Simon prompted.

"Go screw yourself!"

"Tell me about your deal with the warden!" Simon demanded.

"Screw you!" Bullfrog replied calmly.

"What did the warden tell you? What kind of a deal did you make with him?"

But Bullfrog said nothing. He didn't even flinch.

"Did you forcibly rape…Toyboy…over and over again while he was here?"

"Screw you," Bullfrog repeated in the same soft voice. "I don't have to tell you nothin'. I don't have to talk to you at all."

"I suggest you do talk to us," Simon said threateningly. "Or we can make things very difficult for you here."

Bullfrog grunted a laugh. "Do what? You can't do anything to me! I'm in here for three lifetime sentences. There ain't nothin' you can do to me at all. So go screw yourself!"

We all knew it immediately. We weren't going to get anything out of him at all.

An hour later, we were back at that same Denny's restaurant again, only this time we were catching the place at the end of the lunch hour rush.

"You have no idea what I'd like to do to that…monster!" Cynthia proclaimed vehemently.

Simon shook his head. "We're not going to get anywhere with him," Simon said. "We'll have to brace the former warden without hearing Bullfrog's side of the story."

"It still doesn't mean I wouldn't like to…rip his balls off!" Cynthia proclaimed. "Excuse me for the unladylike comment. But he makes me mad!"

Simon and I both laughed. "For the record, I agree," Simon replied.

And then it hit me. It was just an image of something at first, but as Simon and Cynthia talked, that image grew into something…preposterous.

"What if," I said, interrupting their conversation about something else entirely. "What if…we did rip his balls off? Figuratively, of course."

I had their attention now, but they both looked at me like they thought I was crazy. Heck, they were probably right, it was a crazy idea. But as I had learned before, sometimes a crazy idea can work pretty well.

I leaned forward to explain, and believe it or not, they both listened attentively. And then Simon added something that he thought would make the whole thing work even better! And as soon as he was done, dear Cynthia suggested how we could improve on it even more.

And unbelievably, Simon smiled broadly. "This should be good!" he said with a laugh. "This should be real good!

As much as we all wanted to put our plan into action right away, we had to put it off for at least a day in order to set everything up and make it work right. We all had things to prepare for it, but we were all very much looking forward to getting a little something back at Mr. Bullfrog!

That night, I went to sleep, greatly anticipating our little plan for the morning. But sleep was hard to grasp. My brain was too active trying to imagine what things might go wrong and how we could anticipate them.

I should have thought about that a little harder.

CHAPTER

30

I was in my bed, sound asleep, when the explosion nearly threw me and my covers completely off of the bed. I was so dazed that it took me a while to realize I was hearing gunfire outside. A lot of it! Fear gripped me quickly and I fought off the panic enough to grab my gun.

Pariah! I had to find and protect him! In just my boxer shorts, I ran to his room. He was wide-eyed and trembling. "Let's go!" I ordered. "Get out of here!"

My first thought had been that anyone coming into the house would immediately look in the bedrooms to find him. I had to move him to someplace safe! But where?

As we left his room, I killed the light I had just switched on, leaving us mostly in blackness. I didn't want to make us too obvious a target. There was still a faint glow coming up the stairs from the lights that were always left on down below.

"What was that?" Phil yelled as he came out of his room – shotgun in hand.

"Trouble!" I replied. What else could I tell him? He knew as much as I did just then.

Brutus ran to the top of the steps and started barking madly. "Shut him up!" I told Phil quickly.

"Brutus!" He hissed urgently.

But the damn dog kept barking. Phil ran to the head of the steps and picked the dog up. I saw him stop there to stare down the steps before he came back again, Brutus in his arms. "Didn't see anything," he said.

That didn't mean they wouldn't be coming for us. Pariah reached out and took Brutus and hugged him to him…and I noticed that he still had that damn picture folder too! Had he slept with the thing?

"I'm going downstairs," Phil proclaimed. "Coming?"

"Not yet," I replied. "I need to stash them somewhere first…not a bedroom where they're going to look."

He looked around. "Good luck," he said when he didn't see any ideas. "You too," I replied as I grabbed Pariah's arm and started backing further away from the stairs.

Now, where do you hide someone when there was no place to hide? I quickly started opening every door I came too, but with each one, I already knew I would only see a bedroom that wouldn't offer any protection at all. And the first place they would look in each bedroom was the closet so they were all out.

Gunfire! Downstairs! Close! I distinctly heard the roar of Phil's big shotgun. I prayed he was alright. Voices! Spanish voices! Coming from the stairs! I pulled Pariah to the very last door, the bathroom, which was already open. I quickly shoved him and Brutus inside. "Hide!" I told him. "And keep Brutus quiet!" I shut the door quickly behind me and ran halfway back down the dark hall toward the steps. From there I crawled on my hands and knees to keep my profile down. Then I fell and slithered the final few feet on my belly.

From the floor, I peeked around the corner to the stairs. I could just make out someone halfway up. He was moving slowly, but the dim light coming from somewhere below showed me the gun in his hands. Movement further back showed me someone else behind him. Without thinking, I raised my gun and shot the first one! Then, also without thinking, I aimed at the second man and pulled the trigger again. The first one fell on top of the second one, but I was sure I had hit both of them. Talk about lucky!

I was wondering though if my streak of never killing anyone had come to an end. That wasn't why I cautiously made my way down the steps, but it was running through my mind. I could barely see the bodies since they were both lying flat on the steps, blocking anyone from coming up easily…or going down in my case. The first man on top was dead. So much for my streak. The second one was dead too. My streak was really over now.

My hand brushed against the top of the first man's gun. I remembered that I only had the one clip. Not a lot of bullets, and I didn't know how many would be down there. I occasionally kept hearing the roar of Phil's shotgun coming from…the kitchen maybe? That's what I was guessing anyway. I grabbed the gun from the corpse and had to feel it more than see it in the dim light. I quickly figured out that I was holding a sawed off side-by-side shotgun. A nasty weapon for sure. But one that needed reloading often. I searched the corpse's pockets and found them all full of shells. I grabbed as many as my one empty hand could hold. But since I was wearing only boxer shorts, I had no place to put them.

Very carefully, I worked my way over the two dead bodies. As I passed the second one, I searched briefly with my hands for his gun, but I only felt a pistol stuck in his belt. I left it and continued down to the bottom of the steps where I dropped my pile of shotgun shells in a neat little pile along with the shotgun itself. Then I went back up and grabbed the pistol and more shotgun shells.

I now had three guns, an unknown amount of ammunition, and no way to carry it all. I was seriously wishing I had slept in my pants!

I heard the faint sounds of the front door latch opening. I dropped the third pistol, and ran forward with the sawed off shotgun and my own pistol. I saw the door opening slowly. I dropped to my knees in the middle of the foyer. Motionless, I watched as someone carefully pushed the door open with the barrel of his rifle. Even as dark as it was, I could tell by the way he entered that it wasn't one of our guys. As soon as the door was open far enough, I let loose with both barrels of the shotgun at the same time. It kicked enough that I nearly lost the damn thing. But it also threw the body of whoever was coming in right back outside again. I ran forward and slammed the door shut again and this time locked it.

I heard the roar of Phil's shotgun again. How many shells did he have left? It couldn't be many. And since I kept hearing him shoot once in a while, it sounded like they were concentrating their attack more on the backdoor than anywhere else. Of course, since Phil was there blasting away at them, that too would keep most of their attention on him. But that wasn't the only gunfire I was hearing. I was very troubled by the continued sound of an automatic weapon being fired somewhere outside. And it was being fired a lot!

I went back to my little cache of weapons, unloaded the spent shells from my shotgun and replaced them with new ones. There was more gunfire from the kitchen, but not from Phil's gun. I precariously grabbed everything I could carry and cautiously made my way toward the kitchen. Bracing myself behind the wall next to the doorway, I looked in. I saw a shadow move in the distance, but I didn't know if it was Phil or someone else. I quietly dropped everything in my hands except my own pistol which I aimed at the shadow. "Phil?" I called cautiously. The figure turned toward me and I heard Phil's voice a moment later, but not coming from the figure. I fired and whoever it was went down. I didn't see anything else moving. "Where are you?" I whispered all too loudly.

"Behind the island."

I grabbed all the guns and ammunition again, and keeping low, hurried toward his voice. I couldn't see him very well, but I was glad he was there. "Are you alright?" I asked quietly.

"So far," he replied as he continued to watch for anything moving past the other side of the island.

"I brought you a present," I told him. He turned to me and I laid the sawed off shotgun down next to him along with the cartridges I had for it.

"Bless you," he said. "I'm all but out."

"I figured that." I replied. "I found this one just lying around on the staircase. Its owner doesn't need it anymore."

"You got him?" he asked.

"Got *them*." I replied.

"Good. They came in so fast I couldn't get all of them. I know at least one got past me. Just two?" he asked.

"Two. But I had to try the shotgun out on another one stupid enough to come through the front door. By the way, watch out for that gun, it's got quite a kick!"

"Just the way I like them," he replied. "I know it's working that way."

"It's slowing down," I said as I checked around my side of the island again. "Nobody else seems to be trying to come in."

"Sounds like they're awfully busy outside though, he replied. And someone has an automatic something that shoots an awful lot of bullets. He's been blasting away with it all over the place as far as I can tell. Those guards aren't going to be able to hold out forever."

"If they're still alive," I replied.

He didn't answer. Instead he checked to make sure the little shotgun was loaded, then he stuffed the remaining shells into his pockets. Why hadn't I taken the time to grab my pants? Dumb McNair! Dumb!

I was down to just the two handguns now. The one I had picked up from the dead body was heavy so I moved it to my right hand and put my own gun in my left. "Ready?" I asked.

"Marine time again," he replied, and started crawling his way across the floor on his belly. I did the same from the other side of the island.

It wasn't long before I came across the first body. The next one wasn't far beyond it. And then I heard a sound I really didn't like. The awful sound of somebody shooting something major against what I was guessing was the front door. "Got to go!" I yelled to Phil as I got to my feet in a crouch and ran for the front of the house again.

Another blast rocked the front door. A shotgun? It was my best guess. A third one hit not long after. I was just in time to see the door being kicked open. I fired the gun in my right hand. I wasn't used to it though and I was sure I missed. I thought I saw a shadow slip inside. I quickly fired the gun in my left hand but I know I came nowhere close. I dropped flat on the floor and dropped the heavy unfamiliar gun and grabbed my own gun the way I was used to holding it. I aimed at the next shadow I saw and was rewarded to see someone go flying backwards. I was further rewarded by automatic gunfire spraying back at me. Fortunately, it all went over my head and the muzzle flashes clued me in perfectly for my next shot. The automatic fire was silenced – fortunately.

I heard a grunt and some kind of Spanish curse coming from the stairs. Someone had tripped over the two dead bodies there. As much as I worried about Pariah, I dared not move though. I didn't know what else might be aimed at me from the front door. But after a very long few moments of waiting, I saw no other movement. I slithered forward toward the door. Then took a chance and rolled up against the wall next to it. I dared to peek out. Nobody. Nothing. As far as I could see anyway. Which meant I had to stop the man upstairs.

I ran for the steps, not bothering to worry about anyone shooting at me. Since I knew where they were, the bodies there didn't slow me down much. At the top of the steps, I stopped to look. Light! Not a lot, but more than there should be. I noticed the doors to three of the rooms were cracked open. The lights in each of them had been turned on. I saw nobody in the hallway. Where was he? I cautiously moved forward, keeping low, my gun at the ready.

A banging noise came from one of the bedrooms ahead of me. A closet door maybe? It was hard to tell. I focused most of my attention on that room. A moment later I saw the door swing open wide for someone to come out and I dropped down to one knee, my gun already aimed. The man in the room was sharp though, he took the time to check the hallway before he stepped out. I only saw his head for a fraction of a second before he ducked back in again. I knew where he would be, and he knew where I was. I moved from the middle of the hallway up against the side and did my best to make myself as small a target as possible while I aimed at the door again.

Nothing happened. Was this going to be one of those Mexican standoffs? With a real Mexican? Was he waiting me out? I was going to have to move forward…or stay here and make sure he didn't leave until help arrived. But what if help didn't arrive? What if more bad guys came instead? I didn't feel too secure with that scenario, so with my gun more than ready, I carefully crept toward the lighted open doorway.

I reached the wall next to the door with no problem, but now what was I going to do? Was he in there with his gun aimed right at the door? That's what I would do. The odds were not in my favor that way. Then I got hit by another one of those harebrained ideas that seemed to be invading my mind lately. But I could see no other choice than to try it. As fast as I could, I rolled on the floor across the open doorway to the other side while trying to look inside. I was rewarded for my effort by being shot at. Fortunately, he was a fraction of a second too slow and I made it safely. But now I knew he was indeed watching for me at the door. I also knew he was shooting a rifle of some kind. Not that it mattered what kind it was. Any kind could kill me easily!

So how was I going to get at him? Waiting him out again came to mind, but for the same reasons as before, I dismissed it. Going behind him and coming at him from the window sounded nice, but how could I do it? So that was out too. Stuck!

With no other option, I did the stupid thing and of course rolled back on the floor to the other side, but this time I fired my gun somewhat in his direction as I rolled. Great McNair! Real smart! It accomplished nothing except to use up another valuable bullet. Of course he had used another one of his too, which again had come too late.

Both times now I had rolled on the floor. I could see by the hallway floor that his second shot had come a lot closer than his first. Maybe not in timing, but it was certainly in the right direction.

I did think seriously then about yelling out that I was FBI and he should drop his weapon and come out with his hands up, but that sounded so ludicrous even to me that I quickly dismissed the idea. These guys knew I was FBI before they left home. They had come with the distinct purpose of killing me. Well, Pariah really, but I was on their list too.

Since I had rolled on the floor the last two times, I decided to take the high road this time and hopefully confuse him. But as I got to my feet, I was hit with another stupid idea. Not giving myself time to think about it, I launched myself as high in the air as I could as I jumped across the doorway, trying to aim and fire my gun at the same time. I saw the guy! I clearly saw the guy as I crossed the doorway and pulled the trigger. He was crouched down behind the bed with his gun aimed right at the floor where I had just rolled across. His shot rang out at the same time as mine.

Once safely on the other side, I severely berated myself for being such a dumb ass! Stupid move McNair! Stupid! Going back and forth across the doorway like that was going to get me killed real fast. And I was fairly sure I wouldn't like that much.

So I got chicken and decided to wait. And wait. And wait. I'll say one thing for the guy, he was certainly patient. But that didn't mean much. He wasn't going anywhere and he knew it.

I started to hear sounds from downstairs. More people. Lots of people. I was very happy to hear Don's voice calling me. "Up here!" I yelled. "I could use some backup!"

I heard footsteps running up the stairs, then cursing as they tripped over the bodies, then finally more footsteps again. Don finally came into view, with three other agents right behind him. "Are you alright?" he asked as he approached cautiously.

"I think so," I replied. "I haven't had much time to check though." I pointed toward the lighted doorway. "Bad guy. Big gun. He was behind the bed. I don't advise sticking your head in to look."

He surprised me by what he did next. "This is the FBI," he yelled. "You can't get out of there without getting hurt. So drop your weapon and come out from behind the bed with your hands on your head!"

Why hadn't I thought of yelling that? Oh, I did.

But the guy didn't answer. "He likes to shoot more than he likes talking," I told Don.

But Don just repeated his demand for the guy to drop his weapon. But again no answer.

"Are you sure he's in there?" Don asked.

I pointed to the bullet holes in the floor and the wall behind me. "That answer your question?"

Don repeated his demand one more time, then quickly he poked his head around the door frame and pulled it back again. "I didn't see him," he said. "Are you still in there?" he shouted to the room.

Silence returned. "Damn!" he swore. "Back off McNair. We're wearing vests, all you've got on is… Where the hell are your pants?"

"It's wash day," I told him.

He pointed at the agents who had come up the stairs with him and I backed up down the hallway. Using hand signals he told them how he wanted them each to go in. Then, on a silent count of three, they hit the door…and the floor inside…and didn't fire a single shot.

"McNair!" Don called from inside. "Get in here!"

I hoped it was safe, but I stuck my head around the corner before exposing my body anyway. Everybody was staring at the floor on the other side of the bed. One of the agents backed up so I could see. The man was there, the rifle was still in his hands. And there was a single bullet hole right through the center of his forehead.

"Nice shooting, McNair," he said. "I didn't know you were that good with a gun."

It had to be the luckiest shot in the world. Without a doubt! It was only then that I felt my body begin to shake as the adrenaline started to wear off. Only then that I realized how scared I had been. Only then that I realized how I had somehow managed to overcome the overwhelming panic that I was just now realizing was no longer needed. Only then did I remember all the stupid things I had done during the attack, and I couldn't think just then of a single non-stupid thing I had done.

Shaking, I sat myself down on the floor and threw my gun on the bed. My arm didn't want to hold its weight anymore.

"Where's Pariah?" Don asked.

Oh shit! Pariah! Where the hell was he? I scrambled to my feet and ran for the bathroom at the end of the hall. I opened the door. Nobody! Where was he? "Pariah!" I called. "Pariah!" My calls weren't answered by Pariah, but by a single bark from Brutus…from the linen closet! Don got there first and opened the door. And I was treated to the sight of Pariah all scrunched up into the tiniest space I could imagine him fitting in, on the floor of that little closet. The bottom shelf kept his head bent down at a terrible angle. But not only was he in there, but he was holding onto Brutus too! The little dog jumped from the closet and began barking, delighted to be free. I held out my hand and pulled Pariah out and to his feet. My relief that he was unharmed was great. My relief that I was unharmed was even greater!

"How's Phil?" I asked.

"Hit," Don replied. "But I think he'll make it just fine."

"And the guards?"

"I don't know yet. But there's one wounded for sure. It looks like they gave quite a fight."

I could believe it. There had been an awful lot of shooting. "Did we get them all…I hope?"

"I don't know. We haven't had time to find out yet."

Going back to bed was definitely out. But I did go back to my room to finally get dressed. Why hadn't I thought to take two seconds to do that before? It would have made things so much easier. The bodies had been removed from the steps so we had no trouble getting downstairs where all the lights were now on. I could see through the open front door that someone had found the floodlight switches too since the yard was now bathed in light.

There were bodies…everywhere. And as I made my way back toward the kitchen, I tried to figure how many of those bodies I had been responsible for. How many lives had I taken? My fault! I had ended their unfortunate misguided lives. Me. It didn't feel good. But I was still fairly sure that my being killed would have felt a whole lot worse.

I saw Pariah glancing around nervously at every single dead body. "Don't worry, buddy, they can't hurt you anymore." At least I hoped that was the case. I was only just barely holding onto my own nerves as it was. At least I wasn't shaking anymore. Well, not on the outside. On the inside I was a total mess!

Phil was back in the kitchen again, along with more dead bodies. There was a bloody bandage wrapped around his chest and over his shoulder. "Don thinks you'll be just fine," I said, trying to sound encouraging.

"Go to hell, McNair!" he replied. "It hurts like hell!"

"Yeah, I know. I got shot recently myself," I said. "I remember all too well."

"Sorry, he replied. "I know you did. I'm just mad because I got shot trying to do something stupid."

I was very tempted to tell him about all the really stupid things I had just done. But Don was standing right there and I didn't want to embarrass myself that badly in front of my boss! "Did you get him though?" I asked instead.

"Hell yeah I got him! Do you think I'd get shot and not get the guy who did it? Think again!"

Yeah, Phil was going to be just fine. He was probably mostly angry because his beauty sleep had been interrupted.

I took a short tour of the yard – which was teaming with agents and police. The first thing I noticed was the huge amount of wall that had been blown away…the big explosion that had nearly tossed me out of bed. It looked like they had used a bit too much explosive.

Not far from the hole in the wall, I saw all the vegetation shot to hell… automatic weapons fire. Why? Then next garden area was shot up the same way…and the next! Someone knew that Pariah liked to hang out in the gardens and sometimes spent the whole night out there. They were doing everything they could to get to him. They had failed again. This time.

Thoughts of how persistent they seemed to be filled my mind. I was tired of being shot at. Tired of being a target. Tired of other people having to watch my back. Tired of not being able to go back to my dumpy little apartment. Well, okay, after living in this mansion, I wasn't missing my little place all that much. But the point was still valid.

There had to be a better way. There had to be some way to take the fight to them. There had to be! But the real enemy was in Mexico! FBI jurisdiction may cross state lines, but Mexico was another country. How do you stop an enemy you can't reach?

That very thought haunted me for the rest of the night and well into the morning. I didn't know how we could go about doing it, but Pacheco had to be stopped. Doing it just seemed impossible.

CHAPTER

31

It was about seven in the morning when Cynthia came running into the now shot-up mansion. I was surprised and dismayed to see Simon right behind her. Did he need to rub it in my face like that?

"Cliff! Cliff!" she called the moment she saw me drinking coffee in the kitchen.

She ran up to me and actually hugged me. It felt great, but all the joy was taken out of it by Simon's presence. What was he doing there? Had he slept with her last night? Was that why he was with her?

"Are you all right?" she asked rather desperately.

"Shaken, not stirred," I replied bravely. Actually, the fatigue was setting in now.

Simon had been looking wildly around. "Geez McNair, you really throw some party! I wish I had been there!"

"No you don't!" I replied rather emphatically as the hand holding my coffee cup began to shake a little again. As much as I both liked and disliked him, I wouldn't wish that on anybody.

Cynthia almost made me spill the coffee as she grabbed my face in both her hands to hold it still while she looked into my eyes. "Cliff, are you sure you're alright?"

"Like I said, shaken…"

"Yeah, and you're still shaking now!" she said quickly.

"This? This is nothing. I'm just tired now. My…sleep got interrupted."

"Where's Pariah?" Cyn asked. "Is he alright?"

"Pariah's fine. Phil got shot though. They took him to the hospital. He'll be okay…eventually. Pariah's out back somewhere."

She hurried away leaving me alone with Simon.

"So what happened?" he asked.

"They blew up the wall, and then tried to storm the place."

"What did you do?"

I looked at him. "The truth? A lot of stupid things. Very stupid!"

"In other words, you fought back."

"Something like that."

"How many?" he asked.

I had to think about that. "I really don't know. I never heard. There were bodies all over the place but I never thought about counting them. I tried once to figure out how many I murdered myself, but right now it's all one big blur."

"By the looks of this place, you really must have done pretty well for yourself. You're still here and the place looks like a major war zone."

"It was a major war zone! Trust me!"

"Oh, I believe you. I just wish I had been here to see it."

I looked at him strangely. The guy must have an inner death-wish somewhere!

It wasn't long before I packed my bags, along with the few things that Pariah had, grabbed Brutus's leash and other accessories, and loaded up the armored SUV. We had to get out of the mansion. It wasn't safe anymore. I drove Pariah and Brutus to work since I had no better place to keep them. Pariah seemed more than happy to take charge of Brutus, and Brutus seemed more than happy to have a lot more people paying attention to him and loving on him. Lucky dog!

Frank Morris stopped by my office in the early afternoon to apologize. "We dropped the ball on this one," he told me. "There was no phone chatter about when they were going in, so when it did start to happen, one of our guys was too slow to react. We missed this one big time, and I'm sorry."

"There was no way you could have known for sure," I told him – as if I believed it myself, which I didn't.

"Yeah, we should have known. Just like we should have found out that they would have more people than we thought. We're trying now to sort out where the rest of them came from. We're thinking they might be local farm hands. There's a million of them in this part of the country alone."

That actually made sense to me. And now that I thought about it, there had been more men coming at us than I figured they had sent up from Mexico. But then I didn't know much about that operation because they had purposely been keeping the details away from me. Now I really wished they hadn't. "So now what?" I asked.

"It's early stages still," he replied. "We have a lot to sift through. I'll let you know."

Which to me meant – we don't know and you're on your own. Great!

Cynthia showed up at the office a little while later. I saw her wave briefly to Simon before she came into my little office and closed the door behind her.

"How are you feeling?" she asked, her voice full of concern.

"Tired," I replied.

"And how are you feeling about what happened last night?"

"I'm trying not to think about it."

"Why?"

"Because it was difficult."

"I have no doubt. But that's not a reason for you not to think about it."

"I don't see where it's a reason that I have to think about it either," I replied.

"What bothers you the most about it?" she replied.

Her question caught me totally off guard.

"I have no idea. Lots of things. Way too many things!"

"Like what?"

"Like why didn't we get a clue they were coming in the first place? Why didn't we know there would be so many of them? Why didn't somebody warn me? Why did they seem to know so much about the place? Well, that last part I've kind of figured out. The guard must have told them."

She just looked at me for a while. "But there's more, isn't there."

"Like what?"

"Like about yourself. I'm sure this isn't the first time you've had to kill people, but…"

"Actually, it is the first time. I've shot men before…twice, but I didn't kill them."

"So this is your first time."

"I guess."

"And how do you feel about it?"

I had to think about that. "It's a mixed bag really. In the heat of battle, I didn't exactly have time to dwell on it. I just had to act or be killed. I got lucky. Very lucky. Especially since I did some amazingly stupid things. But afterwards, when the lights came on and I could actually see all the bodies everywhere…well…that's a different story."

"How did you feel then?"

"I felt okay, but it wasn't fun to realize that I was responsible for ending so many lives. They were all people…living people. I simply had no choice. I feel bad about it, but I had no choice."

She got up from her seat and came around to my side of the desk and hugged my head. Then she kissed the top of it. "You're a good man, Cliff. A good man. And don't ever let anyone tell you otherwise!"

Yeah sure. But not as good as Simon. Still, I really appreciated her concern.

"Where are you staying now?" she asked as she let go of my head.

"Don is lining up a hotel for us for a few nights. Then we're going to try to get back into the mansion again – if they're finished with it."

"I'm surprised they don't just move you to another safe house.

"So am I."

Simon knocked on the door and I waved him in.

"I just talked to the warden. He thinks he's located everything we need for tomorrow. We should be all set there."

"Tomorrow?" I asked. "We're still going through with it?"

"Do you have a better idea for getting information out of Bullfrog?" he asked.

I thought about that. "Actually, no. But after thinking about it a while, the whole idea sounds more and more corny."

"So what? Somehow I don't think it's going to be all that corny to him."

He did have a point. "So we've got everything ready?"

"I'm set," Cynthia said. "I've even managed to borrow a few…special props."

"And I'm almost set," Simon added. "All I need is one little thing from you."

"From me? What?" I asked.

He pulled a piece of paper out of a folder in his hands and laid it on my desk. "Your signature."

I looked at the paper and what it was he wanted me to sign. "You're kidding, right?"

CHAPTER

32

The next morning I drove Pariah and Brutus back to the office from our cheap little hotel room. To tell the truth, I think all the guards they had in the area were glad to get out of there for the day just as much as I was. I left Pariah in Hannah and Billy's care, and Simon and I got into my big SUV to head toward the prison.

"I found your Clint Green," last night," he said as I drove. "Just where you said he would be."

"Did you learn anything else?" I asked hopefully.

"Not really. Except after talking with him, I'm liking the way his trial went down a whole lot less than I did before. I've got it on my list now to talk with a Mr. Morgan, the head of the firm he actually worked for. I'm hoping he'll know where Green's original trial notes and materials are."

"Including the tape?"

"Including the tape."

I noticed that Cynthia's car was already there ahead of us when I parked. The guards had been alerted to call the warden at our arrival and he showed up to personally escort us through the facility.

"This is very unusual," he said as we walked. "Are you sure this is all necessary?"

"Do you know a better way to make him talk?" I asked.

"No…but it still seems a bit…cruel."

"Do you think a week in solitary will loosen up his tongue?" Simon asked.

"Him? Not a chance."

"That's what we figured," Simon replied. "So we came up with this little strategy."

"It's still unusual."

"Yeah," I replied. "But we think he deserves it!"

The medical wing of the facility had been cleared out as much as possible. Cynthia was already there ahead of us. She was dressed completely in hospital scrubs and was preparing a tray full of what I was guessing were tools found in an operating room.

"What's that stuff?" I asked.

"I can't exactly operate on him without the right equipment," she replied happily.

I was surprised at how into this she seemed to be.

I looked around at what was going to be our little operating room. I had no doubt that it wasn't up to the standards any other hospital would want, but it would be more than adequate for our purposes. What surprised me the most was the center attraction in the room – the odd looking chair.

Cynthia saw me examining it. "I had it pulled in here from the gynecological ward on the women's side," she said. It should work perfectly for us.

"Are you sure?" I asked. "He's pretty big."

"I'm sure," she replied confidently. She pointed at a pile of scrubs. "Now get dressed! Both of you!"

I hadn't remembered anything about hospital scrubs in our original plan. But I followed her advice anyway.

We stood back behind a piece of wire filled glass that looked into the room with the chair as the guards brought Bullfrog in. I was wrong, I thought, he had to be closer to six hundred pounds than four. At least that's how he looked to me right then. Scary! I was nervous despite all the chains they had binding him. He looked nervous too. Awfully nervous. And I think his nervousness fed mine!

It took a long time to get him into the room because he was bound in such a way that he could hardly move. He was forced to take little tiny steps as one of the six guards prodded him along. Getting him to sit down in the chair was the easy part. Strapping him down wasn't! I held my breath as the guards fought with each part of him to secure him to the chair.

When his arms and neck were secure, Cynthia pulled the mask up that had been hanging around her neck. "See you inside," she said. "And don't forget your masks and hats! We need a sterile environment from now on!"

For a minute there, I thought she was serious! Simon, the Warden, and I watched as she entered the room, looking for all the world like any other surgeon you would find in an operating room. She picked up a control box wired to the chair and pushed a button. Bullfrog's nervousness increased as the chair began tilting back. When it was flat, she started giving the guards instructions on how to raise the separated leg portions of the chair. Bullfrog fought as hard as he could, but even he was overpowered by the strength of the six guards.

"What are you doing?" he yelled. He didn't get an answer from anyone. Only more and more straps to hold him more and more motionless.

And then, while the guards were still securing his legs, Cynthia took a pair of scissors and started cutting his clothes away. He really yelled then. But as before he got no answers. It took some time, but eventually she had him stark naked. She picked up the control box for the chair again and his legs started raising up and separating even wider – and despite his huge size, he couldn't do anything about it. Cynthia directed the guards to add a few more straps in key places, and to tighten a few others. Then she shooed them out of the room.

She looked at the window where we were waiting. "We're ready now."

That was our cue. I stuck the odd little paper hat on my head and pulled the mask up so that it hid most of my face. I turned on my tiny little recorder and headed into the room with Simon.

"What's going on?" Bullfrog roared as we walked in. If I hadn't seen with my own eyes how thoroughly the guards had strapped him down, I would have been much more afraid than I already was.

Simon approached the bound mass of muscle and fat on the table. And then he pulled down his mask.

"This is an operating room," Cynthia cautioned. "We need to keep it sterile!"

"Tough!" Simon replied without looking at her. He looked straight at Bullfrog. "Remember us?" he asked.

Bullfrog's eyes went wide, I saw him try to look over at me and I lowered my mask too so he could see my face. He turned to Cynthia. She shook her head but lowered her mask too. "You're the ones from the FBI," he said nervously. "What's going on?"

"I'm just getting to that," Simon replied. He held out the piece of paper that I had signed the day before in front of Bullfrog's face. "See this? Read it!"

I watched as Bullfrog did his best to read the document, but he was obviously having trouble. "What the hell does it mean?" he yelled. "How am I supposed to know what some of those words are?"

"Oh!" Simon said as he withdrew the paper. "Maybe I better read it for you. This is an order, signed by the governor himself!"

Actually I had signed my own signature where Simon had listed my name instead of the governor's, but Bullfrog wouldn't know that.

"What's it say?" Bullfrog asked.

Simon began reading what had looked to me like a completely authentic order from the Governor of the State of Georgia. The document was complete with a colored state seal on top and everything. If I hadn't known better when I signed the thing, I would have sworn it was absolutely legitimate! Except for my name being on it of course.

"Wait, wait!" Bullfrog began yelling. "What does all that mean?"

Simon looked confused – what an actor! "Oh! I guess I can try to translate it if you like."

"Hell yes!" Bullfrog roared.

"Well, basically it says here…in light of your refusal to be of any help in our investigation, and in light of your past behavior toward others – particularly one Thomas Clayton…he's the one you know as Toyboy…

and in light of your past crimes for which you're already serving three life sentences...."

"What's the bottom line?" Bullfrog roared.

"It's an order from the governor directing us to remove and modify your genital area, neutering you and performing any other corrections because of said procedure that the doctor deems necessary."

"Say what?"

"It means," Cynthia replied. "That I'm going to cut your nuts off and do anything else to you I feel I'd like to do!"

Bullfrog panicked. "What? You can't do that! You can't! You can't!"

"I'm afraid we can," Simon replied over top of his panicked ranting. He held the paper up. "This is the order – signed by the Governor himself! Sorry Bullfrog. But I'm afraid it's a done deal!" He looked up at Cynthia. "Doctor, are you ready?"

"Hey!" Bullfrog yelled. "You're not a doctor! She's not a doctor!" he yelled. "She can't do this!"

"Oh, but I am a doctor, and I certainly can do it," Cynthia replied calmly. Over top of Bullfrog's protests she asked, "Can I start now?"

"He's all yours," Simon replied as he took a step back to watch.

Bullfrog was screaming and struggling for all he was worth, but he couldn't move much at all from the neck down. My job was supposed to act like the doctor's nurse – assistant in my mind. I pushed the cart holding the tray of surgical tools over toward Cynthia and she pulled it into place right behind her as she took her place between his legs and raised her mask. I took the cue to pull my mask back in place too.

And then Cynthia did the most astonishing thing...she began massaging his massive naked sexual organ with her latex covered hands.

"Hey! Hey! Hey!" Bullfrog suddenly started yelling, a lot less strenuously than his previous ranting. "What are you doing?"

"What do you think I'm doing," Cynthia asked as he started to swell under her ministrations.

"Damn!" Bullfrog exclaimed. "Damn!" He certainly sounded a lot happier than he had a few moments before.

When Cynthia determined he was ready, she stopped and moved away from him.

"Hey! Hey! What are you doing? Don't stop now!"

I'm glad you enjoyed that so much," Cynthia said as she picked up a hypodermic needle off of the tray and plunged it into a tiny bottle, because I'm afraid it's the last erection you're ever going to have."

"What? What do you mean?"

"I mean," Cynthia said as she squirted out some of the liquid she had drawn into the syringe, "once I remove your balls…." She quickly swabbed a tiny area with some alcohol laden cotton and plunged the needle into him just above his raging hard organ. "You won't ever be able to have a hard-on again!" She pulled the now empty syringe out of him and Bullfrog began yelling frantically again.

"You know," Simon said, "technically, there is a way out of this for you."

"Excuse me a minute," Cynthia said as she tapped with her finger on his still somewhat swollen sex. "Can you feel that?"

"Feel it? Yeah, of course I can feel it! What the hell did you do to me?"

"Nothing yet," Cynthia said, "just some local anesthetic for the pain."

"The pain?"

"Yes. You wouldn't want me to do this without it, would you?"

"No! I don't want you to do it at all!"

"Just let me know when it goes numb," Cynthia replied. In the meantime…." She looked back to Simon.

"As I was saying," Simon continued, "technically, the Governor left you a way out of this…"

"What? What? What way out? Just tell me!"

"All you have to do is cooperate fully," Simon supplied.

"Can you feel that?" Cynthia asked. I saw her tapping with her finger on his now mostly shrunken organ.

"Feel what? Hey! Hey! What did you do? I didn't feel nothin!"

"He's almost ready," Cynthia told Simon.

"Hey! Hey! What do I have to do?" Bullfrog asked Simon.

"Well, that's a good question," Simon replied. "For starters, we want to know everything there is to know about the deal between you and the former warden."

"Sure! Sure!" Bullfrog replied quickly. "Anything! Just get her to stop!"

"Clamp!" Cynthia said to me and pointed at one of the super weird contraptions on the table.

"Hey! Stop!" Bullfrog yelled. "I'm cooperating. Tell her I'm cooperating."

"Just ignore me," Cynthia said as she fussed with the clamp. "You just tell them what they need to know. I'll stay busy here. Oh, you may feel some slight pulling and tugging, but hopefully that's all you'll feel."

"What? What? Hey! I'm cooperating! Stop her!"

"So how about it?" Simon said to him, "What did you and the warden cook up?"

"Hey! Look! He came to me! He said to make life miserable for the squirt! I could do anything I wanted to him! Hey! Hey! What are you doing? I can feel that?"

I looked and saw that she had actually connected the clamp to the loose skin of his scrotum and she was pulling fairly hard on it.

"You can feel it?" Cynthia asked. "Hmm… I thought I gave you enough pain killer to totally numb everything, but your body mass is so much that it's not working as well as I thought it would."

"What? Stop! I'm talking! I'm cooperating!"

"Like I said," Cynthia said without looking up at him, "just ignore me."

"What?"

"Bullfrog!" Simon said to get his attention. "What about the deal? You said he told you to do anything you want to him?"

"Yeah! Yeah! Anything! Just so long as I didn't kill him. He said it would be real bad for me if I actually killed him."

"Scalpel!" Cynthia said to me holding out her hand.

That one would have been easy for me to figure out if there hadn't been three of them on the table. I went with the one she pointed to."

"Scalpel!" Bullfrog roared.

"Relax," Cynthia said, her concentration seemingly totally on what she appeared to be doing. "You shouldn't feel a thing."

"But! But!"

"Bullfrog!" Simon yelled. "The deal! You just couldn't kill him? Anything else?"

"Yeah! Yeah! He said Toyboy had raped several kids and now he really wanted to see him suffer for it."

"See," Cynthia said softly to me. "Very little bleeding. Now we can open him up completely."

"Hey! Hey! What are you doing? I'm cooperating! See? I'm cooperating fully! Stop her!"

"Bullfrog!" Simon said to get his attention again. "What else did he tell you?"

"Nothin! Nothin! I swear! That was it!"

"See," Cynthia said softly to me, "Now we can just pull them straight out like this. Easy access. Hand me the thread to tie it off with."

I was guessing she meant the spool of thread on the tray. I handed it to her.

"Bullfrog," Simon said again, trying to regain his attention. "What did you do to Clayton…Toyboy?"

"What do you think? I had my fun with him!"

"Snips," the doctor said pointing at another piece of equipment.

"Hey! Hey! Stop!"

"You had your fun with him?" Simon asked. "What does that mean? Exactly what did you do?"

"You know! I raped his ass. I stuck it to him good. Both ends. Tell her to stop! Tell her to stop!"

While he was talking, Cynthia had pulled aside the drapery on the cart and had pulled out a plastic tub of chicken livers from the second shelf. What I saw in it looked absolutely disgusting. She reached into the tub with one of her instruments and pulled one out. "There," she said, sounding very satisfied as she held it up to show me. See how easy that was? She was holding a bloody ball of livers that looked all too much like what I was guessing the real thing would look. I can't begin to tell you how disgusting it appeared!

"Hey! Hey! What did you do to me! You can't do that! You can't! Make her stop! Make her stop! Put it back! Put it back!"

"Oh relax!" Cynthia said to him. It was only one! You still have another one. You'll never miss it!" She turned to me. "Tray," she said, nodding at an empty glass container on top of the cart. I handed it to her and she dropped the bloody mass into it. "That's one."

"Hey! Hey! Put it back! Put it back!"

"Bullfrog!" Simon yelled at the panicked prisoner to get his attention. "What else did you do?" he asked.

"What else? What else? I don't know! I had everyone else have fun with him too!" he said.

"Snips!" Cynthia said to me again. This time I knew what she wanted.

"Hey! Hey! She can't do that! She can't do that! Don't!"

"Bullfrog!" Simon yelled to get his attention again. "Shortly before he left here, you hurt him bad. What did you do?"

"Tell her to stop! Tell her to stop!"

"Then tell me what you did!"

"I nearly killed the little shit! He bit me right on my.... Dumb shit nearly bit it off! I nearly killed him for it! Now tell her to stop!"

"Too late," Cynthia said as she held up another bloody mass from the hidden tub so that he could see it.

"No! No! I told you everything! Everything! I cooperated! I cooperated! Put it back! Put them back! Put it all back!"

"Bullfrog!" Simon yelled again. "What did the Warden do when you almost killed him? What did he do?"

"Huh? Nothin'! He didn't do nothin'! He retired! Quit! I didn't even talk to him again! Now get her to stop! Get her to put them back! She has to put them back!"

"Anything else?" Cynthia asked Simon.

He shook his head. "I'm good."

She looked to me. I was still speechless. I knew what we were going to do. The basic idea had been mine to begin with! But I was still speechless!

"In that case...." She picked up another hypodermic needle and plunged it into another tiny bottle. She grabbed her alcohol swipes and wiped another patch of skin just above his now totally shrunken organ. Then she plunged the needle into him.

"Hey! Hey! What are you doing? I cooperated! What are you doing?" Bullfrog yelled.

Cynthia just looked at him very calmly. "Oh, that's just because this next part could hurt more so I'm giving the anesthetic a little boost. I figured as long as I'm here, I'm just going to remove the rest of what's there as well. You don't need it anymore anyway."

"What? What? You can't do that! Tell her she can't do that! I cooperated! I did! You said if I cooperated, she wouldn't do anything! You said the governor left me a way out!"

Simon leaned over him with a big smile on his face. "I lied!"

"What? What? You can't do this! You can't!"

"Oh relax," Cynthia said again. "I understand that this procedure can have a very calming effect on people. And since you won't have all that testosterone coursing around through your system anymore, you're going to be a much calmer, much more amiable person. But don't worry, you'll still be all male…technically. Of course, you'll have to sit to pee from now on, but don't worry, you'll get used to it. It's easy. I've done it that way all my life!"

I saw Bullfrog's eyes roll up in his head and his body immediately went limp.

"Damn!" I said, "Did that sedative you just gave him work that fast?"

"It shouldn't," Cynthia said with some concern as she quickly came out from between his legs and moved to his head. She raised each of his eyelids and stared at his eyes for a moment. Then she stood up and shook her head. "Imagine that, he fainted!"

CHAPTER

33

The three of us stopped again at the same Denny's restaurant we had visited twice before. We were all pretty much giddy with laughter as we sat down. "I can't believe he fell for it!" Cynthia proclaimed as she took her seat.

"Fell for it?" I said. "Shit! I knew what was going on, and I think I fell for it too!"

"Hey McNair," Simon said, "let me have that recorder you've got. When we get back, I'd like to get your tech guys to help me edit it down so we can use it when we talk to the old warden."

I handed the little recorder over and he stuck it in his pocket. "So what's our next move?" I asked. "The former warden?"

Simon shook his head, "Not yet. Like I said, I want to hit him with parts of this tape when we talk to him. In the meantime, I'm trying to get a lead on some of the jurors from Clayton's trial."

That part confused me a little. "The juror's? Why?"

"Because I want one of them to confirm what the transcripts said. There's always little things that get left out of the transcripts or get talked about in court and then thrown out. I want to see if any of them remember anything that might be important."

The guy was sharper than I thought. I hated him! I liked him...sort of, but he was definitely sharp!

When we got back to the office, I went straight to see Don. "Any news on another safe house for us?" I asked.

He shook his head. "No, not yet. We're trying to work out something more…permanent!"

"Permanent?" I asked. "Like what?"

"Permanent!"

I love it when he gives me so many details. "In the meantime," I said, "I'm going to put Pariah back to work again."

"If you think he's ready, go for it. I take it you have something in mind?" he asked.

"I've had our profiler working on digging up some candidates that could lead us to their Texas operation."

He nodded. "Just keep me in the loop."

Simon was waiting for me when I got back to my office. "I just talked with a woman who was on Clayton's jury. She's willing to talk if we can see her today."

I looked at the mound of paperwork on my desk which had somehow mysteriously grown a bit in my absence. "I'm ready now," I said. I wasn't the least bit interested in doing battle with papers that could somehow regenerate so quickly by themselves.

Mrs. Moorhead was an elderly woman. But then, after twenty years, nobody who had been on the jury was going to be a spring chicken anymore. "What can I do for you officers?" she asked.

"It's Agent!" I replied. "Agents McNair and Cantrell. I'm FBI and he's Justice Department."

"Oh! I'm sorry," she said. "I didn't know there was much of a difference."

I decided not to enlighten her.

"Ma'am," Simon began, "do you remember the Thomas Clayton trial twenty years ago?"

"Sure I do," she replied. "It was the only time in my life that I ever had to sit on jury duty. It was so exciting! I mean, yes it was terrible what that Mr. Clayton did! But to someone like me, it was still exciting!"

"I'm glad you feel that way," Simon said kindly.

"Why are you asking about that now?" she asked. "That was a long time ago!" Then she leaned forward. "Did that man get out of prison and start raping girls again?"

"No Ma'am. Nothing like that at all. We're just looking into some old cases, trying to find…patterns. Was there anything about that trial, anything at all, that stuck out as odd to you?" Simon asked.

She seemed to think about it for a moment. "No," she finally said. "Even I thought it was really a very straightforward case. And Mr. Clayton's lawyer didn't seem to put up much of an argument to try to defend him. So he must have done it! And then when the judge told us about all the other girls he had raped…."

"Wait a minute," Simon said quickly. "Other girls?"

"Why yes. The judge came in to see us just before we started discussing if we thought Mr. Clayton was guilty or not. He said something about being sure we would reach the right conclusion so we could stop a man who was suspected of raping many other girls. I mean, we all would have voted him guilty to begin with, but that simply made it so much easier."

"Did the fact that he was suspected in other cases ever come out during the trial itself? Perhaps as something that was removed from the record?"

"No…I don't think so. I'm pretty sure that we heard it first from the Judge."

"Mrs. Moorhead," I asked. "Do you remember anything from that trial about Mr. Clayton's lawyer having a video tape he wanted to show?"

"No…not that I remember. The whole thing didn't really last very long."

"Thank you, Mrs. Moorhead," Simon said. "That's all we need. You've been very kind."

Neither of us said a word until we were back in my SUV. "Was that jury tampering?" I asked.

"Blatant!" he replied. "Now we have to talk to a judge too!"

Once back at my office, I called John, Hannah, and Billy into my office. I also had Brent Jackson come down too. "We're going to start working Pariah again," I told them. "And we're specifically trying to target the breaking house in Texas." I turned to Brent, "Were you able to come up with any possible cases for us?"

"You know this is all going to be mostly a shot in the dark kind of thing," he said. "But I've identified several files that I think we could start with."

"Good! Let's pick one and set it up."

Brent disappeared for a few minutes and came back with six case folders. "These are the ones I think we should look at first," he said.

"Which one do you suggest?" I asked.

"Any of them. Just pick one."

We discussed each of them for a few minutes, but as Brent had indicated, they were all likely candidates. So in the end, we decided to choose one scientifically…we flipped a coin. Literally! Since there were six folders, we did them two at a time and gradually narrowed it down to one winner. Only then did we open it to see who the lucky candidate was. Andrea Ipollino – no surprise that she was from Texas.

I handed the folder to Billy. "See if you can get the parents to agree," I told him.

Everybody left except John. "Back in business again," he said.

I nodded. "Once again," I confirmed. "Except this time, Pariah said he wants to help us. We're not asking him, he wants to help."

"How about the Mexican's?" he asked. "Any news on what they're up to next?"

I shook my head. "They won't tell me anything! It's more than a bit scary."

"I can imagine. Just hang in there and let me know how I can help."

"Thanks! And by the way, I'm sorry you're having to cover so much for me lately while I've been otherwise occupied."

"Huh!" he grunted. "Since you and Pariah have solved so many back cases, the truth is that we've got less to do. You've made life easier on everyone! You just keep doing what you have to. Let me worry about the rest."

It's nice to know you've got friends you can count on.

Simon came to see me late in the afternoon. "What's happening?" I asked.

"I'm heading back to D.C. later today," he replied. "We've reached the point in the investigation where anything we do is likely going to alert Chermont or Brecker. I want to do some sniffing around up there before I come back again and tackle what's left."

"Alert them?" I asked.

He nodded. "Any of the people we interview now could very likely pass that interview along to Chermont…or Brecker. I don't want to make my job harder than it already is." He reached into his pocket and pulled out the little recorder I had given him. "Thanks," he said. "Your tech guys have been most helpful."

"Did you get what you want?"

He pulled his cell phone out of his pocket and flipped around the screen for a few seconds. He held it up so I could hear. Bullfrogs voice came through loud and clear, telling all about what he did to Pariah. But what I noticed, was that I heard nothing of what we were doing to him. He just sounded…excited about something.

"Nice!" I said. "But even I know that won't hold up in court."

"I don't intend it to. I only want it as corroborating evidence for when we talk with anyone else." Their statements are going to be much more important!"

Yeah, no doubt about it, as much as I despised him, he was damn good!

"Which reminds me," he said. "You didn't happen to have another one of those little recorders listening in on our conversation with Mrs. Moorhead, did you?"

Busted! I reached into my pocket and pulled it out and handed it to him. "How did you know?"

"Just a guess. How many of those things do you have by the way?"

I pulled open my desk drawer and pulled out four more. "An even half dozen," I replied. "They're very small, very handy, and a whole lot less conspicuous than my phone. Besides, when I want to pass on a recording, I don't lose my phone either."

He smiled. "I may have to get one…or two." He held up my latest little recorder. "I'll get this back to you in a little while. I'm going to add her statement to what I already have."

Unbelievably, Don moved Pariah and I back into the mansion. That had its good points, but also it had some bad ones. The good points included the fact that the wall was being repaired quickly and I felt a lot safer there than anywhere else. The wall patch was currently nothing more than bare cement block, but I figured that was a lot better than the gaping hole. The bad part was all the bullet damage that was literally everywhere. I couldn't turn to look at anything without seeing some kind of destruction.

Phil was moved in with us too, but not to take care of us. Nor was it for us to take care of him – I had other jobs to do anyway. Instead, they hired a woman to cook and take care of the house – us included…that is, until Phil was well enough to take over again. Her name was Samantha and I immediately associated her name with the character on the old TV show, "Bewitched." This Samantha however looked nothing at all like Elizabeth Montgomery! This Samantha was older, and black, and had a commanding way about her that seemed more like she came straight from Marine basic training than anywhere else. While she wasn't heavy in the least, she certainly knew how to throw her weight around! I think Don picked her out especially because of that!

The day Phil came back from the hospital, he and I sat out on the back patio, watching them working on the wall. "They really tore this place up!" he complained as he looked around. "It'll never be the same."

"No, especially if the government is footing the bill."

He laughed. "You've got that right!" A minute later he added, "Man, that was some night!"

"Yes it was!"

"You were great!" he said. "Running off after those Mexican's with a gun in each hand. Like you were some cowboy in a western – Wyatt Earp or something. Shootout at the O.K. Corral!"

I laughed. "You didn't do so bad either. But if this was the O.K. Corral, then you would have been Doc Holliday. And you looked more like G.I. Joe than some fake old wasted doctor!"

"G.I. Joe? Really?" He sounded pleased. "Well, just like Wyatt Earp, you shot the bad guys and didn't get shot yourself!"

"This time!" I replied. "I was lucky! Real lucky! You shot as many or more bad guys than I did!"

He rubbed his bandages. "Maybe," he replied, "but not so lucky for me."

"But you're still here!"

He smiled. "Yeah, there is that!"

It was three days after Simon left before we were able to send Pariah out looking for Andrea. The parents agreed and flew into Atlanta along with the original case officer from our El Paso office, Sam Trent. I had met Sam before, professionally, when I used to work narcotics. The El Paso office was a fairly small one so everyone worked whatever cases came up. Technically, Sam was the case officer for three of the six girls Brent had picked out – I just didn't let him know that.

Sam was not too keen on coming to Atlanta, at least not to work with a psychic. The parents of the girl were only there because his Director had ordered him to convince them to come. It looked like our Director was still keeping a closer eye on things than I thought.

We set up the interview room as usual, and as usual, Pariah threw another fit when the company lawyer walked in and asked the parents to sign the paper stating that they knew he was a child molester. There had to be a way around that. I made a mental note to ask Simon the next time I saw him.

Cynthia took Pariah's blood pressure again – not that I had any clue as to why – and just before we began, Pariah turned to the mother and asked, "If I find her, will you feed me?"

The mother was flabbergasted…as was I. "Don't worry, Pariah," I said. "We'll make sure you get well fed." Why did he insist on asking that? We kept him well fed three times a day and he had even started putting on a little weight. I made another one of my little mental notes to find out about it.

The mother put her hands on Pariah's back, he closed his eyes, and went off somewhere. And five seconds later I saw him shaking his head. "Bad place. Not good," he said. He opened his eyes to look at me. "Girl is dead," he pronounced, "but she's in a bad place."

"Dead?" the mother asked, terrified by the pronouncement. She pulled her hands away from Pariah and started crying.

The father held her. "It can't be!" he replied stubbornly. "This man can't possibly know if she's alive or dead! I was against this from the start! Even Agent Trent was against it. Don't believe him, dear. Stay positive! Andrea is alive! We just have to find her."

I had expected something like this. They never want to believe. Sometimes not even after we find the body. "Please," I said. "Bear with us. We warned you in advance that this sometimes happens. Now that we think she's dead, let us find her body for you."

"Why?" the husband asked. "She's not dead! There's no point in this man's mumbo-jumbo magic upsetting my wife any more than she is."

"Please," I said again. "If you don't think she's dead, then you keep believing that, but help us continue with what we're doing. We've never failed yet to find who we're looking for. Never!"

The mother looked frightened by my pronouncement. Tearfully, she extracted herself from her husband, and after giving it some thought, put her hands back on Pariah's back. And Pariah closed his eyes once again.

"Bad place," he said again. "Bad place."

"What makes it so bad?" I asked.

It was a moment before he answered. "Don't know. Can't tell. Feels bad."

"Tell me about the place Pariah."

"Hole. Bad hole."

"Okay, Pariah, where is the hole?"

"Going up. Nothing."

"What do you mean nothing?"

"Desert. Hard to find landmarks."

"Okay, Pariah. You said the hole is bad. Tell me about it."

"Square, but long."

"Rectangular," I prompted.

He nodded. "Tractor not far away."

"The hole was dug by a tractor? Is it a cemetery? Is she in a grave?"

He shook his head. "No. Big hole. Very big. Deep."

"Does it look like she just fell in and couldn't get out?" I asked.

"No. Can't see her. Under the sand."

"Okay Pariah. Try going as high as you can. Let's see if we can figure out where that hole is."

"Going up. Road a little way from hole. Going up. Straight road, very straight. Long road. Up. River in the distance. Long river. No cities. Um… strange."

"What's strange?" I asked.

"Shiny spot. Trying to go closer. House. No, not a house. Trailer. Shiny trailer like you live in. Chairs out front."

"Somebody has a house trailer out there?"

"Trying to get closer. Hard. Very hard. Not sure. Trying. Can't get all the way. Trying. Can't get closer."

"Pariah, how well can you see it?"

"Pretty good."

"Describe it."

"Shiny all over. Rounded top. Big tank outside like for gas."

"Pariah, would that be gas for the car or gas for the house, like propane?"

"Not sure. Don't think it's for car."

"Pariah, is there a name or a logo on the tank?"

"Red diamond and I think an oil well in it."

"Diamond and Derrick!" Sam Trent suddenly pronounced. I know the company…I use them myself.

"Can we get records from them of all the trailers they service like this one out in the desert?"

"I'm sure we can," he replied.

"Then once we have that, we can start narrowing down the search."

It took us a day to get coordinated and come up with some leads from the propane company, then two more days of trying before Pariah was able to lead the authorities to the hole. An hour later, while we were still trying to wrap things up and talk with the parents, we got a phone call telling us why Pariah had thought it was such a bad place. The hole was being used as a body dump. They found four other bodies in the same hole – so far. And evidence of another hole not far away. When they called back another hour later telling us that they had positively identified Andrea's body, Sam Trent was an instant believer.

I was very pleased whenever Cynthia dropped by for dinner. I just couldn't allow myself to express that the way I would have before Simon entered the picture. She usually sat with Phil and I for a little while, then went out to talk with Pariah. If it was anywhere near dinner time, Brutus was usually missing. But then I had noticed that while Samantha was cooking, she kept slipping the little dog bits of food. Brutus wasn't going far from the kitchen anytime she was cooking.

The day after we had wrapped up the case on Andrea Ipollino, Cyn was back at the mansion again. As I watched her talking to Pariah, I wondered how many times she had talked with Simon since he had gone back to Washington. Did she know when he was coming back to Atlanta? I figured maybe I could ask her about it later, just to give me an idea of how fast I could proceed on the next case for Pariah.

Dinner, as always, was good, just different from the way Phil cooked things. Cyn seemed to really like the fact that Samantha cooked more vegetables than either Phil or I cared about.

After dinner, Phil took off to redress his wound and Pariah took off to wander the backyard with Brutus again. Cyn and I occupied two of the chairs out on the patio.

We sat there together in silence for a few minutes. I got the impression that there was something bothering her. But did I dare ask what? Was it my place to ask anymore? I decided to broach my question about Simon. But as I turned to ask, she belted out her own question.

"What did I do?" she asked. "Did I do anything that turned you off? Or did you just get tired of me?"

Huh? "Tired of you? What do you mean?"

"I mean, for a while now you've suddenly been more distant, you haven't even asked me out to dinner. Nothing? I thought that maybe it was because of the attack here, but now I'm pretty sure it wasn't. So what was it? Anything specific? Or have you just lost interest?"

"Lost interest?" I couldn't believe it! "What about you and Simon?"

"Simon? What about him?"

"I thought you and he were…. You know."

"Simon? And me? Whatever gave you that impression?"

"Well, I think it was the way he looked at you all the time and you seemed to look at him the same way. And then you both showed up real early in the morning after the raid. I figured you two had slept together. And let's face it, I'm not built anything at all like he is. And of course… he's got money."

She stared at me openmouthed. "Cliff! You're jealous!"

"Me? Jealous?"

"Yes you are! You're jealous of Simon! Admit it!"

"Me?" I stared at her for a few moments. "Maybe," I said softly. "By the way, do you happen to know when he's coming back?"

"How would I know that?" she asked.

"Well, aren't you two…."

"Cliff! I haven't talked to him. He's married! He's got two kids!"

I was shocked. "Well how was I supposed to know?"

"Didn't you ask?"

"It's not exactly the kind of thing a guy asks another guy," I replied.

"Well he was wearing a wedding ring!"

"That was a wedding ring? With a diamond that big?"

"Sure!"

"Impossible!"

She stared at me for a few moments. "So you've been avoiding me because you thought I was going out with Simon?"

"Something like that," I admitted.

"And yet you still tried to be friends with me while giving us some space?"

"I'm sorry!" I blurted out. "I like you! A lot! Okay? I wanted to be around you. But what chance did I have against someone like him?"

She was smiling at me. "You like me?"

It was my turn to stare at her. Instead of answering, I got up from my chair and stood over her. Then I leaned down and lifted her entire body out of the chair and into my arms.

She giggled and kissed me – on the lips this time. "Simon is awfully handsome," she said teasingly.

"Shut up woman!" I carried her all the way into the house, all the way up the stairs, and laid her gently down on my bed.

Then I showed her just how sinful I was capable of being too.

My heavenly Cynthia was back again!

Now I just had to figure out why she never wore dresses!

CHAPTER

34

A week after the Andrea Ipollino case, we tried again. Pariah found this one alive. She was living in Canada with her boyfriend and hadn't told anyone. The following week we did another one and found her hooking for a pimp in San Francisco. The file we picked out a week later was another of Sam Trent's files. And unfortunately, the girls name was on the list of bodies they pulled out of the same hole with Andrea. Between the two holes, they had uncovered sixteen bodies so far. Somebody had been awfully busy there.

I was starting to get really nervous though about not hearing anything about the Mexicans for several weeks now. What were they doing? Did they give up? I asked Don several times. He told me to just stay careful! What was that supposed to mean? I even approached Frank Morris about it, but he pushed me off too. I did get the sense that he was more than a bit nervous about the issue. What weren't they telling me?

And then two things happened at the same time. I got a call from Sam Trent, and Simon decided to return from D.C.

The call from Trent came early in the morning and it was a special request for Pariah's services on a case that was only a few days old. The only thing with this case was, we would have to bring Pariah out to Texas. The missing girl's name was Patricia "Patty" Paloma. There was no father in the house and the girl was the principal care-giver to her mother who was suffering with a liver that was shutting down and couldn't travel. On the one hand the request sounded reasonable enough – especially since it was such a fresh case. On the other hand though, it would mean transporting and protecting Pariah on a difficult trip – if he would agree to go. And then of course there was the other little nagging thing that worried me. We would be taking him right into the Mexican's backyard. Not good!

I took my concerns directly to Don and he in turn took them to the Director. I had no doubt that the Director probably phoned his opposite at the El Paso office. Bottom line? Yes, everyone was concerned. Yes, everyone was worried. But it had been a month now and we hadn't heard a peep out of Pacheco. I was told that finding this girl would look very good for the FBI's image, but that I should look into it and make the decision myself. Not much help!

If it wasn't for the fact that the girl was the only one who could really care for her mother, I would have passed it up immediately. But I could just see the headlines, "FBI refuses to help sick old lady find her missing daughter." That was the last thing I needed on my head. But I just had all these other nagging worries about it. So I did the best thing I could at the time, I put off deciding what to do about it until later.

And it was a good thing I did, because right after that, Simon showed up in my office. I hadn't even heard he was coming back! I felt secure enough now with Cyn to welcome him back gladly. No reservations whatsoever.

After exchanging a few pleasantries with him, he pulled out a piece of paper and laid it on my desk in front of me. I had seen more than enough warrants in my career to recognize it immediately. What surprised me about this one though was that it was a warrant for the arrest of Harold Morgan, the head of Morgan and McCaffery law firm – the firm that had employed Pariah's attorney Clint Green.

"You're arresting him?" I asked. "We haven't even talked to him yet.

He just smiled and pulled another document out. "I have this one too that I can use at my own discretion," he said as he laid another warrant on my desk. Basically it called for a raid on the entire company and seizure of all documents and materials pertaining to any and all cases over the last twenty-five years. The warrant would pretty much shut the company down!

"I can't believe this!" I gasped.

"Believe it!" Simon said. "I just hope we won't have to issue that second one because it's going to take a lot of time and manpower to handle."

"I believe it!" I replied. "When are you going to issue the arrest warrant?"

"I'm going to hand it over to Wimberly right now. Let him find some upstanding agents to handcuff Morgan and bring him in. Then I thought you and I might have a nice little chat with the man."

I smiled. "This should be interesting!"

He nodded. "Very! Especially since I can pretty much guarantee that his career as a lawyer is about to be officially over."

It wasn't until after lunch when Simon came back to my office again to tell me that our "guest" had finally arrived. I immediately dumped my paperwork and followed him to the interview room. We stopped for a moment in the room on the other side of the glass to try to size the guy up. There were two men in the room waiting for us. I had to ask someone which man was Morgan – the guy on the left. The other one was his partner McCaffrey. They both looked like typical lawyers who had been around a long time. Morgan looked tense, but confident. McCaffrey looked wary. I wondered if this was the first time either of them had been arrested.

Simon and I went into the room with them.

"I protest this arrest!" McCaffrey immediately declared. "You have no legal grounds to arrest my partner and no valid reason to put him through this shameful procedure! And especially not for arresting him in front of all our company employees!"

I stood in the background while Simon smiled and took a seat at the table across from them. "No legal grounds? That's kind of a silly argument for a lawyer to pose. I can assure you that the arrest warrant is all the legal grounds I need. And as for valid reasons…well, that's what we're going to talk about right now."

"I hope you're prepared for a major counter suit against you for this!" McCaffrey returned angrily.

"Mr. McCaffrey, I can assure you that I'm well prepared for a whole lot more than that. Now, just for the record, let's get the formalities out of the way, shall we?" He paused waiting for more protest. When he didn't get any he said. "This is Simon Cantrell of the Justice Department, council to the Attorney General of the United States. With me is also Special Agent Clifford McNair of the FBI here in Atlanta. This is the initial interview with Harold Morgan, head of the Morgan and McCaffrey law firm of Atlanta, Georgia. Present with Mr. Morgan is Mr. McCaffrey, also of said firm. Now gentlemen, can we get down to business?"

I had been a bit stunned when Simon announced that he was council to the Attorney General. I know that Morgan and McCaffrey were stunned too. Suddenly they didn't look so confident anymore.

"Um…" McCaffrey said. "What's this all about?"

Simon ignored McCaffrey and spoke directly to Morgan. "Do you remember hiring a young attorney by the name of Clinton Green?"

Morgan looked startled. "I can truthfully say that I don't remember anyone by that name working for our firm in any capacity."

"I'm not surprised," Simon replied. "It was twenty years ago now."

Both Morgan and McCaffrey looked astonished. "Twenty years ago!" McCaffrey said. "What possible…"

"Please let me finish!" Simon said, cutting him off. He turned back to Morgan. "Twenty years ago you hired a young lawyer named Clinton Green straight out of law school. You immediately assigned him the task of defending Thomas Clayton who was implicated in the molestation and rape of William Chermont's daughter, Stacy Chermont. Now don't you think that was odd?"

"That was twenty years ago," Morgan replied testily. "What possible bearing can that have on anything now?"

Simon smiled. "I see that you remember him now."

"Mr. Morgan did not say that he remembered him," McCaffrey argued.

"But he does remember the case," Simon replied. "And I think he remembers it very well."

"That's your opinion, not fact!" McCaffrey said.

Simon ignored him. "Mr. Morgan, don't you think it's strange that a young lawyer gets assigned as the sole lawyer on such a case as this as his very first assignment? He wasn't even given the opportunity to sit in on any other cases just to watch or even act as second chair where he could learn procedures first. And believe me, he made more than a few blunders in the procedure department."

"Don't answer that!" McCaffrey warned.

"And don't you think, Mr. Morgan, that it's odd, that that same young lawyer was dismissed…fired…right after that case?"

"If he lost…" Morgan started to say.

"Don't answer!" McCaffrey cut in.

Simon went back to smiling again. "Here are a few more…odd things that I noticed about that case. I think it's odd that Green was assigned to what should have been a high-profile case. I think it was odd that he received no support from your company during the case at all. I think it was odd that he was fired so soon after the trial."

He paused before beginning again, his voice now growing louder and more stern with every word. "My list of odd things seems to go on and on! Because I think it's odd that right after the conviction, Mr. Clayton sent letter after letter asking about his appeal, until you, personally, sent him a letter telling him there would be no appeal and your firm was dropping him from their client list. Why did you do that, Mr. Morgan? Why was he denied any appeal?"

I could see that both Morgan and McCaffrey were shaken. But as usual, McCaffrey warned, "Don't answer!"

"Your company was charged with defending Mr. Clayton, yet you purposely set him up to be convicted before the trial could even begin. You provided inadequate counseling! There's a big ethics question right at the top of my list of things to charge you with, Mr. Morgan. And that list is quickly growing."

"Why are you bringing this up now?" McCaffrey asked. "As you said, this allegedly happened twenty years ago."

"I'm bringing this up," Simon replied, "because in the last few months, Thomas Clayton has become an item of national interest."

"What's that supposed to mean?"

"Let me put it this way. Would I be here from the Attorney General himself, for a case like this, if Mr. Clayton wasn't of such high interest?"

"What's he done?" McCaffrey asked.

"That, I'm afraid, is very highly classified."

"Then it's also hard to believe."

"And it doesn't matter that you don't believe it," Simon replied, "because I'm still going to shut your company down and run both of you into the ground! You, Mr. Morgan will be going to prison."

"You have no grounds!" McCaffrey protested.

"Oh?" Simon replied to Morgan, "Did I mention we found a rather large bank deposit to one of your accounts, made by check from Mr. Chermont right after the trial? One hundred thousand dollars went into one account and was immediately split up into four of your other personal accounts. And don't you think it's odd Mr. Morgan, that you should receive such a large amount of money, at that particular time, from Mr. Clayton's accuser?"

I was floored – as was McCaffrey! Morgan looked awfully uncomfortable, but he held his silence.

"Where are all the materials that Clinton Green collected for the trial?" Simon asked.

"What materials?" Morgan asked.

Simon consulted a piece of paper from a file he had. "Several notebooks, interview recordings, all the letters Mr. Clayton sent, copies of all the letters that were sent to Mr. Clayton, and one video tape!"

"I have no idea where they would be," Mr. Morgan replied.

Simon's smile broadened. "I'm so glad you said that." He pulled the other warrant out of his file folder and passed it across the table. Both of them looked at it and scrutinized it closely. "That's a warrant authorizing me to search and seize pretty much anything I want from your entire company. We're going to go through every case, every computer file, every little scrap of paper. And I suspect we're going to find a lot more than just this one case where you've made...mistakes. And even if we don't, how long do you think a process like this could take? Weeks? Months? Years? Will your company be able to survive that? You, of course Mr. Morgan, you don't have to worry about it. You're going to prison!"

Both of them looked very worried – Morgan more than McCaffrey. "There must be some way we can avoid this?" McCaffrey said.

"I want all those materials I mentioned right here in this building by nine A.M. tomorrow morning, or this warrant gets served! And I mean absolutely every piece of material pertaining to this case!"

"We'll let you know," McCaffrey replied.

"*You'll* let me know!" Simon replied. "He's going to jail. I'm sure he'll be out on bail soon enough, but in the meantime, you're going to have to take care of business for him."

"You've been awfully busy while you were home," I said as we were walking back to my office.

"I had to do something to fill my time," he replied. "Actually, I set a bunch of people looking for things and we got lucky."

"So Chermont what…bribed him?"

"That's what it looks like."

"Why?"

"My bet is that the tape will explain a lot. I just wish I had a copy of the letter that Chavez mentioned that Morgan had sent to Clayton."

"You mean you don't have anything?"

He shook his head. "I was making it up. Hopefully there will be some in with the Clinton Green materials."

I thought about things for a minute. "What if Pariah kept the letters?"

He stopped cold. "Did he?"

"I'm not sure, but if he did, there's only one place they could be. It's a long shot, but do you want to take a little trip out to the mansion later?"

He smiled. "Love to!"

"So what's next?" I asked as we resumed walking. "Wait to see what Morgan and McCaffrey come up with tomorrow?"

"Not this time. I'm trying to move as fast as possible now. Now I check on the latest warrant I applied for – to arrest the former Warden. He's defiantly going to jail when I get done with him!"

"I think it's about time."

"Way overdue!" he replied. "And once I get him wrapped up, I expect we'll be hearing from Nathan Brecker. If not, then I think we should definitely hear from him once we have a little talk with the judge! He's going to be in a bit of hot water too!"

"Wow," I said. "It sounds like you're really moving fast. How long do you expect all this to take?"

"I'd like to start arranging a court date by the end of the week. I'd love to file some kind of action against Brecker too, but I seriously doubt I'll come up with any direct evidence against him. He's always been way too smart to make any mistakes that are likely to be found."

"So what then? What happens after you file?"

"Then we wait."

"Wait?"

"For a court date. And that's likely to be months away."

"Like most other cases," I replied.

"Exactly!"

It was good news and it was disappointing news. But on the whole, it was very positive. And now that I had a basic timeline, things kind of fell into place for me as to what to do about using Pariah to find the Paloma girl.

As soon as I got back to my office, I made a few quick phone calls and one long one to Sam Trent. Then I called Billy and Hannah into my office. "Will either of you have any problem getting away for a few days starting tomorrow?"

"Why?" Hannah asked.

"Where we goin?" Billy asked at the same time.

"I want you two to check on some things regarding a girl named Patricia Paloma who's only been missing a few days now. This is a special case where we'd have to take Pariah out to Texas in person. Sam Trent can fill you in on all the details."

"You think she could be a better link into Pacheco's operation?" Billy asked.

"Yeah, I do. But that's not the real reason I'm sending both of you out there. I want to know something else entirely!"

CHAPTER

35

It was looking like the warrant for the arrest of the former prison warden wasn't going to come through until the next morning at the earliest. So I drove Simon in my big SUV out to the mansion.

"I can't believe they have you back here again," he said as we drove in the gate.

"I feel safer here than anywhere else," I replied.

I saw him noticing the extra guards as I parked the car next to Cynthia's little car. As we entered through the new front door, I saw him looking all around at the bullet holes. "Phil calls the new decorating style, 'Early O.K. Corral'." He grunted more than laughed. Pretty much my reaction too.

"You were damn lucky that night!" he said. "Both of you!"

"I still have nightmares sometimes," I replied.

We found Phil and Samantha in the kitchen. Phil and Simon shook hands, then I introduced Simon to Samantha. "Finally a healthy one around here!" she declared as she looked him over.

"I try," Simon replied.

"Well maybe you can teach some better habits to all the other ones who live around here!" she said while looking straight at me.

Simon laughed. "I'm afraid he may be beyond anyone's help!"

"I think you're right!" she replied. "If it wasn't for that shrink doctor of his, he'd probably eat nothing but TV dinners and hamburgers."

Hmm…someone had been talking to her about what was in the refrigerator back in my apartment! "Hey!" I replied. "Those TV dinners have lots of healthy stuff in them!"

Samantha just stared at me like she was giving me the evil eye.

"Let's go out back before she skins me alive," I suggested.

"Are you and the doctor getting close?" Simon asked.

Instead of replying, I led him outside to where Cynthia was sitting in the shade watching Pariah wandering around the yard. I walked up to her and gave her a kiss. "We have company," I told her.

"Simon!" she cried enthusiastically. Then she jumped up and gave him a hug and a kiss on the cheek. Why didn't she greet me that enthusiastically? At least she only kissed him on the cheek!"

"We need to talk to Pariah and find out if he saved any of the letters from his attorney," I told her.

"I don't remember him mentioning any," she said.

"But there's a lot of things he won't talk about either," I replied. "Let's hope this isn't one of them."

The three of us went out to talk with Pariah. Brutus immediately started barking at Simon again – good dog – except that what he wanted was for Simon to scratch behind his ears. I needed have a good long talk with that dog sometime!

I had this sneaking suspicion that Pariah liked lawyers about as much as I did, probably less, so I decided to go about asking him from a different direction. "Pariah, we have some news about your case. We just arrested the head of the law firm you hired for your defense. He was the man who sent you the letter telling you there would be no appeal."

For once, I saw astonishment on his face. "I didn't do it! It wasn't me!" he said.

"Yeah, we know. We're still working on clearing that up. Pariah, do you remember Simon? He's the one that found the evidence to put Mr. Morgan in jail. He needs to know if you happened to save any of the letters between you and your attorney, Mr. Green."

"Letters," he said. "Not many. I wrote. Lots. Never heard back. Then no appeal. No hope."

"Pariah," Simon said softly, "we know now that what they did to you was wrong. But do you still have the letter saying there would be no appeal?"

"Letter," Pariah said again with a far-away look in his eyes. Then he turned and walked away from us. But he was heading toward the house. Since Samantha hadn't called us to dinner yet, I found that strange. So I followed him…we all followed him.

He went directly up to his room and grabbed the plastic bag I had sealed his old plastic bag in that we had picked up from the little cubbyhole he had created for himself in the woods. He set it on the bed and tried desperately to open it, but his fingers simply weren't up to the task.

"Can I help?" I asked.

He seemed frustrated and also defeated, but he backed away and I attacked the knot at the top of the bag with my own hands. It came loose a minute later and I pulled his old dirty trash bag out. Pariah grabbed his bag and dumped it out on the bed. I didn't remember seeing any letters in there before, but I had only looked quickly – mostly to make sure he didn't have any weapons.

The smell when he dumped it out was pretty awful, as was the look of everything in there. "Pew!" Cynthia said as the odor hit her nose. "We need to do something about that stuff."

I didn't tell her I had wanted to throw it all out the day we had found it.

Pariah searched through the few clothes in the bag, then he grabbed an old red checkered flannel shirt. He carefully unraveled the ball it was in, and out popped two old rumpled envelopes onto the bed. "Letters," Pariah said backing away.

Simon moved in and grabbed them. Not one, but two letters. I could see from where I was that both envelopes bore the logo of the Morgan and McCaffrey law firm.

Pariah came over and took the envelopes from Simon. He looked them over and then pointed to one of them. "First," he said handing them back to Simon.

"You got this one first?" Simon asked. "Thank you," he said.

We watched as he opened it. He read for a moment then said, "It's a letter from Clint Green," he said. He started reading.

"Dear Mr. Clayton,

I'm sorry things didn't work out the way I hoped they would. Rest assured that I will get you an appeal date as soon as possible. I am confident we will have much better luck then. I am sure that a different judge will allow the tape that proves your innocence into evidence and the original decision can be reversed. I will be in contact with you shortly about the appeal.

"It's signed of course by Clinton Green," he finished.
He opened the second letter and read it.

"Mr. Clayton,

I regret to inform you that Clinton Green no longer works for this firm. The appeal you continually ask about is not going to happen.

From this point on, this company will no longer be representing you. You have been convicted of a heinous crime, now it's time to pay the penalty for your actions.

"This one is signed by Harold Morgan," he finished.
"Talk about stern!" I said.
"Yeah!" Cynthia agreed.
"May I have these?" Simon asked Pariah. These can help me nail Mr. Morgan to the wall and make him suffer for what he's done to you."
Instead of answering, Pariah just nodded and pushed his hands toward Simon as if trying to give him the letters. I realized then that there were tears falling from his eyes. Heck, there were almost tears coming from my own eyes, especially when Cyn walked over and held him to her and let him cry a bit on her shoulder. Thanks Cyn. Compassion was one of the biggest things taken away from him. As little as it was, that simple act made me feel better to watch.

Billy and Hannah were noticeably missing the next morning as I knew they would be. The materials from Morgan and McCaffrey were supposed to be here by nine o'clock. Unfortunately, I didn't get out of our morning meeting until nine fifteen. I hurried down to see what was going on. Instead of heading into the room where Simon would be with McCaffrey, I went into the observation room instead.

I saw Simon facing four lawyers this time. I figured that both Morgan and McCaffrey had hired outside lawyers to represent them. Most of what they talked about was somewhat Greek to me, but at one point Simon pulled out the letters he had gotten from Pariah last night and passed them across the table so the other side could read them. A few minutes later, he got back not only the letters from Pariah, but also a small brief case that one of the new lawyers handed over.

Simon opened the case. I couldn't see what was in it from where I stood. But he nodded to the men, and they all got up and left.

I went in to see Simon. "Sorry I was late," I said. "Don's meeting went longer than I planned."

"You didn't miss much," he replied.

"They didn't look too happy when they left," I noted.

"Actually, they should be happy. I'm not going to serve that other warrant and shut down their company." He turned the case so I could see in it. "And look what we have here."

The case contained several notebooks, a collection of letters, several old cassette tapes, and two old video tapes. "Two?" I asked.

"I'm betting one is a duplicate, and the other is the original that Green tried to submit as evidence."

I reached to grab one and he stopped me. "Don't!" he said. "I'd really like to have these fingerprinted to see who's been playing with them first."

Have I mentioned before that I considered the guy to be good? "How about the warrant for the prison warden, Hugh Ogilvie?"

Don Wimberly said he would send someone out to arrest him as soon as it came through. We'll find out then.

It was late morning by the time Simon called and told me Ogilvie had arrived. "Don't bother coming down yet," Simon told me. "He's yelling loud and clear for his lawyer. I think he's going to need one."

Ogilvie's lawyer must have liked him an awful lot, because he was there in less than forty-five minutes. Simon gave them a few more minutes to "confer" with each other before we went to see them – even though we had yet to tell them what they should be conferring about.

Ogilvie was dressed in jeans and what I was guessing was an old work shirt. His lawyer wore a nice looking suit – of course.

"What's this about?" his lawyer asked immediately.

"I'll get to that in a minute," Simon replied. "I just need to get the formalities out of the way first." He raised his voice a little for the recording, even though the microphones could easily pick up the sound of a pin dropping. "This is Simon Cantrell of the Justice Department, council to the Attorney General of the United States. Also present is Special Agent Clifford McNair of the FBI offices in Atlanta. This will be the initial interview with Hugh Ogilvie, former prison warden for the State of Georgia. Present and representing Mr. Ogilvie is...." He looked at the attorney for his name.

"David R. Grouse," the lawyer replied.

"Thank you, Mr. Grouse," Simon said. "To make a long story short, Mr. Ogilvie, we are looking into the treatment of one of your former inmates, Mr. Thomas Clayton. He was a prisoner at your institution for the last sixteen years of your term there."

I saw Ogilvie immediately look far more uncomfortable than he already was.

"Do you remember Mr. Clayton?" Simon asked.

There was a distinct pause before he looked to his attorney. The attorney nodded that he should answer, but it was another few moments before he opened his mouth. "I do."

Simon nodded. "Yes, I think you should remember him. Tell me Mr. Ogilvie, why is his medical file so thick?"

This time he didn't bother checking with his attorney before answering. "Well…many prisoners get hurt, some more than others. He just happened to make a habit of it."

"That's very interesting, and I have no doubt true. So tell me, according to our medical staff who we asked to go through his records, why were all the details as to how his injuries occurred left out of the file? According to them, it looked like those comments had been purposely left out."

I saw his eyes widen again and he fidgeted in his seat. "Don't answer if you don't feel comfortable with the question," his lawyer advised.

"Mr. Ogilvie," Simon continued, "we had a few interesting interviews with some of the current inmates who knew Clayton very well. In particular, his cellmate Angelo Chavez and another one better known as Bullfrog."

Again the widening of the eyes and he shifted in his chair.

"According to Chavez, it's common knowledge that you made a deal with Bullfrog right after Clayton arrived at your prison. You asked Bullfrog to make Clayton's life as miserable as possible for as long as possible. The only caveat was that he couldn't kill him. Why did you do that?"

"I suggest not answering," his attorney said.

"It's okay," Simon replied. "We can have the testimony of a few hundred prisoners to back up what happened over that entire sixteen year period. In fact, here's a little bit of what Bullfrog had to say himself." He pulled his cell phone out and found the file he wanted and laid the phone on the table. Bullfrog's excited voice came through loud and clear outlining the warden telling him to abuse Clayton as much as possible. I saw Ogilvie start to look very uncomfortable, but it was the startled look on his attorney's face that impressed me the most.

As soon as the recording had ended, Simon turned the recorder off. Then he stood up and leaned angrily over the table and banged his fist on the top. "You purposely set Clayton up to be physically and mentally destroyed. And you let it go on and on for sixteen years – despite the injuries to him. He was raped repeatedly, multiple times, day in and day out! His bones were broken over and over and over again because he tried desperately to resist. And you, Warden Ogilvie, did nothing at all to stop it. And then finally, just before you retired, he was hurt so badly that he could no longer speak properly or put two words together. He was left permanently brain damaged. Yet you simply sent him back to his cell with no further medical treatment."

He paused for a moment before continuing. His voice softened, but only a little. "And tell me this Mr. Ogilvie, why, why, why…wasn't he given the opportunity for parole?"

He waited for an answer. I expected Grouse to tell him not to answer, but the guy looked to be too much in shock. When nobody said anything, Simon lowered his voice, but it was full of angry threat. "Mr. Ogilvie, I'm going to put you away for a very long time and let you stay with all those gentlemen in your old prison. What do you think they might do to their former warden? Hmm? Personally, I hope they treat you exactly like they treated Mr. Clayton."

"I want a deal!" Ogilvie suddenly blurted out.

Simon looked totally surprised. "Why should I even contemplate a deal with you? I have more than enough evidence to bury you for a very long time!"

"Give us a few minutes to confer privately," Grouse said.

Simon straightened up and shook his head. "Confer all you want." He turned around and faced the mirrored wall. "Recorders off!" A tiny almost unnoticeable red light at the top corner of the mirror went off. "Knock on the door when you're ready," Simon told them. Someone will get me."

We left them then and went to the observation room to watch. We couldn't hear anything they said, but I knew it wasn't going to be good for Ogilvie, no matter what he gave them.

It was maybe five minutes before the lawyer got up and knocked on the door. "Let's finish them off," Simon said as he turned toward the door. "Start recording again!" he ordered.

"My client wants full immunity for all of his actions," the lawyer stated as we walked back in.

"He's not going to get it," Simon stated flatly. "In fact, I have yet to hear any reason why I should consider any kind of deal with him."

"My client has knowledge of other parties, outside of his office, that he can divulge…"

"You mean like William Chermont?" Simon interrupted.

"How could you possibly…" Ogilvie looked astonished.

"Mr. Chermont has been a very busy man," Simon replied.

To tell the truth, I was somewhat surprised myself when Simon had said it. But it really only made sense, knowing what we already did.

"I'm sorry, Mr. Ogilvie, no deals!" He turned to me. "We can go now," he said.

I followed him out of the room. "You surprised me with the Chermont connection. When did you dig that up?"

"I didn't. It was just a wild guess. But he doesn't know that. I'll let him and his lawyer sit there for a while. We'll book him, then the real negotiations will begin. And in the process I have no doubt that Ogilvie will give me all the tiny details of what went on. But he's still going to prison for a very long time!"

I have long been convinced that somewhere on my desk, in the stack of paperwork waiting to be done, is a male and a female file folder. And I am also convinced that those two folders are reproducing like rabbits! No matter how hard I try to reduce the stack, every time I turn around it grows again…larger than before. It's crazy! And it always seems to happen when I'm not looking!

I had been working on the stack yet again, when Simon entered my little office with a piece of paper.

"The results are in already on the fingerprints on those VCR tapes," he said as he laid the paper in front of me.

I looked at the paper. Tape One listed Clinton Green's name and that was it. The list for Tape Two was also short. Clinton Green and Nathan Brecker. "Not much here," I said.

"No, but at least we know that Brecker got the tape – which he should have.

"Wait a minute," I said. "If Brecker saw the tape, why did he continue to prosecute Clayton? He knew Clayton was innocent."

"We'll probably never know for sure," Simon replied. "But knowing what I do about Chermont, I could hazard a guess."

"What's that?"

"If Brecker told Chermont about the tape, and Chermont's daughter still insisted that Clayton had raped her, then he would have gone with his daughter's word over everything else. Most likely, he told Brecker to make the tape disappear. That would explain why the tape never made it into evidence."

I considered that and quickly realized it was more than possible.

"What I found most interesting," Simon continued, "was that there were no prints from Morgan or anyone else in that law office. And it also proves that the tapes got no further than that in being submitted as evidence."

"That doesn't prove anything though," I noted.

"No, but I still find it unusual," he replied. "I asked the lab to send the tapes over to your tech guys. Want to go see what's on them?"

"I thought you'd never ask!"

The tapes had been delivered to the tech lab by the time we got there, but they were still sealed in individual plastic bags. We had one of the tech guys load up the first one so we could watch it. Unfortunately, it was four hours' worth of video. There was a running timestamp on the bottom of the image. We had the tech fast-forward to the end of the tape and then start playing the video backwards. It still took a few minutes to get to the area of the tape we were interested in.

The camera angle came from behind the counter and slightly above so it could get everybody coming to the cash register as well as everybody coming in the front door. The result was that we got a semi-decent shot of everybody who came in to buy something. As person after person went backwards on the screen, I tried to remember the face in the picture of Clayton from his original arrest. It was a bit hard since he looked so different now.

"There!" Simon suddenly said. "Is that him?"

I looked intently at the man on the screen. He was buying two different types of ice-cream. "I think so," I replied. "I can't be sure without a picture to really compare it to, but I think that's him."

We had the tech guy run the tape backwards a bit more. We watched as Clayton backed out of the store and out of sight. "Okay," Simon said, run if forward now."

"Wait! Stop it right there!" I said. "Go forward a few frames. There!" I said stopping him again. Through the plate glass window of the store, I could just see the front of a car pulling in. "Can you get us a blow up of that license plate?" I asked.

"Sure thing," the tech said.

We waited while he played around with the image on the screen, then he hit the print button. A minute later I had a black and white, fairly grainy picture of the license plate on the car.

"How much image fixing is on this?" Simon asked.

"None on any of it," the tech replied.

"If we can read everything this well, and can identify the face in the photo, then there's no way this tape could have been too grainy to be used for evidence," Simon said. "I want copies of the whole tape. Another copy of this guy driving in till he leaves. And stills of his face and that license tag. Then do it all over again and clean it up as much as possible."

The tech made some notes on a pad. "It's going to take a while," he said.

"Just get it right!" Simon replied. "This is very important! Now, how about the other tape?"

It took only minutes to figure out that the second tape was an exact duplicate of the first one.

"I'll check the metadata on the tapes," the tech offered. "If I see anything out of whack, I'll let you know."

Tech guys can be so good sometimes. Now if they could just get my computer to run faster!

CHAPTER

36

It was late in the afternoon when Simon climbed into my big SUV and I drove him out towards the home of retired Judge Hawthorn. The neighborhood was exceptionally nice, but then I had guessed that it would be. Simon had told me that the Judge had been retired for about the last four years. Beyond that, I knew nothing more about him. If Simon knew anything else about him, he didn't tell me.

We rang the doorbell and were greeted by his wife. We both showed our ID cards and were allowed to come inside while she called him in from his garden out back. We waited in their comfortable living room. After seeing the outside of the house, I was surprised to note that the room wasn't overly fancy. In fact, it looked very lived in! It also contained lots of pictures of kids. I guessed grandchildren.

"What can I do for you gentlemen?" the Judge's deep voice boomed from the doorway. I saw an elderly gray-haired man with a slightly bent-over back standing and smiling at us. He came in and shook hands jovially with both of us. "I don't get many visitors anymore except for the kids," he said as he took a seat, sinking down into one of the chairs. "Now, how can I help?"

"Judge Hawthorn," Simon started, "We're investigating a case that you presided over about twenty years ago."

"Twenty years!" the judge exclaimed. "Isn't that a bit long? I doubt I'll remember much from back then!"

"I think you'll remember this one. It was a rape and molestation case involving the daughter of William Chermont."

His gray eyebrows went up momentarily and he sat back in his chair. "Ah. That case," he said.

"You do remember it then."

He nodded. "Somewhat anyway. What do you want to know? I'm sure you have the transcripts."

"Yes, we have them, but it's some other information we've come across recently that has been the most enlightening."

"Oh? Like what?"

Simon paused before replying. "Before the trial, the defendant's lawyer tried to get a video tape admitted into evidence, but you wouldn't allow it. I've seen the video, Judge Hawthorn, it's not as grainy and unviewable as you claimed it was. In fact, it was rather good quality for the equipment at the time. Why did you dismiss that evidence?"

The judge's face clouded. "I'm not willing to discuss that matter."

"I think you should," Simon said politely.

"Well I think I shouldn't!" he replied.

"Why is that?" Simon asked. "Something to hide?"

The judge's face got angry. "Do you know who I am?" he asked.

"Yes, I know exactly who you are," Simon replied. "And more importantly, I know exactly what you've done."

"What do you think I've done?" he asked testily.

Instead of replying, Simon pulled out his cell phone and played the entire interview with Mrs. Moorhead.

"Where did you get that?" the judge asked.

"We talked with her just a few days ago. How many other jurors will remember the same thing?"

The judge got up from his seat and walked over toward the fireplace. He stared at one of the pictures on the mantle for a moment, then he picked it up. "I would think...they would all remember it," he finally replied without looking at us.

He turned around and handed the picture to me. I saw a picture of a teenage girl.

"Biggest mistake I ever made in my life!" he said. "But sometimes desperate times call for desperate measures."

"Why was that?" Simon asked as he took the picture from me.

He walked back to his chair and sat down. "My oldest daughter," he said as he pointed to the picture. "She had leukemia. Medicine wasn't up to what we can do today, but the bills certainly were! Fantastic costs kept piling up. But what could I do? She was my daughter! Finally came the time when the doctors wanted to try one more procedure, but I was out of money and out of credit. Couldn't get a loan to save my life...or my daughter's life in this case. And then William Chermont walked into my office with a minor little proposition for me. Just sway the jury so that his daughter will get the justice she deserved. As I said, desperate times call for desperate measures. I took his money – in cash! Paid off the doctors a little at a time so as not to arouse any suspicion. I swayed the jury all right, but I shouldn't have bothered, the stupid lawyer they hired didn't have a case to begin with. Especially not up against Chermont's lawyer." He closed his eyes for a moment. "The cancer came back two years later and took her."

Simon set the picture down on an end table nearby, then very softly asked, "Is that why you didn't allow the video tape into evidence?"

"Partially. The lawyer...Brecker I think, visited me beforehand – before the kid even tried to get the tape admitted. Dumb kid! He should have known better. He convinced me not to allow it – especially in light of the deal I had worked out with Chermont himself. But to tell the truth, I figured any wrong doings I had done in that case would quickly be overturned in the appeal. Weren't they?"

"He never got the chance at an appeal. His lawyer was fired and the head of the firm personally took it on himself to notify Clayton that he would be getting no appeal."

"He can't do that!"

"I know. Clayton didn't know. He rotted for sixteen years in prison – under another one of Chermont's little deals with the warden. He was raped and beaten every day for sixteen years. He's out now. Homeless. Brain damaged. All of his bones were broken repeatedly in prison so many times that he can hardly walk, hardly use his hands. He calls himself Pariah now. And the name fits perfectly."

The judge shook his head. "Huh! I always thought there would be an appeal. So Chermont really stacked the deck?"

"Overly."

He nodded.

"What are you going to do?"

"To you?" Simon said. "Nothing! The most we could really do anyway wouldn't amount to all that much. I am going to insist on your testimony in court though."

He nodded. "Gladly! It shouldn't take much to overturn the decision. But after so many years, is it worth it?"

"In this case, it's not only worth it, it's vital!"

"What now?" I asked Simon as I drove back toward the office.

"Now I try to get us a court date!"

I knew from long experience that once the date was finally arranged, we were looking at a long time. Months…at least.

I had barely gotten back to the office when Billy called me from Texas. "Nothing yet, Boss. No sign of anything. Do you want us to keep looking?"

I thought about that. "What's your gut telling you Billy?"

"My gut? My gut says you're right. But so far we haven't found the slightest sign of a setup."

"Okay, you've got till tomorrow noon – your time! Call me then. I'll probably want to talk to both of you then."

"You got it boss. If there's anything at all, we'll find it!"

Billy was good. Very good! Young and a bit inexperienced, but he was still good. And so was Hannah, just at different things. If they couldn't dig anything up between them, then there was a good chance everything about the case was legitimate. But something inside told me there was something wrong. It was just too convenient!

So what the heck was I going to do about it?

I stressed over that question for the rest of the day and all the way back to the safe house. Cyn wasn't there this time, but I sat out back for a while with Phil and watched as Pariah went from garden spot to garden spot.

I went to bed that night dreaming about being ambushed somewhere out in the lonely deserts of Texas, while at the same time bullets were bouncing off of the windshield right in front of me. Disturbing dreams. Nightmares!

Early the next morning, Simon visited me in my office again. "I'm going to the airport now to head home," he said. "I filed for a court date first thing this morning so now we'll have to wait and see what date things finally get settled on. I expect Brecker to be beating down my door by the time I get home. Then of course he's going to try to delay everything pretty much permanently while I try to push things faster. I'll let you know when we finally settle on the date to actually start the proceedings.

"Thanks," I said. "I'm looking forward to it. I know Pariah is too." We shook hands and he walked off again. He had only been back in Atlanta a few days, but he had accomplished an awful lot in that amount of time. I looked at my stack of paperwork that looked bigger than it had a minute ago. I wished I could accomplish so much so fast.

My problem now was trying to figure out what I needed to accomplish out in Texas. Yes, we needed to find the girl – one way or another. But I was still betting that Pacheco was just sitting there waiting for us to come directly to him. Waiting to spring some kind of a trap. But so far we had no inkling if a trap existed or not. It was a no win situation. If I didn't go it would look very bad that the FBI had refused to do something we were capable of, but on the other hand, we could all get killed.

So what was I going to do? Since my mind didn't seem to want to come up with any answers, and it also didn't seem to want to do anything about the mystery concerning the growing stack of paperwork on my desk, I did something far more interesting. I picked up my phone and called Cynthia…and had to wait until she had time to call me back. Doctors! It was an hour before she had time to reach me. "What are you doing for lunch today?" I asked.

"Whatever you like," she replied.

I smiled!

I waited until after we had ordered lunch before I told her. "I'm probably going to be taking Pariah on a little trip tomorrow," I said.

At first her face seemed to brighten, then I saw her get serious. "And you're not taking me."

"No. I don't dare!"

"Why not?"

"Because I think it's going to be too dangerous."

"But you're taking Pariah."

"Only because I have to."

"Then you should take me too."

"I wish I could. I really wish I could! But I'll be worried enough about protecting just him, let alone worrying about you as well."

I could see she was going to argue with me again, but something stopped her and she nodded. "I can kind of understand that."

"Thanks," I replied. "Because I really do wish I could take you with us. But the fact is, I'm already having nightmares over the trip."

"You are?"

I nodded. "It's been a long time since I've heard anything from the Mexicans. I'm sure Pacheco didn't just give up. And this trip will be going right into his backyard."

"Where are you going?"

"Texas. El Paso. Well, somewhere outside of El Paso."

She smiled. "Are you going to have to ride horses to get there?"

"Horses?"

"Well, isn't that what they do out there?"

"Not exactly."

"Too bad," she replied. "I had one when I was a little girl. I took riding lessons for a few years. It was fun."

"You had a horse?"

"Of course!"

Rich kids!

Billy called me again from Texas a few hours later. "Did you find anything at all?" I asked him.

"Sorry Boss," he replied. "Both Hannah and I came up empty. It's looking more and more like this is legit. And Boss, the mother here is one sick old lady."

"So you don't think there's any threat?"

He was hesitant about answering. "I can't find one if it's there."

"Okay, but what does your gut tell you?"

"That we should run for the hills."

That was my feeling as well. "Okay. Noted. Put Hannah on the line."

"Cliff?" I heard her ask a moment later, "What's up?"

"Hannah, did you talk with the mother at all?"

"Oh yeah. Since her daughter isn't here, I've been kind of helping out with taking care of her. Cliff, she's going downhill fast! The doctors have given her three months without a liver transplant. I'm not sure she's going to make that. And caring for her is pretty much a nightmare. Not to mention she really wants her daughter around."

"How about a nursing home?" I asked.

"Around here? Cliff, this place is so small it's pitiful!"

"How about anything that doesn't sound quite right – about anything?"

"Not that I've been able to detect so far."

"And what's your gut instinct?" I asked.

She paused for a moment before answering. "On the surface, I think we need to get Pariah on this fast. But…well…I've got nothing at all to go on. It's just that something is making me nervous."

"I understand," I replied.

"Make the arrangements with Trent. Pariah and I will fly out tomorrow. Tell Billy I want tons of security, twenty-four hours a day… and then double it! We're coming out, but I'm nervous as heck about it!"

With that done, I figured I better let Don in on the decision. Oh, and I hadn't broached the subject with Pariah yet either. Well, if he wouldn't do it, we could always back out of the arrangements. And backing out wouldn't bother me in the least.

That night, during dinner, I asked Pariah about going to Texas with me the next day. A small part of me wanted him to decline.

Before Pariah could answer, Phil jumped on it. "Texas! Where in Texas?"

"Outside of El Paso somewhere."

"El Paso! Heck. Do you know how close to Tombstone that is? Hell, Wyatt Earp, you're heading right back out to the O.K. Corral!" And then he laughed. He actually thought it was funny! I was scared to death!

And of course, that's when Pariah said, "Yes. Go to Texas."

Doomed!

That night, in my dreams, I saw all of us walking straight into the mouth of a monster. Was I the one who was becoming psychic now? I hoped not!

And then another thought crept into my mind. I was going someplace where I could get killed. And I still hadn't seen Cynthia in a dress!

Talk about life being unfair!

CHAPTER

37

Pariah and I boarded a small FBI executive jet at a private airfield just outside of Atlanta. As nervous as I already was about the trip, there was no way I was going to try to walk Pariah though the busy Atlanta Airport. Besides, the way we travelled, there was a lot less security checks than for a normal flight. For instance, my gun was expected!

While I carried a small travel bag onto the plane, Pariah carried nothing. I was worried about how he might handle flying. Would he be nervous? Would he throw a tantrum over something? He didn't. In fact, he mostly seemed like a kid walking through Disney World. He kept looking at this and looking at that as if it was all some fun ride. In other words, he was enjoying himself. I only wished I could say that I did. I was just too worried to really enjoy it – despite riding in the executive jet. Why didn't I cancel the trip? Dumb McNair! Dumb!

Thanks to the time zones, technically, we landed an hour after we took off. Actual flying time was several hours more though. We landed at a rural airstrip that was even smaller than the one we had taken off from. I was very glad to see Billy, Hannah, and Sam Trent already there and waiting on us. As we drove away from the airport, I saw the jet taking off again. I felt like we had been abandoned out in the middle of nowhere. Actually, I wasn't far off.

Sam drove us straight to the Paloma house…or shack. Okay, it was a house. It was just very small and very poor…as were all the houses around it. But the tiny town was in the middle of nowhere. Literally! I could see no reason for the town's existence in that barren place. As we parked the car, I noted four armed men outside the house. Sam saw me staring at them. "FBI and Border Patrol," he said. "They'll stay with us as long as we're here."

I had hoped for more men. Like an entire army!

Maria Paloma not only was frail and sick, she really looked it. A neighbor woman was sitting with her and left as soon as we walked in. Hannah introduced Pariah and me to her. She reached out from her bed with her hand and did her best to shake my hand, but all we really did was to lightly hold hands for a moment. Then she reached out to Pariah.

As she reached her hand out, I saw her looking intently at Pariah's mangled face...just as he was looking at her pain laden face. Slowly he brought both his crippled hands up to hold her frail hand. The two of them seemed to stare at each other for a long time. Both of them ravaged harshly by life – only in different ways.

"I will find her," he said. And I was immediately struck by what he didn't say. He didn't ask if she would feed him.

"When do you want to do this?" Sam asked.

But as he asked, I saw Pariah sit down on the edge of Maria Paloma's bed and bow his head. He was still holding her frail hand between his. "I think we've already started," I replied softly. Quickly, I searched my pocket for my little recorder and switched it on.

"Girl is alive," Pariah said. "Girl is fine, not sick. Sitting up in bed reading a book. Bedroom looks...nice. Bars on window. Can't get out that way."

"Great, Pariah," I said. "Now let's try to figure out where she is. Can you go up?"

"Bond is good. Mother sick, but bond is good. Going up. Up through roof. Outside. Higher. House is...very big, very nice. Men. Men all around. Some with guns. Big pool behind house. Trees around pool. Trees in front."

"Okay, Pariah, I know you like trees. What else?"

"Only trees I see. Nothing else. Desert all around the house. Dirt road leading to house, that's all."

"So the trees look like they were planted there?"

"Yes."

"It sounds like nice landscaping," I said to Trent. "Can you go higher, Pariah?" I asked. "What else can you see?"

"Going higher. Higher. Desert. Lots of desert. Higher. See river way in the distance, but in the other direction."

"What do you mean the other direction?"

"When I found the girl in the bad place. River was one way. On other side of river now."

"Mexico!" Billy blurted out before anyone else could say it.

Out of the corner of my eye, I noticed Sam Trent hurrying out of the room. "Pariah, can you see anything else that might help us?"

"Going higher. I think…small town. Trying to go closer. Going closer. Going down. Closer. Down. Closer. Can't get there. Too far away."

"Pariah, can you describe the town at all?"

"Small."

He wasn't giving any other details though. "Okay, Pariah, go back to the house and let's look around there."

"Going back. Back. Back. Nice house. Big house. Two stories. Red tile roof. Several small buildings around house. Some close, some far."

He wasn't being much help yet. I saw Trent come back in with a laptop computer. He booted it up. "Okay, Pariah, go back into the house and look around. Tell us what you see."

"Going in. Back to girl. Girl closing book. Getting off of bed."

"Here," Trent said bringing the laptop over to me. "Does the house look anything at all like this?"

"Girl opening door."

I was suddenly caught between being surprised by what Pariah was saying and by the picture Sam Trent was showing me.

"Pariah, can you look at this picture and see if the house looks anything like it?"

Pariah opened his eyes and blinked. Then he looked at the picture on the laptop screen. "Yes, that's it," he confirmed.

"Pacheco's house," Trent said. "He doesn't have to look anymore. We know where it is."

I was stunned! How had Sam figured it out so quickly?

"Girl going downstairs," Pariah said.

I realized that his eyes were closed and his head was bent again. Going downstairs? Was she being held captive or not?

"Man talking to her. Spanish. Why are you down here? Um…supposed to be upstairs? Speak fast, hard to follow."

I was astonished. He spoke Spanish!

"He can hear what they're saying?" Trent asked sounding more surprised than I was.

"I didn't know he spoke Spanish!" I replied. I noticed that Trent looked more surprised than I thought he should be. But then I remembered that the last case we had done with him, the girl had been found dead. Pariah had nothing to listen to then. He had no idea what Pariah could really do.

"Something about Uncle Carlos."

Uncle Carlos? Suddenly my attention was totally riveted.

"Girl going around man. Going. Going. Opening door. Going in. Man behind desk talking on the phone. Fast Spanish. Man is angry at girl. Supposed to be upstairs. Just got call. They're there now! Could be watching now. Hurry! Girl running. Running upstairs. Running. Back in room. Closed door. Looking out window. Looking up at the sky."

And then it hit me. "Pariah! Stop!" I said as I literally pulled his hands off of Maria Paloma. "Everyone into the car. Now! Run!"

"What?" Trent started to say.

"It's a trap! A trap! Now move!" I literally dragged Pariah as fast as I could all the way out to the car. Billy and Hannah got into the backseat on either side of him. I jumped into the passenger side of the front seat.

Trent wasn't moving all that fast though. "What's your hurry?" he asked. "There's no trouble here."

"There will be!" I yelled. "Now floor that gas pedal right away or I'll drive and do it myself. Hurry!"

Trent didn't hurry all that much but he did get the car going at least somewhat fast.

"Sam," I said urgently. "Forget the speed limit. Floor it!"

He turned and smiled at me. "What speed limit?" He finally pushed the car as fast as he dared on that lousy road. "Where we going?" he asked.

Good question. I wanted to say the airport, but there was no hanger there, no building we could safely hold up in. "We need someplace safe where they can't get at us!"

"There's a ranch about ten miles up the road where we arranged for you to stay," Sam suggested. "It's about as secure as we get out here."

"Then see how fast you can get us there!" I replied. I turned around to speak to Billy – and noticed that there was nobody following us. Where were the guards? "Where are the guards that were supposed to stick with us?"

"We probably left so fast they haven't had time to catch up yet," Sam replied.

So much for adequate protection!

"Billy! Call that plane back here as fast as possible!"

Billy got out his phone. "Boss!" he soon exclaimed. "No cell coverage here!"

Great! Just great! "Is there phone service where we're going?" I asked.

"Yes, definitely," Sam replied.

Five minutes later, Billy called from the back seat. "I've got cell service!"

I turned around quickly, but he was already punching in the numbers. And as I was watching him, something caught my attention out of the corner of my eye. Way back behind us there was another plum of dust being kicked up on the road. "Oh shit!" I said, my voice more controlled than it should have been. "Somebody's following us."

"Probably the guards," Sam said.

"Better be!" I muttered.

Unfortunately, that was when Hannah said, "Cliff! Off to the right!"

"Shit!" I exclaimed. "More company. My gun was in my hand fast. I heard Billy talking to Don and I turned around fast. "Give me that phone!" Half a second later I nearly screamed into his cell phone. "Get that plane back here now! We're in a trap and there coming after us!"

"Cliff, are you sure?" Hannah asked.

I pointed toward the vehicle coming straight at us on the right. "There's no road over there Hannah! They're not out there for a joy ride!" I turned back to the phone. "Don, get us some kind of help and fast, or we're not going to be around much longer." I could see the vehicle coming from the right now. It was a pickup truck with the back end loaded with men. And guns. "Shit!" I said, "They're definitely coming after us! And they've got more men than I've got bullets!"

I could hear Don yelling something in the background, but I wasn't paying enough attention to him to make any of it out. Most of my attention was focused on the truck coming at us from the right. And then I checked the vehicle coming up behind us. Another pickup with men. The guards wouldn't be driving a pickup truck loaded with men in the back. "Don!" I yelled into the phone. "We've got bad guys in the truck coming up on our rear too!" I didn't hear what he said, because that was when the first bullets started flying past our truck.

Sam started weaving. He was pushing the car as fast as it would go and we were bouncing all over the place. The good news was that we were far enough ahead of the other trucks that they couldn't cut us off. The truck on the right reached the road and was now behind us. We heard occasional shots, but nothing hit the car.

I turned to look behind and saw that Hannah had pushed Pariah as far down toward the floor as she could get him. Bless you Hannah!

The trucks were big and new and obviously had a lot of horsepower. The car we were in was lighter and seemed to have a pretty good engine. As far as I could tell, we were holding our own…distance wise. No…the truck behind us was very slowly gaining!

"There's the ranch!" Sam yelled.

I looked, but what I saw wasn't exactly good. "Don't stop!" I yelled. "Keep going. If you slow down they'll be on us too fast!"

I was relieved that he passed the place up. Our crazy fast ride continued. I needed a plan. A way out. A way to safety. "Is there any place we can go to get away?" I asked.

"Around here? There's nothing but open space out here!"

The truck behind us was gradually getting closer and I was gradually getting more desperate. "Billy! Try leaning out the window and getting a shot at their tires! Slow them down!"

Billy and Hannah both looked at me like I was crazy. Yes, I know I was crazy, but just then I didn't care! Billy let his window down and leaned out as far as he could, took aim as best he could and fired four well spaced shots. All to no avail.

"We're bouncing around too much!" he complained as he pulled himself back into the car and let his window up again.

Well, it was worth a try. What else could I do? I heard Don yelling at me from the phone I had forgotten was in my hand. I put the phone back to my ear. "What?" I asked him.

"Where the hell are you?" Don asked.

"Where are we?" I asked Sam.

Instead of answering, he reached over and I handed him the phone. "We're about three miles past the Winslow ranch heading west over the old desert road," he told Don. Then he handed the phone back to me.

"You got that?" I asked. But what I heard was him relaying the message to someone else. Then I heard him clearly again, but his question made no sense to me. "What do you mean what kind of vehicle are we driving? What difference does it make? We're in the one that's being shot at! It's a four door sedan! White! Being followed by two big pickup trucks full of big guns!" As if to emphasize the point. A bullet hit the back end of the car and the bang reverberated loudly inside. "See!" I told him.

I turned the phone off and handed it back to Billy. We couldn't expect help. We were in the middle of nowhere. We would have to get out of this ourself!

Slowly the pickup behind us gained more and more and a few of the shots started to hit us. Hannah and Billy both tried to keep low behind the back seat. Then the rear window exploded, showering them with glass. I took aim through the open back window and fired. As far as I could tell, my shot did nothing at all. Then Billy took aim and fired, followed by Hannah. I saw the truck swerve to avoid their shots…and saw the second truck uncomfortably close behind it.

More shots came at us, but an occasional shot from one of us seemed to keep them back a little way. At least it seemed that way. The only problem was, I was almost out of bullets!

And then something passed overhead, very low, and incredibly fast. And then it happened again! It happened so quickly it scared me more than I already was. The truck behind me swerved and I saw the truck behind it swerve too. Only then did I take the time to look and realize that a fighter jet had just passed right over our heads. Two fighter jets!

I watched as very slowly they climbed back up into the sky and started turning. It took them forever and they were almost out of sight by the time they started returning. In the meantime, the truck behind us had gained a

little and now the bullets were coming at us faster! We fired back again –
my gun emptied after only two shots. Useless!

The roar was like the loudest continual thunder I've ever heard. The
ground began to explode in a long line that ran from the desert right at the
road…then right over top of and through the truck behind us. The truck
exploded like someone had set it up for a Hollywood movie. The men in
the back went flying through the air in all directions.

And then the jet behind it hit the second truck. It didn't explode,
but the results were just as dramatic. The truck flipped and rolled several
times.

It had lasted a total of two seconds. That's all the time it took for the
jets to take out the enemy before they were climbing skyward again. Sam
slowed down the car and eventually brought it to a stop. We all got out.
The jets were circling overhead.

I phoned Don again. "I don't know how you arranged it," I said, "but
thank you from the bottom of all our hearts!"

"Thank the Director," he replied. "It seems he had some pull with the
Air Force. They diverted a couple of jets over your way."

"How soon can you get us out of here?" I asked.

"Not till tomorrow. The jet is halfway home now and needs refueling.
And that strip near you doesn't have lights. You're going to have to stick
it out for the night."

"Just make sure you get it back here early!" I replied before hanging up.

"Can we head back to the ranch now?" Sam asked. "My luggage is
there and I think I need to change my shorts."

It sounded awfully cliché, until I realized a few minutes later that he
really wasn't kidding!

CHAPTER

38

he ranch Sam took us to was exactly that…a ranch. I don't know what else I had expected, but somehow I wasn't expecting to see horses and cattle all over the place. I felt oddly out of place. Cyn had said she liked horses, but I had never even ridden one – well, except for some pony rides when I was a kid.

Sam took off to change the minute he got there and Hannah was kind enough to introduce Pariah and me to the owners of the ranch, Chet and Sharrona Winslow. Since Billy and Hannah had already spent a few nights there, they had already picked out their bedrooms. Billy was sharing one with Sam, which meant that I would be sharing mine with Pariah. Actually, I had no problem with that. I wanted more than ever to keep a close eye on him now.

The Winslow's were gracious hosts and gave Pariah and me the ten-cent tour of the place, including the stable. I had noticed the cattle smell the minute we had arrived and got out of the car. But the smell of horses in the stable was a bit powerful. Actually, I guess it was the horse manure that I was smelling the most. I was surprised to see Pariah walk right up to one of the stalls and start stroking the head of one of the huge beasts. "Pretty horse," he said. "Pretty horse." We wound up leaving him there with Hannah to watch over him as my tour continued with the other areas of the ranch close to the main house.

The authorities didn't start showing up until nearly two hours after we got to the ranch. Sam had spent a good part of that time on the phone

380

and all of us had to tell what happened several times to several different people. I knew the drill so I didn't get too upset about it. Once they tried talking to Pariah though, they soon gave up. I was glad for their presence though because the guards that had been assigned to us never did show up. We found out later that they had all been killed back at the Paloma house.

Hannah was kind enough to keep a close eye on Pariah while we were busy with the authorities. I noticed that they spent most of the time in the stable. I guess he and Cynthia had something in common about the horses. But then, he couldn't smell the manure. Lucky for him!

Later that evening, I had trouble sleeping. I noticed Pariah was having a little trouble too, but at least he was laying in bed attempting to sleep. I paced around the room trying to figure out where we had gone wrong. I finally pulled my little recorder out of my pocket. Since I never turned it off, it had long since run out of recording space. I turned the volume down so as not to disturb Pariah any more than necessary and started it at the beginning.

As the recording played, my mind once again saw everything that I had seen at the Paloma house earlier. I remembered seeing Sam leave the house quickly. I remembered him coming back with his computer just as Pariah was going back to the girl's room. I listened again as the recording replayed Pariah confirming that the house in the picture was the same house he was at. How did Sam guess which house it was that quickly? Pariah had given us almost no details at all about it. Very few. There had to be thousands of places that could fit the little description he had given us at that point. How did Sam know? Lucky guess?

I continued playing the recording. I stopped it and replayed sections several times. And then I got to the section where the girl was talking with her "Uncle Carlos!" It was there that I had realized that we had been placed in the middle of a trap. Once again I listened to the words.

"Supposed to be upstairs. Just got call. They're there now! Could be watching now. Hurry!"

I went back and listened to them again. How did I know it was a trap? I had almost nothing to go on. I was nervous and worried about it, but

I had no real reason. I played the section one more time. Someone had called. Who had called? From where? But it couldn't be one of us, we had all been there…except for the few minutes that Sam had gone back out to the car to get his computer.

I thought about that. How did he know about the house so soon? I backed the recording up again and started it from the beginning. And this time, something Sam had said came through with more meaning. *"He can hear what they're saying?"* He had been astonished to learn that. Had he seemed worried about it too?

Carlos had told the girl we could be watching. From what Pariah had said, it didn't sound like Carlos knew that Pariah could hear everything as well.

How did Sam know it was Pacheco's house? Who had called him? Carlos didn't know Pariah could hear everything. Sam didn't know Pariah could hear everything. It was thin. It was crazy. But I couldn't sleep.

I grabbed my gun and made sure it was fully loaded. Then I stuck it in the small of my back and pulled my shirt over it so it wouldn't be seen. I knew Pariah was still awake. "I'll be back in a few minutes," I whispered. He didn't even roll over to look.

I went over to Billy and Sam's room and knocked softly on the door. Sam opened it. "Anybody sleeping?" I asked.

"Not even close," he replied. He let me in.

"Billy, do me a favor, go sit with Pariah for a few minutes," I said. "Sam and I need to discuss some 'grown-up' stuff."

Billy grunted, but he got up and left. I went over and sat on Billy's bed. "What's up?" Sam asked.

"I just need to talk," I said. "And sometimes it's not good for the junior agents to hear that the senior ones have troubles."

He laughed. "Yeah. I know what you mean. So you were scared shitless too?"

"More than you'll ever know!"

"At least you didn't mess your shorts! Damn, I thought you were great! You didn't panic. You managed to think clearly through the whole thing!"

"I wasn't great, you were! That was some piece of driving you did."

"Once I got started," he replied.

"Yeah, you were awfully slow to get going."

He said nothing to that.

"I was wondering some things," I said.

"Like what?"

"Pacheco's house… How did you know it was that house so soon? There's got to be thousands of houses like the one Pariah had described at that point. Maybe hundreds of thousands! But you managed to pick the exact house right away."

There was something in his eyes that showed worry. "Lucky guess," he said.

"Yeah…very!" It was time to lay another part on him. "And did you notice that when Pacheco was talking to the girl, he didn't know that Pariah could hear what went on as well as see everything?"

"I…missed that part," he admitted.

"If I remember correctly, you didn't know Pariah could hear things either."

"Nothing was said about him hearing anything when we worked the Ipollino case," he replied. "It kind of took me by surprise."

I nodded. "Yeah, Pariah can definitely do that. He's a very surprising guy. But while we're at it, did you happen to notice exactly what Pacheco said to the girl?"

"What was that?"

"He said that someone had just called him to tell him that we were there with Pariah.

"To tell the truth," he said, starting to sound a bit worried, "it was all happening so fast, I didn't really notice."

"Yeah, well someone tipped him off. Someone who was right there at the house. Someone who knew exactly what was going on."

He stared at me. He didn't look exactly amiable anymore. "What are you saying?" he asked.

"You were the only one who left the house! You were the only one who could have called him!"

He stood up quickly. I saw how angry he looked. And I also saw him glancing toward his gun on the nightstand. He lunged quickly for it. I tried to get at my own gun but my damn shirt tail was in the way. So I did the next best thing, I rolled over backwards onto the floor on the far side of the bed. I hit the floor just as his gun exploded. A piece of the wall blew away throwing bits of plaster all over me. From the floor I finally freed and brought up my own gun. Now that I was on the floor on the other side of the bed, he couldn't see me, he had to climb over top of the bed to get at me, and I saw him coming before he could get another shot off. I pulled the trigger and was rewarded to see him thrown backwards.

I scrambled to my feet and ran around the end of the bed, but before I could get to him, I saw him bringing his gun up again, I ducked down just as he fired…and missed…luckily. I saw him getting to his feet with his gun still aimed at me. His right shoulder was bleeding heavily. I rolled back to the other side of the bed. But that was when the door opened and Billy ran in. I watched in horror as Sam turned toward him with his gun raised. I pulled my trigger again, but he was standing sideways trying to aim at Billy and my shot caught him in his left arm. His gun went off as he was thrown sideways. I scrambled to my feet again and saw Billy dropping to the floor in agony. I didn't have time to help him just then. I had to focus all my attention on Trent.

I'll say one thing for him, he didn't give up easily. He was shot in the right shoulder and now his left arm, and he was still trying to roll over far enough to shoot at me again. I was on my feet though and faster than he was. I jumped on top of him grabbing his gun arm to keep it away from me. Being shot the way he was, he didn't have much of a chance against me and I quickly stripped the gun out of his hand and threw it a few feet away. I was tempted to punch his lights out, but I rolled him onto his stomach instead. I saw his necktie on his suitcase and I used it to tie his hands behind his back. Just then I didn't care that he was bleeding or shot twice. I just wanted him safely out of commission.

I finally turned to help Billy and saw Hannah on top of him through the open door. She was pressing down on his bleeding leg. "How is he?" I asked.

"I think he'll be okay," she said. "I just need something to help stop the bleeding."

I grabbed the first thing I could think of, the pillow from Sam's bed, and pulled the pillow case off. "Here, use this," I said as I bent down over them. "How're you doing?" I asked Billy. His face was contorted in pain.

"It hurts like shit!" he replied angrily.

"I know. We'll get help as soon as possible."

"I called for an ambulance already!" Chet Winslow said from the end of the hallway. "Is it safe to come down there?"

I glanced back at Sam. He was fidgeting and rolling desperately around, probably trying to get his hands untied. "Safe enough," I replied.

He was there quickly and pushed Hannah out of the way. I watched as he examined Billy's wound, then he pushed the pillow case back over top of it again and motioned for Hannah to keep the pressure on it. "I could pull the bullet," he said, but it doesn't look bad enough that it can't wait for someone more qualified.

"How long do you think before they can get here?"

"Probably about forty-five minutes to an hour. He'll keep till then."

I glanced back at Sam Trent. "Better make sure they send two ambulances."

Chet went into the room. He looked briefly at each of Sam's wounds. "I'll get something to bandage him up with too."

I went back to my room to check on Pariah. He was huddled on the floor behind the bed on the far side of the room. "It's safe now, buddy," I said. "I've got him all tied up in the other room. He can't hurt us now."

He popped his head up over the edge of the bed, but he didn't move any further. He was fine so I left him and went back to keep an eye on Sam.

Chet was back a few minutes later with an assortment of bandages. "I'll do it," I told him as I grabbed some of the bandages. "Close the door on the way out."

He looked at me somewhat surprised, but a minute later, I was alone with Sam. The door was shut, but Billy and Hannah were right on the other side of it. They would hear what was going on, but they wouldn't be able to see it. I had to settle for that.

Everyone had been keeping me pretty much in the dark about what the Mexicans were doing. I was going to get what answers I could while I had the chance. The fact that I was going to be somewhat torturing Sam didn't even enter my mind. I was tired of being shot at and was determined to take it out on someone.

I rolled him over so he would be on his back. He kicked furiously at me so I grabbed his legs and sat on them. Then I used my belt to tie his ankles. He was breathing through his teeth and cursing at me. I knew the pain from his wounds had to be horrendous. And I was only going to make things worse.

"Settle down, Sam," I said. "You're bleeding all over the place and I need to bandage those wounds."

"Go to hell, McNair!" he returned angrily.

His anger was only what I expected. I pulled out a long narrow strip of bandage and started wrapping it tightly right over top of the wound on his left arm. He hissed at the added pain. "Who did you call?" I suddenly demanded. "Was it Pacheco himself?"

"Go to hell!" he said again.

I grabbed both the ends of the bandage and pulled as hard as I could. He screamed at the pain. "Was it Pacheco?" I demanded again.

"No!" he cried out as his body contorted in agony.

I didn't let up on the pressure.

"Who then?"

"Miguel! I only know him as Miguel!"

I eased up a bit.

"And what was supposed to happen?" I asked.

"Go to…. Owww!" he yelled as I pulled on the bandages again. "They were supposed to come in and shoot you! All of you!" he said. I eased up a bit on the bandages and tied a knot over top of where the bullet hole was.

"I'll kill you McNair!" he screamed.

"Yeah, yeah. You and Pacheco and everybody else. I'll add you to the list." I started tying another knot. "And what were you supposed to get out of it?" I pulled the knot tight.

"Oww! What do you think? Money!"

"How much?" I asked.

"I got fifty thousand before," he said. "I get another fifty when you're all dead!"

"Looks like you're not going to collect that other half," I said as I moved from his arm to his other shoulder. Something about what he had said raised another question though. "You said you got fifty thousand… before. How much before? Before what?"

"Go to hell!"

I looked at the wound again as I grabbed more bandages. "Hmm," I said. "This one is bad. I should have tackled it first. Sorry, but I'm afraid this one is really going to hurt!"

It's amazing the things he was willing to tell me because he was grateful for my first aid training. As I bandaged his shoulder tightly, making sure to keep extra firm pressure over top of the wound itself, I learned that Pacheco had known in advance that Sam was going to be coming out to Atlanta for the Ipollino case. And that Miguel had grilled Sam rather strenuously about it afterwards. I learned that Maria Paloma really did need a liver transplant and that Pacheco had promised to find her a liver just as soon as we were all dead. Sam didn't know if Pacheco was really Patricia Paloma's uncle or not. In fact, he rather doubted it.

And then, as I was making sure to keep extra pressure right over the wound…to help it stop bleeding…I learned some other things too. Like the fact that Sam had been getting drug kickbacks for years from Miguel. There were lots of drug smugglers running their stuff across the river. All Sam had to do was go after everyone else and leave Pacheco's operation alone.

The one thing I was really disappointed about though, was when I asked him about the location of the white slavery breaking house. He seemed to have no knowledge of the place at all. Of course, he was wracked with some awful pain spasms while he was trying to remember, so maybe that clouded his memory. But overall, I got the impression that he really didn't know.

When the emergency medical techs finally showed up, they were so impressed with my bandages and how nice and tight they were, that they decided to leave them that way until he got to the hospital. See, it pays to attend all those first aid classes and pay attention!

One of the county sheriffs was kind enough to give us a ride to the hospital so we could stay close to Billy. I had everyone pack their luggage too, there was no way I was going anywhere else except to the airport. While I was waiting to find out about Billy, I talked on the phone several times with

Don to keep him updated and to make sure the plane would wait for us since I had no doubt that we would be a bit later than I originally planned.

The El Paso FBI office sent about a dozen people out to the hospital to talk with all of us, especially me. Since both Hannah and Billy were able to confirm everything that Sam had told me, we ran into very few difficulties. Their biggest problem was that after yesterday's attack and now Sam Trent, we were seriously taxing the manpower of their small field office. I got the impression that they would all be very glad once we left. An opinion I very much shared.

Once Billy had been sufficiently taken care of, as far as that hospital was concerned, he was presented with a pair of crutches to use after he left the hospital. We were all loaded into one car with a second car in front of us and a third car behind us. For the first time since we had arrived the day before, I felt like we were getting the protection we were supposed to get. Although it felt more like they were running us out of town and were making sure we got on the plane and left. That was fine by me.

The jet was waiting for us at the small airstrip and after a very short delay to get the engines started again, we finally left Texas to go home. I was more than glad to get out of there. We never should have gone in the first place, but I had only myself to blame for that decision.

Home would be so good!

How was I supposed to know that a few hours after taking off from Texas…the sky was going to fall.

CHAPTER

39

No, the sky didn't fall because of a problem with the jet. It didn't fall because of the Mexicans either. The sky fell when I stepped off the plane and saw Cynthia running straight at me – wearing a dress!

I was so dumbfounded that I stopped dead and nearly fell to my knees. The dress was just this simple little red and white print thing with tiny straps over her shoulders. The only other thing she had on was a pair of flip-flops. But...wow! I couldn't believe my eyes! I didn't get to see it very long though before she came running up to me and threw her arms around me. Yes, we kissed. Obviously! But it was the way she greeted me that had me so stunned.

"Cliff! I was so worried about you! When Don called last night and told me about the attack and the planes...and then this morning he said you had to shoot someone else.... Damn it, you had me so worried!"

I hugged her tighter for a moment then looked into her eyes. "Yeah," I said. "I love you too!"

Do you have any idea how many tears those simple four words can cause?"

Before they shipped Billy off to the local hospital and Hannah, Pariah, and I were shipped off for a few days of rest, we were taken back to the office and once again interviewed extensively. But eventually I was released into Cynthia's loving care…as long as we remained at the safe house and didn't go anywhere else. They were now very much afraid of another quick reprisal from Pacheco and his crazy Mexican friends. But I was beginning to wonder how much more reprisal he could make. We had to have taken out most of his organization in the last few months. Unfortunately, hired hands are a dime a dozen. And I knew that Mexico was loaded with them.

The day I started back to work again, Don asked me to stay behind after our morning meeting. I was a bit surprised when he asked Frank Morris to join us.

"Geez McNair," Frank said as he walked in, "Jets? Fighter jets?"

What could I say? "Well, you know how hard the Air Force has been trying to recruit me. It's looking more and more sure like I'm going to sign up now."

"They wouldn't take you no matter how hard you tried to get in!"

"What? Hey, I'm prime material for them!"

"Maybe, but your too much trouble! Way too much!"

In other words, he had something to tell me, and I had a feeling it wasn't going to be good. "What have I done now?" I asked.

He shook his head. "You've made it to the big time now," he replied. "Pacheco has reinstated the bounty on your head, only he's added a couple of zeros to the number."

"Zeros?" I asked, my concern growing.

"Fifty thousand," he replied.

Well, I had definitely come up in the world. I didn't feel so measly any more. The only problem was, having a fifty thousand dollar bounty on my head would mean nothing but trouble.

"And Pariah?" I asked.

"One million!"

Ugh! Once again I felt paltry next to Pariah. But a million dollars for Pariah's head was major trouble! Big time trouble! I don't think I've ever heard of anyone with a bounty that big on their head before.

"What are we doing about it?" I asked.

"We're trying to work with the Mexican government to go after Pacheco," Don told us.

It was what he didn't say that had me wondering. "And?" I asked.

"And so far, they're not playing ball. But it's still early stages."

Not good! "So what am I supposed to do in the meantime?"

"Hide!"

They sure know how to take the fun out of life!

Since Pacheco was going after me, I decided to up my game by going after him...or at least after his white slavery business. We knew from the New York raid that there had been branches in Hong Kong, Texas, and Europe. So far we had found and shut down New York and Hong Kong. But even after repeatedly trying to target their Texas operation, we had found nothing.

I called Brent Jackson and Hannah into my office for a little chat. "We're getting nowhere with the cases we're trying to profile now," I told them. "I want to change what we go after. Let's look at a wider range of girls – mainly younger, and let's only try to take the most recent cases we can find. And...I want to try to run two operations a week from now on if we can."

"Wow!" Brent exclaimed.

"That's a lot of work!" Hannah added.

"I know, but I'm getting tired of not being able to strike back at Pacheco. And if these people are missing, then we can only be doing good."

My phone rang then so I dismissed both of them. Unfortunately, it was a call summoning me to the Director's office. I don't know why, but the entire trip up there, I felt like a school kid being sent to the Principal for disciplining.

His secretary waved me right through and I found him waiting for me. I took one of the chairs in front of his desk.

"Recovered from your trip to El Paso?" he asked.

"Yeah, and I'm ready to get out of that safe house. I'm going stir crazy."

He smiled. "That's not the way I heard it. I heard you've been enjoying yourself immensely these last few days. When you had company that is."

I'm sure I blushed. "Well, Cyn has been great. But it would be nice to take her out somewhere else for a change. And I'm paying rent on my apartment, but I haven't been there in a long time."

His smile vanished. "That's a good point. I'm going to have your lease terminated and all your things moved into storage until we can get this bounty business taken care of. You should be comfortable enough at the safe house for now."

"Cancel my lease?" I couldn't believe he would want to do that.

"Is your apartment any better than the safe house?" he asked.

"Not even close!" I replied.

"Then you should have no problem with it. You can get another place once we're sure that it's safe for you."

"And how long do you think that will be?"

"We have no idea. We're still trying to work out a deal with the Mexican government to go after Pacheco, and they're still putting up roadblocks. Eventually, they're going to have to give in."

"But there's no telling when."

"No telling," he agreed.

Well, so much for my stockpile of frozen TV dinners. "So can I take Cynthia out on a date somewhere?" I asked.

"Not unless you clear it first and you're surrounded by guards at all times."

I couldn't believe it. The President didn't get that much protection! "Isn't that a bit much?" I asked.

Instead of replying, he leaned forward. "McNair, this is important so I need you to think carefully before you give me an answer."

I mentally gulped. Something else was about to come at me that promised to be trouble. "Okay," I replied tentatively.

"You've been Pariah's handler since the beginning. How comfortable would you be remaining as his handler for the long term?"

"The long term? What's that mean?"

"Indefinitely…for now."

Basically, forever! But I didn't even have to think about that one. "I'd be very comfortable with it," I replied. "I've grown rather…fond of him… and his eccentricities."

He nodded as he sat back. "Good. Just checking."

I wondered what that was all about. Somehow I suspected that there would be more to it than what I now knew…which was nothing.

"Now," he said, "we have to come to an agreement about something else."

An agreement about something else? Which automatically meant that he was about to tell me how things were going to work. "What's that?" I asked, immediately knowing that I should fear what he was about to say.

"Calling the Air Force in to rescue your tail like that cost us a lot!"

"I'm sure it did," I started to say.

"Not money wise, although we'll probably get some kind of a bill for it, but in favors owed!"

Oh!

"The CIA has been asking to use Pariah again for the last few months. So has DEA, and I know every other agency is licking their chops to use him too."

"I'd rather not send him back to the CIA!" I said quickly. "After what they did to him last time…"

"Don't worry," he said, "we're going to maintain control of him from now on. And nothing we ask him to do will ever happen without at least you present to work the case with him."

That much made me feel better. I took a minute to think about things. "If we work with the CIA, it's going to take a lot of coordinating. Just coordinating things within the FBI on some of these cases takes a lot. We often take days to complete a case."

He nodded. "I'm sure that's going to be the case most of the time," he replied.

Which meant that this was already a done deal – it just hadn't fully set in until now. "When do we start?" I asked.

"I'll let you know," he replied. "But most likely, soon."

I nodded. "I had wanted to step up our search for Pacheco's breaking house in Texas," I told him.

"Do it! We'll just have to work any special requests in with what you're already doing."

As I walked back to my little office, I had the impression that life just got a lot busier and a lot more complicated. First I had been told that Pariah and I had whopping bounties on our heads, and now everybody in the world wanted to use Pariah's services. There was something very wrong and worrying about that. Very wrong!

Before we could set up the first case to try to find Pacheco's operation again, the Director called us to work a situation for someone else. Not the CIA surprisingly, but the Coast Guard. A boat full of tourists had gone missing from a fishing trip and the air search so far had turned up nothing. Several family members from the missing tourists were quickly flown from Miami to Atlanta. The lawyer sent Pariah into one of his usual tantrums and Pariah set the family members agog by asking if they would feed him. One of the men there braved holding Pariah's hands, and off he went.

"Water! Lots of water," he said. Tiny boat. Raft. Crowded. Water in the boat. Everybody tired. Sleepy. Look sick."

"So they're alive?" I asked quickly.

He nodded. "Alive. Man is sleepy. Sick. But alive."

"Good, Pariah. Very good. Now can you go high? Can you try to see something for us?"

"Going up. Going up. Water. Lots of water. Ocean. Going up. Up. Water. Nothing but water."

"No other boats?" I asked.

"Looking around. Look… Maybe. Speck on the horizon."

"Can you go closer to it?"

"Trying," he said. "Trying. Trying. Hard. Can't go much further. Can't make it."

"How close are you?" I asked.

"Can see that it's a boat. A ship."

"Can you see a name on it, or anything?" I asked.

"Not close enough. Still far off."

Struck out!

"Okay," I said. "Let's go back to the raft."

"Boat is heading closer," he said.

"It is? Is it heading right for the raft?"

It was a moment before he answered. "Not really. But it's coming closer."

"How long do you think it will be before you can see the ship better?"

"Don't know," He replied. "Long time."

The boat must have been far off. "Okay Pariah, let's break the connection and we'll try again in a little while."

I had the man let go of Pariah. "We'll try again in half an hour," I told everyone. "So far, finding that ship may be our best bet."

I could see the looks of astonishment on the faces of the people there. I knew how they felt. But I also saw hope in their eyes.

Half an hour later, a woman took Pariah's hands and he tried again. "Good connection," he replied. "Better than before."

"My husband," the woman said. "How is he?"

"Sleepy, sick. Like other man.

"So he's alive?" she asked.

"Yes," Pariah replied.

"Okay Pariah, go up and try to see the ship."

"Going up," he said. "Up. Up. Up. See ship. Closer now."

"Okay, now…"

"Going," he said without my prompting. "Trying to go closer. Closer. Closer. Trying."

"Pariah, do you think you'll be able to see a name on the ship this time?"

"Closer. Trying…. Trying…. Big boat. Very big boat. Tall boat. Very tall boat. Many decks. Many decks. Trying…. Trying…."

"Sounds like a cruise ship," someone said.

Which sounded very right to me. "Pariah, can you get close enough to see the name of the ship yet?"

He didn't answer. I could see the intense concentration on his face. "Doll… Doll…"

"What is it buddy? Can you make it out?"

"Trying," he said. "Trying. Still far. "Doll…something. Then maybe Queen? Hard to tell. Long way off."

"Dolphin Queen?" one of the people there suggested.

"I think so," Pariah confirmed. "Way off yet."

"Pariah, which side of the ship are you looking at?"

"Left side," he replied.

"So if the ship turns left, they'll find the raft?"

"Not all the way left, just a little bit."

"Great Pariah! Great!"

I had them break the connection. I knew that the guys in the observation room had already sent the order to find out where the Dolphin Queen was.

It was twenty minutes before they told us the ship had been located and the Coast Guard was sending planes into the area as fast as possible.

Half an hour later, another of the people there tried their luck with Pariah.

"Ship is heading for raft now, but is still way off."

"Great Pariah! Great! Can you go higher and see if you can spot any planes?"

It was a moment before he replied.

"Plane heading this way. Flying toward ship, not toward raft."

"Good Pariah. Which way does the plane have to turn to fly over the raft?"

It took a few back and forth tries, but eventually the right direction was relayed to the pilot and Pariah confirmed the correct heading. A few minutes later, Pariah told us that the plane had just flown low over the raft and was now turning around.

"People in raft waking up. Waving at plane," he said. "Plane dropping something into water. Floating in water. Men jumping out of plane now."

Through Pariah, we were treated to a description of every phase of the rescue operation. The cruise ship pulled up close by and sent a boat over to take everyone off the raft, but a Coast Guard ship showed up shortly afterwards to take the people from there. There were more than a few tears among the people in the room with us. I wondered what the people in the raft would have thought if they knew how they had been rescued. Well, they would all probably hear about it soon enough. Word of what Pariah could do was about to spread even more.

That part I wasn't very happy with.

A few days later, I got a call from Simon. "We've nailed down the court date for Pariah's appeal," he told me. "Great! When?" I asked.

"Four months from now."

I wasn't exactly thrilled with the answer, but I knew that it was better than most such cases. The court system needed someone like Pariah to clear up their backlog.

In the meantime, we continued doing our job. We tried to find a few missing people. We worked kidnapping cases. And we did favors for the other agencies. The CIA used us a number of times for things I'm not allowed to talk about. The DEA used us several times to check places out or to see what the drug dealers were doing before a major raid.

I began to feel more and more like a prisoner behind the walls of the safe house. Cynthia's comforting presence most nights was the only good thing about the situation there. Phil was quickly back to his old self, but he was spending his time now going back and forth between his own house and trying to help out Samantha. I began to see less and less of him.

Repeated requests for updates on the Mexican situation were bringing me no information. I began to feel so closed in that I finally did the one thing that I probably shouldn't have done. I blew my top and threw a bit of a temper tantrum!

But it got me out of the safe house…for a few days at least.

CHAPTER

40

We left the safe house in the dead of night, Cynthia, Pariah, and me. Actually, we weren't alone, but only the three of us occupied the big SUV that I had begun to think of as mine. We left the house following another SUV with two other agents in it, and we had a third SUV following behind with two more. I soon began thinking of the other agents as our prison guards. They were supposed to keep their distance, but we weren't going anywhere without them.

I would have preferred to just go with Cynthia alone, but somehow taking Pariah with us became an unstated requirement. Still, we were getting away for a few days...sort of.

It was just a few weeks before Pariah's long overdue appeal trial. The brutal summer heat had backed off and there was a definite chill in the air. The colorful leaves had finished turning and were now falling off the trees to blow across the roads and pile up wherever they happened to land.

We followed the lead SUV north up to the hills. Up into the mountains of Georgia. Up to the area where Pariah had loved seeing the trees. The government had rented us a little cabin on a mountain top north of the town of Blue Ridge. Actually, they had rented three houses, all in a row. We were flanked by our FBI guards at all times. Still, they were trying to keep their distance.

It was still dark when we arrived. We couldn't see the outside of the house but the inside was beautiful – once our guards declared it was safe for us to enter that is. We installed Pariah in the bedroom on the main floor so he wouldn't have to climb the steps, and Cynthia and I occupied the other bedroom upstairs. We slept late that first day – no surprise.

A week. A full week of doing nothing. Staring at the trees with Pariah. Wandering around the shops in town like regular tourists. Taking a train ride to see…more trees. And having to deal with an overly lazy horse on a mountain trail where I was mostly concerned with trying to spot any hungry black bears that might be lurking a little too close in the woods.

We had fun! We relaxed! And in the process, we started to learn things about Pariah. Something happened to him on that trip. He started opening up to us more than he had. We sat and watched a movie on TV, and for the first time since I could remember, he joined us. We laughed and told stories…and he laughed too. And one afternoon, sitting out on the back deck of the house, overlooking a view that was to die for, Cynthia started talking about some of the crazy phobias she had come across in her career.

Cyn and I laughed at a few, and that's when Pariah said, "Not crazy. Not funny. Serious. Bad. Difficult."

We stopped laughing quickly. "What do you mean, Pariah?" Cyn asked.

He had to stop to collect his thoughts. "Some things not easy," he said. "Fear of animals. Fear of dark. Fear of anything!"

I expected Cynthia to say he was right, or to apologize or something, but instead she asked, "What are you afraid of, Pariah?"

And surprisingly, I watched as he thought about it for a few moments and then replied, "Small places. Shower room. Men around when I can't get away. Can't undress. Hurting."

All his phobias came straight from prison.

"Pariah," Cynthia said as she turned her chair to look straight at him, "tell me about your fear of small places."

I fully expected him to ignore her like he usually did. But again he fooled me. He closed his eyes so he wouldn't have to look at her. "Always in small places. Always where I couldn't get away. They hurt me. Did things to me. Made me do things. Always. Always. Always. Tried to stop them. Tried and tried. Hurt me. Hurt me. Over and over. Hurt me. Too many. Too strong. Tried to stop them. Couldn't stop them. Hurt me. Did things to me. Made me do things. Bad things. Over and over and over."

He didn't open his eyes. Instead he sat there with his head back as if looking up at the sky. I had no doubt he was seeing again the horrible things that had been done to him for sixteen years in prison.

"We're getting back at them now," I told him. "Most of them have already been arrested. Your appeal trial is only a few weeks off. You know they're going to exonerate you."

"Didn't do it," he said with his eyes still closed. "I didn't do it."

Cynthia leaned forward. "Pariah, you know that part of your life is over. You know they can't hurt you anymore."

He shook his head. "Still afraid. Fear still there. Can't get away."

"Pariah," Cyn said, "would you like us to help you get past that fear?"

It took a few minutes, but eventually he opened his eyes and looked right at her. "Make fear go away."

It wasn't easy, especially for Pariah. It wasn't easy for me either since it turned out that despite how much he liked and trusted me, I was a man and therefore he still harbored a little fear of me. Often I saw Cyn and him talking…in the distance. Often I saw Cyn pointing at me. And just as often I saw Pariah shaking his head – stubbornly.

I felt left out. I felt jealous. I felt…hopeful. I wanted Pariah to be normal so badly, yet I knew that with his brain damage, he never could be. According to Cynthia, the best we could ever hope for would be some kind of compromise. But still, that would be an improvement.

At Cyn's request, I phoned Don and asked for an extension to our little vacation. He said no until I lied a bit and told him that Cynthia had made huge strides in Pariah's progress toward getting well. He called back a few minutes later to tell us to enjoy another week. Way to go Don!

I distinctly remember the day the three of us went shopping in the little tourist district again. We walked into and out of every shop. Pariah, as usual, drew distasteful looks from everyone, everywhere he went. Cyn was still trying to coax him into taking a shower, but it seemed that that was one of his major phobias. I wonder why?

There was one little shop though that specialized in t-shirts, and since the weather had now grown colder, sweatshirts. Cyn saw one she liked with a black bear on the front and held it up to her body. "Isn't it beautiful?" she asked.

"Sure is!" I replied. Although I was referring more to her than the sweatshirt.

"I'm going to buy it!" she declared.

"Go for it!" I replied. She had already bought three others since we left home.

Then she did something odd, "You should get one too. Just like it! It would look good on you!"

"Me?"

"Don't you like it?" she replied.

"Love it. But you've got that one already."

"We could have matching sweatshirts," she suggested.

Like it or not, I was soon the proud owner of a matching sweatshirt – only in a size that was a bit larger than hers.

She slipped hers on in the store and "encouraged" me to do the same. "Twins!" she declared.

I wouldn't have exactly put it that way. We were leaving the store when I realized that Pariah wasn't right with us. In the stores, he always followed closely because everyone looked at him so strangely. I couldn't blame them, and I couldn't blame him for being afraid. But when I discovered he wasn't with me, I felt a brief moment of panic.

A short search found him back at that same pile of sweatshirts. He was looking through them. He held one up. "Twins," he said. And then… believe it or not…he smiled. Yes, it was perhaps the ugliest smile on Earth, but to me just then, it was beautiful.

"You want one?" I asked.

Unbelievably, he nodded. I was astonished. He never wore anything but the same old clothes, day in and day out. We couldn't get him to remove them for anything – not for sleeping, and certainly not for washing – him or the clothes. He smelled pretty awful, but Cyn and I had long gotten so used to it that we hardly thought about it anymore.

And now he wanted a new sweatshirt. I didn't even have to think about it. I would have bought him a whole new wardrobe if he asked. We took a few minutes and found one we thought would be the right size, and a few minutes later, the three of us were a matching group. As dirty and smelly as he still was, it was a vast improvement.

Since it was still a bit early for dinner, we chanced taking Pariah into a fairly nice restaurant with us. There were only a few other customers in there at the time. The staff was very accommodating to all of us, especially after I flashed my badge where Pariah couldn't see me doing it. Cyn and I ordered the local trout and we arranged for the chef to make an order of scrambled eggs for Pariah.

As we waited, I saw the food being brought out to one of the other tables. When the waiter left, the family there looked at each other, held hands, and bowed their heads in prayer. Pariah stared at them and watched intently. When their prayer was through, they raised their heads and dropped hands. And Pariah said, "Amen." He watched the family intently while they ate.

Pariah's actions reminded me of something though. It was a long overdue question. And now that he was trying to open up a little, maybe he would open up a little more. "Pariah," I said, "why do you always ask the people if they will feed you?"

He looked at me with a somewhat surprised look on his face. "Important," he said. "Very important!"

"Why?"

He seemed to think for a moment. Then he pointed at himself. "Pariah," he said. "Outcast. Ugly. No good. Not liked. Not wanted. Hated. Alone. Hurting. Hungry. Very hungry." He paused to collect his thoughts again. "People want my help. Want a miracle. Want loved one…found." He looked back and forth between Cyn and I for a moment. "Do they want help enough to offer something back? Are they willing to share a scrap of bread with someone like me?"

Once again, he had astonished me. And then I remembered that he had been Stacy Chermont's Sunday School teacher. So underneath it all, he had been somewhat religious before. And now it seemed he still was.

And then he surprised me again.

He held up one finger and said. "One! One woman gave me food. One!"

"But that's because I told the others that I would feed you instead. That was my fault."

He shook his head. "I know. I can tell. None of the others would have fed me. None."

"How do you feel about that?" Cynthia asked.

He shrugged his shoulders. "Expect it."

"But you still helped them. You helped all of them."

"Can't not help," he replied. "Not right."

And he was right. For all the bad things in life, for all the bad people in the world, some of us had jobs that forced us to deal with all those bad people. It was our place in life to face things that others would never dream of. And rarely ever did we get much more than a simple thank you…if that.

I don't even think I tasted my fish. My mind was too occupied with wondering about Pariah.

Once we returned to the cabin, Cyn and I took our sweatshirts off and threw them in a pile on the back of the couch. I specifically watched Pariah to see what he would do. I was surprised to see him remove his as well. As if he was copying us. But to be truthful, he was fully dressed underneath, so it was no big deal.

But Cynthia moved in quickly. "Pariah," she said, "you've got that beautiful new sweatshirt. Wouldn't you like to have cleaner clothes to wear under it?"

I held my breath as he stared at her and thought about it. Very tentatively, he nodded his head, but only slightly. He looked very distrustful all of a sudden. I could almost see him running out of the cabin away from us.

But Cyn kept her cool. "If you'd like anything you're wearing washed, you can give it to me now…or if you like, you can leave it outside your door when you go to bed tonight, and I'll have it ready for you when you get up in the morning."

There was no mistaking it – fear! I could just see the wheels in his head turning, remembering. His fear of removing his clothes because all too often it meant he would get raped. Or hurt. Or both.

At Cyn's silent urging, we left him to consider the question.

That night, Cynthia left our bed a short while after we had turned in for the night. When she didn't come back, I went looking for her. I found her downstairs at the cabin's little washer and dryer. The washer was running. "Pariah's?" I whispered.

She nodded. "I think he gave me everything he had on."

Amazing!

I stayed up with Cyn until the washer had finished, until the dryer had finished…and until she had folded everything perfectly and placed it right outside his door. Only then did we go back to bed – and hold each other. But all night long my thoughts remained on the sudden changes in Pariah. Would he continue to improve?

When I got up the next morning, the clothes were missing from in front of Pariah's door, Pariah was missing from his bedroom, and his new sweatshirt was missing from the stack with ours. I found him outside on the back porch, watching the birds and the trees as usual. He never said a word about his clean clothes. I didn't say anything either. And neither did Cynthia a little while later.

Now if we could just get him to take a bath!

The last few weeks before his trial ticked slowly away. We worked a case where Pariah found the girl, but we were totally stumped over what to do about it. He found her, but we couldn't figure out exactly where she was. Pariah couldn't make heads or tails of the strange writing he saw. From what he described, the closest we could guess was that the girl was now one of several wives in some Sultan's harem somewhere in the Middle East. Although both Don and the Director claimed it wasn't, I considered that our first lost case.

We worked a kidnapping where Pariah found the little boy in a houseboat at a marina in Florida. We worked another drug bust for the DEA where a shipment was being collected right at the dock where the cargo ships were being unloaded in Savannah. Right after that we worked another of the cases from our stack of missing girls. This one Pariah found in the basement of some bozo outside of Chicago who had this weird thing for collecting female "specimens." Talk about sick!

And then there was the case of Andrea Remington, a pretty little fourteen-year-old, red-haired pixie from North Carolina. This one was a kidnapping because several people saw her being grabbed by two men and dragged into the back of a van. The van had been driven away by a third person. But after three days of waiting, there was still no ransom demand. So Pariah was asked to lend a hand.

As was sometimes the case, the father was dead set against it, but the mother's concern won out over his disbelief and distrust. I saw Mr. Remington glancing several times with distaste at Pariah before we even started. And after the lawyer had finished, I heard him mutter something about a damn child molester. I didn't want to know what else he had said.

The mother was just fine with touching Pariah or holding his hands, but the father wouldn't hear of it. "You stay away from him, Beth," he said. "I'll handle this piece of filth myself!" Such a nice man.

He took a chair facing Pariah, and of course that was Pariah's cue to ask him. "If I find her, will you feed me?"

I saw the father's eyes bulge in disbelief. "Feed you? You piece of human garbage! I'd just as soon ram your ugly head down the nearest sewer hole than feed you!"

"Mike! Stop it!" his wife demanded.

"Shut up, Beth. Let me deal with this." He turned back to Pariah, "How dare you ask if I'll feed you? You ought to still be in prison. Feed you? My tax dollars fed you every day you were in jail. And they probably gave you a whole lot more than that. Feed you? How dare you ask me that! You…pervert!"

We were all stunned. And then, Pariah did something I had never seen him do before. He got up from his chair and walked out of the room. And mentally, I applauded!

"You know of course," I said to the father, "we have proof now that he didn't do it. That he was framed."

"Then why did they make me sign that damn paper?" the father replied vehemently.

"Because he hasn't had his appeal trial yet," I replied.

"Then he's still hasn't been found innocent! I have no doubt, that if he was as innocent as you say he is, then the lawyers wouldn't have made me sign anything!"

"Mike!" his wife interrupted angrily. "Stop acting like a moron! We're here to find Andrea. They told us before we agreed to do this that he had been convicted of rape. Now Mike, think about Andrea! Your daughter! My daughter! That's the only reason we're here!"

He didn't look very convinced. In fact, what I saw on his face instead was more like pride…pride that he had told Pariah off and put him in his place.

"Hell!" he finally said. "Let's get this show on the road."

"Huh!" I grunted in surprise. "After the way you just acted? You just insulted him so badly that he walked out of here. He has never…I repeat never done that before. Just like he has never ever failed to find who we're looking for…alive…or dead! And after that, you expect him to help you? I'm with him!" And after saying that much, I walked out of the room too. I found Pariah down by the vending machines. "Come on, Pariah," I said. "Let's go home."

Cynthia joined us only moments later and we all walked out of the building together and drove back to the safe house. Morons!

Unfortunately, I got a call from the Director later that night telling me that the Remingtons had had a change of heart and he wanted us back to try it again in the morning.

"If," I said, "Pariah will agree!" I hung up on the Director before he could say anything else.

We did go back the next morning and Cyn showed up as expected too. Although none of us wanted to be too friendly with them. I was hoping for at least some kind of apology from Mr. Remington, but we didn't get anything from him at all.

This time, the mother won out and decided she would be the link Pariah needed to find her daughter.

"If I find her, will you feed me?" Pariah asked.

She looked him straight in the eyes. "Yes!" she said. "If that's the only thing you want, then it's the least I can do for you – whether you find her or not!"

"Oh for heaven's sake!" the father said as he rolled his eyes.

"Shut up, Mike!" she said to him. "You and your big mouth have caused enough trouble already!"

I thought about giving her a medal, but I was fresh out!

Pariah held out his gnarled hands and she never hesitated in taking them. Pariah closed his eyes and bowed his head. "Dim light. Gloomy. Three girls. Working. Two men watching. Holding small clubs."

"Pariah," I said, "Is she alive?"

"Yes, alive. A little sick, but otherwise okay."

I knew from experience now that a little sick usually referred to how drugged the girl was. "What's she doing?" I asked.

"Packing bricks into box."

Packing bricks into a box? That didn't make sense. "What do you mean? Can you describe it better?"

"Taking white bricks from pile and packing them into box."

White bricks? Strange. "What are the other girls doing?" I asked.

"Same thing. No!" he suddenly exclaimed.

"What happened?"

"Man with club kicked one of the girls. Wants her to move faster."

Packing white bricks into boxes. Something about that triggered a memory. "Pariah, are those white bricks wrapped in plastic or anything. Or do they look like normal regular bricks to build houses with?"

"Not for houses. Bricks are wrapped. Bad bricks!" he said. "Make people sick!"

"Drugs!" I exclaimed. Pariah said nothing.

"Okay, Pariah, good. Now let's try to figure out where those girls are. Okay? What else do you see around?"

"Nothing. Just this room. No windows. No doors."

"No windows and no doors?" I asked. This was sounding crazy. "Okay, Pariah, let's just go up first and try to figure out where this place is."

"Going up. Long way up. Oh! Horses. Pretty horses."

"Horses? How far away are the horses?"

"Right above white bricks. Pretty horses."

"Pariah. How high are you?"

"On the ground now."

"So where the girls are is someplace under the ground?"

"Under the horses."

"The horses. Pariah, is it a pasture of some kind?" "Stable. Like at Texas ranch."

"Pariah does it look like the stable you were in out there? At the Winslow ranch?"

"No. Different place. Big stable though. Many pretty horses."

"Okay, Pariah. Can you go up high? Let's see if we can find something to pinpoint where they are."

"Going up. Up. Up. Very good connection. Can go very high."

"Good Pariah, what do you see?"

"Cattle. Horses. House. Stable. Other buildings. Going up. Good connection."

"So it's a ranch?" I asked, just to be sure.

"Looks like it," he replied. "Going higher. Very high."

Since he had mentioned a ranch, I started to wonder if they were in Texas. "Pariah, do you see a river from where you are?"

"Small river. Tiny river not far from stable."

"But no big river at all?"

"No."

So maybe it wasn't Texas.

"Okay, Pariah, you said you saw a house. Let's concentrate on that. Can you go there?"

"Going down," he said. "Down. Down." And then suddenly his voice was panicked. "Something wrong with girl! Going down fast! Down! Down into ground. Down in room. No! No! Don't! Don't!"

"Pariah!" Cynthia said, "Calm down! Take it easy! Calm! Calm!" Her fingers were over his wrist now, taking his pulse.

But it was like Pariah didn't hear her. "No! Don't! Beating girl! Kicking girl! Hitting with club! No! No!" "Pariah!" Cynthia yelled trying to break his concentration. "Stop! Calm down!"

"Stop!" Pariah shouted, there were tears in his eyes now. "No! No! No!" "Cliff," Cynthia said. Break the…"

Cyn never finished what she was saying. Instead, Mrs. Remington screamed slightly in surprise. "Where…" but she didn't finish her question.

The room went deathly still for a moment as we all realized that Pariah had suddenly disappeared.

"What the hell kind of circus trick is this?" the father asked.

"Shut up!" I yelled. "Nobody move! Nobody move or say anything!"

We waited in silence, each of us desperately looking around the room at each other.

"Come on, Pariah," I said softly. "Come on! Find a way back, Pariah. Come on, buddy! Find us, Pariah. Come back…"

Other than my soft encouragements, you could hear a pin drop in there. And then suddenly the room exploded with sound again. Mrs.

Remington screamed, but her screams were not the only ones in the room. Just as had happened once before, Pariah was back, rolling on the floor with the girl in his arms.

"Andrea!" Mr. Remington yelled. I was surprised at how fast he moved. "Get your filthy hands off my daughter!" And before I could react, I watched as he delivered a horrible kick right to the side of Pariah's head.

I was stunned – especially when Pariah fell limp. The father was ranting angrily at Pariah. I ran at him as fast as I could, but not before he delivered yet another kick to Pariah's shoulder. I tackled him and threw him to the floor. And I punched him in the face with every bit of strength and anger I could muster.

The panicked girl was screaming and trying to get off of Pariah's now limp body. Cynthia pulled her away – then actually pushed her toward her mother! She bent over Pariah trying to examine him.

"How is he?" I asked.

"Not good!"

All through the helpless waiting, all through the ambulance ride that seemed to take forever, all I kept seeing in my mind was Mr. Remington's big boot connecting with the side of Pariah's head. Over and over again I saw it. And it made me sick!

He was alive, but that's all we could say about him. He certainly wasn't conscious.

They wouldn't let me near him at the hospital. Cynthia either. We waited and waited for word that never seemed to come, and when it finally did, it wasn't what we wanted to hear at all.

He was seriously hurt. In a coma. Not likely to survive.

CHAPTER

41

We met the next day in the conference room. The Director, Don, me, Frank Morris…and Simon, who had flown in during the wee hours of the morning.

It was only three days before Pariah's trial had been scheduled to start. Three days!

"What do we do?" the Director asked.

"He's still alive?" Simon asked.

"Technically," the Director replied.

"I move that we proceed with the trial," Simon said. "Only I'm going to have to refile this a little differently so that we do this on behalf of Pariah."

"Can you do that?" the Director asked.

He nodded. "I think so. If we can't, then we'll go about it a different way. But it will mean more rescheduling and wasting probably months of time. Maybe years."

"I'd like this finished fast," the Director said.

"The one thing that Pariah wanted," I said. "In fact, the only thing that he ever wanted, was for everyone to know that he was innocent – *before* he died."

Everyone stared at me, but nobody said a word. They didn't need to.

"I'll proceed," Simon finally said. "And we'll hope to God that he lives!"

"Amen!" the Director added.

What followed next kind of surprised me since they were discussing security for the trial. And they were talking about lots of security. And then the word Mexicans started popping up over and over again. And now I was listening very closely! Especially to the part where they were hearing chatter since last night about how angry Pacheco was again. Had we found part of his operation?

Frank used the phrase, "terrorist activities" more than once and told us how he was coordinating efforts with the Atlanta police.

Suddenly this simply little trial wasn't sounding so simple anymore.

"I guess that's it!" the Director finally declared when all decisions had been made. "Anything else?"

"Just one thing," Simon replied. "I think you should be aware that we've had Chermont and Brecker under light surveillance for a while now. A few weeks ago, Brecker flew into Atlanta and met with Judge Foster who will be the presiding judge for Pariah's trial."

"What did they talk about?" the Director asked.

"We don't know. But I can make some guesses. We may have more of an uphill climb for this thing than I thought."

Nobody said a word. The Director finally closed his file folder and walked out to end the meeting.

I didn't attend the first day of the trial proceedings since Simon told me they would only be selecting the jury and nothing else. At his advice though, Cynthia and I were very early getting there the next day. At his suggestion, we took a seat on the bench at the end of the very first row. The room filled up fast. I was surprised when I realized that Simon was saving a seat right next to me. "Are you expecting someone else?" I asked.

He smiled. Since Brecker decided to play his games with the Judge, I decided to play one of my own. I invited an old friend who I think may be helpful."

Just before the trial started, an elderly gentleman walked in and shook hands with Simon. Simon pointed him toward the bench right next to me. The man sat down and shook my hand, but he didn't give me his name.

Judge Foster came in. We all stood up. His gavel came down. And the trial started.

"Mr. Cantrell," the Judge said. "Where is your defendant?"

Simon stood up. "You'll notice Your Honor, that the petition has been refiled so that we are now proceeding on behalf of Mr. Clayton instead of having him here."

"This is ridiculous, Your Honor," Brecker suddenly exclaimed as he stood up. "This is a twenty year old case and he doesn't even have a defendant anymore! What's the point? I move for an immediate dismissal."

"We don't need a defendant!" Simon argued back. "We're doing this on Mr. Clayton's behalf!"

"This is highly unusu…al," the Judge finally finished. I noticed he was staring at the old gentleman sitting right next to me. "Um…welcome, Judge Benson," he said. "It's not often that we have such a distinguished visitor from the Supreme Court in our midst."

Judge Benson? Supreme Court? And I was sitting right next to him? I had even shaken his hand!

Benson stood up. "I'm only here to observe as a favor for some friends," he said. "There are a lot of very highly placed parties in all areas of the government who are interested in these proceedings." He sat down again.

Judge Foster looked very surprised. "As I understand it, Mr. Clayton has already served all sixteen years of his sentence. What possible interest can the government have in this case and why is this being brought up now?"

"I'm sorry, Your Honor," Simon replied, "but the Government's interest in Mr. Clayton is highly classified. We're bringing this up now because Mr. Clayton was illegally denied his right to an appeal. So this proceeding is very overdue!" He then picked up a plastic sealed letter. "I have here a letter from the head of the law firm that Mr. Clayton employed for his defense. The letter specifically tells Mr. Clayton that there would be no appeal. The head of that firm is now awaiting separate proceedings against him and is declining to speak on the matter here. His letter however speaks for itself."

Simon handed the sealed letter to the bailiff, who in turn passed it to the Judge who grunted a bit after he read the name. "No wonder I haven't seen Mr. Morgan in a while." He looked back at Simon. Since the government has such a big interest in this case, does that have anything to do with the increased security that I'm told practically has this entire building under lock-down?"

"It does, Your Honor," Simon replied.

Judge Foster looked back at Judge Benson for a few moments. Then he turned to Brecker. "Motion to dismiss these proceedings is denied! You may begin, Mr. Brecker."

"Your Honor," Brecker said as he stood up again. "How can we proceed if the defendant isn't here to question?

"I admit it is highly unusual," the Judge replied, "but under the circumstances I'm afraid you're going to have to do the best you can." He turned to Simon. "I hope you have a good reason for Mr. Clayton's absence."

"I do, Your Honor, but I'd rather save that for the defense portion."

"It better be good then," Judge Foster replied.

"Oh, it is, Your Honor. I'm sure you'll find it very interesting…and enlightening."

The Judge nodded. "It better be!"

"Now Mr. Brecker. I'm waiting."

We listened as Brecker, then Simon addressed the jury. Then Brecker went on the attack – although I had the impression that he was a little off because Pariah wasn't there for him to point at.

I got my first look at Stacy Chermont. What little background I knew about her was that despite her father, she had led a somewhat ragged life. Evidently she had been though several marriages and was now using the Chermont name again. She had no arrests – on record, but that didn't mean that her father hadn't managed to smooth things over for her. I was surprised when she managed to speak about her rape so clearly after twenty years."

"Cross examine!" the Judge said when Brecker was finished.

"Your Honor," Simon said standing again. "The defense is declining the cross-examination at this time, but we would like to reserve the right to speak with Ms. Chermont later."

"So ordered," the Judge said.

The rest of what Brecker had to say was very limited. The judge ordered a fifteen minute break in the proceedings. And then it was Simon's turn.

The first thing he did was to pull out a couple of very large pictures. "Your Honor, I would like to submit two pictures for everyone's inspection. He handed them to the bailiff who in turn handed them to the Judge. "The first is a picture of Mr. Clayton before he went to prison. The second is a picture of him when he came out."

I saw the judge look closely at the pictures. "This can't be the same person, Mr. Cantrell."

"I assure you, it is."

The Judge nodded, then handed the pictures back to the bailiff to hand to the jury so they could be passed around. Simon waited until everyone had seen the pictures – including Brecker and Chermont.

"What's the purpose of this?" Brecker suddenly challenged.

"Your Honor," Simon replied. "Since Mr. Clayton is noticeably missing, I only want to give everyone a sense of who we're dealing with."

"The Judge rolled his eyes. "Move on, Mr. Cantrell."

"Your Honor, I'd like to call to the stand Doctor Cynthia Westmore."

Cynthia was quickly sworn in and Simon addressed the jury. "Doctor Westmore is one of Atlanta's leading psychiatrists. She has studied Mr. Clayton extensively in the last six months." He turned to Cynthia. "Doctor Westmore, please describe Mr. Clayton's condition when you first met him."

"Yes," Cynthia agreed. "While he was in prison, Mr. Clayton sustained severe injury to almost every part of his body. Almost all of his bones were broken multiple times, particularly his hands and fingers. He was raped repeatedly nearly every day he was there, and shortly before he was released he received a major trauma to his head that has left him permanently brain damaged and his communication skills are now highly impaired."

I wasn't sure how highly impaired Pariah's communication skills were, but I didn't think it mattered.

Brecker was quickly on his feet. "I object!" he declared. "We have no way to corroborate Doctor Westmore's claims and in any event, what possible bearing can any of this have on the facts of this case?"

"He has a good question," the Judge said to Simon.

Simon smiled then went back to his briefcase where he pulled out a stack of files. "I have here Mr. Clayton's medical reports and x-rays. I think that should be sufficient evidence to back up the Doctor's claims."

He turned them over to the bailiff who tried to hand them to the Judge, but the judge waved him off.

"And what bearing does any of this have on this case?"

Simon smiled. "You asked me to explain why Mr. Clayton isn't here, so that's exactly what I'm doing."

The Judge looked at him dubiously. "Proceed."

"Doctor Westmore," Simon said, "what is Mr. Clayton's current condition now?"

"Several days ago, Mr. Clayton was attacked and received a severe blow to the head. The blow has placed Mr. Clayton in a coma. We are currently unsure as to his eventual outcome…but I'm afraid it's not looking promising."

Simon looked up at the Judge. "Your Honor, as you have heard, Mr. Clayton is of particular interest to the government. It was Mr. Clayton's only wish that he be exonerated of all charges before his death. Now it seems, we have to hurry a bit."

"Objection!" Brecker called. "None of this is reason proving that Mr. Clayton did not rape my client! Previous proceedings have already established that fact!"

"Proceedings that were flawed!" Simon returned. In any event, he was illegally denied his right to an appeal. We are simply exercising that right at this time on his behalf!"

Judge Foster looked back and forth between Simon and Brecker. Then he glanced one more time at Judge Benson beside me. "Thank you Mr. Cantrell for enlightening us as to Mr. Clayton's absence. I'm sure we all will pray for his speedy recovery." He looked to Brecker. "Mr. Brecker, do you have any questions for this witness? Or can we move on to other matters?"

Brecker had no questions so Cynthia was dismissed.

And then Simon called Hugh Ogilvie, the former prison warden. The minute he had been sworn in, Brecker was again on his feet objecting. "This man can't possibly add anything pertinent to these proceedings," he argued furiously. "He didn't even meet Mr. Clayton until after sentencing had been pronounced!"

The Judge looked a Simon. "Mr. Cantrell?"

Simon just smiled back broadly. "We were just getting to that exact point," Cantrell replied. "If you'll allow me to proceed, I promise that in a moment you'll find very good reason to listen to everything that Mr. Ogilvie has to say."

"It better be good, Mr. Cantrell, or I'll have it all stricken from the record."

"Thank you, Your Honor." Simon turned to the jury. "I want you all to know that Mr. Ogilvie here is testifying as part of a plea bargain we worked out with him. So any and all wrong-doings on his part are not going to be dealt with here." He turned back to Ogilvie. "Mr. Ogilvie, will you please enlighten everyone as to exactly why you are part of these proceedings?"

Ogilvie paused for a moment as if summoning up the courage to speak. "I was the one ultimately responsible for Mr. Clayton's abuse in prison and also for altering Mr. Clayton's records so that he was denied any chance at parole. I did this because I received a visit from Mr. Chermont shortly before Mr. Clayton arrived at the prison. Mr. Chermont offered me a lot of money to make Mr. Clayton's life as miserable as possible for as long as I could."

"And how much money was that?" Simon asked him. "Fifty thousand the first year. Then an additional fifteen thousand for every year I could keep him there."

"I object!" Brecker protested immediately. "This doesn't concern the case between Mr. Clayton and my client in any way at all!"

"Sit down, Mr. Brecker!" the Judge ordered. "Mr. Chermont made it part of the case the minute he bribed the warden. Now I want to hear everything that this man has to say!"

We were then treated to a horrific accounting of just what the warden had arranged with Bullfrog and what he knew was going on in his prison. By the time Ogilvie was finished, Brecker had little to cross-examine about, and the rest of us were simply sick!

The Judge decided to call a halt until after lunch. Frankly, after Ogilvie, I wasn't sure I felt much like eating.

After a long lunch, the trial started again. This time Brecker objected the minute that Simon announced that he was calling Mrs. Moorhead, former juror in the original Clayton trial. "I object!" Brecker declared again. "This is another witness who has no bearing on the fact that Mr. Clayton raped my client's daughter!"

"Oh but it does have a bearing," Simon replied. "More so than Mr. Ogilvie's testimony."

The Judge looked dubiously at Simon. "Proceed then."

Mrs. Moorhead was sworn in, after which she told everyone that she was so excited to be there. It was exciting to me too, only in a different way.

A minute later she told everyone how the Judge in the original trial had walked into the jury room and told everyone about Mr. Clayton being suspected of multiple rapes and that he had been certain their decision would put Mr. Clayton in prison. I saw the jaw of Judge Foster drop wide open!

When Mrs. Moorhead was finished the judge didn't even give Brecker a chance to question her. He thanked her and dismissed her. Then he turned to Simon. "I have enough evidence here to end this right now," he said.

Simon shook his head. "Not really. All you have right now is her statement. I'd like to call Judge Hawthorn to the stand next."

The retired Judge was quickly sworn in. For some reason, he appeared to be very comfortable in the chair, although he did look up at Judge Foster and say jokingly, "This is a strange place for me to sit. Everything looks so different down here."

Judge Foster didn't laugh.

The Judge wasn't on the stand very long at all. But by the time he had told everyone about the bribe he had taken from Brecker on behalf of William Chermont, Judge Foster himself was looking very uncomfortable.

Foster turned to Simon. "Now can I put an end to this farce?" he asked.

"Not yet, Your Honor. We still haven't produced any proof of Mr. Clayton's innocence."

"There is no proof!" Brecker suddenly argued.

The Judge turned back to Simon. "I take it you have some kind of direct proof in this matter?"

"We do, Your Honor. The video tape that Judge Hawthorn refused to allow into evidence."

"I object!" Brecker yelled again.

I saw Foster struggling with something within himself. "A twenty year old tape can't possibly…"

The old Supreme Court justice next to me suddenly went into a coughing fit. He was loud enough to disturb the whole trial. When it ended, he simply held his hand up and said, "Sorry."

Foster seemed to change his position quickly after that. "As to the video, in light of…other evidence, I think the court should view this tape."

Simon already had everything arranged. A large video monitor was brought out and we were all treated to a viewing of the pertinent section of the tape – unaltered. Then Simon played the enhanced version. Then he started showing the enhanced pictures, including the one of the license plate from Clayton's car.

"Are you finished now, Mr. Cantrell?" the Judge asked him. "Or can we put an end to this?"

"Not yet," Simon replied. "There's still one big question left. Who did rape Stacy Chermont. I'd like to recall her now to the stand."

This time, Stacy seemed a lot less confident.

"Ms. Chermont," Simon began, "I want to thank you for providing us with such an exact testimony earlier. Your memory seems to remain very clear."

"Well it should!" she replied.

"Yes, it should!" Simon agreed. "But the thing that interested me the most, was that everything you said…everything…was almost word for word your exact testimony from twenty years ago. Why is that, Ms. Chermont?"

"Objection!" Brecker shouted. "The rape was a traumatic experience. My client should remember it perfectly!"

"Remember the rape, yes!" Simon retorted. "But to give us word for word testimony again? I think not!"

"The witness will answer the question," Judge Foster decided.

Stacy looked a bit sheepish. "Um…I had to go over it with Mr. Brecker," she replied. "He helped me to remember the details better."

"I see," Simon replied. He turned to Brecker. "Thank you Mr. Brecker for helping her to provide us with so many facts."

"It's part of my job," Brecker replied.

"Yes it is!" Simon noted with a smile. He turned back to Stacy. "Ms. Chermont, we've just seen evidence that Mr. Clayton was nowhere near where you were at the time of the alleged rape. Please explain how it is that he was able to be in two places at the same time?"

Stacy was beginning to look worried. "I don't know," she replied. "All I know is that he raped me."

Simon nodded. "Okay. Ms. Chermont, let me ask you this then, who is Vincent Brown?"

Stacy's eyes immediately went wide with surprise. "You have no right to bring him up here!" she shouted.

"I have every right!" Simon replied firmly. He pointed at the people in the room. "I have three witnesses out there who are willing to testify that you and Vincent were in a very heavy relationship at the time that Clayton was supposed to have raped you. Now please tell us who Vincent Brown was!"

She stared angrily at Simon.

"Tell us!" Simon demanded.

"Objection!" Brecker yelled.

"Sit down!" the Judge ordered. "The witness will answer the question!"

"Now who was he?" Simon asked a bit more civilly.

"My boyfriend," Stacy finally replied.

"Your boyfriend," Simon repeated. "You didn't get raped by Mr. Clayton at all, did you? You and Vincent Brown got it on instead!"

"No!" Stacy shouted. "No!"

"Yes! Now why did you blame Clayton instead?"

"Because he raped…"

"No he didn't! We know he didn't. Now who raped you?"

"Objection!" Brecker roared again.

"Sit down and shut up!" Judge Foster told Brecker. "I've had just about enough of you!"

"Who raped you?" Simon asked a bit quieter.

Stacy didn't answer.

"We know it wasn't Clayton, so somebody had to do it!"

Still Stacy remained silent.

"Was it your father?" Simon suddenly asked as he pointed his finger straight at William Chermont.

"Objection!" Brecker yelled.

"No!" Stacy said at the same time.

"Well if it wasn't your father? Who are you protecting?"

I noticed now that there were tears starting to fall from Stacy's eyes. "You don't understand," she said.

"Well enlighten us then. Who raped you?"

"He would have killed him."

"Who?" Simon asked. "Who would have killed who?"

"Daddy," Stacy said so quietly I almost didn't hear her.

"Your father?" Simon asked. "Your father would have killed someone? Who?"

"Vince," she finally replied.

"So your father didn't exactly approve of your boyfriend."

"He thought I was too young!" she replied quickly. "And besides…."

"What?"

"Vince was black. Daddy didn't like that at all."

Simon moved back a little way away from her. His voice was slightly softer as he said, "So you weren't raped at all, were you?"

Stacy Chermont stared at the floor as she softly replied, "No."

"You and your boyfriend Vince got it on, and you got pregnant in the process. Am I right?"

Stacy didn't answer out loud, but finally nodded. She looked up at Simon. "He would have killed Vince!" she said as tears started to fall from her eyes.

"And why did you blame Mr. Clayton for it?" Simon pressed. "Because of the argument you had earlier that day?"

Stacy looked at the floor without responding for a few moments before she nodded again. Then her head came up with a bit of defiance in her eyes. "He was always spouting off all that 'holier than thou' nonsense at me! Over and over and over again. You can't do this! You can't do that! It's wrong to do this. It's wrong to do that! You're going to go to Hell for the way you live your life!" Her defiance seemed to double. "He deserved it, the bastard! What right did he have to tell me how to live my life?"

Simon stared at her for a few moments in silence before speaking. "So you blamed Mr. Clayton to protect your boyfriend Vince."

Stacy's voice softened, but still held a note of irritation. "Mr. Clayton kept hounding me over the way I lived. He wouldn't let up. I hated it!" Her head bowed slowly down toward the floor again. Very softly she added, "Vince got me pregnant that day. The pregnancy made me sick…and I panicked."

Simon shook his head. His voice was just above a whisper, but it rang loud and clear in a room where you could have heard a pin drop. "Maybe you should have been a little more open to what Mr. Clayton was trying to tell you."

Simon backed further away from her and looked at the jury, then at the judge, then he addressed Stacy again. This time, his voice was full and strong. "So Mr. Clayton spent sixteen years in prison. Where he was raped repeatedly every day. Where he had all his bones broken over and over again. Where he was finally injured so badly that he became brain damaged. His pregnant wife and unborn baby died from the stress while his house and everything he owned were being taken away. And when he finally was free from prison, he was left to wander the street a homeless invalid. Incapable of working. Incapable of doing anything except hunting for food." He paused for just a moment. "All because of one little lie from a girl who was afraid to tell her father the truth!" He shook his head. "Such a shame."

Simon looked up at Judge Foster. "I think we're finished here."

"I think so too," the judge replied.

Just to finalize the issue, the jury was sent out to deliberate. But they were back a few minutes later to return a verdict of not guilty for Clayton. No surprise there.

The Judge turned to the bailiff. "I want Mr. Chermont, Stacy Chermont, and also Mr. Brecker taken into custody immediately. Then he turned to Simon. "And I have a check in my possession, given to me by Mr. Brecker on behalf of William Chermont – in return for not admitting a certain video tape into the proceedings."

He banged his gavel on the desk and it was over. Clayton had been exonerated!

The only problem was, would he ever know it?

In a crowd of people, Cynthia and I made our way outside to head home. But we had to stop on the steps of the courthouse because I saw the Director himself giving a news conference there. We moved closer so we could hear better.

"On behalf of the United States government," the Director was saying, "we are glad to have this issue finally resolved. It has always been Mr. Clayton's wish that before he died…"

He was suddenly interrupted by another of our agents urgently coming up to whisper in his ear. The Director looked at him with a troubled look on his face. I immediately started looking around for Mexicans with guns!

The Director went back to the microphone. "I'm afraid…," he started to say, then backed up and collected himself.

I started to get a really bad feeling.

"Excuse me," he apologized. "It has always been Mr. Claytons wish, that before he died, everyone would know he was innocent.

"Mr. Clayton has indeed been found innocent. Unfortunately, this message is too late. I have just been informed that Thomas Clayton passed away a few minutes ago."

CHAPTER

42

It was one of those spring-like days that Georgia often gets in the middle of winter. The sun was shining and the most anyone needed was a light sweater to guard against the temperature. A perfect day for a memorial service.

Cynthia and I sat in the first row of chairs and listened to several people speak about Pariah…or now Thomas Clayton as he was being referred to. I had been asked to speak, but I had declined. Every time I thought about it, my throat clogged up too badly. How could I speak about him if I couldn't talk?

There was no body, no casket. He had actually been buried three months earlier in a private ceremony two days after the trial. But now a tall obelisk shaped monument stood on top of his grave. A monument carefully designed so everyone could properly remember him.

When the speeches were over, I glanced around. A lot of people. A lot! But then I had made it my mission in life to contact every person I could — *personally*, about Pariah's innocence and what he had done, and what had been done to him. And I had started with a certain Italian chef named Joe.

Far behind the seats, in a special section, there was a huge amount of donated food. We had told everyone that it would be given to the homeless shelters on Pariah's behalf. Of course, when I had talked with everyone, I also took the time to explain why Pariah had insisted on asking each of them if they would feed him. There was enough food collected now that they were going to need a bigger truck than planned to carry it all away.

Off to the side of the affair, everyone was just now heading toward the tables where Joe the chef had prepared a spaghetti lunch for everyone. There was one main table, with one place elegantly set – candle and all. The plate was loaded with spaghetti covered in sauce. The chair had a piece of material draped over the arms so no one could sit in it. Pariah's place. The place of honor.

"Ready?" Cynthia asked me? "It's about time to go."

"Not yet," I replied.

With her arm in mine, I walked up to the monument for a better look. The artist had done a magnificent job of carving the name of every person Pariah had ever found – alive or dead. The entire bottom portion was filled with names on all four sides. As I walked all the way around it, I ran my hand over several of the names, trying to remember each and every case in detail.

We came around to the front again and I stared at the name inscribed in big bold letters and ran my fingers over it. "Thomas Clayton." But the artist had carved a line through Thomas Clayton, crossing it out.

Below that he had carved, "Pariah," and I ran my fingers longer over that name…letting them linger for a moment. But that name too had been crossed out.

My fingers fell to the one remaining name on the monument. The one name that meant the most to me.

"Hero."

CHAPTER

43

I don't live in Atlanta anymore, and while I'm still technically attached to the FBI, I no longer work for missing persons. In fact, I don't do much actual work for the FBI at all. Instead, I spend most of my time trying to learn how to manage our ranch and become a little more competent at horseback riding where we live somewhere in the state of Idaho. I'm sorry I can't be more specific than that.

With Pariah gone, the FBI decided I was too well known, and there were too many memories of what Pariah and I had done together for me to continue to be effective in Atlanta. So in their infinite wisdom, the FBI moved me to someplace more remote. In fact, very remote. Not that I mind all that much.

I married my wife Cynthia in a private little ceremony at the ranch. It was a very pleasant and touching affair. Mostly touching – but we won't go into that here!

Cynthia isn't a psychiatrist anymore. Instead, when she isn't helping out at the ranch, she works as a social worker and psychologist for the city that's not too far from here.

And together, we do our best to take care of my Uncle Tom.

When we first got here, Uncle Tom was recovering from some plastic surgery that was necessary after a major traffic accident he had. I'm happy to report that they were able to reconstruct his nose just fine and he can once again breathe out of it. He's not too fond of his false teeth, but he's trying to get used to them. The accident caused him some mental difficulties that Cyn is slowly working on with him, but that is looking more and more hopeful. He's also still having a lot of problems because of the arthritis that has twisted and gnarled so much of his body so badly, but that's to be expected I guess.

Mostly, Uncle Tom just sits on the porch swing and looks out at the beautiful scenery surrounding our ranch – the horses, the mountains, and of course, the beautiful forest of trees in the distance. His little puppy, Laura, a miniature white French poodle, is never far from his lap.

He seems to be happy and content right where he's at, doing just what he's doing.

Cyn and I stay busy with the ranch and of course her social work.

Oh, and occasionally, we do little favors for the government.